THE SCARCE MAN

THE SCARCE MAN

James Frie

iUniverse, Inc.

New York Lincoln Shanghai

The Scarce Man

iUniverse, Inc.

For information address:
iUniverse, Inc.
2021 Pine Lake Road, Suite 100
Lincoln, NE 68512
www.iuniverse.com

This book is a work of fiction. All characters and events exist in the imagination of the author and do not represent real events or locations. Some locations, businesses and organization in the story are real and were included to provide the reader with believability. The author has nothing but the highest admiration and respect for those businesses and organizations.

ISBN: 0-595-33296-X (pbk)
ISBN: 0-595-66827-5 (cloth)

Printed in the United States of America

"In the beginning of change, the patriot is a scarce man; brave, hated and scorned. When his cause succeeds however, the timid join him, for then it costs nothing to be a patriot."—Mark Twain

CHAPTER 1

▼

The man who thought of himself as a patriot lay hidden in a row of thick juniper shrubs on the edge of a low hillside. The shrubs were sharp and uncomfortable, but he was protected to some degree by the ghillie suit he wore over his black jeans and dark blue sweatshirt. He had purchased this top quality ghillie from one of the many Internet-based vendors he had used to acquire his collection of wares.

It was a warm May evening and, although there were not many insects around yet, he had brushed a few off his face. He knew that, in a couple of weeks, there would be a full contingent of Minnesota mosquitoes to cope with on the nights he would be out.

He shifted his position, eased himself off a root, and then realigned his sights on the bright kitchen window of the house across the street. The Ruger Mini-14 rifle felt cool and comfortable in his hands although a trickle of sweat slowly made its way down the middle of his back. He had no telescopic sight on the rifle but felt he wouldn't need one at such a short distance.

He studied once again the visible parts of the interior of the house. Not much had changed from the reconnaissance mission he had made here the week before. The house was a large, open-designed rambler in a wealthy neighborhood across the street from the Normandale Golf Course in Edina. The house was occupied by The Honorable Judge Edward R. Borgert and his wife. He could see the judge in the living room to the right sitting in a large recliner watching TV. Borgert's back was to the patriot, who, nevertheless, could clearly see the top of his head.

The Borgerts didn't appear to value their privacy; although their house had many large windows facing the golf course, none of them with curtains or shades.

The patriot smiled to himself, imagining the Borgerts looking at the house for the first time and discussing with each other how nice it would be to be able to look across the street and up the little hill to see who was golfing on the ninth hole that day. He wondered if they objected to the juniper bushes which partially blocked their prized view.

The patriot spent a lot of his time visualizing scenarios in his mind. His vivid imagination allowed him to enjoy his time alone when he could escape his many aggravations by mulling over his ideas. Although he almost let himself continue picturing the life of the Borgerts, trying to recreate their conversations, their hobbies or even their sex life, he concluded he didn't have time for that right then. All of that could come later, when he would relive the night in his mind. He brought himself back to the present and again reviewed his escape plan. The night was dark, and he could hear no voices. Off in the distance a stereo was playing rap music—probably some spoiled rich kid showing off the car Daddy got him. The patriot didn't like rich people and especially didn't like their kids. He was certain that the current generation was doomed by a lifestyle of comfort and easy access to money and credit.

Behind him lay the ninth hole of the course and a little farther back there was a little cluster of buildings which housed the grounds equipment. His car was parked in between the grounds' sheds, and he had little fear that anyone would see him leave. Sunday nights were quiet in that area with little traffic. When his work was done, he knew he could run to his car in less than two minutes and that any police responding to the area would go to the Borgerts' front door on the other side of the course.

Just then, Judge Borgert got up from his chair and walked into the kitchen. He removed an ice cream container from the freezer, spooned a hefty amount into a bowl, and sat down at a small table facing the windows. Borgert, a large man, was bathed in light from the row of small track lights on the kitchen ceiling. He began to eat the ice cream methodically.

The patriot checked the other windows again but could not see the judge's wife. He wondered whether she was home or in another part of the house. He lifted his head and looked up and down the street once more for anyone walking. He saw no one.

As he lined up the rifle's rear peep sight around the front post, he paused. A muffled distant voice said something, and the rap music died immediately. He was about to take a big step. His life would change forever after this night, he knew. He would forever be a hunted man and knew that the government would shut him away in a prison if they caught him. He also knew from experience that almost all hunted men were eventually caught. He felt that if he could stay free long enough to accomplish his goal, the risk would be worth it. He had planned long and taken the steps he knew were important so that he would be exposed as little as possible. He had his tools, he had made his list, and he had carefully looked over his areas of operation, as he liked to think of them. Still, there was an element of unreality to it all. Up to this point it had all been an exercise in thought and theory, but if he carried out his plan tonight, there would be no going back.

He checked once again to make sure the top of the front sight was centered on Borgert's chest. The rifle rested comfortably on his left palm. Sliding his right index finger into the trigger guard, he pushed the safety forward until he heard it click off. He had loaded five fully jacketed .223 shells into the rifle's magazine and had a full twenty-round magazine in his jacket as a backup. He tightened up the slack on the trigger until he met resistance. He then took a breath. As he let it halfway out, he squeezed the trigger. The rifle surged easily against his shoulder, and the bark of the report didn't seem very loud at all.

Judge Borgert was amazed to see his picture window shatter before his eyes. At the same moment, he felt as if he'd been punched in the chest. The wind was knocked out of his lungs and he rocked back in his chair. He felt no pain. For a split second, he thought there had been a gas explosion. Then he felt another blow to his chest but then nothing at all when the patriot's third shot hit him just under his left eye.

The patriot was up and running while the echo of the last shot rang through the still neighborhood. His night vision had been partially ruined by the bright muzzle blasts, but there was enough ambient light for him to make his way across the ninth green and over to the sheds. With his heart beating fast, he slid the rifle into the case on the back seat. He slipped the ghillie suit over his head and threw it in the rear of his three-year-old dark blue Ford Explorer. Closing the hatch as quietly as he could, he got behind the wheel. After taking a couple of seconds to get his breathing under control, he started the engine. He pulled out onto the road and drove down the uninhabited portion with his headlights off. He turned them on as he neared the next intersection and stopped for the stop sign. He made his way through the neighborhood to eastbound Interstate Highway 494 and joined hundreds of other cars.

CHAPTER 2

▼

Detective Phil Deane, of the Edina Police Department watched the sun come up and rubbed his eyes with the palms of his hands. Judge Borgert had been killed at about 10:30 the night before and Deane had been called in shortly thereafter by the on-duty patrol supervisor. Edina, an inner-ring suburb of Minneapolis, is known as a wealthy city, where many of the Twin Cities' rich and famous live. Its population of about 47,500 does not yet suffer too badly, in spite of its close proximity to Minneapolis crime. Edina had not experienced a homicide in over six years, and the killing of Judge Borgert was definitely out of the ordinary compared to the type of cases Deane usually worked. He had been at the Borgert home for over seven hours now and had a sinking feeling in the pit of his stomach that there would be no quick arrest for this one.

The crime scene teams who had been called upon to assist were from the Hennepin County Sheriff's Office and the Minnesota Bureau of Criminal Apprehension (BCA) and had almost finished collecting evidence inside the house. Deane had been told that the BCA's best homicide investigator, Mike Rawlings, would be meeting with him to discuss the case later in the day after Deane was finished at the house.

The judge's body had been taken away to the Hennepin County Coroner's Office for autopsy, and the kitchen area around him had been carefully photographed, fingerprinted, and vacuumed. The bullet which had struck Borgert in the face had passed through and exited the back of his head. The Crime Lab deputies from the Sheriff's Department had been having a difficult time finding the slug, even though they had covered every square inch of the area behind where the judge's body had been.

When a person is murdered, the police and crime scene teams understand the need to maintain an open frame of mind when trying to recreate what had taken place. It is important to keep assumptions to a minimum in order to prevent the investigation from charging off in the wrong direction. A slow, methodical search and careful documentation of the scene are critical to make sure that investigators have a solid set of facts to draw upon when they begin the process of trying to determine motive, one of the critical elements in a homicide investigation. The motivation for murder comes from within the mind of the killer. Sometimes that mind is diseased, confused, mistaken or altered by drugs or alcohol. The investigator tries to determine motive by looking, for example, into the life of the victim. Most murder victims are killed by people close to them. Rage, greed, and jealousy are the issues which usually send people off this planet early. For this reason, most murders are solved within 24 hours of the crime. Usually there is little question as to who did the killing. The questions for most police investigators are: why did they do it and where are they now? Homicide investigators in large cities cite the twenty-four-hour rule, which states simply, that, if a murder isn't well on its way to a solution within one day, the chances of solving the crime dwindle with each passing hour.

Phil Deane had been a cop for 21 years and an investigator for 13. He thought himself lucky to work for a department that didn't have to deal with a lot of violent crime. Just a few blocks away in Minneapolis, his fellow investigators were working on their twenty-fifth murder of the year. They could have it, Deane thought. Deane was a good cop and knew that he couldn't rush the crime teams. And right now, they were frustrated.

The two bullets which struck Borgert in the chest had remained inside his body. During the autopsy, they would be recovered, and the paths they took through the tissue would be plotted. Those paths would provide a direction from which the shots came and, possibly, the distance from the body to the shooter. That information would not come until later in the day, however, and the matter of finding the third slug was critical. Bullets normally travel in straight lines, so investigators label a bullet's final resting place as Point A; the point it exited the body as Point B; the place it entered the body as Point C; they then try to determine the place it was fired so they can label it Point D, by tracing off an imaginary line through the points into space. Unfortunately, bullets sometimes go off in different directions once they encounter bone. Often they break up, sending shards of lead and copper jacketing off in several directions. Also, the body may twist before falling, or may be moved later by the killer, paramedics, family members or the first police on the scene. Any movement of the victim makes the process of recreating bullet paths difficult.

In this case, it didn't appear as if Borgert had been moved. The blood spatter analysis done by the crime teams immediately after taking photographs was pretty straightforward. Blood, as the saying goes, is thicker than water, leaving the body and striking surfaces uniquely based on the height and direction from which it traveled. Blood drops which fall straight down leave a round drop mark. Blood traveling at an angle leaves a tear drop-shaped mark with the tip of the tear drop pointing in the direction of its source. The more elongated the drop shape is, the greater the striking angle. The back of Borgert's head had been a mess. A large amount of blood, skull, and brain tissue had been blown out onto the kitchen surfaces immediately behind him, therefore, the crime teams were confident that Borgert had been shot and died right there in the kitchen chair, eating his Neapolitan ice cream.

Deane would have liked to leave and start interviewing people closest to Borgert, but he knew it was best if he stayed until the end. Besides, the first person he needed to interview was Mrs. Borgert, who was still sleeping.

The crime had been discovered by an Edina patrol officer named John McCarron, who had been called to the neighborhood on a fireworks complaint. As he cruised down Countryside Drive he saw Borgert, through the window, sprawled on his kitchen chair. When he looked closer, he saw the broken glass and the blood. As he called for backup and a supervisor, he realized his hopes for a quiet night were gone. The shift supervisor, Sergeant Erdahl, arrived, took McCarron and one other officer, and entered the house to secure the scene and look for other victims or any suspects who may have been lingering inside. Finding all the doors locked, they had to enter through a poorly made patio door at the rear of the house. Although the door was locked, the Borgerts hadn't put a rod in the door's track, so Erdahl was able to shake the door up and down and dislodge the locking pin. This old police trick he'd learned years before, when the citizens of Edina would call the police for help after locking themselves out of their own homes. The three officers searched the entire house, staying well away from the kitchen area to preserve any evidence. None of them wanted to get yelled at later for blundering around and messing up the scene. Besides, it was apparent from looking at Borgert that he was beyond any help they could provide.

Their search of the house revealed no suspects, but it did reveal Mrs. Borgert in her bed, sound asleep. The officers looked at each other and then at the nearly empty bottle of Absolut Citron vodka and the glass with just a few remaining slivers of melting ice on the bedside table. Erdahl had tried to shake Mrs. Borgert awake, but she just mumbled groggily and tried to push him away.

"Jesus Christ!" Erdahl said to the others. "I bet she's a three-five." Erdahl was referring to her blood alcohol content. He was close. When the ambulance came and determined that Judge Borgert was well and truly dead, they loaded up Mrs. Borgert and took her to Hennepin County Medical Center. There, doctors determined that her blood alcohol level was .37 and climbing. Her fairly normal breathing indicated that Mrs. Borgert had made frequent forays into the lower portions of vodka bottles. The doctors replenished her fluids intravenously and moved her to a detox room to sleep it off.

Phil Deane's team of officers and investigators were canvassing the neighborhood and speaking to everyone in a three-block area. They had barricaded off the street in front of the Borgert home and staked off the hillside across the way with yellow crime scene tape. The crime lab had decided not to look around on the street or hillside until daylight for fear of missing something. The lieutenant in charge of the Sheriff's team, Gary Hamner, had requested that the golf course not allow anyone to play until it could be checked. Deane had sent one of his younger investigators off on that happy errand. He knew the management of the course would be very displeased with that bit of news, for today was shaping up as fairly nice after a long, drawn-out stretch of miserable weather.

"I'll be goddamned!" came a voice from the living room. One of the crime lab men had discovered a small hole in a picture above the fireplace. He removed the picture and found that the hole continued underneath into the paneling. In the shallow hole, he could just barely make out the end of a lead slug.

"Okay," said Lieutenant Hamner, "let's not get ahead of ourselves here. Bobby, get the saw and cut that section out of the wall. How the fuck did it go from there to there?" He asked pointing into the kitchen and back at the fireplace. He stood there for a moment and then walked purposefully back to the kitchen. Behind Borgert's recliner was a kitchen island holding a row of heavy Cephalon pots and pans. Hamner moved a couple of the pots gently and found a dent in the side of a heavy two-and-one-half quart cooker. The dent appeared fresh, and there was a groove inside the pot where the black cooking surface been taken off.

"Look at this, folks," Hamner said. "I bet the bullet went through Borgert, hit this pot, and then glanced off at an angle into the living room. Bag this pot as evidence after you photograph it, and we'll check it for traces of lead and copper."

"Odd that the dent was facing the other way, away from the body." said a female deputy.

"Yeah, but that countertop is smooth. Look at how all the other pots have lids on them. This one's lid is lying alongside it. I bet the shot glanced off it with enough force to knock the lid off and re-direct the bullet's path, but not enough to knock the pot over. See how it's nestled up against the others? This shit's heavy cookware."

Deane knew that they'd keep looking for a while anyway, just to make sure nothing had been missed. He believed that the slug in the wall would match the ones in Borgert's chest, but all the bases had to be covered. In the meantime, the outside crime team had just finished searching the street and had found nothing. Deane had initially thought the shooting may have been a drive-by, but now it seemed as if the angle for that was wrong. The Borgert house sat up a little higher than the street, and it was beginning to appear as if the shot had come from at least the same level, if not a little higher. That meant the hill. Two crime techs had moved up there with metal detectors slowly probing the bushes and the grass. Deane saw one of them bend down and look at something. He took a numbered plastic tent-shaped evidence marker from his pocket and set it down. Deane knew that meant that something had been found which was worth marking and photographing. He resisted the urge to run up there and look. He was getting sick of waiting here, and the coppery odor of Borgert's blood. He knew that the team up on the hill wouldn't appreciate him running around and trampling their evidence. Just then another marker was put down.

A dark blue Ford Taurus drove around the barricade and pulled up in front of the Borgert house. Dean's initial flash of annoyance increased when he saw a man and woman step out dressed impeccably in dark blue business suits and expensive shoes. He didn't need to see the windbreakers with "F.B.I." emblazoned in yellow on the backs to know that the feds had arrived.

"Oh, no," Deane groaned to himself, "just the very last fucking thing I need right now." He walked out and met the agents in the yard. Both simultaneously pulled out their ID cases and flashed their badges at him.

"Good morning," Deane said, trying to keep his voice pleasant. "I'm Detective Phil Deane of the Edina PD. What can I do for you?"

"Special Agent Frank Olivetti," said the man, who was of medium height and stocky. He looked to Deane to be about 40 years old and combed his thinning hair straight back from his forehead, like Michael Douglas in *Wall Street*. His dark skin and piercing look harkened back just one generation to his Italian ancestors. Deane shook Olivetti's hand and found the grip hard and dry. Deane thought that Olivetti's nice suit and expensive watch hid a personality that could get menacing under the right circumstances. "This is Special Agent Hazel Loomis. We're from the Minneapolis office. We understand a Dakota _ was killed here last night." Loomis appeared to be in her late twenties and seemed to feel out of place at the crime scene. She wasn't long out of the Academy and, therefore, had not spent much time dealing with the uglier side of law enforcement. She was pretty, but kept true to bureau policy of downplaying her feminine assets and projected a businesslike demeanor.

"That's right," Deane said, "Judge Edward Borgert. Someone shot him three times, probably from that hill, there." Deane pointed at the bush line.

"Hmm," said Olivetti. "You sure it wasn't a drive-by?"

"Don't think so, the angle's wrong. Crime Lab is still working the scenes. Who called you? Last I heard, murder wasn't a federal crime."

Olivetti looked around at the house and the hill across the street. "It isn't. We were called because crimes against government officials have taken on a new priority since September Eleventh. We want to determine if this incident might be terrorist-related. We're here to see what you have and offer any type of assistance you might need."

"Well," Deane said, "it's pretty early in the game yet. We've just started to gather our evidence. None of the neighbors have given us anything useful yet. The victim's wife is in Hennepin County Medical Center, so we haven't been able to talk with her yet."

"Yeah," said Loomis, "I looked in on her a little while ago. The doctor said she's still sleeping it off."

"We have some threats on file from specific terrorist groups which we can reference once your investigation gets rolling," said Olivetti. "Nothing specific against this judge, but we'll show you what we have. Could be he got killed by someone he sent away, too."

"I doubt that," Deane chuckled. "This guy let everybody go. Maybe he got shot by a prosecutor or a cop, but I doubt if it was by a defendant."

CHAPTER 3

▼

The patriot woke up Monday morning at 8:25. He'd had trouble getting to sleep after his night's excitement. His drive home had been uneventful. Even so, he had driven very cautiously back to his house in Hastings. He didn't want to do anything that might draw attention from the police.

After getting home, he had gone into his workroom in the basement and disassembled the Mini-14. He gave it and the magazine a good scrubbing. He took out the remaining two rounds in the small magazine and the twenty in the larger one and put them back in the box. He then took the cased rifle and ammunition out to his garage and laid them on the hood of his car. He pushed aside a small metal cabinet in which he kept his motor oil, washer fluid, and other vehicle maintenance items. Using his power screwdriver, he removed four Phillips screws from a piece of plywood wallboard which was attached to the two-by-fours at the back of the garage. The previous owner had insulated the entire garage against Minnesota winters, covering the insulation with plywood instead of Sheetrock. This made a convenient hiding place when the patriot had first realized the need for one. The panel, a patch piece that took up the space between the end of an eight-foot section and the door, was 20 inches wide and five feet high. The patriot had removed the insulation from this space and lined it with a thick polyurethane barrier to keep out moisture. The cased rifle and the ten boxes of ammunition fit easily into the space, as did the manila envelope which held his intelligence information. When he replaced the panel and screwed it into place it looked perfectly natural. He slid the metal cabinet back in front of it.

The patriot eased his muscular six-foot-one-inch frame out of bed and walked to his bathroom to relieve himself of the brandy he'd drunk the night before sleeping. He went to the living room of the modest three-bedroom rambler and turned on the Channel 11 morning news. The pretty blonde anchorwoman had just finished some small talk with the meteorologist, who got the first say on any news station in weather-obsessed Minnesota. She turned to the other camera and said, "First up this morning, news of a shocking murder in a quiet neighborhood in Edina. Let's go to Tammy Nelson, who is reporting live from the 6600 block of Countryside Drive. Tammy?"

The camera cut to another pretty blonde woman, this one standing one house down from the Borgert residence. She was clutching a notepad in one hand and a microphone in her other.

"Thank you, Margaret," Tammy said. "Police here in Edina are investigating the shooting death of a Dakota County judge who lived in this house right over here." She gestured to the Borgert home. "Last night at about 10:30 police were called to investigate a report of what were thought to be fireworks in the neighborhood. When they arrived, they found the body of Edward R. Borgert sitting at his kitchen table. We don't yet know how many times he'd been shot, or if police have a suspect. We do know that the judge's wife, Marjorie Borgert, was taken from the scene by ambulance to Hennepin County Medical Center. A spokesperson for the hospital has told us that Mrs. Borgert was not injured in the attack but would not release any other information on her condition. Neighbors expressed shock when they learned of the crime this morning."

The camera cut to an interview with a woman who lived down the street. She said that, while she didn't really know the judge or his wife, they seemed like nice people. She thought it was "terrible" that anyone had been killed so close to her home and said she intended to keep her children inside more from then on.

Tammy came back to wrap the story. "Judge Borgert was appointed to a vacancy on the Dakota County bench five years ago after being a partner in a successful law practice in south Minneapolis for over 20 years. His time on the bench was marked by several controversial decisions which drew criticism from police and prosecutors in Dakota County. Police working on this case have refused interviews to this point, but a press conference has been set up for 4:30 this afternoon. Margaret?"

The anchorwoman came back in a split screen with Tammy and asked, "Do we know if police believe the judge's wife may be involved in the murder?"

"We don't know that at this point," Tammy replied. "We do know that there is no police guard on Mrs. Borgert at this time, which would tend to suggest that she is not a suspect, but we will stay on the story and let you know when we know more."

Margaret said, "Thank you, Tammy. More violence in Israel occurred last night when Hezbollah extremists clashed with Israeli forces today near the West Bank." The patriot shut off the TV and chuckled over the fact that the news had said that Borgert's time on the bench had been controversial. That was putting it mildly, he thought.

Borgert had been despised by police and prosecutors for his extreme liberal bias. He routinely stepped outside of mandated guidelines when sentencing those few criminals whose cases actually made it that far in the clogged justice system. One of the more glaring examples was when Borgert refused to send a four-time-convicted child molester named Andrew "Randy Andy" Stoughten to state prison. Borgert read a notation on Stoughten's pre-sentence investigation report that young Andy had been molested by his uncle and that he suffered from fetal alcohol syndrome, thanks to his mother's appreciation of vodka gimlets during her pregnancy. Borgert said that he thought that Stoughten was "actually as much of a victim as his victims" and sent him to a halfway house in Hastings, Minnesota, instead of Stillwater Prison, as was required by law, due to Stoughten's criminal history. He also ordered Stoughten not to use the Internet in the future to meet the young boys he liked to befriend and then molest.

Borgert had also been criticized by the media for letting a carjacker named Tyrone Clemens out of jail without bail so he could have his drug addiction treated. Clemens failed to show at the treatment center, choosing instead to go on a five state crime spree. He committed five rapes and four armed robberies and beat a 73-year-old man to death in Missouri, when the man tried to prevent Clemens from stealing his car. The man didn't care about the car as much as he did the cremated remains of his wife, which were on the front seat. Clemens had been sentenced to death by a Missouri judge who said he didn't give a rat's ass about Clemens's drug problem and that the State of Missouri would cure it for him once and for all.

The patriot went over to his computer and turned it on. He logged onto the internet and checked his emails. He had a few from friends forwarding jokes and cartoons. He typed in a URL and entered a site which sold weapons, knives, ammunition and other items which interested him. He clicked on a link labeled "Fun Page" and scrolled down to read any new postings. Site members could post messages, jokes, ideas and rants using their site alias. Some of the postings were obviously put up by people with limited intelligence. One read, "Fuckin Jews. Tryin to get us into another goddammed war over there. I say we're giving bombs to the wrong side. Give a few to the sand niggers and let them wipe out the fucking Jews for all time!" It was signed "Rebel Yell".

The next one read, "Fuck you!!!!! Why give any of those barbarians bombs? Why not just drop them on all of them?? Nuke the Holy Land!!" That one was signed "KKKlem."

The patriot thought that Rebel Yell would probably fire back with some other ignorant remark and KKKlem would probably keep it going. Maybe they'd meet and fight it out: two bucktoothed, lumpy-headed, cousin-fucking hillbillies swinging lead pipes at each other. The patriot wondered if KKKlem was actually in the Klan or if he just liked the name. Probably some guy who sat in the library in Birmingham, Alabama, and shot his mouth off on the free computer.

The patriot had spent a good deal of time surfing such sites, finding others who, like him felt that the country was desperately in need of change. He spent a lot of time dwelling on what people needed to do to get over the politically correct, socialist mind set which seemed to be flowering in America. Every group had a beef with the nation. Every group thought they were getting the shit end of the stick. And for some reason, the government was paying attention! The patriot believed that everyone, from the Somalis to the Klan had the right to express their opinion. Others were free to disagree. Wasn't that what America was founded on? Now, though, if someone has an issue with something, everyone else had to "feel their pain". He recalled a news story from late the previous year in which a small town on the East Coast had given up a seventy-year tradition of having Santa Claus and the Mayor light the town Christmas tree. Apparently, two families expressed their feeling that they would be "excluded" if such a ceremony was carried out. To the patriot's way of thinking, the mayor should have said, "Sorry you feel that way, but since the rest of the city enjoys the tradition, we will be continuing on with it. Attendance is not mandatory." But, for some reason, the wishes of a handful of people ended an enjoyable time for hundreds of others. It wasn't as if the tradition was "whipping the Christmas midget" or some such thing, he thought.

He remembered how his father had despised people he considered odd or different. He used to rant at the sight of hippies and Vietnam War protesters on TV and tell his young son that the nation would be far better off without them. In stores or restaurants, the patriot's father would point out people with strange hair styles or unusual clothing and say, "Jesus Christ! Look at that excuse for a human being." His son had learned those lessons well, even though he came to despise his father as he grew older.

The patriot had come to the conclusion that truth in all things lay in the middle. He had read widely the feelings of extremists and found that their views, whether they be to the far left or the far right on the political spectrum, were flawed. Extremists tended to ignore anything which didn't support their position. In doing that, they missed important facts. The Klan railed against Jews and blacks and maintained that there was a conspiracy among Jews to use civil rights and threats from the black community to bring down the government. At the same time, they suspected the government was secretly controlled by Jews in Russia and had been since before Franklin Roosevelt was in office. The patriot wondered why Jews in Russia would want to bring down a government controlled by Jews in America, if they were members of the same conspiracy. The ultra left railed against the government claiming that it was using police and federal agencies to whittle away civil rights. They suspected that the government wanted a "1984" society in which everyone was constantly watched and their actions controlled. Then there were people like Ted Kaczynski, the "Unabomber," who thought computers were the root of all evil, and spent his time living like an animal, writing a rambling manifesto and sending mail bombs to universities. The patriot had read the manifesto, and thought Kaczynski was very intelligent. However, he would take a good idea and then go off on a tangent which the patriot couldn't follow.

He knew that, in the mountains of Idaho and in the remote stretches of Kansas, lived reactionaries in compounds. Some marched behind the Confederate flag, others behind a Nazi swastika. None of them ever seemed to merge with any others, and their membership ranks ebbed and flowed with the seasons. They spoke of "the next revolution" and how all the concerned white men needed to be willing to become involved in order to wrestle control away from the Communist/Jewish/Black/CIA forces who wanted to ruin America.

The patriot thought that the truth was somewhere in the middle, yet the plan of action he'd decided was called for certainly was not. Concerned about the country, he felt a revolution was badly needed. The country needed to be restored to what it once was.

The events of September Eleventh still pissed him off. Every time he saw a picture of the World Trade Center on fire he became enraged. All the pictures which had flooded the Internet in the following months, such as crying firemen raising the flag over a huge pile of rubble or of the shrine erected near the site by those who'd lost family members, tore at him. He saw the video of Bin Laden gloating over the deeds and would have happily killed him himself. He was glad to hear George Bush talk tough to the terrorists and happy when the bombs began falling in Afghanistan, but thought Bush was still not the leader the country needed. When he saw the Al Qaida fuckers burning the US flag, he threw a glass against the wall. "How dare they!!" he had raged. "Look those filthy ignorant savages! What have they ever given the world? They've never helped a neigh-boring country in a time of need, never given the world art or poetry. They jump around in front of any camera put in front of them and had the absolute FUCK-ING nerve to criticize America?? What is their nation in comparison? It looks like a fucking cat litter box! Not much in the way of purple mountains majesties or fruited plains, that's for sure. If they have a national anthem, it probably had the words, 'Shit Abdul, I've got sand in my eye again!'"

He was concerned that America's children were being shortchanged in school. He spoke at work once with a co-worker whose wife was a public school teacher. The man was saying that his wife was so disappointed that American children scored so much lower in math than did kids from Belarus. She had thought that the state needed to stop funding all the defense industries and give more to the schools. The patriot told his co-worker that he was pretty confident that the gov-ernment of Belarus spent far less on education than did the United States and that, just perhaps, pouring tax money into the problem wasn't the answer. Maybe if the schools spent less time teaching cultural diversity and social awareness, he said, they would have more time for the basics and could again turn out kids who could read and write, add and subtract. The co-worker said that the patriot was not raising kids and, therefore, had no say. The patriot pointed out that he paid property taxes to fund an education system he didn't believe in.

There were vicious people out walking around because the most talented law-yers became defense attorneys and the ones who couldn't land a plush office in a partnership applied to the County Attorney to work for less money than the patriot made.

It made him angry that a former gang member from Chicago now lived in Minneapolis and had miraculously changed into a "neighborhood youth leader." The press kissed his ass every time he were on TV claiming that the PO-lice had executed another innocent black youth who was just running through an alley at one a.m. and that the gun he was carrying wasn't even loaded.

He was sickened by the mousy-haired, aging hippie woman who kept showing up on the news trying to raise support to shut down the nuclear power plant which had been safely supplying electricity to the neighborhood she had recently moved into for thirty years. She had just been arrested for trespassing and disor-derly conduct after she chained herself to the front gate for the third time. She had also been fined for slashing tires in the plant's employee parking lot. As the police were dragging her away she screamed to the reporters that she would be back. "If we can't have no justice, there can't be no peace!!" she screamed. The patriot smiled when he thought of the fact that his manila file of intelligence information contained facts on her, too. He would visit her soon.

The patriot felt that if he could do his work quickly and efficiently enough, he might be the person who could bring together the others in the country who felt as he did, the working people who thought as he did about things. If he could keep active long enough to gain attention he felt sure that many people in the nation would support his actions. He would use the media to get his ideas across. People would come to understand that he wasn't a nut, but a patriotic American. Maybe history had chosen him to be the next force which would shape the nation. He thought that, even though this idea seemed grandiose, history was full of examples of ordinary men who guided America toward a different, better direction. Maybe there would be chaos for a while, but even if nuts like the Nazis and the Klansmen did support him, the more stable leaders of the movement would eventually take control. The patriot honestly didn't want to be famous or a hero, but he truly felt that America needed someone like him at this point in history.

The patriot shut down his computer and stretched. He went to his basement and began his exercise regimen. He had been lifting weights regularly since his divorce three years before. He liked how working out had helped lift the depression he'd felt after his wife, Amber, had left.

He started out by lying on the carpeted floor and doing fifty sit-ups. He did them wrestler-style, by flexing his knees to his chest with each sit up. He then turned on his stomach and did fifty push-ups, balancing on the first two knuckles of his fists and touching his chest to the floor with each down stroke. He then lay down on his weight bench and gripped the free weight bar. He loaded 275 pounds on the bar and took a short breath before lifting it off the rest. He bench-pressed the bar five times and set it back on the rests. The patriot felt the strain in his chest and shoulders but wasn't tired. He continued with shoulder presses, triceps presses, and bicep curls and finished by working on his calves and quads by doing knee bends with a 150 pound bar on his shoulders. By the time he was finished, it was time to get ready for work. It was always hard to go back after his string of four days off, but he was a punctual man. He enjoyed being punctual and was annoyed by people who weren't.

He took a shower and toweled off. He combed his short hair and shaved. He had considered growing a moustache but every time he tried it grew out with four different colors. Most of the guys at work had them, but he just didn't like the result. The last time he grew one a guy said it looked like he had a calico cat under his lip. He went to the kitchen and had a bowl of Rice Krispies and peanut butter toast. He wished he had a grapefruit, but he hadn't had time to go to the store. Working the 3-to-11 p.m. shift made him lazy.

He returned to the bedroom, and pulled on the stiff work trousers, and laced up his brown lace-up Hi Tech combat boots. It seemed as if it would be warm today, so he pulled on a V-neck mesh T-shirt. Putting on his work clothes took a couple of minutes. He then walked back into the living room and made sure all his doors were locked. He took a look out front onto Pine Street. and saw that everything seemed normal. He remembered that he was now a hunted man. He would have to be very careful from now on.

The patriot thought of himself as a hunter, although he didn't hunt animals. He had often dismissed offers from co-workers to take him along deer hunting by saying, "No thanks, I like animals more than I like people."

He was both the hunter and the hunted. The thought was exciting! It made his pulse quicken and his breathing sharp and clear. All of his senses were alive and his thoughts were focused. His mission had begun and there was no going back now.

He walked into the attached garage and took out his car keys as he reminded himself that all thoughts of his secret life had to stop now. He had to focus on his public life. It was critical he keep the two separate. It was the only way he could survive until the job was done.

Every hunter needs good camouflage. The patriot thought he had that angle pretty well covered as he slid behind the wheel of the big Ford Crown Victoria. Deputy Tony Bauer was starting his afternoon shift for the Dakota County Sheriff's Office.

CHAPTER 4

▼

At 2:30 on Monday afternoon, Phil Deane and the crime lab team leaders sat down in the conference room in the Edina Police building. Lieutenant Hamner was joined by Agents Olivetti and Loomis from the FBI and Agent Mike Rawlings from the BCA.

Rawlings was the head of Major Crimes Investigations at the state's criminal investigation bureau. He was 55 years old and eligible for retirement, but after having spent 31 years as a cop, no other lifestyle appealed to him. Rawlings had left the Marine Corps in 1970 after serving in Vietnam and joined the St. Paul Police Department as a rookie patrol officer in 1971. He'd made Sergeant and then Detective and had scored a number of successful investigations in Minnesota's capitol city before being wooed away by the BCA. They hadn't used money as an incentive, but rather the opportunity to head up the statewide crime team that was called out to help Minnesota's smaller police agencies when the unthinkable happened in their town. He enjoyed challenges and was known as a very savvy investigator. Rawlings was modest and preferred to nudge less experienced detectives in the right direction rather than point out their mistakes. He also had the grace to stand back later and let them take the credit when the case was finally solved. Rawlings didn't crave kudos or media attention. He derived his job satisfaction from seeing the bad guy go down.

They all sat down at a large wooden conference table and opened their files after Deane, as the host, arranged for a coffee urn to be brought in.

"Okay," Deane started out, "let's go over what we know. Our victim apparently sat down at his kitchen table a little before 10:30 p.m. to eat a bowl of ice cream. The TV in the next room was tuned to Channel 5, so he probably had just finished watching the news. Someone lying in the bushes of the golf course fired three shots from a .223 rifle through his window. We're confident no one gained entry to the house. We have recovered three spent shell casings in the bushes. What do we know about them?"

Lieutenant Hamner fielded that one. "They're not a common brand, I can tell you that. Casings for most rifle shells are yellow brass; these are painted Army green. The bases of the shells are stamped 5.56 X 46, and there is some kind of a symbol I can't make out on them. This can be good for us. If they had been standard Remingtons or Winchesters, we might be looking at thousands of sources. Once we track down where these were made we should be able to follow some lines of distribution."

"Maybe we can help there," said Olivetti. "We can fast-track the rundown on these through ATF."

"I'm sure we have the brand in our files," answered Hamner, who somewhat resented the feds stepping on his dick just then. "I just haven't had a chance to run them through yet."

"I'm sure you do, Gary," said Deane, "Your guys haven't let me down yet. But you do have a lot of other evidence to process here. Let's farm out what we can here so we can get the most accomplished. Run them for fingerprints, though, just in case, and work the slugs so we have solid bullet tracks to take to court."

"We'd be happy to air freight anything you needed to the lab at Quantico," offered Olivetti.

Hamner had taken just about enough weight on his manhood and decided to say so. "Well, why don't you air freight…" Hamner began, until Deane put a restraining hand on his forearm.

"Lieutenant Hamner was about to thank you for that thought," said Deane. "However, his people are VERY good at what they do, and I'm sure they'll handle it just fine. We do appreciate the offer, though."

"I didn't mean any offense," said Olivetti, "I was told to help any way we could."

"No need to apologize," said Deane. "What else do we have?"

Hamner took the ball. "All of the casings bear the same stamp. Let's send one to ATF after we glue it and then we can analyze them for ejector marks."

"What?" asked Agent Loomis. "Glue it? Ejector marks? What do you mean?"

"It's a very effective way to get faint prints from small areas, like a narrow shell casing," answered Hamner. "We put the casing in a small sealed tank with a portion of super glue near it. The fumes condense on the print and bring them out so we can see them easily. Ejector marks are small impressions left on a shell casing by the rifle's ejector mechanism. Different brands of rifles eject shells differently and, therefore, leave different marks on the shell. They're pretty unique, just like the rifling on a slug. Could help us ID the kind of rifle used." He considered ending with a dig on Loomis's FBI Academy training, but he was bigger than that.

"Sounds good," said Deane. "Moving on: Mrs. Borgert is awake and I've got an investigator with her now. So far, she remembers nothing about last night and has no idea who might want her hubby dead. We asked her if there had been any strangers nosing around lately and she remembered a brush salesman coming by last week. We're checking any complaints in that area for door-to-door sales and researching City Hall's issued-permits list. Neighborhood canvas came up empty. A few people heard the shots but we still haven't found out who made the initial call. We located a dog-walker who talked with the first officer. He was to the north and two blocks away at the time and saw nothing of value. Any luck with trace evidence in the bushes?"

"We should be able to look through the vacuum bags today, yet," answered Hamner. "No impressions really. The ground was pretty solid under there. No footprints around either. We had dew last night, but no tracks leading away, so I guess it set in after our man took off."

"Okay, now I have another question." said Deane. "Maybe Mike here can help me with this one. How much do I tell the press at 4:30? Murder is not exactly my bread and butter."

Rawlings cleared his throat. "Good question, Phil. Press coverage is helpful when you're looking for Joe Blow neighborhood criminal, but I doubt that's the case here. This was an organized crime scene. I think he thought this out, possibly made a visit or two to the area before. Following this line of thought, it's a good bet our man is closely monitoring any press coverage. Give him as little as possible. Tell the press what we know about the caliber of weapon and the fact we've recovered casings. He knows we have these. Tell them we are following up other leads which you are not allowed to disclose at this time. You might want to read from a prepared statement, but don't get drawn into the question and answer game. You're on the right track checking on strangers in the neighborhood. It's kind of off the beaten path, so the residents probably notice strangers. I might also suggest, on a CYA level, that you have a sit-down with your chief first."

"The boss is pretty good, here," Deane said. "He leaves us pretty much alone, so 'cover your ass' isn't what's on my mind."

"That may be," said Rawlings, "but this is the kind of case that will have a lot of important people asking why someone hasn't been caught in the next few days. Those questions will be directed at him, and he'll be coming to you."

"You seem pretty confident that we won't catch anybody," said Deane.

"Frankly, I don't think you will, right away," Rawlings said. "This guy has an agenda. Maybe he was just after Borgert, maybe not; we don't know yet. Until we do, this is a stranger-homicide and one with press interest. That makes things uncomfortable."

"You're doing wonders for my confidence, here," Deane said with a grin. "Well, let's get going on our chores. Call me when you have some answers." Deane handed business cards all around and stood as they all filed out. Rawlings lingered behind and faced Deane as the last of the others had walked out.

"I don't mean to be the pessimist, Phil," Rawlings said. "We'll eventually find this guy. By the way, is Borgert's address and phone number listed in the book or in information? He was a pretty public guy there for a while when the press had their finger in his eye."

"I don't know," Deane replied. "It's a good point. You're wondering how our guy found him if he isn't?"

"Worth looking into," said Rawlings. "If he targeted Borgert, he had to find him first."

Deane picked up a Minneapolis White Pages and flicked through to the Bs. There were twelve Borgerts, but no Edward on Countryside Drive. He picked up a phone and dialed 411. He asked for Edward Borgert and was transferred to a recorded voice which told him "At the customer's request, the number you are requesting is non-published."

"Hmm," Deane mused. "I'll do an Internet search after the press conference. I hope this means Borgert got killed by someone who knew him."

Rawlings picked up his briefcase and left. Deane walked down the hall to the Chief's office. He knocked and his boss, Chief James Roosevelt, told him to come in. Roosevelt was an imposingly large black man in his fifties. He had worked the north side of Minneapolis for 25 years, working his way up from patrol to Sergeant and eventually to Captain. Over the years he had taken college courses and graduated, earning his Bachelor's in Criminal Justice from the University of Minnesota and a law degree from William Mitchell Law School. He served as chief of Chaska, Minnesota PD, and was hired as chief of Edina two years before. Roosevelt had acquired an understanding of the political world during his time as a police administrator but hadn't forgotten what it was like to wrestle a pissy drunk into a squad car or how it felt to carry the charred body of a baby out of a burned home and turn it over to the medical examiner. He knew the stresses of police work, and had a reputation for being pretty easy going with his men, and was on a first name basis with them.

"Well, Phil," Roosevelt sighed, "isn't this some shit? What do we have?"

Deane went over the scene and the evidence and covered Rawlings' suggestions about what to tell the press.

Roosevelt winced a little and said, "That's pretty thin. The reporters won't be too happy with that little bit. Are there any areas we could expand on?"

"I'm open to suggestion," Deane said. "The fact is we don't have a hell of a lot now. I haven't done a lot of these, but I don't want to give away too much."

"These reporters can be a pain in the ass," Roosevelt said. "If they find we're hiding something they'll make a big deal out of it. I've had calls from the city manager, the mayor, and the county attorneys of Hennepin and Dakota already."

Deane felt his stomach souring and wished he had some Maalox. Between being up all night, spending the day trying not to step on Borgert's gray matter, guzzling coffee, and now getting signals from his boss that the world was watching, he felt as if he was developing a world-class ulcer.

"Boss, it's the first day. We've got a lot of ground to cover, and I'm all for telling these reporters to go pound sand. I'm open to suggestions, as I said, but if I have to run everything past them as it crosses my desk, I won't get much done. Do you want Stanley to handle it?" Deane was referring to Captain Stan Polaski, Edina PD's information officer who, as such, usually dealt with the press.

"Normally, I'd say yes," Roosevelt said, "but not on this. The press will want to see a real live detective. I know you've got stress here, too, so I'll trust you to play it as you see fit. I'll give them a little speech, then turn it over to you. Once it's over, we can let Stan handle the inquiries until we announce the arrest you'll be making tomorrow." Roosevelt grinned broadly after his little joke and reached across the desk and slapped Deane on the arm. Deane returned a little sickly smile even though he caught the underlying message, which was, "Don't fuck this up."

The press conference was held in the large roll call room, which was empty after the afternoon shift had filed out following their 3:00 p.m. shift briefing. By 4:25 the chairs were full, and there were four cameras set up in the back. Channels 4, 5, and 11 were the CBS, ABC, and NBC affiliates in the Twin Cities area. The local WB and Fox channels were there, too, as were a number of radio station and newspaper reporters. Donald Lentzmeyer, the Hennepin County Attorney, was also on hand.

Chief Roosevelt stood up and said, "I think everyone is here, so let's get started." He paused, knowing from experience that the TV would begin coverage from this point. "As you know, last night someone committed a cowardly and vicious act of violence on Countryside Drive. Judge Edward Borgert, a District Court Judge in Dakota County, was murdered in his home. Investigators from the Edina Police Department, the Minnesota Bureau of Criminal Apprehension and the Hennepin County Sheriff's Department are investigating this crime. I'd like to introduce you to Phil Deane, the investigator who will be heading up the search for the person responsible for this act. He has served this city well for over twenty years and has been on this case since the body was first found. Phil?"

Deane rubbed his sweaty palms on the sides of his trousers and stood up behind the podium. "Good afternoon, everyone," Deane began. "Last evening at about 10:30, one of our officers was called to the 6600 block of Countryside Drive to investigate a noise complaint. He discovered a kitchen window shot out on the street side of a house at 6617 Countryside Drive. Inside was the body of the homeowner, Edward Borgert, age 58. Mr. Borgert had been shot three times, twice in the chest and once in the face, with a high-powered rifle." At this, several of the reporters grimaced and some shook their heads.

"We have recovered three shell casings from a line of bushes along the edge of Normandale Golf Course across the street from the Borgert house," Deane continued. "We are working with the FBI and the Bureau of Alcohol, Tobacco and Firearms to trace the manufacturer of these shells. An autopsy has just been completed on Judge Borgert's body, and I have not yet been briefed on the findings. Investigators are following up several leads and interviewing neighbors now." Deane realized he'd run out of steam and didn't know where to go from there. He looked at Roosevelt and at Lentzmeyer. Neither of them stirred.

"Perhaps, Mr. Lentzmeyer would like to comment at this point," Deane said hopefully.

The County Attorney stood up next to Deane and cleared his throat. "Well, ah, it would be premature for me to comment at this time. I was briefed by Chief Roosevelt earlier in the day, but I, ah, have not had the opportunity to review any reports and statements at this point. My office will certainly provide legal assistance to Investigator Deane, here, and to any other officers, if needed." He sat down leaving Deane standing there feeling like a cigar store Indian. Deane wondered why Lentzmeyer came at all if he had nothing to offer, then it occurred to him: Lentzmeyer is a politician.

"Well, I am prepared to answer your questions at this point," Deane said. Immediately hands went up and reporters stood. One of them in front asked, "Do you have a suspect?"

"We are following up several leads at this time, but I am not at liberty to reveal any suspect information as it may hurt our case," Deane replied.

Another reporter followed up with, "So, you DO have a suspect, then?"

"I said I cannot answer any questions about suspects at this time, for the reason I just stated."

A female newspaper reporter asked, "Is Mrs. Borgert a suspect?"

"We do not feel Mrs. Borgert is a suspect at this time," Deane answered.

"Could she become a suspect?" Another reporter asked.

Deane smiled and said, "Anyone could become a suspect, even you." Deane thought that was pretty clever until the reporter speared him by saying, "So, that means you have no suspects at this time. Do you believe this case may go unsolved?"

Christ, thought Deane. *I sure stepped in dog shit that time.* Aloud he said, "I believe we will solve this case. I meant, by my poorly worded answer, that we are keeping an open mind and following up all leads."

"Do you have evidence to believe that the judge was killed by a former defendant as a result of a vendetta?" asked a male reporter from a radio station.

"Please folks," Deane said, "I said that I couldn't answer any questions dealing with suspects. We are very early in this investigation."

A female reporter asked, "Detective, why was Mrs. Borgert hospitalized last night?"

Deane weighed how best to avoid THAT particular land mine. "Mrs. Borgert's medical records are private and confidential. All I can say is that she was not injured and her illness was not connected with the death of her husband."

The same reporter then said, "A source at the hospital had said that Mrs. Borgert was intoxicated when she was admitted. Do you have any comment on that?"

What a bunch of fuckers!" Deane thought. "I will not comment on that," he answered, "other than to say that we should all remember that Mrs. Borgert's husband of many years was brutally murdered in their own home. I can only imagine the grief and shock she is experiencing and the disgust she will feel if she is unlucky enough to hear that last question." *Take that, bitch!* thought Deane.

A male TV reporter waved and asked, "Detective, the FBI was on the scene of the crime this morning. Are they concerned that Judge Borgert's murder may have been a terrorist incident?"

"The FBI has offered their help in this investigation. The man was a judge and, as such, a representative of our government," Deane answered. "We've found nothing yet to indicate this act was carried out by terrorists, but, as I said, we are keeping an open mind."

Chief Roosevelt stood and raised his hands. "My friends, I think we've covered all the ground we can cover today. Please direct any further inquiries to Captain Stanley Polaski, our Media Liaison. Thank you for coming." He took Deane by the sleeve and they walked out of the room as reporters continued to ask questions.

"Jesus!" Deane said as they stepped into the hall. "If I interrogated a suspect like that, you'd be giving me days off."

"Yeah, well, the thing to remember about reporters is they're looking for a comment from you that they can trim down to about five seconds for the nightly news," Roosevelt told him. "Doesn't matter if it makes you look like an chump or helps tell the story. In fact, it's better if it makes you look silly. Don't ever, EVER, smart ass a reporter like you did just then. They'll take you out back and tan your ass! Then I will!"

"Sorry, boss," Deane said. "I'm beat and I've never been through the mill like that before."

"All right," Roosevelt said, calming down. "Finish what you need to and then get some sleep. Get someone over to that radio station in St. Paul. Be back bright and early tomorrow and go about catching this guy. I won't have G.I. Joes running around doing Lee Harvey Oswalds on citizens in my town."

CHAPTER 5

▼

Deputy Tony Bauer pulled into the big Dakota County Government complex on Highway 55 in Hastings. As a patrol deputy, he had a take-home squad car and was free to go directly on to his patrol area from home. Because today was his first day back after four days off, he wanted to stop in the office, read through the department memos, and review any incidents which had recently occurred in his area of responsibility.

Bauer worked the 1130 area, the southernmost patrol sector in Dakota County. It is a large county, with well over a quarter million residents. It contains the Twin Cities suburbs of Burnsville, Lakeville, Rosemount, Apple Valley, Eagan, and many other, smaller cities. It also contains the cities of South St. Paul and West St. Paul, both of which are actually south of St. Paul, the state capitol. The Dakota County seat is Hastings. The majority of the northern half of the county is urban, and most of the southern half is rural farmland. One of the fastest growing suburban areas in Minnesota, Dakota County is considered part of the so-called seven county metro area.

Tony Bauer had worked the 1130 area for four years. Prior to that he had worked in the sheriff's Jail, and the Transport, and Warrants Divisions for seven years. He had always yearned for a patrol assignment and enjoyed the freedom of working the road. He knew the gravel roads around the farming communities of Castle Rock, Randolph, and Vermillion very well. He had gotten to know most of the troublemakers and thought of his sector as a large, spread-out, small town. He worked alone, and while he was considered a friendly and competent cop, he preferred it that way. His sergeant, Mike Fitz, had been making noises lately that he thought Tony should put in for training to certify him as an FTO, or a Field

Training Officer. In that capacity he would be used to train new patrol deputies. Bauer remained noncommittal, saying he enjoyed his privacy. He had considered the advantages of such an assignment, the extra pay, and the chance to try to shape the new people into the type of cop he thought the country needed more of. But he also knew that, more and more, he had begun to appreciate his freedom. He liked the privacy of cruising the back roads, listening to talk radio and thinking. On quiet nights, he enjoyed pulling into some secluded spot, turning the police radio up and sitting on the hood of the car looking at the stars. Doing this he found it was easier to keep from thinking about the things that upset him, such as his ex-wife, and he could close his eyes and let his mind wander over more tasteful subjects. He had already decided that he would not think about the previous night's events or do any other related planning while at work. He intended to keep his work life and private life completely separated so there would be no slipping up.

He had been forced to do some of his intelligence work while on duty. He knew that once he had used his work resources to get the data he needed, he would have to steer clear from then on. His MDC, or Mobile Data Computer, which was the laptop computer the county had installed in his car so he could be dispatched to calls more efficiently, had been very handy in getting addresses like Judge Borgert's. He simply had to open up the QDNS (or Query Database Name Search) screen and enter whatever information he had. The Minnesota State Department of Motor Vehicle's driver's license files would supply him with every record close to the one he was looking for. He was then able to call up the full driving record of the person he was looking for, including driving violations, height, weight, eye color, and address. Even addresses which were non-published were available to him this way. He could then print them out on a small printer mounted between the squad car's bucket seats. He had used his home computer to access county property tax files to get some information, but the DMV files were much easier to browse through. The manila envelope in the compartment in the garage contained a number of these records.

Tony used his key tag to buzz open the doors leading into the secure inner offices of the sheriff's department. He walked into the large patrol office and greeted co-workers who were either sitting around a large office table drinking coffee or parked in cubicles talking on phones. Some were writing state accident reports on standard forms and others were typing at word processors. Greetings were called out to him as he walked over to the coffee machine and poured himself a cup.

"Big Tony," said Mike Fitz, with a smile. "Did you enjoy your days off?"

"Yes I did," Bauer answered. "Very much." He turned to Todd Erickson, who worked the adjoining 1140 sector, and asked, "Are we going to give 'em hell today or just fuck off?"

"Fuck off," Erickson replied. "I'm so tired I can't see straight."

"Bonnie wearing you out after work?" Fitz asked with a grin.

"Shit, I wish. Between the four-year-old who's decided something is living under her bed, the two-year-old who's teething and the Jehovah's Witnesses who insist on ringing my bell not once, but five times, to discuss the Lord, I haven't gotten three hours combined sleep."

"The evening shift is a pain," Fitz agreed.

Han Nguyen, one of the department's Hmong deputies agreed. "Well, how about when you have to work late and then turn around and be in at 0900 for court and then find out the guy is gonna plead guilty and you're not needed at all?"

"Why complain about that?" Bauer asked. "You get paid two hours of overtime and then go home for a nap."

"Because the whole day is shot. I don't live close to court like you."

Mike Fitz clapped him on the shoulder and said, "Wait until you rotate to nights. Then you get to work all night, go to court at nine, go home when the guy doesn't show up, drive across the county for in-service training from one to five p.m., and then be back at 10:30 that night for your eight-hour shift!"

"There's a cure to that," said Steve Bennington, who was a fifteen-year man with a notoriously seditious attitude. It was Bennington who changed the screen savers on the computers to urge people to vote for whoever was running against the Sheriff. He also enjoyed drawing telescopic sights on the faces of registered sex offenders, whose images and histories were posted on a bulletin board. Bennington had once been given a reprimand for putting an auto joker on the Lieutenant's car engine, after the distracted supervisor nearly had the crap scared out of him when the device screamed and smoked on ignition before issuing a loud, although harmless, explosion. "Work nights, arrest no one, claim you slept through in-service training, and then call in sick for your shift. Life is short."

Mike Fitz grinned and shook his head. "Can't you keep from polluting the newer guys? They turn fast enough as it is."

"I think of it as 'Team Policing,' a concept I'm surprised you, as a line supervisor, seem to be unfamiliar with. I believe in sharing my years of hard-earned experience with the younger men," Bennington said with an affected air of insult.

"What about the younger women?" asked Bauer.

"The High Sheriff keeps me away from the women. I think he fears my mojo." There was a general round of laughs and jeers over that remark.

"Yeah, you're very concerned for the younger men," said Nguyen. "My first day on the road alone and you put a child seat behind the wheel of my squad!"

"It was never proven that was me!" complained Bennington, laughing.

"That's Steve's motto," said Fitz. "'Admit nothing, deny everything and demand proof.'"

"Don't forget the last part of that," Bennington reminded him. "'Make counter-accusations.'"

Bauer picked up the Metro section of the Minneapolis paper and the state section of the St. Paul Pioneer Press. He slipped them into his briefcase and sat down to read the memos. Bennington retired to a computer and began typing a report. A short time later a very large lieutenant named Gus Schultz ambled in with some papers for Mike Fitz. Gus was 6'8" and weighed well over 350 pounds. Behind him, a huge, gray-haired day-shift deputy named Ernie Engleman came in from his shift. He was only about 6'3", but Ernie's impressive stomach strained the buttons on his uniform shirt front. His hands were massive from the years of farming he had done growing up and still did.

A young Hispanic deputy, who had just started training, leaned over to his FTO and whispered, "Are all the old guys around here so big?"

His training officer looked at the two man-mountains and said, "Yeah, cops were big in the Jurassic Era."

Bennington saw the lieutenant and said, "Gus, I have a question about this report I'm doing. Is the correct plural in this sentence 'hard-ons' or 'hards-on'?"

The lieutenant, who had a large monthly desk blotter in his office with the 56 remaining days to his retirement highlighted with big red numbers, shook his head and said, "I'm not sure. Why don't you write to Miss Manners and ask her?"

"Okay, thanks," said Bennington with a nod.

Tony Bauer finished with his reading, gathered up his briefcase, and went out to his car. He got behind the wheel and put his briefcase on his front passenger seat behind his large nylon case; this case contained his ticket book, maps, code books, two extra magazines for his .45 Glock duty sidearm, and four extra boxes of 12 gauge shotgun shells for the Remington Wingmaster which was mounted above his head on the protective Plexiglas screen behind the front seats. He had one box of slugs and three of double-ought buckshot in the glove box. The case also the contained extra pens, report forms, micro-cassette recorder and tapes, and other items he needed to do his job. The car's truck contained another larger container which held tools, flares, a 100-foot tape measure, a blanket, first aid kit, fire extinguisher and a large bundle of plastic Flex-Cuffs. The trunk also contained his traffic direction vest, hat, tools, tape measure, blanket and raincoat.

Bauer started the car, adjusted the ride of his holster and ballistic vest, and drove south. He called his dispatcher on the radio and said, "1130, clear", telling her that he was available for call.

"1130, clear," replied the female voice.

Bauer drove through Hastings to County Road 47, which would take him southwest to his patrol area. He tuned in his favorite conservative talk radio show, where an argument was raging between the host and a black man, who was telling the host that it was not possible for minorities to be prejudiced.

"That's a ridiculous argument," said the host. "Why is it wrong for me to refer to you with a racial slur and okay for you to do the same to me?"

"Because you have the power," the caller answered. "You white people own everything, you have all the top jobs, you make the laws, and you spend all your time figuring out how to keep us out."

"How do you justify the practice of so-called 'Equal Opportunity Employment,'" the host asked, "when a government agency runs an ad for employees and puts in it, 'No white male applicants accepted'? Can you imagine the furor if it said, 'No blacks need apply'?"

"It's the same thing," said the caller. "There were ads like that for years, and the unspoken message when a black man or a black woman shows up to apply today is the same—get out!"

The argument went on awhile with neither side making any ground. After the caller hung up, the host said, "Liberals have a corner on the market of hypocrisy. They always have. One set of rules for me, one for you, unless I disagree with them, then you have to change them. Liberalism is the new fascism. 'Either agree with me, or you're wrong and I hate you!'"

The next caller was a young woman who told the host that she felt sorry that he had such a small penis that he needed to vent his frustrations on people who had greater IQs and had had the advantage of a better education.

"See, that's exactly my point," said the host. "I have an opinion that differs from hers, so she concludes that I am sexually frustrated and stupid. When did God die and leave these people in charge? Conservatives think liberals are wrong, but liberals think conservatives are bad."

Bauer got a call to go to a farm east of Farmington to take a vandalism report. When he arrived he was met by a farmer in his fifties, whose face had spent almost all of its life outdoors in Minnesota. The man waved Bauer over to the cow barn, and Bauer parked near the edge of the grass. As he got out, the farmer came over and shook his hand.

"Can I help you?" Bauer asked.

"Well, I don't know," the farmer answered. "I suppose you can't do much but the missus said I should call. Last night somebody got in the milk house. Come on in." He led Bauer into the barn. All the cows were out in the pasture but their smell and the smells of hay and manure were strong inside. Bauer had grown up in the city but enjoyed farms and respected farmers for the hard, honest work they did. He followed the farmer to the milking machinery. Bauer could see a huge wet area around the equipment. Some of the pipes were bent, and milk dripped out of several places in the stainless steel, where someone had used a crowbar or some other tool to break the piping at the joints and seams.

The farmer scratched his head and said, "There's a lot of damage there. What's more, I can't get replacement parts in time to collect milk tonight or tomorrow. Normally I could store it in there," he pointed to a large tank, "but they tore out the wiring for the refrigeration and, just to be nasty, took a piss in there, so I had to empty everything out and sterilize it."

"Christ," said Bauer. "How much will it cost you to repair all this?"

"It's not the cost so much. There's $500 there easy, but it's the time and the lost milk."

"Any idea who would have done this?" Bauer asked.

"Well, I have a guess it might be that Eddie Fischer down the road. His dad's upset with me over a land deal, and I called the game warden on him a few weeks ago, when I saw him hunting on my land out of season. He's not all there, you know, upstairs, and I can't think of anyone else who'd do this."

Bauer nodded. He knew Fischer well from many calls in the past. He also remembered him from working the jail. Fischer was a bully. He was a big, biker-looking guy who seemed to threaten somebody once a week. He usually picked on women or men he could intimidate. He would call people on the phone and threaten them and then refuse to answer the door when the police came to talk to him. Bauer remembered one time when he was brought to jail for making terrorist threats to a business in Farmington. He whined and kissed the jailers' asses until he got released. As he walked out the door of the jail, Fischer told the deputy, who was safely inside the glass control room and, therefore, unable to kick the big slob's ass, "Thanks! I'm off to fuck your mother!" He then hustled out the door.

"Yeah," said Bauer, "I believe it. I know if I go over there he'll just hide in the house. Did anyone see anything?"

"No, we go to bed early. My dog used to guard the house at night but he died a few weeks ago. I guess I need a new one."

"A big one," Bauer agreed. "I'll write this up, and the detectives will be in touch."

He left the farm and thought about how one man could work so hard, put everything into the profession of feeding other people and how another one, a thirty-year-old who still lived with his parents and never did an honest day's work in his life, could live so close to each other and be so different. He shook his head and thought how easy it was for the worthless guy to cause so much trouble for the hardworking one. It wasn't fair.

Bauer stopped for a salad at a diner in Lakeville and then passed the rest of his shift quietly. He read the papers' accounts of the untimely death of Judge Borgert. He received a call about an alarm at an auto repair business but was told to disregard it before he got there. He helped a couple of housewives exchange information after they crashed their cars at a wide-open intersection in Castle Rock. The two kept apologizing to each other, saying, "I don't know why I didn't see you! I feel like such an idiot!" "So do I!"

As Bauer walked back to his car, one of the women asked him under her breath, "Did you smell liquor on her breath?"

As 11:00 p.m. neared, Bauer pointed his car toward home. He hoped he wouldn't get a last-minute call because he had to get up early in the morning. He had a job to do.

CHAPTER 6

▼

The patriot drove east into the rising sun and adjusted his sun visor. He was wearing a large pair of reflectorized aviator sunglasses, but the sun was still low in the sky and pretty bright for a man who'd just gotten up. He steered his Ford Explorer down Highway 61 and watched for the turnoff to County 18 Boulevard. He was getting closer to the Mississippi River, and the surrounding terrain was gradually sloping downhill.

The false handlebar moustache he wore irritated his upper lip, as did the baseball cap on his head. The patriot didn't normally wear hats, but this piece of work had to be done in the early morning, and a disguise was called for. He had bought the moustache at a theatrical supply store, and it was stuck to his lip with a gentle adhesive. He was beginning to sweat and was concerned the gum would work loose, even though the girl at the store promised him it wouldn't. He knew that a moustache added ten years to the estimated age of the wearer and a hat concealed not just hair color, but length and style, as well as a good portion of the upper face. He turned up the air conditioning to help relieve the discomfort he felt from wearing a cotton shirt and oversized hunting jacket. The day was warm enough already to go without a coat, but he needed it to hide the Browning Hi-Power 9mm he wore in a jackass shoulder holster rig; he also wanted the long, unsnapped sleeves to conceal his hands, should he need to put on the surgical gloves he had in his coat pocket. A hunting jacket, jeans, and baseball cap were pretty much the standard form of dress where he was headed and, above all things, he wanted to blend in. He had brought some other items along for quick improvisation in case Plan A failed.

He turned north onto County 18 Boulevard and was grateful that the sun was no longer in his eyes. It would now be just a short ride through the town of Eggleston and then a right turn onto Sturgeon Lake Road. He passed a sign indicating he was headed toward the Prairie Island Nuclear Power Plant, owned and operated by Xcel Energy on land owned by the Sioux Indian Nation.

Sarah Ehrenberg slowly stirred and rolled onto her stomach in the morning light. She had a massive hangover caused by the beer, wine, and pot she'd ingested late into the night before. As she turned she was suddenly aware of the presence of someone else in her bed. She was startled for a moment and then realized that it was George. She lifted her head to look at him and immediately regretted it, when a shaft of pain cut through her head like a lightning bolt. She fought down a wave of nausea and lay her head back down on the pillow.

Ehrenberg, a forty-one-year-old woman, lived alone in the small little house about a mile from the nuclear plant. She had spent a good portion of the three years she'd lived there making the plant management and workers wish she'd settled elsewhere. She was committed to environmentalism, activism, vegetarianism, and a lot of other "isms" except for fascism, which she felt was a creeping cancer in the "land of the free." She supported People for the Ethical Treatment of Animals, Greenpeace, the American Civil Liberties Union, The Green Party (because the Democrats had become too moderate), NAACP, the American Indian Movement, and a host of other causes, into which she threw herself with a passion. She considered the American government a fascist state and clung to every cause and persuasion which clashed with the mainstream of American ideals. She had been in jail fifteen times for disobeying court orders, trespassing, disorderly conduct, assault, damage to property, attempting to incite a riot, and burglary. She had managed to avoid any lengthy jail terms because the very judges and prosecutors she hated were reluctant to press for tough sentences against activists. It was thought better to let them off quietly than to make them martyrs and cause others to feel sorry for, and then emulate, them.

Ehrenberg had friends in the Native American community and considered herself an "Indian Apologist." She hated her white race for their persecution and attempted extermination of the people who had welcomed them to the New World. She regularly attended powwows and potlatches, joined in the dancing and singing, and enjoyed it when the talk turned to politics and conflict.

She had attended a powwow the night before; that's where she had run into George. She chuckled to herself when she thought that she had done more than "run into" George. She again turned her head to him, gingerly, this time, and looked at the mass of black, unruly hair that fanned out over the pillow. He was lying naked on the sheet, and she admired the size of his back and the curve of his butt. A lot of Native American men didn't have much of a butt, but George did. She saw the row of red fingernail marks she'd put in his lower back the night before and felt a little guilty, but then realized that George hadn't complained. In fact, he seemed to like it.

They'd danced together at the powwow and eaten wojapi. She had intended to stay longer, but George had asked her if she wanted to get out of there, and she liked the idea. She'd driven him to her place because George had no car and was currently staying with his brother's family. They drank a 12-pack of Budweiser and then switched to red wine. Ehrenberg had a pretty heavy buzz going when George took out a quart-size zip-lock bag of fine smoking Mexican green. They took it into the bedroom, where Ehrenberg got out her bong, and the night really got going.

She'd lost track of time in a very visual daze when she realized that George was pulling off her sweater. She eagerly joined in and soon both of them were naked and rolling on the sheets. George had a little trouble doing his part at first, due to the amount of depressants his body had absorbed, but Ehrenberg knelt on the floor between his legs and showed him why she'd gotten the tongue stud. It wasn't long at all before George was ready and mounted her. Ehrenberg enjoyed sex and wasn't shy about telling him what she wanted. George, for his part, was happy to oblige the somewhat homely white woman as long as she popped for booze and let him get his rocks off. This took some time, as she was in no hurry to let the session end too soon, and kept moving away whenever she thought George was getting close. Finally he'd had enough with the teasing bullshit and pinned her down onto the bed. He pumped her vigorously until he released and then collapsed on top of her. They'd had another, less trying session about an hour later and then both passed out.

Ehrenberg considered finding out if George could be persuaded to go for a little morning romp, but decided against it. Better to let him wake up. She'd fix him some coffee and breakfast and then see what would happen if she just dropped her robe on the floor and crawled onto his lap on a kitchen chair. *A man can't do too much complaining with a nipple in his mouth,* she thought with a smile.

She dozed off of a few minutes and then heard someone knocking on the front door. She tried to ignore it, but the knocking continued. She hated to get up but thought it would be better to get rid of whoever it was before they woke up George and pissed him off. She pulled on a black sweatshirt that had the word

"Choice" on the front, slid on some cutoffs, pulled the bedroom door closed behind her, and stumbled down the hallway to the living room.

The patriot had parked around the corner from the little gray trailer house just off Sturgeon Lake Road. He walked slowly but directly around the block and up the front walk. He looked around discreetly; the street looked quiet. A red pickup with a man in it had passed him as he got out of his Explorer, but it didn't seem as if the driver had paid any attention to him as he went by. The patriot saw that the woman's car was parked on the road out front. It was a Chrysler K wagon with about 15 bumper stickers on it. One said "Itchin' for an incident," another said "You can't hug your children with nuclear arms." The patriot had read them before on his trips here. He stepped up onto the wooden landing and knocked. He had to knock for a couple of minutes before he heard movement in the house. He tensed, knowing that he would have to move very quickly. He couldn't be sure if there was anyone else in the house. His previous surveys of the house and neighborhood had led him to believe that the woman lived there alone. He had seen other cars there, though, and he intended to spend as little time in as possible.

Ehrenberg looked out her front door and saw a man in a hunting coat and baseball cap standing on the step. It took her a second to realize that the man had on a Cleveland Indian's hat and she was instantly angry. The stupidly grinning Indian's logo of "Chief Wahoo" was the most offensive creation she'd ever seen. She had once been arrested for throwing a soup can full of urine on a Cleveland player when he was leaving the Minneapolis Metrodome after a game against the Minnesota Twins. That incident had made local and national news as well as ESPN.

Ehrenberg opened the door and said, "What do you want? It's pretty goddamned early to be knocking on doors."

The man said, "I'm Barry Green from *Time* Magazine. We're doing a story on nuclear power plants and talking to people who live near them. I'd like to ask you a few questions because you've been the most vocal critic in your area against the Prairie Island site."

Ehrenberg considered that for a minute, thinking; *Time Magazine is a national forum. Hell, it's an international forum! Why did he have to come NOW, though?*

"Can't you come back in an hour or so?" she asked.

"Sorry," said the man. "I have to be at the Prairie Island offices to interview the managing director in an hour. After that I have to go to Monticello, and I have an early flight." He smiled, hoping to look apologetic.

Ehrenberg thought it over for a second. Monticello was where Minnesota's other nuclear plant was. It sounded as if this article was going to lean heavily on the side of the energy industry. If she didn't take this opportunity, it might never come back again.

"Come in," she said and stepped back. The patriot stepped up into the house and closed the door behind him. Ehrenberg walked in front of him toward the kitchen and was going to tell him how the Native Americans who lived around here wouldn't like his choice of hats when she felt, more than heard, him step up behind her. The patriot didn't look very big in the hunting coat, but he had a lot of muscle mass and moved smoothly. She was startled, feeling the rush of air as the space between them disappeared in a split second, and said, "Oh!" as she began to turn around.

The patriot had pulled an awl from the front right pocket of the coat. An awl is a leather-working tool which is used to punch holes in thick hide. This one had a door-knob-shaped handle and a seven-inch steel shaft which ended in a point. The patriot had used the shop grinder in his garage to put a needle-sharp point on the end. He grabbed Ehrenberg's hair on the left side of her head with his powerful left hand and curled his fingers into a fist. In the same motion, he pulled the stunned woman's head back against his chest and pinned it there. He pushed the point of the awl into Ehrenberg's right ear and rammed the handle in as far as it would go. The steel shaft easily pierced her ear canal and went through the thin bone of the skull. The patriot drove in the awl's entire length and pushed it through the center of Ehrenberg's brain.

Ehrenberg's body convulsed but did not fall, nor did she cry out. The awl had cut into the parts of her brain which controlled the essential functions of breathing and circulation. The patriot held her for a moment and twisted the awl handle around in a grinding clock-wise motion, causing further damage to her already doomed brain. As her body shook more violently, he eased her down onto the floor. He pressed his right knee onto the middle of her back and let go of the awl. He took hold of her jaw with his right hand while still gripping her hair with his left. He pressed down forcefully with his left hand and savagely twisted her jaw around to the right and up and was rewarded by the sound of her spine snapping just under her skull. Ehrenberg's body immediately went limp.

The patriot stood up and looked around. Killing the hippie had taken no more than thirty seconds. He heard no movement in the house and decided the woman was alone. He pulled the awl out of Ehrenberg's head and wiped the blood on her sweatshirt, leaving two red V's showing against the black back of the garment. He pocketed the awl and took out a handkerchief, which he used to pull the door closed behind him. He'd been certain to touch nothing inside the house. He walked at the same pace around the corner and back to his car.

George Fast Horse woke up and stretched. He had a pretty big hangover, but he was no stranger to them. He wondered where the woman—*what was her name again?*—had gone. He thought she was pretty plain looking, even for a white woman, but she had been a good lay. He might come back again, but he figured that she might be the kind who would want to show him off to all of her friends; that would get to be a drag. He got out of bed and pulled on his underwear and jeans. He walked out into the hall and down to the bathroom. He took a leak and decided she must be in the kitchen. He thought he'd have some breakfast, just to be social, and then hike up the road to the gas station where he could call his buddy, Noah, for a ride.

George walked into the living room and stopped still. He looked down at the body of the woman—*Damn, why can't I remember her name?*—and froze. He felt his head clear and his balls shrink up into the pit of his stomach as he realized that no one could have their head all the way around looking at their own back and still be alive. He saw a small trickle of blood seeping down from her right ear. He stood there for a few minutes in complete shock. How would he explain this? He knew if he called the cops it would be good old George who got hauled off to prison. "Well, you see, we just met last night. I don't know how this happened. I was sleeping!" *Yeah sure. They'd believe that all right.* Then it occurred to him that he'd fucked this woman six ways to Sunday last night! His jizz was all over her and the bed! "Oh, shit!" George breathed. "Oh, shit! Shit, shit, shit!"

George was overcome with fear and panicked. He ran back to the bedroom, grabbed his boots, shirt, and coat and pulled them on as fast as he could. He ran out the back door and into the little yard. He looked around and then had an idea. He went back inside and found Ehrenberg's car keys on the kitchen table. He tried to step around her body in the living room to get out the front door, but he began to shake so badly when he looked at her again, he just couldn't. He ran out the back door again and around the side of the house to the front. He jumped into the wagon and started it up. He saw that it had an almost full tank of gas, which was enough to get him away from there. He jammed the car in gear and stepped down on the gas. The tires squealed as he pulled out from the curb and sped down the street.

Mrs. Bowman, who lived next door to Ehrenberg, was outside watering her lovely tulips, which were just blooming. She kept pretty close tabs on the goings-on at the house of that terrible woman next door, but she hadn't seen the first man leave. She had seen the second, though.

CHAPTER 7

▼

Cecelia Bowman finished watering her tulips and then raked her little backyard. All the while she was doing her spring chores, she kept an attentive eye on the house next door. Mrs. Bowman had lived in her little row house for thirty years. She had moved there with her late husband, Dewayne, when he got the job at the new power plant. He'd died ten years before of a heart attack, and she'd decided to stay on. The house wasn't too big, and the yard wasn't too much work, yet. Their three children were all long grown-up and had moved away, and many of the friends she and Dewayne had spent time with were either dead or had left when the neighborhood had started to decline.

Cecelia was a devout Catholic, and prayed every day for Dewayne, and lately had begun to wish that she could join him. Life just wasn't any fun anymore, and she hated getting old. She couldn't pray for such a thing, though. That would be a sin. She went about her days and passed one after the other, waiting for the day she'd be called.

Life had gotten a little more lively when that crazy woman moved in next door. Cecelia had seen her so many times on TV being dragged off to jail and screaming about the government and nuclear power and what not. She'd watched some of the strangest characters she'd ever seen come and go from that house and wondered what could be going on inside. Cecelia just couldn't understand why any woman would go to such lengths to cause trouble.

When the woman first moved in, Cecelia had tried to talk to her. She told her about Dewayne working for the nuclear plant since it opened, and the woman asked her if he'd died of cancer. She had told her, no, that he'd had a heart attack.

The woman had said, "Too bad, cancer would have been more fitting." After that, Cecelia would have nothing more to do with her.

She finished raking and bagged the old, dead grass and sticks and piled the bags along the curb for the trash man to pick up. It was getting close to 10:00 a.m., and she was going to go turn on *The Price Is Right,* but she still hadn't seen any movement next door. She'd woken up at midnight the night before when the crazy woman had brought the Indian home. Cecelia hadn't slept well in years and woke up at the slightest noise. She'd seen the Indian tear out of there in the woman's car but hadn't seen the woman. The Indian sure looked wild-eyed when he took off, like he'd seen a ghost, and the back door was standing open, too.

Cecelia jacked up her courage and walked over to the woman's front door. She knocked lightly, figuring she'd ask the woman if her phone was working if she answered. She knocked a little louder and still no one came. Cecelia cupped her hands around her eyes and looked in the front door window. It took a second for her eyes to adjust to the dark inside, but when she saw the body on the floor, she began screaming. She ran to her house and was still screaming when the 911 dispatcher took her call.

Sarah Ehrenberg's house sat just outside the boundary of the reservation in Goodhue County. When the first deputy on the scene realized what had gone on in the house, he wasted no time calling in an investigator. The investigator called the sheriff and the sheriff called the crime lab of the BCA. By the time a fully equipped crime scene team was set up in the house, it was 1:15 p.m. Ehrenberg had been dead for over six hours.

The first deputy to the scene had finally calmed Mrs. Bowman enough to get the story out of her. He and the investigator determined that the Indian male seen leaving the house driving Ehrenberg's car was their prime suspect. They called their records department and pulled Ehrenberg's file. They had the dispatcher run what is called a QMO check using Ehrenberg's driver's license number (this is a query which provides police with a list of all the registered vehicles and trailers owned by someone). The DMV responded immediately with one vehicle registered to Ehrenberg. It matched the description given by Mrs. Bowman, so the next task issued to the dispatcher was to send out a nationwide message to law enforcement agencies, with special attention to those in Minnesota and Wisconsin. The message read:

**********BOLO**********BOLO**********BOLO**

    To all law enforcement agencies, special attention, Minnesota and Wisconsin…for the Goodhue County, MN Sheriff's Office…please stop and hold for investigation of homicide: Gray 1988 Chrysler K station wagon, MN LIC/ 760FPH, numerous bumper stickers on rear. Vehicle is listed to Sarah Elizabeth Ehrenberg. Driver is described as Native American male, 6' 220 lbs, long black hair, jean jacket, jeans. Age 30-45. Driver is suspected in the homicide of the vehicle's owner and should be considered armed and dangerous. If vehicle is located, please impound for crime scene processing. If suspect is located, please hold on charge of Probable Cause Murder, and contact the Goodhue County Sheriff's Office immediately. Auth/Detective John Pappas.

The BOLO (Be On The LookOut) message went out before noon and was broadcast to all police cars in Minnesota and western Wisconsin.

Mike Rawlings and the BCA crime team wrapped up the Ehrenberg crime scene at 8:15 p.m. The woman's body had been taken away to the Ramsey County Medical Examiner's Office in St. Paul for autopsy, although anyone who saw how grotesquely twisted her neck was knew that it had been broken. It didn't appear that she'd suffered a fall: there were no ladders or chairs around which she might have been standing on; there were no other abrasions visible on her which would have indicated a nasty tumble. The blood in and around her ear, although there wasn't very much, was yet to be explained. Rawlings had been filled in about Ehrenberg's political history by Detective Pappas, the primary investigator on the case. Rawlings had seen the woman on TV and remembered he had wished she would shut up. Well, Mike, he thought to himself, somebody else had that very same thought. The black light his team had run over the bed sheets and Ehrenberg's clothing had showed a lot of semen residue. They had taken samples for DNA testing, they also took the sheets, which were liberally covered in hairs, both head and pubic, some of them clearly too long and dark to be the victim's. On the bedroom floor they had found a glass bong covered in fingerprints, some large, some small. A plastic baggie of marijuana also yielded fingerprints as did the Budweiser bottles and a couple of glasses on the kitchen table.

    Rawlings's team sealed the house with crime scene tape and piled the bags of evidence they had collected into their van. Rawlings promised to call Detective Pappas the next day with the initial findings. Pappas had figured he should catch some sleep while he could. Once the car was found, he'd probably be going for a ride.

    What he didn't know was that the car had just been found.

Officer Tom Blount and his new partner, Jason Bandy, were on their way to a theft call in the 2000 block of Emerson Avenue North in Minneapolis when Bandy said, "Tom! Wait, go around the block!"

"What?" Blount asked with a little exasperation in his voice. "Did you see Elvis?"

"No, I think I just saw that car they're looking for down south in that homicide they told us about at roll call. It was by that little grocery store."

Blount chuckled and decided to humor the new kid. At the same time, this was getting a little old. He didn't mind someone being conscientious, but this kid wanted to solve the Kennedy assassination. He turned the corner and went back around to Olson Memorial Parkway. He slowed as they went by the store and he read the plate on the wagon.

"One piece-of-crap K car, license seven, six, zero, Frank, Paul, Henry," Blount said. Bandy clawed through his briefing notes (he'd kept all that he'd accumulated in the four months since he'd been released from the Minneapolis PD's rookie school) and found today's entry.

"760FPH! That's it!" he cried. "That's the car from the murder in Goodhue County! Suspect is an Indian male with long hair, wearing jeans and jean jacket!"

"Well, he ain't in that car," said Blount.

"What do we do?" Bandy asked.

"Go on to our theft call. It's almost break time," Blount was joking but it caused Bandy to choke.

"What?? Go? A theft call? It's a murder! This guy killed somebody!"

Blount laughed and said, "Calm down, junior, I wasn't going to deprive you of your big arrest. We're going to call a supervisor." Blount dialed the duty sergeant on the cell phone and was waiting to be transferred when he saw an Indian guy with a long pony tail and jeans walk out of the store with a bag and head toward the car. "Say, Jason, what was the physical description on that suspect?" he asked Bandy, who was again digging in his bag.

"Ah, six foot, 220, 30 to 45 years. Why?"

"Because he's getting into the car," Blount said.

Before Bandy could reply, Blount dropped the phone, grabbed the radio mike and put the car into gear. He cut across the street and said, "455 requesting backup, Olson Memorial Parkway and Penn. We are stopping felony suspect in Assad's Grocery." Blount dropped the mike, hit the red lights, and screeched to a stop behind the Chrysler, blocking it in. Blount and Bandy jumped out but stayed behind the open doors of their car. Blount pointed his pistol at the driver, and Bandy yanked the shotgun out of the rack. He jacked a round into the chamber and leveled it on the Chrysler's driver compartment.

"Driver!" Blount yelled. "You're under arrest. Do exactly as I say and you won't be hurt! If you disobey my instructions, I will take it as an aggressive act, and you will be shot, do you understand?" The driver nodded.

Just then the first of several squad cars pulled into the lot and took up positions around and behind the wagon. George Fast Horse was on his way to jail, just as he figured.

Fast Horse was brought to the Hennepin County Jail on a hold for the Goodhue County Sheriff's Office. Because there was no warrant or formal charge at that time, the jail staff called Goodhue County dispatch when Fast Horse came in and asked them to come pick him up as soon as possible. The Goodhue duty sergeant called John Pappas on his cell phone and told him that his suspect had been arrested. Pappas called the shift supervisor at the Hennepin County Jail and asked who they had. When he was told, he chuckled. He'd known George for a long time as a thief and a doper. Murder seemed a little out of his line, but even criminals try to "improve" themselves, he thought. He asked if the jail could hold him until the morning. No, the jail sergeant said, there were no Hennepin County charges pending on him, so he would have to be picked up right away. Hennepin's jail in downtown Minneapolis was always full and the staff would not bend rules to pack in any more than were necessary. Pappas said he would contact the arresting officers to see if they would put a charge on Fast Horse for possession of stolen property. The jail sergeant gave him the name and number of the Minneapolis duty sergeant for the precinct where Fast Horse had been picked up.

Pappas got through to the supervisor and repeated his request. The sergeant asked, "Do you have a signed stolen report on the car?"

Pappas was afraid that would come up. "No, the owner was murdered. No relatives around to sign the stolen report." Minnesota law required the owner or a representative of the owner to sign an affidavit that a car has been stolen before any prosecution can take place. This prevented people with scores to settle from calling in auto theft reports and then getting a kick out of imagining how the cops would soon be shoving guns in the face of the person they'd just loaned their cars to.

"Well," said the Minneapolis sergeant, "no stolen report, no stolen. Sorry."

Pappas thanked him and hung up. He called the Goodhue County shift supervisor back and asked if there was anyone available to run up to Minneapolis and get George. The shift was short, but the sergeant said he'd round somebody up or go himself. Pappas thanked him and reminded him that Fast Horse was not to be questioned. He asked that whoever transported him have a tape running and to be sure to advise him of his Miranda rights as soon as he got him in the car. That way, if George wanted to ramble on and volunteer information on the hour long ride back, it would be admissible in court.

Pappas went home and set his alarm for 5:00 a.m. He wanted to get an early start on the day.

CHAPTER 8

▼

Wednesday was a busy day for Phil Deane. He had spent all of the previous day running down leads and following up on evidence from the Borgert murder. By Wednesday, the preliminary autopsy results were available, as were the initial ballistics tests. They showed that the slugs in Judge Borgert's body were the same caliber and type as the one found in the wallboard behind the hanging picture. The bullets had deformed severely when they bounced around both in the room and inside of Borgert's body. The .223 shell is very small and light and travels at an incredible 3300 feet per second. One of the shells in the judge's chest was fragmented, probably from having to pass through the double paned window glass. The crime lab was unable to tell yet if they would be able to get any rifling marks from the shells. Deane hoped they would get some evidence there as the rifling—marks left on the outside of a shell as it passes through the grooves inside a gun's barrel—would be crucial in comparing them to a weapon, should they find one.

The investigation had not turned up any leads with regard to door-to-door salesmen in the Countryside Drive neighborhood. On a brighter note, the Bureau of Alcohol, Tobacco and Firearms (BATF) had identified the shell casings used by the killer. The bullets were made in Russia and imported to the United States under the brand name Barnaul. They were an inexpensive brand of ammunition sold generally through Internet sites and at gun shows. Unfortunately, Barnaul does not mark shells with lot numbers, so it would be impossible to tell where the shells were sent to by the importer. Any routing information would be on the shell boxes themselves. The BATF agent Deane spoke with told him that if he developed a suspect they could trace any ammunition boxes they might find back to the supplier.

At some point on Wednesday evening, he heard about the murder of an environmental activist in southern Minnesota. He hoped the cops working that case had better luck than he was having.

On Wednesday morning, Detective John Pappas carried his case file on the Ehrenberg murder, a tape recorder, and a cup of coffee to the Goodhue County Jail. He set up the recorder in an interview room in the jail and asked the detention officer to bring George Fast Horse in. A few minutes later, Fast Horse was led in, wearing handcuffs and a brown jail smock with matching trousers. His hair was pulled back in a ponytail and tied with a piece of kite string. Pappas looked at him and tried to read the expression on his face. Fast Horse looked worn down and depressed. Pappas hoped that he would be inclined to talk about the murder.

Pappas turned on the tape as soon as the jailer left and took out a pad and pen. He began by reading Fast Horse his Miranda warning from a sheet of paper he had brought with him.

"George Fast Horse, I am Detective John Pappas of the Goodhue County Sheriff's Investigations Division. Today is May 8, 2002. We're at the Goodhue County Jail and the time is 11:15 a.m. I'm investigating the death of Sarah Elizabeth Ehrenberg on the morning of Tuesday, May 7, 2002. Before we continue I'd like you to direct your attention to this sheet of paper. I'll read it to you and ask you to follow along. I'll then ask you to initial each point as we complete it, okay?" George nodded. "Is it all right if I call you George?" Pappas asked. Again George nodded. "George, for the purposes of the tape, I'll ask you to make all your responses verbally, okay?"

"Okay," George said.

"George, line one reads, 'You have the right to remain silent. Anything you say can and will be used against you in a court of law.' Do you understand that?"

"Yeah," replied George.

"Could you initial in the box at the end of the sentence?" Pappas offered a pen and George scrawled his initials.

Pappas continued, "'You have the right to an attorney. You can have an attorney present with you at any time while you're being questioned. If you cannot afford an attorney, one will be appointed for you before any questioning, if you wish.' Do you understand that?"

"Yeah."

"Okay, Initial that box." George complied. "Continuing on, 'You can decide at any time to not answer any questions or make any statements.' Do you understand?"

"Yeah." George signed the box without prompting this time, having gotten the hang of it.

"Last part," Pappas said. "'Having these rights in mind would you like to give a statement about what happened yesterday morning?'"

George looked at Pappas. "What's the point, man? You ain't gonna believe me anyway."

"George, I'm willing to listen to anything you have to say. I haven't made up my mind about what happened in that house."

"Riiight," said George, drawing out the word so the emphasis wasn't lost.

"George, you know I have a job to do. I want to find out exactly what happened to that woman. If you had anything to do with her death, maybe you had a good reason." George shook his head. "Listen George, if you tell me exactly what happened, I'll write it up that way. If I've found you've lied here, I'll write that up, too. You've known me for years. Have I ever bullshitted you or done you wrong?"

"No."

"Okay, if you want to give a statement, I'll listen. Initial the last box on the form and we'll get started."

George wrote in the box and pushed the paper away, almost as if it was a disease. Pappas put the paper in the file and got started.

"George, yesterday at about 10:00 a.m., a neighbor of Sarah Ehrenberg saw a man fitting your description run from the back of Ehrenberg's house and take her station wagon. A sheriff's deputy later found Ehrenberg's body inside her house. She'd been killed, and it was apparent she had company with the man since the night before. Earlier today I showed a photo lineup to the neighbor, and she picked your picture out of a group of six men roughly resembling you. You were found in Ehrenberg's car in Minneapolis last night."

"Well, shit, John, sounds like you've got it all figured out," George said. "Just send me to the gas chamber and go have a steak."

"George, calm down," Pappas said in an even voice. He knew when to let a suspect blow off steam and when to bear down. "I told you I'm willing to hear your side. Why don't you tell me if you were with Ehrenberg that night and what happened."

George slumped back in his chair. He ran a hand over his face and said "Yeah, I was with her. I met her at the powwow Monday night. She hangs out around the reservation a lot, likes Indians, likes to tell us she's one of us, you know." Pappas nodded. "Well, we left there and she drove us to her place and we had some drinks."

"About what time was that?" Pappas asked.

"I don't know, maybe midnight." Pappas made a note on his pad.

"Okay, what happened then?"

"Well, we drank some Bud and some wine she had and then went into the bedroom. I had a bag of shit and we smoked some in her pipe."

"So, you smoked some marijuana in a bong?" Pappas asked.

"Yeah, my pot, her bong. Seemed fair, she bought the beer."

"Okay, go on."

"We got pretty shitfaced. We smoked and then got horny and got it on. You know."

"You had sex with her?" Pappas asked.

"Yeah, a couple times."

"Was she conscious?"

George took exception to that. "Yeah, fuck, man! What do you think? Christ! Think I'd fuck a passed-out woman?"

Pappas thought George probably might, but didn't say that. "Sorry George, I'm just trying to get the facts right." George pulled himself together and went on.

"Right, well, she was awake and didn't mind it, neither. Look at the scratches on my back it you don't think so." Pappas made a note of that, intending to have photographs taken of those scratches and any other wounds George might be sporting. Maybe Ehrenberg fought back.

"Well, we got it on a couple times and then we went to sleep. Next thing I know, it's morning, and I get up to find her on the living room floor. I didn't touch her, but I could tell she was dead."

"How?"

"You just know, you know? Besides, her neck was all fucked up. Twisted around. Made me freak."

"Then what happened?"

"I freaked! I looked at her and knew I was fucked. I knew you guys would pin it on me so I took off. I wasn't thinking. I grabbed her keys and I…I couldn't even walk past her. It made me sick to just see her like that. I ran out the back and took off in her car just to get away. Later I realized that was stupid, too, but I needed to get away."

"Where were you going?"

"I was going to go north to Red Lake, but then I tried to find my cousin in Minneapolis. He wasn't around, and I talked to some guys who told me he was somewhere else. After a while I got hungry and stopped at the grocery store for some food. I pretty much figured there wasn't anywhere I could go. I thought about coming back, but I couldn't do that, either. I was just kind of depressed. That's when I got caught."

"So, you're saying that someone else killed Sarah while you were sleeping? You never heard anything?" Pappas asked.

"That's right. I know you don't believe me. Look, I'll take a lie detector test if you want."

Pappas thought about that. Lie detector tests weren't admissible in court in Minnesota. A lot of guilty criminals offer to take one figuring they can beat it. If they can't they're in no worse shape because the jury will never know. A police officer usually offers a test if he has doubts about his case or if he intends to use a failure as ammunition for a follow-up interrogation.

He had a witness who saw his man flee the scene; the suspect stole the victim's car; the suspect's hair, fingerprints, and DNA would be shown to be all over the house—he had a great case. Why, then, did something feel wrong about this, he wondered. Pappas thought he'd try another tack.

"Why was there blood in Sarah's ear?" He asked.

"I don't know," George answered. "I told you I didn't kill her. She was alive when I saw her last. Did she get shot?"

"I don't know, I'm asking you."

"Well don't, 'cause I don't know." George said.

"Okay, tell me what you know about Sarah. You said she hangs around, likes to kiss up to your people. How do you feel about people like that?"

"I don't give them much thought," George said. "It's fine to be white and say you worry about Indians and feel bad about shit in the past, but you can go back to your white world and kick back. To tell you the truth, its all bullshit. Look, we are who we are, you are who you are. I wish I was Mdewakanton Sioux so I could get rich off the casino and live like a king, but I'm not. You know how many Sioux show up trying to prove they have enough Mdewakanton in them to qual-ify? The tribe has a council to handle them."

"I know that," Pappas said. "So you don't like those people?"

"I don't know. Maybe some mean well, maybe they're just doing it for them-selves, I don't know. The point is, they don't accomplish anything. Nothing changes. A hundred white women can come to a powwow and tell me they wish my ancestors would have wiped out all of their ancestors four hundred years ago, but it won't change anything. I'll be on the reservation and they'll live in town."

"So why did you go home with her, if you think they're all full of shit?" Pappas asked.

"Cause I figured I could get a piece of ass, maybe," George shrugged. "I'll drink anybody's beer if they wanna give it to me. I don't get too many women, you know? I ain't rich or pretty. That woman wasn't even that good-looking, but she offered the beer and the bed and it was a better deal than I had lined up that night, so I took it. I wish I'd gone back to my brother's place that night instead."

"George, I'd have an easier time believing you if there was someone else in the house or if someone else was seen leaving there. What do you think we should do to the guy who did this?"

George thought about that. He decided there was no way out of this one, so he might as well be honest. "I didn't kill that woman, John. I know it looks bad for me. Whatever. If you find who did do it, throw his ass in jail forever. I don't know his reason, but it's pretty cold to kill somebody like that." He paused and then said, "You know, when you asked me before if she was awake when I fucked her, I got all mad and said I wouldn't have. But, you know, I might have, with enough drink in me. I'm no angel, but I couldn't kill somebody like that, even if I do think they're full of shit."

After the interview was over, Pappas called Mike Rawlings and went over what had been said.

"I don't know, Mike," Pappas said. "It seems like I've got an open-and-shut case here, but something just doesn't feel right."

"Well, it sure sounds as if you've got an attractive suspect. He had the opportunity, we don't know about motive yet or how exactly she died, but he sure behaved like a guilty man, stealing her car, and tearing off like that."

"I know, but George has always given it up to me before."

"Well, the stakes are higher now. Maybe he's more afraid of life in the can than he was about doing short time in the county jail. Let's see what the autopsy shows, and maybe he'll change his tune."

Tony Bauer went about his normal routine and went to work. He'd slept in a little late Wednesday morning because he was short on sleep from the day before. He'd gone home after killing the hippie and tried to take a nap, but couldn't. The neighbor was mowing his lawn, and the phone rang a few times. He'd gone to work and had run his ass off all night because of a rash of vandalism that had happened the night before. The day car had taken a bunch of them, but he was sent on seven that the earlier guy couldn't get to, plus five of his own. Plus he got called to a family dispute where a bratty fifteen-year-old kid wouldn't turn down his blaring music and kept calling his mom a "cunt". Bauer asked the parents if they wanted him to arrange to have the kid placed in a foster home. They wrung their hands and looked at each other and said, no, they just wished he could talk to the boy. Bauer tried to talk to the little shit through the door, but he just turned the music up louder. He told the parents he thought the kid wanted attention and that his suggestion was to give him some by placing him some-where. The dad told him he thought that placement was a "perfectly awful" idea and that they didn't want junior in some frightening place. He said they would take care of the matter and ushered Bauer to the door. Mom got in her parting shot as he left, saying, "I thought the police were supposed to help people." Then, just before he was supposed to go home he got a call about a domestic near Hampton. He found a broken-down dump of a trailer outside of town and heard screaming as he pulled up. He ran into the house and found a twenty-three-year-old scumbag beating the shit out of his pregnant nine-teen-year-old fiancée with his belt. He cuffed the guy, who didn't have the stom-ach to turn the belt on the big cop who'd just thrown him across the room, and waited until backup arrived before taking any statements.

The woman, it turned out, was less than grateful that Bauer had stopped the whipping she was taking, and pleaded with him to let poor Jesse go. She said he was just upset because he'd lost his job and things were tight, what with the baby coming and all. Then the girl's mother showed up and listened to the tale with a cigarette dangling out of her mouth and said in a whiskey-and cigarette-ruined voice, "I don't see what the big, goddamned deal is. My husband's blackened my eye more than once. It's part of being married!" By the time Bauer had booked the turd and finished the reports, he was two hours overtime.

On Wednesday the call load was a little lighter. After just a couple of vandal-ism calls, he caught up with a drunk driver who was being followed by a person reporting him on his cell phone. The dispatcher had transferred the caller to Bauer's car phone, and he was able to catch up to the guy in about 10 minutes. The caller said the guy had been all over the road and had even been in the ditch once. Bauer could see weeds dragging under the rear bumper. He pulled the guy over and asked for the driver's license. The guy was shitfaced and said, "Isn't it on the back of the car?" And then laughed, like it was the funniest thing he'd ever heard. Bauer asked him how much he'd had to drink and he gave the standard DWI answer, "Two beers." After failing the sobriety tests, referred to as "Stupid

Human Tricks" by Mike Fitz, Bauer asked the guy to give a preliminary breath test. The guy took the tube of the PBT in his mouth and puffed out his cheeks and crossed his eyes, pretending to blow. Bauer'd had enough and arrested the guy. By the time he'd booked him and done the report, it was time to go home. Bauer was glad, because he had someplace to be after work.

CHAPTER 9

▼

After calling the dispatcher and saying that he was "10-7," or out of service at the end of his shift, Tony Bauer parked his squad car in his garage. Unhurriedly, he changed clothes and organized the things he would need for the night. He changed into dark slacks and a dark polo shirt. He put on his shoulder holster rig and verified there was a full magazine of 9mm shells in the Browning Hi Power before he snapped it in. He took a dark blue trench coat out of his bedroom closet and carried it out to the garage. He hung the coat on a nail and set about opening up his hidden storage area in the wall. From the cubbyhole he removed two items and then closed the compartment. He considered leaving it open so he wouldn't have to go through the whole process when he got home, but he knew it was best to be consistent and keep any evidence hidden at all times.

He hid the items away in his clothing and put on the trench coat. The patriot got in his Explorer and used the remote to open the garage door and drove out.

Wallace Berry shut off the TV and decided to do a little reading before bed. He got up and turned up the thermostat in his apartment, for a spring cold front had moved through, bringing a little rain and wind and dropping temperatures. He went into his bedroom, changed into a T-shirt and a pair of gray sweat pants and climbed into bed. He considered reading the novel he'd started but knew that he should read the response to the lawsuit he'd filed on behalf of a paralyzed sixteen-year-old boy named Joshua Carpenter, who wanted to play football for his high school team. The school had told the boy he wasn't qualified to play due to his disability and Josh's mother approached Berry, who was the head of the Minneapolis chapter of the American Civil Liberties Union. Berry took the position that Josh was being discriminated against under the Americans With Disabilities Act and filed suit on his behalf to force the school district to allow him on the team.

The suit had made headlines and Berry had been interviewed along with Josh and his mother by all the local TV news programs. There was the expected conservative response from people who wrote letters to the editors of the papers, saying that the suit was stupid and that anyone with common sense should understand that a person who was confined to a wheelchair could not play a sport like football. Even Josh's father, who had divorced Josh's mother when Josh was two, had been interviewed saying that the suit was just a stunt by his ex-wife to spread her kooky views and further spoil their son. Berry intended to press on with the suit and thought he had a good chance to win or at least force a compromise. School districts were notoriously shy of fighting legal battles, especially when they were denying opportunity to a student.

Berry felt that school sports were a holdover from an earlier, more uncivilized, era. He felt that sports created division between the kids who had athletic talent and those who didn't. He remembered the feeling of being the last kid picked when the phys ed teacher made the class choose up sides. He had always been physically small and was afraid of getting hurt in contact sports. He remembered well the games of dodgeball held in the gym on rainy days when the strongest kids always grabbed the loose ball and threw it hard at the smaller, weaker kids. Berry had known he would be one of the first "out" and dreaded the stinging impact of the rubber ball when it would hit him. He had come to hate sports because someone always won and someone always had to lose and the loser always seemed to be him. He applauded a movement he'd seen in some school districts toward moving away from scorekeeping so that a sport could be enjoyed by everyone without the loss of self-esteem which came from losing.

Wallace Berry had made it through a very trying school career and gone on to college and had come to enjoy the academic lifestyle he'd found there. Participation in sports wasn't mandatory and he'd found plenty of other kids who felt the same way about them that he had. A fulfilling homosexual lifestyle had also blossomed there for him and he felt none of the stigma which he thought would be focused on him. Law school had been even better, and he'd considered becoming a professor because he felt so at ease in the campus environment. But he realized that as an attorney he could bring about real change in society, the kinds of change which would make America into a better place.

Shortly after joining the ACLU as a staff attorney, Berry had worked with the Minneapolis City Council to close all but one of the city's gun stores. He helped write ordinances which made the buying and selling of firearms so paper-work-intensive and so heavily regulated and taxed that it would no longer be profitable. He looked at guns as just another way of one person exerting control over another. He had pressured schools to stop saying the Pledge of Allegiance and had engineered the disbanding of a Lutheran youth group after Berry had worked to get a court order forcing them to allow in a homosexual boy. The group was not willing to obey the order and opted to fold rather than comply. Berry considered this a great victory.

Wallace Berry felt that the names which had been used to describe him by enemies were badges of honor. He enjoyed being referred to as a "skinny faggot" as well as a "godless atheist." He fully agreed that he was a "prissy intellectual" and felt that it was better to be a "socialist cocksucker" than it was to be a "red-blooded American boy." Berry had seen too many bad examples of what an American man was supposed to be like in the movies. Wallace Berry had found that, through the law, he had the power to bring about change. He truly believed that he could help move the country away from its pioneer, rough-and-tumble roots and toward a more civilized, thoughtful, intellectual lifestyle. He planned to fight one battle after another, and if he couldn't change the country, he would try his damnedest to change his little corner of it.

He was about to meet a man who thought the same way.

The patriot drove through the commercial district of Burnsville and turned into The Oaks apartment complex, an upscale group of apartments in the southern part of the city. He was wearing his false moustache and a plain dark baseball cap as well as a pair of large, clear glasses. He was tired and debated whether or not he should have planned this night's work. He knew that tired people make mistakes and he had been determined to be as safe as possible. He decided that he would take care of the problem at hand and then take a couple of days off.

He checked his watch and saw it was 12:15 a.m. He thought that his target would be sleeping by now, since it was a Wednesday night. He had followed the pervert a few times and noticed that he tended to stay out late and bring home boyfriends on weekends. During the week he had proven to be a creature of habit, as were most people, and the patriot counted on him being confused and half awake when he rang his doorbell.

Berry lived in a security building which had locked front doors that required a security code to open. He had considered waiting until a resident was entering and using that opportunity to pass through, but he didn't want a confrontation with anyone. A week before he'd been here and tried a gamble which had worked and he felt it would work again tonight. He pushed the call button for the manager in room 100. He pushed it a second time and a voice cracked from the speaker. "Yeah, can I help you?"

"Police," the patriot said, "I have to speak with one of your tenants."

"Okay," the voice said and the door buzzed, just as it had the week before. The patriot smiled as he walked in the entryway. He quickly walked up to the second floor and down the hall to apartment 242. He took out his wallet and opened it to reveal his badge and ID card. He knocked on Berry's door.

Wallace Berry had just fallen asleep and was startled by the knock on his door. At first he thought he'd dreamt it and then heard another insistent knock. He got up and turned on his bedroom light. The clock read 12:21 and he wondered what this could be about. He went into the living room and turned on a light. Berry looked out the door's peephole and saw a man with glasses and a baseball cap. The man knocked again and Berry checked to make sure the chain was on before opening the door.

"Yes?" he asked. "What is it?"

The man showed Berry an open wallet with a badge and police ID. "Wallace Berry? I'm from the Burnsville Police and I have to talk to you."

Berry was surprised. What could the police want? "What's this about?" he asked.

"Would you open the door, sir? I have to discuss a serious matter with you."

"About what?" Berry asked.

"Well, sir, its about one of your co-workers, he's been hurt. Could you open the door, please?" The patriot hoped that Berry wouldn't keep carrying on the conversation through the chained door. He knew that he could pop the chain off with a quick thrust of his shoulder, but he didn't want Berry yelling and alerting the neighbors.

Berry considered the request for a moment. He wasn't sure why the police would come if a friend was only hurt. He figured it had to be serious. He was tired and it didn't occur to him to wonder why the police would send a plainclothes cop in such a situation as opposed to a uniformed one. The patriot had more cover story to go with, if need be, before he broke down the door. As it turned out, it wasn't necessary. Berry closed the door and slid off the chain. The door opened and Berry said, "Come in, officer."

The patriot walked in behind Berry said, "Are you alone, sir?"

"Yes, why?" Berry asked.

"Well, I have some bad news for you and I don't want to leave you alone. Can we sit down?"

Berry rubbed his eyes and turned to lead the way into the kitchen. He had a sinking feeling in the pit of his stomach, wondering what could have happened to one of his friends. The patriot reached into his coat and grasped the handle of the stun baton. It was hanging from a looped strap around his right shoulder. The baton was 20 inches long and hung to his knee from the strap. The patriot pulled the baton out and pointed the electrode end at Berry's back. He flicked on the power switch and jammed the baton's end into Berry's right kidney as he closed the apartment door. The baton crackled and 500,000 volts surged from the electrodes through Berry's body. Berry stiffened and all of his muscles spasmed as the electricity coursed though his small frame. The patriot held the baton against Berry's back for a few seconds until the little man was no longer able to maintain his balance on his toes and fell to the floor. The patriot knew that Berry would be incapacitated for a minute or so, but he wasted no time. He grabbed Berry by the hair with his right hand and lifted him to a kneeling position. Using his left arm to reach around the front of Berry's neck, the patriot brought his left hand around to a point just behind Berry's right ear, grasped his right forearm with his left hand, and flexed the muscles in his left arm, and simultaneously pulled backward with his right forearm.

This maneuver was known in professional wrestling as "the sleeper." In police parlance it was known as a "carotid neck restraint." This hold very effectively allows the user to temporarily shut off the blood supply to the victim's brain by squeezing the carotid arteries shut. The patriot had learned this hold while working in the jail and had used it successfully several times. It was a safe hold unless the subject's carotids were shut off for too long.

Wallace Berry was a very small, unathletic man. He could never have fought off the patriot under any circumstances, but with his nervous system disrupted by the incredible voltage of the stun baton, he was totally helpless. He felt the patriot grab the hair on the top of his head and lift him off the floor. He felt the solid arm slid around his neck and begin to squeeze and his conscious thought ended just a few seconds later. He had made no sound at all.

Feeling Berry go limp in his arms, the patriot let him slide to the floor. He knew Berry would be unconscious only for a minute or two, so he took a few seconds to quickly check the apartment. Walking through the bedroom and bathroom, he discovered that Berry was alone. He walked back into the hallway where Berry was lying and rolled him onto his back. The patriot reached into his boot and removed a Tanto knife from a sheath clipped to his boot top. He felt Berry's ribcage with his left hand and easily found the sternum and the space between the fourth and fifth rib on Berry's left side. The patriot jammed the knife into the space and down into Berry's heart. He then reversed his hold on the knife's handle and drew it along Berry's rib line in one savage motion, pulling the knife out toward the armpit, cutting Berry's heart in half and opening his left lung.

Blood immediately welled up in the huge opening in Berry's chest. The patriot pulled out the knife and wiped it on Berry's sweatpants as he had wiped the awl on Sarah Ehrenberg's shirt. Returning the knife to the boot sheath, he straightened up, went into the kitchen, took a damp washcloth out of the sink, and used it to wipe off the doorknob he'd touched. He held the cloth over his hand, using it to open the door and then to pull it closed behind him. As he walked out of the building, he used the rag to wipe the front door handle and the apartment buzzer. He then threw the rag in the complex dumpster before he drove away.

CHAPTER 10

▼

The patriot got out of bed Thursday morning and turned on the local news. He'd been trying to keep up with events by reading the papers and catching the news whenever he could, but there hadn't a lot of coverage about his actions. A couple of the local stations had done a piece on the death of Sarah Ehrenberg showing passing shots of crime scene tape around the small house and investigators conferring with each other on the lawn. The "Red Star" (a term he used for the liberal *Minneapolis Star-Tribune*) had done a small piece in its Metro section, but, all in all, the patriot was a little surprised that her murder had made such a little splash. It was almost as if the press was happy she was gone. He thought that attitude was strange considering how many stories she'd given them over the years. The local police hadn't released any information about her death other than to say it was "suspicious," and that the case was being investigated.

He didn't believe it was time to move on to the next phase of his plan, but this morning's news gave him a lot to think about.

"Good morning, everyone," the anchorman said with a serious look on his face. "This morning we have news of the death of a prominent local activist, an arrest made in the death of another, and continuing coverage on the murder of Judge Edward Borgert. First up, let's go to Wendy, who is live in Burnsville at The Oaks Apartment complex, home of Minneapolis ACLU President Wallace Berry. Wendy?"

Wendy was standing outside The Oaks holding an umbrella and was trying to manage it and the microphone while fighting against the wind. She reported how Berry's body had been found and said that the police were treating it as a homicide, although details hadn't been released. She ended by saying, "Todd, we hope to have more details later in the day on this. As you know, Wallace Berry was a champion of numerous causes. Some of those causes were unpopular in the area. Whether or not it was his activism which cost him his life remains to be determined."

Todd thanked Wendy and said, "Investigators in the Goodhue County Sheriff's Department announced that they have arrested the man they believe is responsible for what they have now declared as the murder of Sarah Ehrenberg. Ehrenberg, who was a noted environmentalist and animal rights activist, was found dead on Tuesday May seventh at her rural Welch, Minnesota home. Later that night, Minneapolis Police arrested a man driving her car in Minneapolis named George Fast Horse." The news put a mug shot of Fast Horse up on the screen. "Goodhue County Sheriff Charles Cooper issued a statement early this morning saying that investigators with his department have determined that Fast Horse was seen by a witness running from the victim's house early on Tuesday morning." Here, the news replayed the tape of the investigation going on at Ehrenberg's house and the patriot got another look at the detective, who he figured had to be BCA, if he was running from one city to another. He listened as the reporter said, "Fast Horse allegedly took Ehrenberg's car and drove to Minneapolis where police arrested him. Sheriff Cooper said that Fast Horse has admitted that he was with Ehrenberg at the time of her murder, but has denied killing her. Investigators believe they have enough evidence to bring the case before a judge later today to charge him with Second Degree Murder. Sheriff Cooper said that the Goodhue County Attorney may convene a grand jury to determine if Fast Horse should be charged with First Degree Murder. Sheriff Cooper did not release details of how Ehrenberg died, but said that it had been determined that she was murdered."

The patriot was stunned by the report. He hadn't considered the possibility that someone else would be accused in Ehrenberg's death. His mind mulled over the implications as the anchorman went on to the next story.

"Edina Police today announced that they are no closer to locating a suspect in the shooting death of Judge Edward Borgert. Borgert was shot to death in the kitchen of his Edina home on Sunday night. Police say they are still speaking to neighbors and are looking into the backgrounds of some individuals whom Judge Borgert had sentenced. They also want to examine records of cases Borgert handled when he was an attorney for a Minneapolis firm. They say it's possible that Borgert may have been killed by a former defendant or possibly by someone associated with his former practice who may have carried a grudge against him."

The news moved on to a fire in St. Paul and the patriot turned the set off. He was disturbed by the arrest of the man in Goodhue County. He wondered what they had meant when they said that Fast Horse had been present when Ehrenberg died. He knew that he hadn't searched the house after the killing. Was it possible that someone else was in there? Did the man get a look at him? It sounded like whatever story Fast Horse had told wasn't being swallowed by the cops.

The patriot was upset about the announcement both because an innocent man had been jailed, but more so because the arrest would divert attention from what he was doing. The news had just reported the deaths of two prominent activists so close together; it was only a matter of time before someone linked them together. He had always planned to tell the press about what he was doing and why, but decided to wait in order to buy as much time as possible. His list was lengthy and he wanted free rein for as long as possible. He was glad the Borgert case seemed to be stalled, but knew that if he tipped his hand, he would have the combined resources of several local, state, and federal agencies breathing down his neck. He'd been a cop long enough to know that no one can keep from getting caught for very long, especially when they don't intend to go on the run.

It would be premature for him to go public at this time. He felt sorry for Fast Horse, but he felt that he was doing something which would bring important changes to the country if he could only have a little more time. From the look of Fast Horse's mug shot, he looked like some jail time might do him some good, anyway, the patriot thought. Just the same, he began to plan the safest way to contact the media when the time came.

Detective John Pappas took the call from the Ramsey County Coroner's Office at his desk on Thursday just after lunch. Deputy Coroner Dr. Jenny Haugeruud told him she had the preliminary autopsy results on Sarah Ehrenberg for him.

"Let me guess," Pappas said, "she died of a broken neck?"

"Well," Haugeruud began, "yes, I think the broken neck killed her, but it was incidental to another fatal wound she'd received. Your killer shoved something long and thin into her right ear and into her brain before her neck was broken. We took a measurement of the wound canal and it looks to be something like a sharpened screwdriver or an ice pick with a shaft about 7 inches long and about 1/8 inch in diameter."

"Christ!" Pappas said. "It went all the way into her brain from her ear?"

"Yeah, and while there, it did a hell of a lot of damage. It looks like the killer twisted the object around inside to increase the trauma."

"Oh, shit!" Pappas breathed.

"Yeah, pretty grisly," Haugeruud agreed. "The injury to her brain would have killed her in pretty short order, but the tests show that her heart was probably still beating when her neck was broken. Now, as to how that happened, we found some bruising and separation of the rib and spine cartilage in the middle of her back. There were no marks around her neck to indicate a noose or any form of instrument was used to break the spine. Her chin had a faint bruise on the left side, and there appear to be finger marks to the right of her mouth, like a hand-print. I believe someone knelt on her back, grabbed her chin and twisted her head around until it broke."

"Holy shit!" Pappas said. "Can a person do that? I mean, is it physically possible?"

"It would take a lot of strength," Haugeruud answered, "but you would have a lot of leverage in that position. Keep in mind, too, Ehrenberg was in no position to fight back. The damage done to her brain was devastating, and it's a pretty fair bet she was totally helpless by the time her neck was broken."

"Son of a bitch!" Pappas said. "We're charging the guy we caught in her car with the murder today. I've known this suspect for years and I'd have never thought he was capable of something like this. What the hell would have possessed him to do it?"

"I can't answer that." Haugeruud told him. "That's your job. Is your man a cool customer?"

"No," Pappas said. "Our witness tells us he ran half-dressed out the door and burned rubber when he took her car to get out of there."

"Well, I can tell you that there were no defense wounds on Ehrenberg whatso-ever. She had very few marks and there were no hesitation wounds on her at all."

"What are hesitation wounds?" Pappas asked.

"Little, shallow marks in a stabbing. We see them in self-inflicted cuttings a lot where the person hesitates before they cut into themselves. I thought about them in this case because the auditory canal is pretty small and hard to enter, especially if you're struggling with someone. Which reminds me, we did find some loose hairs on the left side of her head. Looks as if they were pulled out by the roots. It is pretty tough to put an ice pick, or whatever, into the auditory canal of a fighting person during the heat of passion. There should be little cuts around the ear opening, where he tried to put it in, but missed. At least some scratches, you know? For instance, have you ever tried to put your car key into the lock when it's pouring rain? Your key bounces all around and goes everywhere but in the lock, right?"

"You found nothing there, though?" Pappas asked.

"Right. It's speculation, but I think your suspect is calm, organized, very strong and very, very goddamned brutal. This was a nasty killing, John. A guy who'd do this would do anything."

"You aren't exactly shoring up my belief that George Fast Horse killed this woman. He's none of the things you just described. How about other evidence?"

"Well, we did find semen in her vagina. I spoke with the BCA lab. They haven't gotten very far into this yet, but they said they found a lot of semen when they black-lighted, is that right?"

"Right," Pappas answered, "all in the bedroom, none anywhere else."

"I didn't see any trauma to her vulva to indicate that she was raped. It looks like she had vaginal sex without a prophylactic, but no signs of force or beating. Any indication from the crime scene guys whether they felt she'd been dressed by someone else?"

"No, nothing was said. She had on cutoffs and a sweatshirt."

"Okay, I'm not seeing rape, here. Maybe sex at weapon point but once again, no tearing of the vagina, no bleeding. The indications aren't there. Maybe they had a big fight the next morning, which brings me to our next point. Time of death is hard to fix here. Body's indoors, heated room, all that. I'm guessing, though, that she died a fairly short time before she was found, certainly no more than a couple hours."

"Anything else?" Pappas asked, afraid of what the answer might be.

"No, not right now. I'll get back to you with the toxicology results when they're available."

Pappas hung up. He pulled the crime scene photos out of the file and looked at the disfigured body of Sarah Ehrenberg. Anger welled up in his throat as he looked at her twisted neck, the bleeding ear where someone shoved a goddamned ice pick in it, for Christ's sake! He studied the look on her face. Pappas had seen dead bodies before, including bodies that had been murdered. He'd seen a bad one before of a four-year-old girl who'd been killed when her mother's drunken boyfriend flew into a rage and drowned her in the toilet. The little girl's face had haunted him for years and he still saw her sometimes when he dreamed. She'd looked peaceful, though, in contrast to the terrible way in which she'd died. Ehrenberg had a look of dismay, as if she were asking, "Why?"

Pappas gathered up the crime photos and made his way to the jail, which was in the same complex as his office in the Sheriff's Department. He walked in and asked the jailer to bring Fast Horse into the interrogation room. When he was led in and the jailer closed the door, Pappas was less than cordial.

"All right, George, I want some goddamned answers and I want them now! No more fucking around, no more fucking philosophy! I want to know what the hell happened in there and I don't want BULLSHIT!"

Fast Horse was surprised by Pappas' attack. "I can't tell you anything!" He told Pappas. "I told you I don't know what happened to her!"

"BULLSHIT!" Pappas yelled. "No fucking way you could have slept through that killing! I'm not buying it! What the hell happened in there? Why did you argue?"

Fast Horse started to get angry. "I told you, I don't know! I didn't kill her! I just found her in the morning! She was dead, and I don't know how!"

"Stop calling her 'she' and 'her'! Use her name! She had a name, use it!"

Fast Horse hesitated. What was her name? He really couldn't remember her name!

"SARAH!!" Pappas bellowed. He was losing his Greek temper, something that hadn't happened in a long time, but he kept seeing her face, seeing her ask "Why?"

"Her name was SARAH!" He yelled in Fast Horse's face. "It was Sarah until somebody shoved a GODDAMNED ICEPICK THROUGH HER FUCKING EAR!! THEN YOU KNELT ON HER BACK AND TWISTED HER HEAD AROUND UNTIL YOU SNAPPED HER NECK! DIDN'T YOU?" With that Pappas threw the crime scene pictures on the table. He picked up the one that showed Ehrenberg looking at the camera with her eyes half closed and that question on her face. "LOOK AT HER! SAY HER NAME!" He shoved the picture in Fast Horse's face.

"NO!" Fast Horse yelled. "NO! NO! NO!" He kept saying it.

"WHY?" Pappas yelled. "Just tell me why? How could you do that?"

"NO!" Fast Horse was sobbing now. The pictures brought the memories back. The panic, the fear. He sobbed openly, unable to hold it in.

"How could you?" Pappas repeated. "How could you hold her, kiss her, share her bed? How could you take her hospitality and then do that to her? What did she do to deserve that? Just tell me!"

"No," was all Fast Horse could say. He was confused. He knew he was a drunk. Could he have done that? Had he blacked out and done that? No. He cried as he remembered her name. He remembered her smile as they had sex. She'd had a nice smile. He didn't know anymore. He didn't know if he'd done it. He'd been a shit sometimes in his life. He'd done some things that he'd regretted later. It all came back. The floodgates opened as he thought of his crimes, his lost jobs, crashing with one relative after another when friends had kicked him out.

Pappas stood over the shaking, crying man. His rage was subsiding and being replaced with a hollow, spent feeling. He looked at the shattered man in the chair and still wondered. He thought that if he'd done it he would have given it up by now. George Fast Horse was no hardened killer. He'd never held out on confessing before. He didn't have the heart to. Pappas tried to reconcile this knowledge with the facts he had in the file. He was spent, tired, and sad. Those cops in cities like New York and LA could have their homicide squads. The whole thing made him sick.

He took one last, long look at Fast Horse as he walked out. He had a lump in his throat and he managed to choke out one last question.

"Why, George? Why?"

George Fast Horse was led back to his confinement cell. It had a set of bunk beds but George was alone in the cell. He sobbed as he was led in and cried openly and loudly when the door slammed. The clanging of the door was so loud, so final. George knew he would spend the rest of his life in a place like this, hearing metal doors slam. He cried and sank to the floor. When the jailer brought him dinner he left it in the food pass opening in the door, untouched.

George cried himself into a stupor and drifted in and out of unconsciousness. Some men when faced with the raw emotion that comes with the realization that they'd made a complete waste of their lives found new strength. Some had religious conversions. George had no strength to draw from. He had never developed real character and never done anything in his life he'd been proud of. He had no reserves, no clean slate to find.

He sat on the floor of his cell for hours, numbed by the mess he'd made of his life. He saw the face of his mother, who had died of scarlet fever in South Dakota when George was five. He'd been afraid then, a little boy seeing his mother covered in a rash, running a high fever. She knew she was dying and worried for her little boy, who was so small and had no one to look after him. It was winter and the room they were in was so, so cold. She wanted to pass something on to him. She tried, but she knew it was too late. With her last strength she held little George's hand and said, "Georgie, be good. Be a good boy."

George knew he'd not been good. Now someone was dead. He'd let everyone down. Just like Pappas he was left wondering why. He gathered the last of his strength to get up and remove the sheet from his cot. He struggled to tear it, but was too drained. Biting the sheet and tearing it with his teeth, he began to cry again, for the waste of it all. He ripped a long, thin piece off of the sheet and wrapped one end around the top bunk frame. He thought of his mother. He felt as if he was dreaming now. He saw his mother with him now in the cell and cried out to her. She was sad, she was crying. George couldn't stand anymore. He couldn't stand to see his mother cry, but yet he couldn't look away.

"I'm sorry, Mommy," George said, as he looped the end of the sheet around his neck and tied the other end to the frame.

"Don't cry, Georgie," his mother said to him. "Be good. Be a good boy."

George Fast Horse let go of life, let go of pain; it was all so easy to do. He let his body go limp and then watched his mother as long as he could, until she faded away.

CHAPTER 11

▼

On Friday morning the patriot saw the news story about the suicide of George Fast Horse in the Goodhue County Jail. The news account was presented in such a fashion that the viewer was led to believe that Fast Horse was overcome with guilt for his terrible crime and had done the honorable thing. The patriot shut off the TV and mulled the problem over in his mind. He had intended on getting Fast Horse released when he came forward in the media, but now the case would, in all likelihood, be closed by the investigators. They would be content to believe they had caught their killer and that he had committed the crime for his own reasons.

The patriot had a glimmer of conscience and felt bad that Fast Horse had died as a result of the political action that was being taken. But the more he thought about it, the less the death bothered him. After all, this was war, the patriot thought. War against the creeping disease of liberalism and socialism was too important to be bogged down by the death of one man. It was a sad fact of life that the innocent often had to suffer more in war than the combatants. He remembered famous photos from the Vietnam War. Photos of executions, dead bodies, burning villages, and crying children. Sacrifices had to be made if the United States had any hope of being saved. It was unfortunate that Fast Horse had gotten in the way, but the course the patriot had taken was too right, too vital to stray from. In World War Two, the allies had dropped thousands of tons of bombs on German and Japanese civilians in an effort to force their governments to end the war. Those civilians had no say in the foreign policy of their countries, but still they died. They died because they had the misfortune of being born in the wrong country at the wrong time in history. They represented their nation, and their nation had to be crushed. It was a war fought between nations, races, tribes. That was how humans organized themselves throughout history. First in tribes, then in races, then in nations. George Fast Horse, by virtue of the fact that he was in Ehrenberg's house that day, was a part of Ehrenberg's tribe and was caught in the crossfire of war. He was no different from the Vietnamese villagers in the pictures.

The patriot felt that people were tribal by nature. It was a trait that hadn't been eliminated, even by millions of years of evolution. Even people in "civilized" nations organized themselves into tribes. A person may be a Boy Scout, a Mason, a Catholic, a Veteran, a Teamster, or a member of any other religion or organization. There were thousands in the United States alone. All of them were organized tribes where the members met and talked about what their tribe represented and how the members should behave. Many people belonged to many tribes at once, but all tribes had similar characteristics. There were rules for each tribe, and a person could be expelled for misbehavior. Often there were dues to pay for membership, and very often the members of each tribe would go to extreme lengths for their tribe. In some religions, people would handle poisonous snakes to show how sure they were of the power of their tribe. Union members had fought bloody wars for their causes. Sometimes members of one tribe attacked another because they didn't like that tribe's rules. They thought those rules were "unfair" and sought to force the tribe to change or disband.

The patriot thought that each tribe had the absolute right to set its own rules and not be forced to change by anyone. He saw liberals like Wallace Berry as outcasts who forced their will on others. The patriot felt that if you didn't like a particular tribe and didn't want to take part in their activities, you should leave them alone and find one that met your own needs. He despised people who pointed their fingers at others and said, "I can't compete by the rules you've set. Change for me, or I will destroy your tribe." And *that* was the key. That was the whole focus of his obsession. He saw people like Sarah Ehrenberg, Wallace Berry, and Edward Borgert as unworthy people who were unable to compete and cried "foul." He saw no disparity in the fact that he was killing people who disagreed with his views because he knew he could compete with them in their world, in their tribes, and on their level. He was smart, strong, athletic, and experienced in life. Anything he couldn't accomplish didn't concern him. He knew that the key was to remind people to live their own lives, to stop expecting the government or anyone else to help them. People had to walk their own path or fall by the roadside.

In the 1800s thousands of Americans migrated west and many died trying. If their wagon wheel broke, they couldn't call AAA. They fixed it themselves or they died. If a person needed water he got it himself, he didn't call a plumber. You could rely on help from a neighbor, knowing that you'd help him someday. Those Americans built the nation. Now people were weak. They did nothing for themselves, and look where the country was now. Unwashed savages from piss ant countries burned the American flag and destroyed magnificent buildings which could never by built in their land in a million years. Worthless barbarians mocked the nation and the liberals of this land *agreed with them!!*

The patriot was so enraged he jumped from his chair and paced the room. He had a burning desire to destroy something. He fell to the floor and did 75 push-ups, but still he was furious. He knew, somewhere in his mind that he had to burn off this anger before he went to work. He couldn't risk tipping his hand and not fitting in. He ran to the weight room and began pumping iron furiously. He'd never lifted so much, but his body was charged with adrenaline. He pumped until his muscles quivered and sweat rolled down his face and chest. The veins stood out on his arms and neck, and he gasped for breath. Finally, spent, he dropped the bar to the floor and collapsed into a chair. When his breathing returned to normal, he was calm. He could go to work and work the last day of his work week. He knew he would have four days off and that he would use them well. The patriot no longer felt bad for George Fast Horse. He had more important things to worry about.

Detective John Pappas sat slumped in his chair in his office with his arms folded across his chest staring at the floor. When he came in, one of the secretaries had told him of Fast Horse's death. Pappas kept going over the last interrogation in his mind and was trying to reconcile the facts with how he felt. He knew that Fast Horse was the best suspect in a vicious crime. He'd tried the nice cop approach in the first interview and the tough cop in the second. There was nothing wrong with a detective altering his approach with a suspect to try to pry a confession out of him. He knew that some suspects needed a shoulder to cry on, some needed a priest, some a father, and some needed to be shouted into a corner until they told what they knew. An investigator had to size up his adversary in an instant and follow his instinct to find the road to the truth, or at least a good imitation of it. Many suspects needed to rationalize what they did and then the investigator needed to nod and agree that, yes, it was perfectly understandable to believe the little five-year-old girl wanted you to pull her pants down and fondle her. The cop and the man inside was crying out to beat the pervert to a pulp, but the investigator needed the confession so the little girl wouldn't have to testify and be traumatized further. It was important to some suspects that the investigator understand that the guy really pushed him too hard this time. They guy shouldn't have said what he did and deserved what happened to him. And the investigator would nod and say, "Yes, I understand completely. It was just too much this time, right. I know. Now, let's start the tape."

Those were the facts, cold and true. But he also knew in his heart that Fast Horse wasn't the type to kill, at least not like that. Not without being pushed way into a corner. Hell, he was in a corner last night and he didn't fight back. Would a cold-blooded killer be bothered by the death of someone he barely knew? Would he be forced to suicide by a rant from a cop in an interrogation room?

Pappas looked at the photos taken of Fast Horse, dead in his cell and sighed when he looked at the slumped body. His knees dragged the floor and his arms hung limp at his side. He could have saved himself easily, but hadn't. The close-up picture of George's face showed eyes half open, with dried tears on his cheeks. Pappas wondered if George cried because of what he'd done or because he was an innocent man who faced life in prison for something he hadn't done.

The phone rang. It was Sheriff Cooper. "John, if you're not too busy, I'd like to see you in my office."

"I'll be right there."

Pappas walked down the hall and knocked on Cooper's open door. He was invited in and closed the door behind him. Pappas sat down in the chair in front of the boss's desk.

"John," the Sheriff said, "I've read the case file to date and I'm confident we had in custody a very good suspect for this murder. I read about your first interview with Fast Horse and I've heard that there was a second. I've also heard that things got a little heated in there. Sound travels through metal doors, John." Pappas nodded.

"I need to know," the boss continued, "what happened in there. I need to know if we had the right man, and I need to know if you got out of line in any way in there."

Pappas stared for a few moments and said, "Chuck, I don't know what to say. Honestly. The evidence says he did it. We can't place anyone else in the house during the time she died. He behaved like a man who'd just done something terrible. I've been going over this in my mind. I've known George for years and interviewed him many times. I've been trying to figure out why I'm so sure he did it and, at the same time, why I just can't believe he did."

"So, what was with the scene in the jail yesterday?"

"George wasn't a professional criminal. He always gave up the truth when he was questioned. He always had a reason why he did it, but he never held out. What bothers me is that he just didn't have the sand in him to kill someone so brutally and then sit there in a jail cell and say, 'Wasn't me.' I could see him killing, for a reason, but not like this, and not without explaining himself."

"So, do you think we need to announce that we arrested the wrong man?" Cooper asked.

"That would open a can of worms, wouldn't it?"

"You know it," Cooper agreed.

"Chuck, I don't know. We can't ignore the evidence. We made a good arrest, that I know. I tried to question him one way, then tried to apply pressure the second time. I've done that before. He insisted he didn't do it. Now he's dead, and I know that if we say we have doubts, we'll be crucified."

"Yes we will." Cooper said. "I've been on the phone with the County Attorney." The County Attorney's office does more than just prosecute in Minnesota. The office also provides legal advice of any nature to county offices and to law enforcement. The office serves as a sort of in-house legal counsel to make sure the county was safe from legal quicksand. "He tells me that the prudent course at this time is to continue on with the assumption we had the right man. We tell the public that the case is still open, in case information on other suspects is developed, but that we are confident Fast Horse was responsible for the murder."

"Okay," Pappas said. He knew it was the only smart play, still, the feeling nagged at him.

"John," Cooper said, "I have confidence in you. I always have. I think you've done everything right so far, and I thing the best thing we can do now is to put this to rest. The county may face a legal problem stemming from a suicide in the jail, but we'll deal with that if we need to. That's my problem. Go home, get some rest, come back Monday, and start on something fresh."

"Okay. Thanks, boss." Pappas got up and walked out.

Mike Rawlings sat at his desk in his office on University Avenue in St. Paul. He had been going over the Berry murder and knew that there was a limited amount of physical evidence to go on. Someone had ripped Berry's chest open with one sawing motion of a knife through his chest. No fingerprints in the room, no witnesses, no obvious motive, nothing. Berry had a strange burn mark near his right kidney on his back, but that had yet to be explained by the coroner.

Rawlings sat there and thought that a lot of people who'd been represented in the media as being very left wing were dying around Minnesota lately. None of them had died in the same way, and nothing seemed to link them, other than the fact that they were known publicly as supporters of very liberal causes. Rawlings had been around long enough to know what happened to cops who ran around like the boy who cried wolf. Still, all three of the murders he'd just finished reviewing had some aspects in common. They were all very organized crime scenes. There were no signs of desperation by the killers. Whoever killed Borgert was a good shot who wasn't afraid to be seen toting a rifle around the heart of Edina. The killers of Ehrenberg and Berry were strong, bold people (most probably men) who struck quickly—in one case in broad daylight—in the victim's homes. All three of the victims had unlisted phone numbers and addresses, yet their killers found them all at home.

He'd never seen cases like this, so close together. Rawlings was a man who spent a lot of time considering how one thing can lead to another. How a child can endure a certain upbringing and turn out a certain way. He'd seen many crimes and been able to see the reason, no matter how warped, why the perpetrator had done it. He knew about all sorts of mental illnesses and how they manifested. He wasn't a psychologist, but could surprise many experienced psychiatrists with his understanding of human behavior. He had worked his way through the University of Minnesota and graduated with honors, but he liked to tell people he was a graduate of "the school of hard knocks." He felt he'd learned more as a patrolman working the east side of St. Paul than he'd learned during the rest of his career. He had impressed a young trainee after they'd taken a burglary report in which a briefcase was stolen. He'd gone outside and looked around for a suitable place where a burglar could look through the contents of a bulky item and dump it so he wouldn't have to be seen carrying such a large item down the street in the middle of the night. He spotted a gardening shed across the street and walked straight over to it, finding the briefcase inside covered in fingerprints. The rookie had been impressed, but to Rawlings it was just common sense.

He had a feeling for people and knew how to read them. He didn't believe in ESP, but he'd seen other older cops do it. He knew it was a fact that police were terrific amateur psychologists; they had to be to survive. Those who got older and didn't become bogged down in the depressing aspects of the job became very savvy. Rawlings was as savvy as they came.

He let himself consider the possibility that all three victims had been killed by the same person. He let his mind drift over motives and imagined what those motives would be. He thought again about how the crimes were carried out and the picture that formed in his mind frightened him enough to make him sit back in his chair. He hoped that such a person didn't exist. The idea of a very intelligent, resourceful, powerful, and totally remorseless killer made him catch his breath.

He hoped he was dead wrong.

CHAPTER 12

▼

Desiree Blevins left the Moon Over Miami Coffeehouse in the Dinkytown area of Minneapolis on Friday afternoon at about 2:30. The twenty-two-year-old had met with her friends Amii and Jeremy to discuss what they had planned to do in the St. Paul suburb of Roseville on Sunday night. She walked down the block to her VW Golf and got in. She knew that what they'd planned to do was risky, but it would be well worth it.

Desiree had grown up in the southern suburb of Apple Valley, a city of about 40,000, the daughter of a massage therapist/holistic healer and a counselor at an alternative learning center. Her parents, Sunshine and Todd, had been together for twenty years but had never married because they never believed in restrictive rites or traditions which bound a person to a certain course of conduct. They were free thinkers, to be sure, and in another time they would have been considered hippies, beatniks, or witches, depending on the era.

Sunshine and Todd had raised their little girl to be her own person. They set very few rules for her and taught her that most rules were only old traditions which had yet to be resolved by the times. They encouraged Desiree to try new things, as they had when they were young, and never, ever punished her, as that would only repress her growing desire to learn and experience new things. They allowed her to make her own mistakes and told her of the ones they had made, but never discouraged her. When Desiree was twelve, she had both ears pierced seven times, at fourteen she had a butterfly tattooed on her shoulder, and at fifteen she had already shared marijuana and psilocybin mushrooms with her parents, who felt those products were part of nature's harvest.

During high school Desiree had developed a deep, abiding love for animals. She was already a vegan, like her mother (her father still ate milk products) and became committed to animal rights. She had protested her school's use of frogs for dissection and had gotten suspended for a week for breaking into the biology lab one night to set all the animals free. As she grew older, Desiree became more involved with PETA and other animal groups. As time passed, she felt that PETA spent too much time trying to win support and understanding through the media, by explaining how they felt and why, to a public who ate beef, pork, and chicken by the ton. The favorite snack food in Minnesota, she had read recently, was meat. Most of the residents of the state thought that animal rights people were nutty and ignored them. The state derived a tremendous amount of its gross product from agricultural food processing, and the raising of animals for food was a large part of that.

Two years before, Desiree had abandoned PETA as a well-meaning but too conservative entity, and helped form a group that only a few knew of, called STS for Stop The Slaughter. STS members like Desiree, Amii, and Jeremy had no intention of speaking with the media. They considered themselves guerillas who would fight to save the lives of animals. They did not believe in the dairy industry, as it forced animals to live for human gain, took away their freedom to breed independently, and stole their milk away from their offspring to put in cartons. They hated pork, chicken, and beef producers. They despised hunters and fishermen and reserved their ultimate revulsion for the research industry who used animals to test everything from makeup to surgical procedures.

Of course, the tactics that the STS members had adopted to deal with their movement brought them into direct conflict with laws. These laws were enacted by legislators elected by farmers, dairymen, sportsmen, and everyday people who enjoyed starting the day with ham, eggs and bacon, and milk on their Special K. Too many Minnesotans appreciated the fine flavor of walleyed pike or a 20-ounce porterhouse to allow any congressmen to take those things away. STS believed that they were outnumbered, and their only hope was to fight a constant battle to turn people away from activities they previously enjoyed. They felt that breaking laws designed to support their opponents was justified since they couldn't get a voice in Congress. Desiree and her friends had committed many crimes, which they called "acts of kindness," such as burglary, criminal damage to property, theft, harassment, disorderly conduct, and obstructing the legal process. They had all been arrested many times and had committed many crimes that they hadn't yet been charged with, such as going to dairy barns late at night and vandalizing the milking equipment.

Each had done jail time, but none had been sent to prison, for they had all been able to convince judges that they were young people who were only standing up for their beliefs. The judges were more than willing to see them as idealistic young kids who just needed to grow up. Desiree and her friends considered themselves soldiers in a cause that was as vital to them as a Jihad was to the Al-Qaida terrorists who had leveled the World Trade Center and left the Pentagon smoking. In fact, Desiree and her friends celebrated the events of September Eleventh, as a victory against convention and money and power-mad fascists. Desiree had told this to the Dakota County Deputy who had escorted her from the jail to the courthouse two months before when she'd been caught in a research facility in Eagan releasing rabbits and mice. The deputy had seemed amused when he asked her if she belonged to PETA, but didn't like her answer when she asked him if he belonged to NAMBLA, the North American Man/Boy Love Association, which is an organization composed of child molesters. They'd fenced verbally during the walk to the court building. The cop had said, "Well, you're a feminist, then. That's so cute." She said, "So you're a Nazi, then. That's pathetic." She told him that his whole viewpoint was obsolete and that he would be swept away by change, like the Neanderthal he was. The cop smiled as they walked, but his smile faded when she told him that someday he would hopefully be crushed beneath the building they were in, like those pigs in New York and she would come and dance on the rubble.

Desiree thought she'd gotten the best of the big idiot. She'd hoped he'd smack her, so she could make a public issue out of it, but he wouldn't take the bait. Still, it was fun seeing him get so pissed. His neck even got red!

Deputy Tony Bauer worked his the last day of his week, a busy Friday night. It started off right away with a call to a house near Lakeville, where a woman reported that she was receiving harassing phone calls from her ex-boyfriend. When Bauer arrived, she told him that she'd left the guy, named Paul, a week before. He was at his home in Rosemount, drunk, and kept calling her to ask her to come back. She said he'd called four times in the last hour, and she was tired of hanging up on him. Bauer asked how she knew he was calling from his home and she told him that the number was on her caller ID. The woman, named Barbara, showed him the phone and he copied down the number. He asked for permission to use her phone and called Paul, who answered right away. Bauer identified himself and told him that Barbara had reported being harassed and told him that he needed to stop calling. Paul said he'd only called because she had left a message on his machine asking him for some personal possessions she wanted back. Bauer asked Barbara if she had called him and she said she hadn't. He told both of them to stop calling each other and went back to his car.

His next call was a burglar alarm at a small cabinet making business east of Castle Rock. When he got there, he found the owner inside, working on a book shelf. Bauer told the guy his alarm was going off and the guy scowled and said, "No it isn't." Bauer considered speaking further with the guy but it was pointless. He said, "Okay, it's not, then," and walked back to his car.

A little while later he was called back to Barbara's house. She had again reported that her ex was still bothering her. When Bauer arrived, she told him that ten minutes after he'd left Paul had called back and asked why she'd called the police. He then called her a bitch and hung up. He'd since called five times and hung up each time she'd answer. As they talked, Bauer was informed of an accident with injuries on Cedar Avenue near 300th Street. That was way back down south again. He asked Barbara if she would consider going to a friend's house for the night, just until her ex slept it off. He suggested she get a restraining order on Monday if he kept bothering her. Barbara said she would.

Bauer got back into his car and heard the dispatcher ask him again if he could "clear" to go to the accident. He told her he was on his way, then turned on his lights and siren and made it to the crash in ten minutes. Someone driving a pickup had tried to pass a tractor and hit a Buick head-on, taking out the tractor with them. The farmer on the tractor had flown off and landed on the gravel shoulder. He was being strapped onto a backboard wearing a cervical collar. The paramedics were preparing to send him to Hennepin County Medical Center by helicopter ambulance. The driver of the pickup, a twenty-year-old man, was thrown around inside the cab of the truck because he wasn't wearing his seatbelt. His right leg had become wedged under the dash on the left side. His passenger, an eighteen-year-old girl, had been thrown through the windshield and was half onto the hood, dead, from a massive head injury. The driver of the Buick, a forty-three-year old woman, had been wearing her seatbelt, but the impact had caused the car to fold around her like a steel blanket. The rescue squad was using the jaws of life to cut the car apart to remove her. He could hear the muffled screams of the woman as the big tool cut the car apart.

Bauer was told that the State Patrol was on the way to write up the accident since there was a fatality involved, so he helped direct traffic around the crash. He got annoyed with the same people who kept driving around and around the flares to get a better look at the mayhem. The driver of the pickup was going to be taken by ground ambulance to Northfield Hospital once he was freed from the dash. Sergeant Fitz asked Bauer to follow him in and obtain a blood sample, as was routine in all serious accidents.

After the unconscious man was removed from the cab of the truck and put in the ambulance, Bauer followed it to the hospital. There, he asked the nurse to get him the man's wallet and have the attending physician draw blood. A short time later she came out and handed Bauer a blood kit, complete with two tubes of blood, and the man's wallet. Bauer copied all the information down and left after he'd filled out the information card inside the blood kit and sealed it up. He returned to the crash scene and turned the kit over to the trooper who was taking pictures of the scene.

By the time Bauer was through, it was 8:30 p.m. He wanted to get some dinner, but was called back to Barbara's house about more problems with Paul. When he got there, she said she'd decided not to leave after all because, as she put it, it was her house, after all, and why should she leave? Now she was pissed and told Bauer she expected him to do something about it. Bauer explained that he couldn't arrest the guy out of his own house without a warrant on a misdemeanor charge of harassing phone calls. He explained that he wouldn't be able to get a warrant on a weekend but said he'd try to reason with him again. He tried to call Paul again, but got no answer this time. Bauer told her it would be best, for her own peace of mind, if she just went out for the night, but Barbara answered that suggestion with a tirade on how the man is always protected and that laws were made by men, and that the woman is just expected to bow to his will. Bauer told her that he had to follow the rules and that there was nothing he could do at that point and left.

Dinner got delayed again when some cows were reported on the road near Empire. Bauer drove there and found the farmer already there, shooing the animals back into the pasture. Next he got called to a report of a suspicious vehicle off the road near Chub Lake. When he arrived, he found a very steamed up Monte Carlo with a pair of female teenagers inside. One girl had her jeans off and was receiving very passionate oral sex from her friend, who was naked from the waist up, showing a pair of big, swaying breasts.

"Jesus Christ," Bauer said and knocked on the window. "Clear out of here!" He told the girls. "You're parked in a 'no muff-diving' zone!" The girls got dressed and drove off.

Finally, it got quiet for a while. Bauer thought about getting something to eat, but by then he was just getting tired. At 10:15 p.m., he got a 911 call to go back to Barbara's residence. She'd called screaming that Paul was there and was assaulting her. Bauer asked for the Lakeville PD to assist him, since her house was close to their city limits. Two of their officers arrived before Bauer and found Barbara being strangled by the drunk and enraged Paul. They'd handcuffed Paul and had him in a squad car when Bauer pulled up. Mike Fitz pulled in right behind him. Bauer went inside to get a statement from Barbara, who blew up at him.

"Thanks for nothing, you big prick!" she screamed. "Why wouldn't you do anything? Why did you let him do this? Look at my door! He kicked it in, it's broken! You call the goddamned police, and they don't do anything!"

Bauer kept his cool and reminded Barbara that he'd tried to get her out of the house to be safe, but she wouldn't go.

"Why should I leave? This is my house! Why do I have to go? He can sit at home, get drunk, and bother me all night, and then drive over here and beat the shit out of me? Why weren't you watching his house?"

Sergeant Fitz saw where this was going and steered Bauer outside. "I'll talk to her," he said.

Bauer went out and talked with the Lakeville cops. "Jesus, what a night," he sighed. "Thanks for coming out here. I'll take this guy to Hastings." Bauer pulled Paul from the Lakeville car and removed the Lakeville cop's cuffs and put his own on him. Paul was complaining that Barbara had kept calling him on the phone and calling him a "bitch" and a "pussy" and telling him that he had no balls. Paul complained that all the laws protected the woman and the man always got the shaft.

By the time Bauer booked the guy in for Domestic Assault and did his report, he had worked an hour-and-a-half-overtime. He went home, poured himself a tumbler of brandy over ice, turned on some music, and let the tension of the night run out of him. He knew he had to limit himself to just one drink because he wanted to get an early start on the day tomorrow.

CHAPTER 13

▼

The patriot rose early on Saturday morning and drove into downtown Minneapolis. The traffic was light as he crossed the east bank of the Mississippi River and entered the Dinkytown area near the University of Minnesota campus. He parked near University and Washington Avenues and locked his car. He knew this mission would be his most difficult because his target kept a very erratic schedule. He had followed her a few times and had not found the patterns that his other targets had displayed. This one slept in different places, didn't seem to have a job, had no specific parking area (parking around the University was very much a hit-or-miss proposition anyway), and had proven very hard to track.

He had her last-known address from her most recent court appearance, of course, and he had watched her walking into the building two weeks before. Still, she'd proven hard to pin down. She spent time at a coffee shop not far away, he knew, but she hadn't been there at the same time of day on any of the four occasions he'd seen her there drinking with friends. Her driver's license still listed her parents' address in Apple Valley as hers. She was unknown on the Internet, from what he could determine, and he had decided that he would have to play this one by ear, as much as he hated the idea. He had chosen early morning on a Saturday because there was actually less foot traffic around at that time than at any other time of day. The student/artist/musician population of Dinkytown stayed up late and got moving late.

Of course, the hardest part of tracking this one was the fact that she had seen his face. He knew that most people who talk to cops don't recognize them even a short time later in civilian clothes, but he thought that this woman would be more leery than most because of her criminal activities. His false moustache was in place, as was his snap brim cap, but he had to stow his sunglasses as soon as he stepped off the sidewalk and into the dark old apartment building. His target's loft was on the top of the five-story cinder block building, so he opted for the stairs rather than the elevator.

The stairway in the building was a disgusting depository of liquor and beer bottles, urine, trash, used condoms, and discarded clothing. The last time the patriot had been in this stairwell he'd found a sleeping teenager slumped on a landing, but there was no one there that morning. He got to the fifth floor and paused to let his eyes adjust to the gloom. He also used the time to listen at the door which led to the hallway. He heard no noise and quietly entered the hall. There were ten apartments on each floor, five on each side, and he estimated they were pretty large from the amount of space between the doors and the width of the building. The woman's apartment was the second one on his left, number 506. The hallway was marginally more clean than was the stairwell, but he still watched his step as he moved down to her door so he wouldn't knock anything over. There was one dingy window at the far end of the hall, and the overhead light bulbs had been broken, so there was very little light to navigate by. The patriot had good night vision and knew that the darkness would work in his favor if he was seen by a witness.

Just as he reached apartment 506, he was startled by a sudden blare of music from the apartment across the hall. It was so loud and the patriot was so focused that it made him spin into a crouch on the floor with his hand on the Browning's grip inside his jacket. He stood and walked quickly back to the stairwell and closed the fire door behind him. He waited for a couple of minutes and heard the music volume lower slightly but it was still evident. He expected that someone would soon pound on the music lover's door and tell him to turn it off, but so far no one had. It seemed that the tenants in this building kept to themselves.

He decided to be bold and re-entered the hall, and walked quickly back to 506. He knocked on the door and waited. He knocked again and heard the song end across the hall. The next song began and the patriot knocked again. He had already decided that posing as a cop or a reporter wouldn't work here. He knew the woman would have nothing to gain by talking to either, so he had decided on a quick frontal assault. When the door opened he had a quick glimpse of the same kind of fake dyed black hair like the woman had. The door chain was on, but the patriot hit the opening door with his right shoulder and the chain flew easily off the frame and he was inside. He quickly closed the door and found himself face to face with a young man, who looked to be about nineteen-years-old. The patriot had planned that this would be a fake robbery and quickly pushed the kid over to a sofa and forced him onto it, face down. He quickly secured the boy's hands using a plastic Flex Cuff and said in a quiet, menacing voice, "If you move or make a sound, I'll blow your fuckin' head off." He tore the kid's T-shirt off and ripped it in half. He wadded up one piece of the shirt and stuffed it into the kid's mouth and then used the other half of the shirt as a gag, tying it around the back of his neck. When the kid was trussed and lying quietly on the couch, the patriot pulled another Flex Cuff from his jacket pocket and used it to secure the kid's ankles. He took a roll of duct tape out of another pocket and tore off a three-foot-long strip. This he wrapped a couple of times around the kid's head, covering his eyes.

The patriot pulled the Browning from his shoulder holster and made a quick search of the apartment. It was very large, and a good portion of it had been converted into what appeared to be an artist's studio and workroom. There were objects lying all around which appeared to metal art sculptures in various stages of completion. There were sheets of tin and copper propped against a wall and a pile of re-bars, four-foot-long rods made of iron that were a quarter inch in diameter, on the floor. The room had a long, sturdy workbench along the far wall with a collection of quality tools hanging above and lying around it.

He checked the bedroom and found one empty mattress on the floor and no one in the bathroom. There was one large closet but it, too, was empty. The patriot walked back to the sofa and removed the gag on the kid. He made sure the kid felt the barrel of the gun in his ear as he pulled the cloth out of his mouth.

"I'm here for one thing," the patriot told him. "I know you don't have it, Desiree does. I want you to answer me quietly and tell the truth or I'll kill you. Understand?" The kid nodded.

"Where is she?"

"I don't know," the kid said. The patriot pushed the barrel of the gun into the kid's cheek.

"Do I have to prove to you that I'm not going to fuck around here?" he asked the kid. "I will. Where is she?"

"I'm telling you the truth," the kid said, his voice calm. "She isn't here all the time."

"When will she be back?"

"I don't know. She lives her own life."

The kid's attitude was too cool for the patriot, who decided to emphasize his point. He stuffed the rag back in the kid's mouth and put the pistol away. He picked up a rebar and held it like a baseball bat. He swung the rebar hard down on the kid's kneecap and heard it crack. The kid's muffled scream almost pushed out the gag, so the patriot rammed it back in. He jammed the pointed end of the rod into the kid's lower abdomen and waited for him to stop bouncing around. After a minute, he pulled out the gag and the kid yelled, "Bastard!" before he could jam it back in.

"You aren't getting the point," the patriot hissed at him. "I told you I'd kill you and I will, and I promise it will be slow and more painful than you can imagine, if you continue to piss me off!" The kid settled down and nodded. The patriot again removed the gag.

"Let's try again," he said. "What's your name?"

"Jeremy."

"Are you an artist, Jeremy?"

"Yes,"

"An artist needs his hands, doesn't he, Jeremy?" the patriot asked.

"Yes,"

"Jeremy, I will cut off your fingers one by one using those tin-snips over there if you don't start answering me."

Jeremy started to whimper and said, "I'll tell you anything I know."

"Good. Are you fucking Desiree?"

"Only sometimes. We don't have a set thing. We leave each other alone, and she can crash here when she wants to. She doesn't really live anywhere."

"When did you see her last?"

"Yesterday at the coffee shop. We were going to get together over the weekend."

"Where?" the patriot asked.

Jeremy paused. "I don't know."

The patriot stuffed the gag in Jeremy's mouth and the rebar whistled as he brought it down again, this time on Jeremy's elbow. Jeremy writhed in pain on the sofa while the patriot held the gag in his mouth. When the boy had calmed down, the patriot pulled the gag out.

"Another lie, Jeremy, and I'll get the tin-snips. Now, you tell me she doesn't live here, and that you're going to meet her, so you two had to have a place in mind. I've followed her, I know a lot of what she's been up to. You don't know what I know, so you'd better start impressing me with your answers, or I'll leave you with just a thumb on each hand to hitchhike with." Jeremy nodded.

"Now, how often have you helped her with her animal rights activities? Remember, you don't know what I know."

"I've been with her a few times. We've been to a lab in Eagan. She got caught that time, but I got away. We broke into a fur dealer once and spray painted a bunch of coats. I helped her last week at a farm breaking up some milking equipment."

The patriot flashed back to the call he'd been on where the dairy farmer had shown him all the ruined equipment and the pissed-in tank. He played a bluff.

"This was the farm down south, by Farmington, on Sunday night."

"Yeah."

The patriot fought down the urge to start breaking more of Jeremy's bones. He pressed the point of the rod into Jeremy's stomach again and bore down. "Where were you going to meet her, and when?"

"I won't tell you."

"What? What did you say?" The patriot was amazed. "I'll tear you to pieces! Where are you meeting her?"

"I won't tell you. You're going to kill her and me, too, or you wouldn't be treating me like this."

"I told you I just want something very important from her. If she gives it to me, she'll live. On the other hand, I'll kill you right now if you don't talk to me! Now tell me what I want to know, Jeremy."

"No!" Jeremy cringed and braced for the impact of the rod. The patriot was getting angry and had spent too much time in the room already. He was having a hard time remembering through his anger where he might have touched things and decided to speed things up. He stuffed the gag in Jeremy's mouth and tied the shirt around it again. He dragged Jeremy over to the workbench and bent him over it, facedown. He grabbed the tin-snips and clipped off the little finger of Jeremy's left hand. Jeremy sagged to the floor and started wrestling around. The patriot knelt on him and held him on the floor until he settled. He pulled the gag loose with one finger.

"Fucker!" Jeremy yelled. The patriot jammed the gag back in.

"You really want me to do this to you, don't you?" he asked. He pulled the gag loose and said, "Answer my question—where are you meeting her?"

"You'll kill her."

"I just want what she has, so tell me now!"

"HELP!" Jeremy screamed before the patriot could jam the rag back in.

"Stupid fucker!" the patriot said. He had to get out of there and the frustration that came with this one going so badly enraged him.

The patriot secured the gag on Jeremy's head and looked around the work area. He saw a large, industrial vise mounted on the end of the workbench. He dragged Jeremy over, wound open the jaws of the vise and put Jeremy's head inside. As he tightened it down on the sides of Jeremy's head, the boy fought against him. As he applied pressure, the patriot pinned Jeremy's body against the bench with his own and twisted the bar tighter. Jeremy tried to maintain some balance but his right knee was shattered and it caused incredible pain to stand. He couldn't fall to the floor because the vise was too high up and all the weight of his body would have transferred to his pinned face.

"Tell me, Jeremy," the patriot said. "Are you going to tell me?" Jeremy couldn't answer. He wanted to. He would have done anything at this point to make the unbelievable pain go away. The gag was too tight to answer and there was no way for him to signal his agreement.

The patriot was no longer worrying about what Jeremy might tell him. He was full of rage and frustration. He'd thought if he could get an early, truthful answer, he might be able to find the bitch and tail her to someplace quiet. Now, he realized, Jeremy might lie to him or start screaming again. He knew he might have to put Ms. Bitch Blevins on hold for a while. He had one more place he could try to lie in wait for her, but he had other targets in mind and she could wait, if need be. Besides, Jeremy now had to pay for the damage he'd done on the dairy farm. He would make an acceptable substitute for Blevins for the time being.

The patriot cinched the vise tighter and Jeremy saw exploding colors in his head. The pain was white hot, and he felt his skull bones flexing. He screamed against the gag and as the vise closed, Jeremy heard his head crack; the last thing he felt was one of his eyes popping out of its socket against the duct tape. His body sagged down and went limp.

The patriot stood back and looked with detachment at the scene. He felt sure that Jeremy was dead, but wanted to be certain. He went to the bedroom, returned with a bed sheet and draped it over Jeremy's body like a furniture cover. He pulled his Tanto knife from his boot, reached under the sheet and cut Jeremy's throat. He already had some blood on his sleeve after cutting off Jeremy's pinkie and didn't want any more. He'd been trained in the dangers of coming into contact with someone's blood and didn't want to risk a disease. The sheet did a good job of keeping the blood from splattering him. He wiped the knife off with the edge of the sheet, wiped down the things he'd touched in the apartment, and left.

Desiree Blevins and her friend Amii Faust waited at the coffee shop for Jeremy, wondering why he hadn't shown up. He was supposed to meet them at noon, but it was now 12:45 p.m. and he still hadn't arrived. They decided to check his apartment so they could begin planning Sunday night.

The members of STS had found out from a friend in PETA about a lab in the town of Lino Lakes, just north of St. Paul, that was using monkeys and dogs in a series of experiments designed to research a new pancreatic pump for the eventual treatment of diabetes. They'd been told that the security company that had been providing a night watchman had gone out of business and the lab was left unguarded until an new company could be contracted with the following week. Desiree and her friends knew they had to get in there Sunday night or they may not be able to get in at all.

Desiree and Amii paid for their coffee and walked out and headed down to Jeremy's. They didn't notice the man across the street waiting at the bus stop. Minnesota's cold winters had inspired the Metropolitan Transit Commission, or MTC, to build glass-enclosed kiosks so people wouldn't suffer frostbite while waiting for their ride. The patriot had taken a position there reading a magazine after leaving Jeremy's apartment. He knew that the coffeehouse was the one place he might pick up Desiree's trail and figured correctly that she might come looking for him after he failed to show at their meeting. He smiled when he saw her walk out the front door.

It was only three blocks to Jeremy's apartment and, by the time they'd reached it, the patriot had closed the gap behind them. He was still on the other side of the street when they went in, so he sprinted across the road and entered the side door. He hoped the women would use the elevator to go up, but he peered into the stairwell, listening, before he started up. He took the stairs two at a time and was at the fire door, peeking through the crack in the partially opened door, when he saw them walking to the apartment from the other way. He saw them go in and his mind raced, wondering what he should do. He may never have another opportunity to pin her down like this. But there was someone with her, and the building was now alive with noise. Music was playing, and he could hear laughter and voices. He had to decide fast. He eased into the hall and headed down it.

Inside the apartment, Desiree and Amii dropped their bags on the couch. "Jeremy?" Amii called out.

"Maybe he left a note," Desiree said. She looked around, but there was nothing on the coffee table where he usually left her notes.

Amii wandered into the work area and frowned at the object under the sheet. She thought at first that it was a sculpture that Jeremy had covered to protect it or something. Then she noticed a foot sticking out from under the sheet.

"Um, Desiree, hey, um,—" she said as she backed away.

Desiree came in and looked. She felt her breath catch as she saw the foot. She froze and grabbed Amii's arm. "What is that?" she asked, knowing what it was, but didn't know what else to say.

"Is it Jeremy?" Amii asked.

Desiree and Amii looked at each other and waited for the other to decide what to do. Both had been around destruction, and both had committed crimes and gone to jail. Both were pretty tough, but neither had faced a situation like this. Desiree had a stronger personality and was the undeclared leader of the little group. She took the initiative and walked forward, dragging Amii along. As they got closer, they smelled a sickening coppery smell. The shoe on the foot was definitely Jeremy's. Desiree took hold of the sheet on the opposite end and slowly pulled it back. She let go as if she'd received an electric shock when she saw the back of Jeremy's head in the vise and the blood all over the floor below him.

Amii wheeled around and ran for the living room. She traveled only a few feet before she fell to her knees and threw up. Desiree ran after her and stopped at the sofa. She wanted to scream, but was too terrified to make any noise. Whoever did this could still be in the apartment. She wanted to run.

"Come on, Amii!" Desiree said. "We have to get the fuck out of here, now!"

Amii nodded but threw up again and was unable to stand. Desiree pulled her up but Amii fell against the sofa, too weak and too frightened to move.

"Come on!!" Desiree cried.

"Wait, shouldn't we call someone?" Amii gasped. "What if he's still alive?"

Desiree hadn't thought about that. She was sure he was dead, and she had no intention of being questioned by the cops. She hadn't shown up for her last scheduled court appearance and figured there was a warrant out for her.

"No, he's dead and we have to leave now!" Desiree said forcefully. She pulled Amii up and grabbed both of their bags. They left the apartment and walked quickly to the elevator. They pushed the down button and waited as the old, noisy elevator creaked and clanked up to the top floor. They saw a man in the elevator when the doors opened, but both women were too shocked and scared to realize that they were on the top floor and he could not have ridden down with the elevator. They got on with him, and the doors closed.

Alexander Shermentov was a Ukrainian student studying English at the University of Minnesota. He hoped to return home to Kiev and teach English to those countrymen who needed to master the language which is used for international banking, the airline and maritime industries, Internet pursuits, and so many other well paying careers in what had been the old Soviet Union. He had considered himself lucky to find a room at the apartment building so close to the campus. He came into the lobby after spending the morning at the library and rang for the elevator. The indicator above the door showed it was on the fifth floor but coming down.

At that moment, Alexander heard two loud pops, about a second apart. They sounded hollow and metallic, like the sound of a baseball bat striking the inside of a steel drum. The elevator made some funny noises, but he hadn't heard that one before. The doors opened, and a large man rushed out past him and went out the front door. Alexander looked into the elevator and saw two women lying on the floor, their heads shattered. There was blood all over the walls and ceiling of the elevator, and Alexander backed away. He'd never experienced violence before, even though everyone had warned him back home how dangerous America was. It occurred to him suddenly that the man who'd just left had actually killed the people in the elevator! He ran out after the man and looked to see where he'd gone. He saw the back of the man, who was walking at a fast pace down the street about 20 yards away. Alexander was very afraid but decided he had to follow him. He took a couple of steps but stopped when the man turned his head and saw he was being followed. The man faced Alexander and opened his coat to reveal the butt of a pistol in a shoulder holster, like those the police wore on TV. The man then pointed his hand like a gun at Alexander and dropped his thumb. The man smiled a very cold smile, and Alexander lost any further interest in following him. Alexander wasn't religious, but when he looked at the killer his mind flashed back to the times he had spent with his great-grandmother in the Ukraine. She had maintained her religion in spite of the pressures the communists had brought against believers. She would tell Alexander of devils and spirits and how there was evil in the world. A cold tingle of fear ran down Alexander's spine, and he nodded to the man that he gotten the point. The man turned and walked away, looking back occasionally to see if Alexander would change his mind.

He didn't.

CHAPTER 14

▼

The Minneapolis Police were on the scene of the shooting of Desiree Blevins and Amii Faust within five minutes of Alexander Shermentov's 911 call. Soon, the lobby was filled with paramedics, police, and onlookers. Two investigators from Minneapolis PD's Robbery-Homicide Division, Sergeant Pete Lincoln and Detective Tom McDowell, arrived in less than a half-hour, hour and a crime scene team from the Hennepin Sheriff's Department had been called for.

Lincoln gave instructions to the assisting patrol officers on hand to begin questioning the witnesses in the lobby and then to begin a door-to-door canvas of the building, asking residents if they could provide any help in the case. McDowell took Shermentov to the building's office and sat him down at a table.

Tom McDowell had been an officer in Minneapolis for nine years and an investigator for three. He had recently been pulled from his previous duty as a burglary investigator to help the Robbery-Homicide Division with the unusual number of murders which had plagued the city so far that year. He was inexperienced in death investigations but was considered a pretty sharp cop when he was on the street and had proven himself a natural when it came to interviewing witnesses and suspects. Homicide investigation is definitely considered the varsity among police detectives, and it is no place for someone who is just learning the ropes. McDowell would be under Lincoln's constant watchful eye and was happy to learn what he could while this assignment lasted. He hoped that one day he would find himself "working stiffs," as homicide investigation is called, full time.

McDowell wrote Shermentov's name, address, phone number, other numbers where he could be contacted, and other personal details on his pad, and, once he had determined that Shermentov liked to be called "Alex", got down to business.

"All right, Alex, let's start at the beginning. How long have you lived in this building?"

"Since the fall term in September. This is my second year at University and I lived in a dorm last year." Shermentov had a thick Russian accent, but his command of English was good and McDowell had no trouble understanding him.

"Okay, do you plan on staying on here for the summer or are you going back to Russia?"

"Excuse me, my home is in the Ukraine."

"I'm sorry, I thought that was part of Russia."

"Not anymore. We are independent." Alex was very proud of his heritage, as are most of his countrymen, and was pleased to no longer be considered "Russian."

"My apologies," McDowell said and went on. "Will you be around in case we need to speak with you further or possibly show you a suspect if we locate one?"

"I will be going back for month of June but returning in July. I want to work and keep up on my English studies."

"Fine, would you write down for me a phone number in the Ukraine where I could call you if something very important came up?" Alex did so. They went over how Alexander had spent his morning and got to his return to the apartment.

"Okay, Alex, what time did you come back? By the way, did you walk or drive?"

"I walk. I cannot afford car now. I think I came back about three, but I am not sure. I am still a little frightened," Alex said with a small nervous smile.

"You came in the front door?"

"Yes, front. I went right to elevator and pushed for up."

"Did you notice anyone out front? Any cars, any other men or women hanging around?" McDowell asked.

"No one. I was alone in lobby, until elevator came down."

"Did you hear anything unusual before the elevator opened?"

"Yes. I heard two sounds. Like bangs, only, what is word, ah, strange-sounding, like inside barrel."

"Like and echo or vibrating?" McDowell asked.

"Yes, like echo. Hollow, that is word."

"Were they close together? Fast?"

"No, like this," Alex said and he slapped the table top twice, about one full second apart.

"Did you hear anything else? Were you afraid they might be gunshots?"

"No, I was thinking, and elevator is old and makes bumps and bangs. I heard nothing else. It was just a short time and then doors opened."

"Can you describe the man who walked out of the elevator?"

"He was moving fast and stepped over one person laying inside. He was about my height, under two meters, big in his body but he had on a coat, like hunter's coat. Had painting of bushes on it."

"Camouflage?" McDowell asked.

"I think that is word, like soldier or hunter wears."

"Okay, Alex, try to think of him from head to toe for me. Was he wearing a hat?"

"Yes, a dark hat."

"Like a ball cap?" McDowell asked.

"No, like older men wear. Round with eyeshade in front. Like Scottish man. You know, snaps down in front?"

"Oh, like a tam?"

"I don't know that word, tam. But like Scottish man."

"Was he a white man?"

"Yes, white. He was wearing big sunglasses and I think he was just putting them on because he was taking his hand away from his face as doors opened."

"Could you tell how old he was?"

"Not then. As he stepped over body, I looked down and saw two people and blood everywhere. I did not look at him again until he was walking out door."

"Okay, you said he had on a hunting coat. Was the coat more green or more tan?"

"Not so green, but some green." Alex answered. "More brown and tan."

"Thank you, could you see his pants?"

"Blue jeans," Alex said after thinking for a moment.

"What happened then, Alex?"

"I followed him out to see where he was going. I know that some people in America do not want to help police and stay away, but I do not like violence. This, killing like this, is very bad. We have not so much in Ukraine. Some, but now that Russians are gone, people help police now."

"Well, I hope you can help me, Alex. You're doing a great job here. Where did he go?"

"He walked that way, toward University. I started to follow him. I wanted to see his car or where he went. I see TV and they say people can tell police license of car so I wanted to do that."

"Did you see his car, Alex?"

"No, he saw me, and I didn't want to follow him anymore." Alex looked down at the table. He felt ashamed for his fear and thought the policeman would think of him as a coward.

"Why not, Alex? Did he run?"

"No, I would have chased him, but he...he saw me." Alex would not look McDowell in the eye and McDowell sensed that Alex was feeling shame.

"Alex, if you were afraid of him, I understand. I won't be disappointed with you for being afraid of a criminal. Sometimes I get afraid of some of the people I meet."

"You do?" That surprised Alex. "But you are policeman. You have gun."

"Yes I do, but there are some very frightening people out in the world. This man you saw shot two women in their heads in a elevator, standing closer than you and I are now. When I find him I will be afraid of him, but I will also be very careful, because catching him is my job. It's not your job, Alex. Tell me what happened."

"Okay. He smiled at me. He stopped, turned around, and smiled at me. He opened his coat so I could see a gun, under his arm, like police wear on TV?"

"A shoulder holster," McDowell said.

"Yes, shoulder holster," Alex went on. "He wanted me to see gun and then he smiled."

"Why do you think he smiled, Alex?"

"He was not afraid, I think, like I was. I think he was wishing I would try to stop him. I think he liked the idea if I would do that. He smiled and then walked away, but first he did this," Alex pointed his hand like a gun at McDowell, as the patriot had done, and then dropped his thumb. "He pointed, like a gun. I knew he meant gun, and I knew he meant he would shoot me if I followed. He walked away, and I called police."

"Alex, I think you did a very brave and smart thing. I think this man would have killed you if you had pressed him. Don't feel bad anymore, okay?"

"Okay."

McDowell went out to the lobby and conferred with Lincoln about what Alex had told him. Lincoln asked a patrolman to put out a description of the suspect on the radio and say that he was last seen on foot walking northwest on University Avenue. They agreed to let Alex go home for now so they could start with tenants on their door-to-door interviews while the crime lab worked the scene in the elevator.

Tony Bauer drove to the apartment complex in Burnsville and parked his Explorer. He went into the Community Building and into the indoor pool area. A party going on around the pool and in the adjacent party room. Most of the guests were members of the Dakota Sheriff's office, and the host was a deputy named Don Sundquist. He lived in the apartment complex and was celebrating the fact that he'd completed his law degree at the University of Minnesota and was going to be moving on to his new career shortly. He was throwing a real bash, complete with barbeque, beer, munchies and sodas for the nondrinkers, of whom there were few. It was 8:00 p.m., and the party was already in full swing.

Bauer would have rather spent the night at home resting after his very trying day, but he felt it was important to keep up appearances. He didn't really know Don Sundquist very well, they were just passing acquaintances, but most of the off-duty deputies from his shift were there, and Bauer thought he'd make a courtesy appearance and then head home early. When he walked in, Sundquist yelled, "Tony!" and held up a drink. Don looked as if he was already three sheets to the wind.

Bauer walked over and congratulated Sundquist on his graduation, asking if he planned to work in the prosecution area.

"Hell, I've gotta pass the bar exam first. Then, I'll have to look for an opening somewhere, but prosecution is my eventual goal. Where's your drink?" he asked with a sloppy grin.

Bauer went to the bar and tapped himself a beer from the keg. The partiers were arranged in knots of three or four and Bauer circulated among them, listening in on the conversations. Cops were some of the few people he felt comfortable around because they were mostly conservative, most of them didn't trust higher authority, and they all had in common the fact that they'd seen life stripped bare. Cops are great storytellers when they socialize and are prone to relating hilarious experiences related to their work. As Bauer moved around he heard one group debating the relative merits of .308 and .223 rifles in sniper work. Now, *that* was a topic Bauer thought he could throw some light on, but decided to pass it by.

Another group was enjoying popcorn and beer, and a road deputy named Joe Burns was telling about the last drunk driver he'd stopped. "So, I'm going north on 61, just into Hastings? This car turns left in front of me and goes north. It's midnight, no headlights, and it runs the red. I see this car turn *way* into the right lane and then weave all over the place. Then, it goes all the way over into the oncoming lane. I hit the reds and the car pulls off to the right and almost hits a signpost. As I'm walking up the car rolls forward again and I have to go back and get in my car and follow. I hit my siren and it pulls over again. I walk up and this really cute blonde, who's just *shitfaced* asks, 'Is something wrong officer?' I ask for her license and she roots around in the car and then hands me a shoe."

"A shoe?" one of the others asked.

"Yeah, a shoe," Burns continued. "I say, 'That's nice, but I asked for your license.' She says, all indignant, 'Are you denying I have one?' I say, 'No, but I'd like you to show it to me.' So she looks around some more and hands me the other shoe!"

Everyone got a laugh out of that. "Then," Burns went on, "all the while I'm reading her the implied consent, she's crying and saying, 'I'm so drunk, I'm so drunk, all I wanted was a ride home.'"

One of the group asked, "So, Joe, did you give her the 'breathalyzer'?" and grabbed his crotch. There was more laughter and Burns smiled and shook his head.

"She was ripped. Seriously. And she was planning to drive all the way to Oakdale like that. Never would have made it."

Another member of the group, a Lakeville officer named Terry Johnson, weighed in with his latest drunk story. "I had a guy last Saturday night who cracked me up. I watched him stagger out of Jimmy's Pub, and he goes out to the line of cars on the street. First he tries his key in one car door, that doesn't work, so he goes to the next one and *that* one doesn't work so he goes to the *third* car in line and still hasn't found his. Then he gets smart and pushes the alarm button on his key chain, his car lights up and beeps and he hops right in and starts it up. I mean, you could almost *see* the light bulb go on over his head when he thought to push the alarm button!"

Bauer laughed along with the rest but found that his laugh was forced. He looked at his co-workers differently now. He wondered if they would understand the path he'd chosen to take. He wondered if they'd understand what he was trying to do. The men he'd always thought of as allies and companions were threatening to him now. They weren't treating him differently, he knew that. He wasn't paranoid, after all. Still, it was uncomfortable being there, and he moved off to the bar and refilled his beer glass.

"Hi, are you Tony?" Asked a female voice behind him. Bauer turned and saw a cute brunette in her mid 20's standing there holding a wine cooler.

"Yep," Bauer answered, "I don't think I know you."

"I'm Tina. I'm Don's wife's sister."

"Nice to meet you."

"Do you work for the Sheriff's office?" Tina asked.

"Yep, I work the south end, evening shift."

"I work for Blue Cross in Eagan, in Marketing."

Bauer nodded, wondering where this was going. "Are you here with someone or crashing the cop party?" Bauer asked with a smile.

"I'm solo," Tina answered. "I would have brought my boyfriend, but he had a prior commitment cheating on me, so I came alone."

Whoa, Bauer thought. *Issues. Big-time issues.* Still, she *was* cute, and she filled out the spaghetti strap top she was wearing very nicely.

"Sorry, I didn't mean to pop off like that." Tina said.

"It's okay, I think everybody here's been kicked in the crotch a few times by love."

"So, what's your kick-in-the-crotch story?" Tina asked, opening another wine cooler for herself.

"I'm divorced. It's been three years."

"You have any kids?" Tina asked.

"No. No kids." Bauer thought about going on about *that* subject, but decided that it was too early. He didn't know this girl.

"Me, either. What do you like to do for fun?" Bauer wondered if she might be dangling a worm.

"I'm pretty open-minded," he replied, not wanting to press too fast. "Lately I've been spending my free time working for Bartle's and James." He said with his voice lowered to a conspiratorial tone. "I hang out at parties and research consumers of wine coolers. So far I've found that," he looked down at the flavor Tina was drinking, "women who drink 'Wild Berry' tend to be hot brunettes who hang out with cops."

Tina laughed and nudged him with her hip. She gave him a look as she took a drink that let him know she *definitely* was dangling a worm. "What else has your research shown?" she asked.

"Well, women who drink 'Wild Berry' also have really nice eyes and are pretty good dancers." Bauer pointed at the end of the room where a stereo was playing and said, "Should we try?"

"Well," Tina pretended to think about it. "If it's in the name of science."

They danced and their bodies gradually got closer and closer. They spent the evening talking and laughing, and it wasn't long before Tina was rubbing his arms and chest and commenting on his muscles, asking how often he worked out. The others at the party were enjoying the scene going on in front of them. Knowing smiles were passed around and Don Sundquist's wife was glad that her sister had latched onto someone who appeared normal, for a change. Tina had dated some real losers, and Tony Bauer had always struck her as the strong, silent type. She hoped something good would come of this.

Bauer excused himself to go to the bathroom, which was down the hall from the party room. When he came out, Tina was waiting for him in the hall, and immediately began kissing him. The two of them kissed and groped urgently, as if they were short on time. Bauer had one hand on Tina's firm buttock and the other on her left breast when Terry Johnson came through to use the can. "Christ, Bauer," Johnson said, "get a room! A man can't take a piss without slipping on the wet spot around here!"

"Let's go," Tina said, and they left in Bauer's Explorer.

About the time that Bauer and Tina had decided that her place was closer and he was trying to steer while trying to keep Tina's eager mouth out of his lap, Mike Rawlings was turning on the evening news. He'd had an enjoyable Saturday, doing some yard work at the house he shared with his wife on Lake Elmo, east of St. Paul. Rawlings had his stocking feet up on a hassock and a bowl of microwave popcorn on his lap. His favorite movie, *The Manchurian Candidate* was coming on at 10:30.

Rawlings was savoring his Orville Redenbacher's and thinking how it was so much better than the off-brand his wife bought on sale when he sat straight up in his chair, listening to the first story of the night.

"Tonight, Minneapolis Police are investigating the deaths of two animal rights activists," the reporter was saying. "Desiree Blevins, age 22 and Amii Faust, age 21, were found shot to death in the elevator of an apartment complex on University Avenue this afternoon. A witness said that a man, described as a white male in his 30's with dark hair and a moustache, walked off the elevator, stepping over the bodies of the two women. The witness reportedly heard two shots before the elevator doors opened.

"Blevins and Faust were notorious animal rights activists, and both had been arrested numerous times for criminal activities related to their cause. Blevins was awaiting trial in Dakota County for the burglary of a research facility in Eagan. Faust had been arrested for throwing urine on a woman who was wearing a fur coat at the Mall Of America last year.

"Police say that they are following up leads in the murders and that they feel that robbery was not the motive." The camera cut to an interview with Pete Lincoln.

"The victims were not robbed," Lincoln said. "This seems like a 'gangland style' double murder. Both victims were shot once in the head at close range. The suspect was last seen walking from the scene." The story ended with a short interview with Blevins's uncle, who said he hoped the killer was caught soon, so the family could "get closure."

Rawlings was reaching for the phone before the last interview was finished. He called the Edina PD and got Phil Deane's home number. Deane answered on the second ring.

"Phil, Mike Rawlings here."

"Hi, Mike, how are you?"

"Mike, did you just see the news?"

"No, I've been working in my garage," Deane answered.

"Well, I'd like to meet with you in my office on Monday at one o'clock."

"Sure, what's up?" Deane asked.

"I want to sit down with you and investigators from Burnsville, Minneapolis, and Goodhue County. I think you all might be looking for the same man."

"Why?" Deane asked.

"Because it seems to me that too many tree-huggers are being slaughtered here, lately."

At Tina's apartment in Eagan, a trail of clothing led from the front door to the bedroom. Bauer and Tina were standing naked at the foot of her bed, kissing passionately. Bauer bent down and circled his arms around Tina's hips, lifted her up and held her to him. He took one of Tina's nipples into his mouth and teased it with his tongue while Tina rolled her head back and moaned softly in pleasure. Feeling her pubic hair rubbing against the hairs on his chest, Bauer grew hard. He moved his mouth to the other nipple, and Tina responded by wrapping her legs around his body. Bauer laid her down on the bed and slid his body down until his face was buried between her legs. Tina wrapped her legs around his neck and ran her fingers through his hair as he gave her moist triangle his undivided attention. When he could take no more, Bauer mounted Tina and slid easily inside her. The two thrashed hungrily together until they both climaxed in a chorus of sound. Tina was a very vocal woman, and Bauer wondered for a minute if someone would call the police when she was screaming during her passion.

Afterward, as they lay back, Tina rested her head on Bauer's chest and ran her fingers through the hair he had there. Bauer chuckled, and Tina said, "Okay, what's so funny?"

"I don't know your last name!" Bauer exclaimed.

Tina laughed, too. "It's Sullivan."

"Hi, Tina Sullivan." Bauer held out his right hand.

"Hi, Tony Bauer." Tina shook his hand.

As they lay there, Bauer became increasingly uneasy. *What the hell are you doing?* he asked himself. It wasn't part of the plan to get involved with anyone at this point. Certainly not the sister-in-law of a co-worker. *This could be bad*, he thought. But how could he cut her loose now without causing bad feelings? Bauer knew he had a job to do, one that was so important that he couldn't abandon it by giving in to lust. He thought for a moment about what it would be like to start a life with this woman, but then he remembered what it had been like with Amber. He'd loved Amber with all his heart, but she had hurt him like no one else in the world ever had, or ever could, he was sure. He didn't know if he could ever trust a woman again. He knew that all women acted pretty much the same. It was impossible to trust another one the way he'd trusted Amber, wasn't it?

"What are you thinking?" Tina asked, as she let her hand run down to his groin.

"Nothing, really," Bauer answered. "I was just wondering if you were real, or just some exotic dream I've been having."

Tina smiled. "A dream, huh? Let's see if this wakes you up!" She slid her hands down his body and slowly ran her tongue down his chest until she took his penis into her mouth. Bauer lay back and decided to put off any decisions about the future for the time being.

Meanwhile, in a dark Minneapolis apartment, the undiscovered body of Jeremy Soderberg hung lifelessly in a vise, waiting to be found.

CHAPTER 15

▼

That night, Tony Bauer had the dream again. The dream was always the same. He had it less frequently now, since he was so focused on his mission. He usually had the dream when he was going through times when he was confused or uncertain. That night he was enjoying a very satisfying night's sleep after his exertions with Tina when the dream came, as it always did, at about 3:00 a.m.

Bauer was in a hospital delivery room. Everything was so white it hurt his eyes. Light reflected blindingly off of the sheets, the walls, the floor, and a tray of instruments. There were doctors and nurses there, and they, too, were in white. They were talking, but he was having trouble understanding them. There was a figure under the sheets on the table. Somehow he knew it was Amber under there, but he walked to the head of the table and looked anyway. His wife was covered from her neck down with a white sheet and she was staring up at the ceiling. Her legs were up in stirrups. In the dream Amber and Bauer were still married and Bauer knew she was there to deliver their son.

Bauer wanted to see the baby. He wanted a son. He felt he *needed* a son. He needed a boy to raise and to teach things. He thought of days spent fishing and playing catch in the yard. Bauer wanted to spend cool fall nights standing on bleachers watching his son carry the football into the end zone for a touchdown. He wanted to cheer on hot summer days when his boy hit the baseball over the fence for a home run. He knew he would be a good father, certainly better than his father had been. He would never get drunk and throw his little boy into the closet for not eating his vegetables. He wouldn't beat him with a heavy strap for breaking a drinking glass when he was carrying it to the sink after dinner. If his little son wanted a pet, he would let him have one. If his boy brought home a kitten, he would never, ever stuff the poor, mewling creature into the garbage disposal and turn it on, like his father had.

The doctors and nurses moved so slowly in the dream. The air felt as if it was made of molasses, and he could hardly move. Amber only stared at the ceiling. He wanted her to look at him and smile or reassure him in some way that everything was okay.

Bauer knew that he and Amber would be good parents. He felt that they had to have at least three kids so all of them would have a brother or sister to play with. He knew how hard it was to be an only child. He remembered what it was like to grow up and to be alone so much. Of course, his mother never left his father; that just wasn't done. "Til death do us part" was the promise that his mother had kept. She kept it even though her husband would come home drunk, grab her by the hair, and throw her around the house just because she asked him where he'd been. She kept it even after she found out he'd been screwing the waitress down at the diner where he ate lunch. She kept it when he lost the mortgage payment in a card game and then took the money she'd been saving for Christmas. She even kept it when her husband had slapped their boy so hard on the side of his head that they had to take him to the doctor with a ruptured eardrum.

Bauer knew that his mother didn't know about all of the bad things his father had done to him. Usually she was out when it happened. She knew that if he was drinking he would find fault with something, and she found excuses to leave the house for a while.

Esther Bauer wasn't a strong woman, and she just couldn't handle it when Vern would get angry with her for something. She knew that he'd been mean to Tony, but she was sure that he really loved the boy and that most of the things that made him angry were her fault, after all. She didn't know that he had once pressed a hot cigarette against Tony's arm while they were going to the store in the car. She didn't know that her husband had bound their son's hands and feet and left him in the cellar for an hour when little Tony had told his father that he was afraid of the dark. Vern Bauer was an unhappy man who had trouble holding a job and making friends because of his moodiness and his temper. He was, by nature, a very critical man and couldn't seem to avoid pointing out people's mistakes to them. He usually did it in a cutting, hurtful way and people tried to avoid him.

Vern Bauer went from job to job, never really mastering any trade. He couldn't get along with his co-workers and never respected any of his bosses. The longest he'd spent at one job was two years. That was driving a delivery van for a messenger service. He worked alone at that job, which was why he held it for so long. It ended one day when he was making a delivery to a woman in an office and she berated him because the package was supposed to have been delivered the day before. Vern wasn't a man who would take what he considered shit, especially from a woman. The customer ended her criticism by telling him, "If your company insists on hiring the retarded, they should at least have the sense to confine them to the loading dock and keep them off of the delivery routes!" An hour later the woman was being treated for a broken nose, and Vern Bauer was out of a job. That incident had resulted in an assault charge and Bauer had also been dragged into the lawsuit the woman filed against the delivery service.

Bauer's father took out his stress on his family, and he had a lot of stress. He was pissed off by everything from traffic to the weather. Life was full of irritations for him and one of the things that galled him the most was his son. It seemed to Vern that his wife was spoiling the boy. He was always running to her and crying about something or other. The kid never wanted to spend any time with Vern, and what good was a son anyway if he didn't learn from his father? Vern was a competent carpenter and had tried to teach Tony how to use tools and how to build and repair things, but the boy kept making mistakes. He would cut the trim pieces the wrong way in the miter box and then run off when Vern would correct him with a backhanded slap. Vern knew it would be his responsibility to toughen the kid up, otherwise his wife would turn him into a limp-wristed faggot.

When Tony was growing up, he would dream of his father dying. He would imagine him crushed beneath a bus or cut in half by a speeding freight train. Sometimes he would dream that he and his father were in the car where his father was telling him that he was a "poor excuse" as he always did, and the car would swerve and roll over. Tony would imagine how he would be thrown free of the car and his father would be trapped inside and how the car would catch fire. He father would cry, "Help me, son! Get me out!" and Tony would just stare and smile as the flames crept over him and made him scream and turn black. When his father had died of a brain tumor when Bauer was 17, he remembered looking down at him in the coffin and fighting to keep a smile from crossing his face. He felt a sense of triumph. He'd finally beaten his father and he had done it with death.

Bauer knew he would never treat his son as he had been treated. He would play with his son. He would show him things and tell him how the world was. He would teach him to say the alphabet and read to him, and be proud as he took his first steps, rode a bicycle around the block, and went off to his first day at school. He would be his son's best friend and his boy would be his.

But in the dream, he didn't understand why Amber wasn't in labor. She should have been crying out as she suffered contractions, but she was only staring at the ceiling. In the dream he wants to talk to the doctor, to ask him what was wrong. He tries, but he can't form the words. He walks to the foot of the table and sees Amber's belly, uncovered by the sheet, but it doesn't seem to be swollen, like that of a woman who is nine months pregnant. The doctor has given her a shot, an IV is running into her arm, and Bauer doesn't know why, but sees the doctor take a speculum and use it to open Amber's vagina. Bauer sees the doctor inset a long pair of forceps and draw out the baby, but the baby is so small. He is small, but perfect and looks just like Bauer. The baby is halfway out of his mother's body and he looks at his father. He turns his head and looks at him and his eyes are *so big!* He looks sad, but he doesn't cry at all. Bauer tries to speak in the dream but he can't. Everything moves so slowly. The nurse hands the doctor something covered by a sterile cloth and the doctor moves it down toward the baby where Bauer can't see. Bauer strains to move and slowly inches his way further to the end of the table and sees the doctor is holding a large syringe and needle. The doctor looks at him and says, "This is formaldehyde. It will all be over in a minute." Bauer opens his mouth to scream but cannot as the doctor pushes the needle into the soft spot on the top of Bauer's little son's head and depresses the plunger. The boy dies and the doctor delivers the rest of his tiny body, placing it in a white plastic trash bag. The nurse carries it away.

Bauer can't speak. He wants to kill the doctor. He wants to grab his throat with is thumb and fingers on either side of his Adam's Apple and tear his windpipe out. He turns to Amber, who is now looking at him. "I told him to do it, Tony," she snarls at him. "I made him do it. I'll never have your child, ever. I'd kill any child of yours!"

In the dream Bauer slowly makes his way to the door. However, that night he woke up drenched in sweat and sobbing right after Amber spoke to him. When he got out of bed, he was relieved to see that Tina was still sleeping. He couldn't deal with her now, not after the dream, and he was afraid of what might happen if she were to question him. He went into the bathroom and ran cold water in the sink, splashing it on his face until he felt he was back in control. He hated the dream more than he hated anything.

Of course, it hadn't really happened that way. Amber had been pregnant, but Bauer hadn't known until a couple of weeks after she'd left him. She'd told him on a couple of occasions before she'd left that she was afraid of him sometimes and that, even though he'd never hurt her, she felt that he was angry too much of the time and that maybe he should see a doctor; however, Bauer thought he could hold it together. He knew that he sometimes flew off the handle at home when things got to him, but it was just so hard to keep everything bottled up at work, and he knew that he could never let off steam on the job or he'd be fired. His police job was too important to him, and he knew that he had to be totally in control every minute.

He'd been surprised and hurt the day he came home from a training class and found that she'd taken most of her clothes and left. She'd left him a letter saying how she needed time alone and that she didn't think they could go on together. She wrote that she would call him. Bauer had tried calling her friends and her parents to try to find her, but none of them would tell him where she was. He thought that, if he could just speak to her, he could convince her that he could change and that everything would be all right. He did his best to go on with his routine, hoping she would call. Then he got a call from the clinic two weeks later. A nurse identified herself and asked for Amber. Bauer didn't want to tell the nurse that he didn't know where Amber was, exactly, so he said that she was sleeping. The nurse told him that she was making a follow-up call and wondered if Amber had been noticing any hemorrhaging or fever since yesterday's procedure. Bauer was confused but knew he shouldn't let on that he didn't know what "procedure" the nurse was talking about. Obviously, the nurse was calling the phone number they had on file for Amber. Bauer asked, "Is bleeding or fever normal? Is it something we need to worry about?"

"No, a little bleeding might be expected but not very much. Most women who have abortions this early in their pregnancy don't show any ill effects, but we would be very concerned about a fever."

Bauer was stunned. He felt physically ill and couldn't speak. He tried to mumble something but the words wouldn't come out. The nurse kept saying, "Hello? Hello?" but Bauer could only stare at the phone. The nurse kept talking and, when she asked if she should send an ambulance, Bauer finally got his composure back enough to tell her that he'd had to put the phone down to take something off of the stove. He assured the nurse that everything was fine, and he hung up. He'd had no idea Amber had been pregnant. She'd never spoken to him about it, and he sank into a chair to try to deal with the revelation. He had to know why she did it. Why had she robbed him of his son? She knew he desperately wanted one. They'd spoken about it many times, and Amber had always promised him that she would have it. He flew into a rage, and knew that, if he knew where Amber was at that moment, he would have killed her with his bare hands. He felt cheated and abused.

When she finally called him a week later, Bauer remembered how she'd tried to sound pleasant and told him how they'd grown apart and that she felt they each needed "a different type of person" in order to be happy. She assured him that she hadn't found anyone else and that she'd been faithful to him, but she said she thought he would be happier with a woman who was "more the stay-at-home type." Bauer had fought to control his anger during that conversation. He knew he could never love Amber again, not after what she'd done to him. He also knew that, if he let go and told her the thoughts that were going through his mind, she might go to his sheriff or even get a restraining order against him. He couldn't risk her jeopardizing his work. So, he listened to her spell out how she thought it would be good if they each spoke to a lawyer and how she wouldn't fight him for anything and how she hoped that he could see how a divorce would be a positive thing for both of them after some time passed.

Amber had talked on and on, thinking he was paying attention, but she couldn't have known that Bauer was wondering if it was possible for him to skin her alive using only the kitchen utensils in the drawer under the phone. He found it was comforting to let his mind play over such images, and it helped him keep in control.

When she'd spoken her piece, Bauer told her that he wouldn't fight a divorce. She asked if it would be all right if she came and picked up the rest of her clothes and her personal things. Bauer told her he would prefer if she did it when he was at work so he wouldn't have to see her. Amber had sounded a little hurt by that and said, "I hope we can keep this from getting ugly. I don't want to hurt you." That was too much and Bauer asked, "I just have one question: the baby you aborted, was it mine?" There was silence on the other end of the phone, and Bauer heard a dial tone after a few seconds. He tore the cord from the wall and threw the phone across the kitchen. He vented his rage in the weight room, pumping iron and tiring his body until he could hardly lift his arms.

The divorce had been fairly painless, and Bauer hadn't shown up in court for the final hearing. He hadn't even seen Amber because they'd worked out all the details through the attorneys. Bauer wondered how he would react if he did bump into her in the mall. He wondered if he might be tempted to follow her. He knew where she lived now, of course, but had avoided seeking her out.

Bauer drank a cup of cold water and toweled the sweat off of his body before returning to bed. Tina was sleeping face down and snoring softly. Bauer looked at her and felt the conflict rise in him again. He missed having a woman in the house with him and had gotten lonely lately, but he knew he couldn't trust Tina with his secrets. He couldn't share his past with her as he had with Amber. He had come to realize that, when he opened himself up to Amber and told her things he'd never told anyone else, she'd turned around and used them against him. He wouldn't make that mistake again. And he was *absolutely* sure he couldn't tell her about the fight he was waging. She seemed nice, and she *was* a good lay, so he had no desire to hurt her feelings. He also didn't want to have bad feelings with her brother-in-law, so he thought it would be best if he let her down easy. He remembered Tina's comment from the party about her boyfriend, so maybe she was just doing a little catting around tonight and wasn't looking for a long-term thing. He decided he would treat her nicely and try to get the message across in the morning that he wasn't looking for a relationship, but that he had enjoyed her company.

The effects of the dream had worn off and Bauer found himself suddenly extremely tired. He closed his eyes and slipped into a deep, dreamless sleep.

CHAPTER 16

▼

Sunday, May 12, was a quiet day in the Twin Cities. The weather had stayed cool and prevented people from enjoying spring activities.

Tony Bauer had awakened with Tina and shared coffee and toast with her before driving home. The morning's conversation had gone well, and Tina hadn't applied any pressure by bringing up the future. She thanked him for the evening when he kissed her goodbye and told him, "Last night was just what I needed." Bauer smiled and walked out to his truck.

At home, the patriot used the time to do some yard work and catch up on his e-mail correspondence. He read the Sunday paper's account of the killing in Minneapolis the day before and was amused to read that only two bodies had been found. He thought that Jeremy must be getting a little ripe by now and someone would soon notice. The patriot thought back to the satisfaction he'd felt as he tightened the handle of the vise. It was a much more appropriate way to punish a turd like Jeremy than to shoot him like the two bitches in the elevator who'd made him waste so much time. He had been rushed in dealing with them, and it bothered him that now the Browning, like the rifle he'd used on Judge Borgert, could be linked to him through ballistic tests if they were found in the future. He had other untraceable weapons at his disposal and knew how to get more if need be.

The patriot had bought his rifle and handguns through third parties and at gun shows. He had made contacts with people who disliked government rules regarding the documentation of firearm transfers. He had destroyed the serial numbers on the guns with a Dremel Tool and kept them hidden away safely in his garage cubbyhole.

The patriot leafed through the Sunday paper and found James Knox's column. He liked Knox and, even though he was still pretty liberal, he found that Knox was better than most reporters at keeping his opinions to himself. He also thought that Knox, by virtue of the fact that he'd had the crime beat for so long, had become somewhat hardened toward criminals, and it showed in some of his stories. Knox had written a nonfiction book called *Public school battle zone,* in which Knox dealt with rising crime in schools and the inability of the juvenile justice system to deal with it. The patriot thought that some of Knox's conclusions were off-base and that Knox had tended to oversimplify the problem when he addressed solutions in his later chapters, but still, he saw juvenile criminals for what they were and called a spade a spade. The patriot had decided that he would approach Knox when the time came and offer him the story. He had considered a call from a phone booth but dismissed it because he thought it might be hard to contact Knox by telephone. He decided to give Knox the story cold and then arrange a way to contact him, if Knox was interested. The fact that Jeremy's body hadn't yet been found made him believe that the time was right to make his story known.

The patriot opened a shopping bag containing items he'd bought several weeks before. He took out a new box of floppy disks and a box of plain white envelopes. He went to his computer and began to write:

Mr. Knox,

I am sending you this disk in the hopes that you will read what I've written and believe that what I'm writing is true. I cannot tell you my name but I understand the need to attach labels to things and to people, so I would prefer if you referred to me as "a patriot".

As of Saturday May 11, I have silenced six people who I felt were not of democratic ideals and exemplified the erosion of personal responsibility and freedoms in this once great nation. I am a student of history and am disgusted to see that the well-thought-out principles of government, set forth by the framers of the United States Constitution and the Declaration of Independence, are being exchanged for those of Marx, Lenin, and Mao.

The new fascism of political correctness and unrestrained liberalism have given us schools which no longer produce informed and well-educated children. Rampant crime, disrupted families, and a population of citizens who, if they bother to vote at all, find that the only candidates running are criminals, half-wits, and perverts. The government of the United States has branched out from its original purpose of providing "life, liberty and the pursuit of happiness" and is now trying to feed us, house us, clothe us, provide us with medical care, and educate our children. It is trying to tell us which foods we should eat, which cars we should drive, and how we should go about repairing our houses and forcing business owners to refuse service to those customers who choose to engage in the perfectly legal (although unhealthy) habit of smoking. What right does government have to order people around in this arbitrary way?

Our government formerly welcomed immigrants who could make their new life in this nation and, in turn, make the nation better through their talents and hard work. Those who came to this country were given only an equal chance, no preferential treatment, and were expected to work for a living like everyone else. Those with incurable diseases, mental illness, and the inability to earn a living were turned away and returned to their home country. Now, we encourage people of foreign birth to come to America even if they are HIV-positive, or have other incurable illnesses. We allow them to become a burden on an already overstressed healthcare system, even though they cannot or will not pay their medical costs. We allow them to live here, speaking their native language, and we provide all needed services though a translator so they will not be inconvenienced by having to learn English.

Our society has grown weak through the efforts of lawyers who fool people into thinking that they are not responsible for their own errors. They help them get out of paying the price for their own mistakes by manipulating a grossly warped legal system, which has long abandoned any shred of common sense.

We have grown weak through the work of activists who believe that their duty is to destroy long held American values and institutions, and who feel justified in using force and violence to overthrow those values and institutions.

We have grown weak through a decline in moral values. People sit enslaved by television programs which depict mindless people and unrealistic lifestyles. Our children grow up wanting to live like their idols on TV and resent the concepts of hard work, right, and wrong and personal responsibility, all of which they need before they can ever hope to live those lifestyles.

Mr. Knox, many people in this country believe, as I do, that our nation MUST return to some of these values in order to insure freedom and a healthy free-market economy for future generations. We are willing to fight and die, if necessary, trying to accomplish that goal. Some things in this world worth dying for. Freedom and democracy are two of those things.

To convince you that I am not a publicity-seeking crackpot, I will tell you how you can go about proving my story.

On the night of Sunday, May 5, I shot Judge Edward Borgert through the kitchen window of his house in Edina. I selected Borgert because of his appalling record on the bench and his inability to enforce the law. Borgert represents all that is wrong with our legal system today. He was a hack attorney who gained the power of a judgeship through political connections rather than through merit. You can confirm with the Edina Police the fact that Borgert was wearing a light blue pullover shirt and was eating Neapolitan ice cream at his kitchen table when I shot him three times with a .223 caliber rifle. I used Russian Barnaul fully jacketed ammunition.

On the morning of May 7, I killed nuclear protester Sarah Ehrenberg in her house near the Prairie Island Nuclear Power Plant. I selected Ehrenberg because, despite the opinion of experts in the field, she, of her own accord and with no expertise, chose to believe that nuclear power was unsafe. She then used all means at her disposal, including committing crimes against innocent employees, to try to force her will upon others. She was a fine example of a fool who knows nothing about a complicated subject, yet screams her opinion about it at the top of her lungs. She was a remnant of the bygone age of the hippies, and the less of them we have around, the better off we will be. I knocked on her door early in the morning and got her to let me in by means of a cover story which I will not relate to you. I shoved an awl into her right ear and punctured her brain. I then twisted her head until her neck broke for good measure. Need more? She was wearing a black sweatshirt that had the word "Choice" on the front.

Shortly after midnight on the morning of May 9, I gained entry to the apartment of Wallace Berry in Burnsville, again by means of a cover story which I will keep to myself. I selected Berry because his work in the American Civil Liberties Union represented everything I have found to be a threat to this great nation. When the Soviet Union fell and the archives of its KGB, the former secret police force, were opened, they revealed strong links between the ACLU and the KGB, an organization dedicated to the destruction of the American way of life. That it was allowed to continue to exist after those facts were revealed is further testimony to how lax our nation has become in recognizing threats. I eliminated Berry by stunning him with an electric stun baton and then slitting open his chest. I'm sure the Burnsville Police can confirm the burn mark on Berry's right kidney. They're probably also wondering what caused it. Now you know.

On Saturday, May 11, I went to an apartment near the University of Minnesota looking for a criminal animal rights activist named Desiree Blevins. Blevins and her friends were vicious criminals who attacked laboratories where important work was being done to cure disease. They also sought to destroy the way of life of dairy farmers by ruining their milking equipment. They threw paint and bodily fluids on people who exercised their right to wear leather and fur and put the welfare of beasts above that of human beings. To my mind, they had become beasts, and I treated them as such. I found an associate of Blevins named Jeremy in the apartment, and he admitted to me that he had joined Blevins in her night visits to farms. I bound his hands and feet with plastic tie wraps and crushed his head in a vise. In a political discussion, I'm sure Jeremy would have considered me "narrow-minded" but when I left him his mind was considerably narrower than mine. Interestingly enough, no mention has been made of Jeremy in the media, and I do not think his body has yet been found. This will be a scoop for you.

Blevins and another cohort came to visit Jeremy later in the day and left when they found he wasn't able to entertain them. I surprised them on the elevator as they were leaving and shot them with a 9mm pistol. I'm sure the police are analyzing the Federal Hydro-Shock cartridge casings they found next to the bodies. A young man with long blonde hair saw me leave the building. The Minneapolis Police will be happy to confirm that once you tell them that they can find Jeremy in apartment 506.

Mr. Knox, you are free to disagree with the path I have chosen. I suspect you will share this with the police who are investigating these deaths. I hold no ill will toward those investigators as they are only doing their jobs, although I am saddened that they haven't seen the light. I believe that many of them understand that the world will be better off without these creatures in it. The only difference between them and me is that I have chosen to take action. The police are bound by their political masters and are forced to follow rules set by others.

Now that you know my story, I hope you will do your job and report it. I hope that there are others who will read it and follow my lead. People need to know that they have the power, the right, and the ability to stand up and fight for a better nation. We need to identify the individuals among us who are acting as a cancer and remove them the same way a surgeon would cut out a tumor.

It is not my desire to become famous. I hope I am never caught, although I believe I probably will be. I intend to continue on with my campaign and, if I am able, you will hear from me again.

Signed,

a patriot

The patriot reread the document and put on a pair of surgical gloves before he removed a new floppy from the package and put it in the drive. He saved the document to the floppy and checked to make sure it was copied before he removed it. He used his computer printer to address an envelope to Knox at his office and placed the floppy inside. He used a wet rag to moisten the seal so that none of his saliva would be a residue to be tested, and he put three stamps on the front for good measure. Later in the day, he drove to St. Paul and dropped the letter in a mailbox near downtown. He drove back home and took a nap so he would be fresh and alert when he went out later that night.

On Sunday evening, Peter Montgomery was engaged in his favorite pastime at his home in Shakopee. Montgomery lived alone in a small rambler house along Apgar Street. He didn't have a lot of friends, so there was little chance of him being interrupted.

Montgomery was starting a new job the next morning and intended to get to bed early so he would get a good night's sleep. He'd been out of work ever since the news story about him was aired and it had taken him quite a while to find a place that would hire him. He finally found a small warehouse in Inver Grove Heights whose manager evidently hadn't recognized Montgomery when he applied for a job as a bookkeeper. The manager seemed quite impressed with Montgomery's college background and said he was delighted to have someone so well educated doing his books for him. The job didn't pay as well as his last one, but, Montgomery thought, beggars can't be choosers.

Peter Montgomery had been very well educated. In fact, he'd spent most of his life studying literature, philosophy, art, psychology, history, theology, languages, and humanities. He had been considered a fine student, and his mind soaked up subjects like a sponge. He had a shy personality which he overcame as he took on knowledge and became respected by his peers. Montgomery could converse intelligently with experts in many fields, and this broad expanse of knowledge was later mistaken for wisdom by some who had come into contact with him once he became established in the position he'd held in his former life. He enjoyed the academic world, but, as his shyness went away, he found that there were certain activities he enjoyed which were better when others were involved.

Montgomery had discovered, to his delight, that his respected position had granted him easy access to young, trusting boys, and that actually engaging in sexual games with those boys had been far more satisfying than playing out those games in his fantasies. He not only had the access to them and the respect of his office to intimidate them into not revealing his passions, but he had the tacit cooperation of his organization to help him remain active for many years. Peter Montgomery had been a Catholic priest for thirty of his 55 years and would still have been one had a groundswell of media attention not exposed him along with many other priests who shared the same tastes.

Montgomery had been a valued member of the clergy in 14 different parishes in Minnesota, Iowa, and Wisconsin during his tenure. He had been first exposed to the lifestyle he eventually embraced in the seminary and carried on with it, moving from one opportunity to another, gradually becoming more skilled at sensing which of the boys in this year's class could be approached and manipulated into Father Montgomery's "fellowship." He developed an almost predatory cunning which helped direct him to those who could be maneuvered into joining in, and then being trusted to stay quiet.

Of course, rumors would circulate after a time, but Montgomery had little to fear. After all, he was considered by those devout Catholics in the parish to be a man of God, a direct descendent of the Apostle Peter. He was a pipeline of the Holy Spirit and a man whose vows put him above human failures and made him, by definition, above reproach. He was the man with whom couples discussed the intimate details of their troubled marriages and listened to his advice as though it were the wisdom of the Lord God Himself. He was the holy man who counseled parents who came to him when their children were misbehaving and they were at the end of their ropes trying to balance their careers and family. Often Father Montgomery would suggest prayer and, if the child was a certain age, and a boy, that the parents consider sending their son to a youth retreat, which he himself would be attending, coming up very soon.

Sometimes the rumors would become the subject of calls to the Archdiocese, and the Bishop found it prudent to bring Father Montgomery in for yet another session about how he needed to pray for strength and guidance to help him conquer temptations. Father Montgomery would adopt a pious attitude and ask for forgiveness, and the Bishop would grant it, telling him how valued a man of his experience and training was to the Church. Father Montgomery would then soon find himself assigned to another parish in another state with a clean slate, no ugly rumors, and fresh new generations of young boys whose parents appreciated the time the new Father spent with their son.

It was with dismay that Father Montgomery saw people's attitudes change toward authority figures. When the lessons of the Vietnam War and Watergate made people cynical about believing what the government told them, they also began to question what the Church told them. It was a gradual process, but soon the ugly rumors that had plagued Father Montgomery were turning into formal complaints, lawsuits, and even death threats from parents who were slowly becoming aware that the good Father and others like him were actually wolves in sheep's clothing. The pressure became too much for the Church to bear, and gradually priests like Father Montgomery were asked quietly to leave. He had done so with regret, knowing that it would be difficult at his age to find the companionship he craved without the trappings of the priesthood to support him.

Plain old Peter Montgomery was awarded a job as Library Director at a St. Paul college and made a comfortable living back in the bookish life where he had begun. The job paid well and he was able to afford a small house in Shakopee and to decorate it with some of the medieval artwork and objects he fancied. He enjoyed talking with the students and discussing subjects with them. When the State of Minnesota established requirements that all employees of educational institutions be required to be fingerprinted to determine if they had any criminal records, Montgomery had nothing to fear. He'd never been arrested in his life. He enjoyed five years at the library until one of his former victims came forward publicly in the media and slapped a multimillion-dollar lawsuit against the Catholic Church, the Diocese of St. Paul, the archbishop, a bishop and the former Father Montgomery. Two weeks after the press announced the suit, four more men came forward and said that they, too, had been molested by Father Montgomery, a man who was now living quietly working in a library for a St. Paul college. It was also revealed that one of his former victims had hung himself at the age of 25 from the shame of his victimization by Montgomery. The night that story came out, the dean of the college called Montgomery and asked him if it was true that he was formerly the same Father Montgomery whom the news had just accused of being a pedophile. Montgomery adopted the same pious attitude which had always gotten him out of trouble with Church officials and said that, yes, he had been a priest and that, yes, he had been served legal papers accusing him of crimes, but that he intended to fight the accusations and be proven innocent. The dean told him that the college had "liability issues" and that he was, from that moment, on "administrative leave" pending a resolution of his legal problems and that the school's board of regents would decide if and when he could return.

Montgomery read the writing on the wall and resigned. The media storm which had followed him after that was unbelievable. He had reporters following him everywhere, asking him leading questions. They spoke with his neighbors, his former co-workers, former parishioners, everybody. His picture was in all the papers along with all the details of his life. He'd never be able to enjoy life in the academic world again, and this saddened him. He was most at home among books and scholars, and the new laws prevented anyone with a questionable past from working with them. It was with regret that he closed that chapter in his life, but he had to go on. He then discovered the Internet and the myriad of things a person could find there if he had the time and the inclination to dig around. He found an abundance of websites devoted to gay men and spent many enjoyable hours looking at pictures of well-built naked young men having sex with each other. He also found that he could go into chat rooms and carry on conversations with the same types of confused and lonely young boys who had formerly turned to their priests but now turned to their computers for the companionship they desired, but couldn't find, in their social lives.

He was sitting at the computer in his home's darkened bedroom now, wearing only an open robe and browsing through some of his favorite websites. He was careful not to visit any child pornography sites, for he knew the FBI had been making a lot of arrests lately by monitoring those. Montgomery went into some of the chat rooms he'd previously had success in, but found no one interesting to go off into a private chat with. He contented himself with pictures of young studs involved in various sexual activities. As he clicked through thumbnail pictures and enlarged the interesting ones, he fondled and kneaded his genitals. He loaded a couple of .mpg movie files and watched short ten-second clips of men eagerly devouring each other. He became very aroused and replayed one interesting film short of two young men in a "69." They were outside near a campfire on an open sleeping bag, and it reminded Montgomery of some memorable youth retreats he'd been on. He stroked his stiffening penis faster as he kept hitting the replay button and watched the action over and over again until he finally had to grab a Kleenex to keep from soiling his robe. It was at that vulnerable moment that the electrical power to his home went out.

The patriot had parked two blocks away from the little house on Apgar Street. and walked the rest of the way. He cut between houses and approached the rear of Montgomery's house through the dark backyard of a neighbor. On a previous visit, the patriot had discovered that the house had an old style electrical system with the fuse box outside on the back wall near a crumbling patio. There was no back door on the house, just a front entry and a door going out through the garage on the side. The side door was flanked by very tall, thick arborvitae. It was into one of these thick bushes that the black-clad patriot hid after he had donned a pair of surgical gloves and shut off the power main for the house.

Peter Montgomery was startled when the power went out. He sat there panting from his orgasm and staring at the dark screen of his computer. "Shit," he said as the realization of what had happened came to him. He got up and looked out the window at his neighbors and saw that their power seemed to be on. The streetlights were working.

He found a flashlight and looked up the number for the power company. He called the number listed for residential outage reports and after going through the maddening process of having to push buttons and select options, finally got a live technician.

"Xcel Energy Electric, this is Dan, how may I help you?"

"Hello, the power seems to be out at my home." Montgomery said.

"What's your name and address?"

"Peter Montgomery, 415 Apgar Street in Shakopee."

"How long has your power been out, sir?" Dan asked.

"It just went out a few minutes ago." Montgomery could hear Dan tapping on a computer keyboard.

"Um, I'm not showing any grid failures in your area, are you aware if any of the homes in your neighborhood are out of power?" Dan asked.

"No, it seems to be just mine," Montgomery answered.

"Sir, I'm not showing any outages on my equipment, have you checked your breaker box?"

"No," Montgomery replied sheepishly, "I'm not very handy with those things. Is that like a fuse box?"

"Yes sir, some older homes have fuses, the newer ones have breakers. Do you have an electrical box in your basement?"

"No, I think it's on the outside of my house."

"Yes, that would be an older style, more than likely a fuse box. Do you have spare fuses?" Dan asked.

"I don't know. I've never had a problem since I moved in here several years ago."

"Well sir, you probably just blew a fuse. I would suggest you check that before making a trouble report. If I have to send a repair crew out and they find it's a blown fuse, you would be charged for the service call."

"Okay." Montgomery sighed. "I'll see if I can find what's wrong."

"You'll find a lever inside the fuse box which shuts the power off. You might try flipping that first," Dan said, trying to be helpful. "Be careful not to touch any bare metal inside the box, though, or you could get a nasty shock. You should also consider having your fuse box moved into your home. It's very unsafe having it outdoors."

"Great," Montgomery said. "Thanks for the tip." He hung up and tightened the sash on his robe before going outside. As he walked around the back of the house, he was thinking about the prospect of being electrocuted and didn't see or hear the figure slide out from the bushes and into the garage behind him. Montgomery found the fuse box and opened it. He saw an array of fuses in two rows and a large switch marked "Main." He pressed on the switch, but found it was very stiff. He didn't know how much he should force it. His robe loosened and flapped open as he struggled reaching up into the box. The robe was a little small and didn't close well over his expanding stomach. He became irritated and tightened his sash again. "Christ," he mumbled to himself. He tried using his thumb next on the switch and applied more pressure. He jumped as the switch snapped over suddenly and the lights inside came on.

Montgomery was startled and somewhat pleased with himself that he had fixed the problem so easily. He closed the box and went back inside through the garage door. He made his way into the living room and was going to turn on the TV for a little while before going to bed when he got the fleeting impression of a person stepping out from the corner behind him. He felt an explosion of pain in his head as the patriot swung his forearm down hard into the side of Montgomery's neck in a police tactic known as a brachial stun.

The patriot was well schooled in hand-to-hand combat and had eagerly attended every ground-fighting school and pressure-point tactics classes which the Sheriff's Department would send him to. He knew about the nerve cluster on the side of a person's neck and how, if it is struck solidly with an arm or a baton, it will cause the victim's body to go limp and the thought process to be momentarily disrupted. The stun causes a sensation all over the body which is similar to a person hitting the ulnar nerve or "funny bone" in their elbow.

Montgomery fell hard to the floor, and his robe burst open, revealing his fish-white belly, sagging breasts and small, limp penis surrounded by flab and hair. The patriot looked down on him with disgust, thinking of the children whose lives had been forever altered by this man's selfish needs. He stepped forward between Montgomery's legs and kicked him hard in the balls, causing him to curl up on his side. Montgomery tried to scream, he wanted to scream, but his voice was choked off by the pain in his groin. He felt a wave of nausea roll over him and vomited on the rug, unable to move his head from the mess. The patriot stepped quickly behind Montgomery and again kicked him hard, this time in the kidney. The pain was so great that Montgomery felt engulfed and smothered by it before passing out.

The patriot saw that Montgomery was unconscious and looked around the room. He saw a variety of Middle Ages artwork and objects on the walls and a suit of armor standing in the corner. He had intended to finish off Montgomery with a quick slice across the throat from his Tanto knife, but then he saw the beautiful sword on the wall. It was a Scottish Claymore with a maroon fringe on the handle, and a four-foot-long blade sharpened along one edge. He took it down from the wall and felt the blade. The tip was dull but the edge seemed fairly keen. He thought about the appropriateness of finding a sword there. The sword was a traditional means of dealing with society's miscreants back in the days of justice by common opinion. Muslim countries still dealt with those accused of high crimes by means of beheading and the patriot had long believed that swift, certain capital punishment was a definite deterrent to crime.

Montgomery was stirring and trying to get onto his hands and knees as the patriot walked up behind him.

"You've been a very bad boy," the patriot told Montgomery. "You've made a lot of people miserable in your life by taking their innocence away from them. Now you have to pay."

"No," Montgomery mumbled. He tried to crawl sideways, but he got caught up in his robe and fell over sideways. The patriot pulled the sash out of Montgomery's robe and looped it quickly around his neck. He yanked the sash hard and dragged Montgomery like a dog on a leash into the middle of the room.

"NO!" Montgomery cried again. His bowels let go, and the reek of vomit was joined by the stench of feces now on the floor. Montgomery knew he was about to die, and an almost forgotten part of him flashed back to his religious upbringing. The old words formed in his mind and he began to mumble the once-so-familiar words of the Catholic Act of Contrition despite his pain and fear: "Oh, my God, I am heartily sorry for having offended Thee, and I detest all my sins, for I dread the loss of Heaven and the pains of Hell…" he began, and then the Claymore whistled down, ending Peter Montgomery's final, long-overdue, attempt at repentance.

CHAPTER 17

▼

James Knox woke up on Monday morning to the sound of his jangling alarm clock and struggled to open one bloodshot eye. The 51-year-old reporter moaned aloud as he slid his carcass closer to the edge of the bed and, through a supreme effort of will, managed to paw at the goddamned noisy thing until he hit the snooze button. His arm dropped off the bed from the sheer agony of it, and he lay there knowing he only had five minutes until it would happen again. He spent that time wisely, taking stock of the parts of his body which he could move without pain and those he could not.

Knox had overdone it again last night. *Been doing that too often lately,* he told himself. But then he realized that wasn't entirely true. He'd been overdoing it for years. He considered resting until the alarm went off again. *That way you'll have your strength back,* he thought. *May even be able to shut it off. Hell, you might even be able to sit up!* But then two things happened simultaneously which convinced him that he had less time than he thought. First, his derelict cat, Jeeves, chose that moment to leap onto the bed and decorate the bedspread with bloody paw prints. Second, his intestinal tract, overburdened with spicy Italian manicotti and two bottles of Peppermill Pinot Noir (not to mention the three brandy manhattans before dinner and the cognac afterward), suddenly locked and loaded and prepared to fire. "Ooohhh!" Knox groaned aloud. "Fuck me!" he cried at the cat, at the alarm clock, and at himself for being such a sad sack. He swung himself to a sitting position and noted in an offhand way that such an unprepared-for maneuver added a fine slice of nausea to the mix. Then he noticed that the act of sitting up added the power of the earth's gravity to the lava that was trying to make its way out of his colon. "Jesus, let me die!" he cried.

The effort of saying that phrase dilated Knox's sphincter and he could feel the load getting away from him. "Aaaahhhh!" He cried and made a break for the bathroom. It wasn't far, but it seemed as if he was running a 100-yard dash with a wolverine trying to claw its way out of his ass. He dropped his shorts in the last couple feet of his journey and threw his shaking frame onto the bowl, but found he had aimed poorly and landed half on and half off the rim. "Mother of God!" he yelled as he slid off the throne and landed hard on the floor, becoming wedged between the bowl and the tub. He could feel the hot liquid escaping now, and he had to marshal all of his strength to push himself away from the wall and get to a kneeling position. From there he grabbed the vanity and pivoted, this time landing squarely on the toilet. He allowed his protesting body to lean back against the tank as he relieved himself of his burden. *Why am I so fucking old?* he asked himself.

There was a day not so long ago when James Knox could have put away twice the amount of food and booze he had last night and shaken it off the next morning with a couple of aspirins and some hot coffee. He remembered nights spent in bars with cop friends drinking bourbon and listening to talk about which criminal was up to what and who had just killed who and which cop was banging which waitress. He also remembered being a young reporter, fresh out of college, crouching against one of the few remaining walls in the city of Hue in Vietnam, hearing the sound of shrapnel clatter on the plaster above him, and wondering why the hell he'd decided he needed to be this close to the fighting in order to get a story. He remembered sharing a bottle of vodka later with some frightened young marines and laughing off the fear, the way everyone tried to do over there. That seemed like a hundred years ago, and there had been so much water under the bridge. Too much, for sure.

His reverie was cut short by the unmistakable sound of ripping material, which let Knox know that Jeeves had decided to sharpen his claws on the bedspread again. Goddamn it!" he yelled and quickly cleaned himself up. He ran into the bedroom and saw the animal crouched down, pulling away at the expensive cover for all he was worth. The evil creature even had the balls to look right at him as he did it, as if to say, "Yeah, motherfucker, look what I'm doing! What are you gonna do about it?" Knox lunged at the cat and it deftly sidestepped him. It feinted left, then went right and tore into the next room, running like Walter Peyton against an inferior defense.

Knox sat down on the bed and looked at the footprints on the bedspread. What he had thought was blood was sauce, he saw, from the bits of cheese and sausage clinging to it. Jeeves must have been in the manicotti dish during the night. He thought he'd put that away, but realized he didn't remember much about the previous evening. He remembered eating, vaguely, but nothing after that. Now he'd have to have the cover cleaned. *The fucking thing probably walked all over the house, too,* he thought. *Well, first things first.* He got into the shower and let the hot water course over his tortured body. He turned the water on cold at the end and stood in the icy stream until his pores closed. Then he got out, toweled off, and took four aspirins, which he hoped would take the edge off the hammering in his head.

After shaving (and cutting himself twice from trying not to look at himself in the mirror) he dressed in his habitual blue jeans, short-sleeved dress shirt, and loosely knotted tie, and went to the kitchen. He surveyed the damage from last night. "There were no survivors," Knox announced to no one, as he looked at the empty bottles, dried dirty dishes, and red paw prints everywhere. Knox started a pot of coffee and piled the dishes into the dishwasher, which, he felt, had to have been invented by a bachelor. He wiped up the majority of the paw prints and decided the ones on the rug would have to wait. He considered some breakfast, but a burning lance of nausea at the thought convinced him to limit himself to coffee.

Once he'd downed a couple of cups he felt slightly human again, or at least strong enough to take on the morning rush hour traffic. He lived in Golden Valley, and it would take about a half-hour drive to the Star Tribune offices, unless someone had fucked up Highway 55. Knox hit the automatic garage door button, backed his midnight blue Mustang out of the garage, and started his week. He had to get the weekend crime reports at City Hall and wanted to do some follow-up with the investigators on that double homicide in the elevator to see if they had gotten anywhere. A lot of killing had been going on lately. A gang war brewing on the north side between the Gangster Disciples and the Home Boyz that had resulted in a couple of shootings, and the usual domestic murders had been occurring. There was plenty of work for a reporter, but Knox was seriously bored with covering how C Dogg shot Tater because Tater chose to wear his red hat today or how Tom killed Mary because the bitch just wouldn't stop *aggravating* him. Once Knox had nearly won a Pulitzer for work he'd done uncovering corruption between the mayor and the City Council. He also had won acclaim for other investigative work he'd done, but lately everything was so bland. Sometimes he wished for a real in-depth, relevant story to come along. It would be nice to feel the old juices flowing again. *Juices!* he thought to himself as he turned east onto Hwy 55. *Any juices you had dried up years ago.* Still, he craved a break in the routine.

Later, Knox would think of that day and the old adage, "Be careful what you wish for; you may get it."

Monday morning dawned hard on another man who was also a veteran of the battle with the bottle. Charlie "Knuckles" Garrity woke to a pounding noise which he thought was coming from inside his head, but soon realized was actually coming from the front door of his apartment. He swung his bony frame out of bed and struggled into a seedy robe that most people would have made into a rag five years before.

Knuckles was 55-years old and looked 70. He was a self-described graduate of "the school of hard knocks" and carried those knocks from the permanent lumps showing through his thinning red and gray hair to the crooked, twisted toes on his flat feet. He had been a boxer in his youth and showed a lot of promise until facing an opponent in his twentieth professional fight in Kansas City. Knuckles was a good middleweight, and known for his left hook, which he had perfected in a gym and his neighborhood on the northeast side of Minneapolis where he grew up. He found himself fighting a French Canadian from a town called Trois Pistoles whom his manager told him would be a "nice warm-up" for a bigger fight he had coming the next month. Knuckles sparred with the Cannuck for three rounds before finally getting the chance to throw the hook. After delivering his Sunday punch, he stepped back, but he was very surprised to see the guy shake his head as if shooing a fly and step into him again. Knuckles threw everything but the kitchen sink at the man but found his rival had a chin like Italian marble. What was worse, when Knuckles got arm weary, the Canadian started tagging him and showed Knuckles how tough Quebec lumberjacks really were.

After leaving boxing for professions that didn't involve French-speaking lumberjacks who hit like Sammy Sosa, Knuckles tried his luck at a number of jobs. He cooked at diners, roofed houses, loaded freight, tied iron, bounced bars, dug graves, and cleaned windows. He finally landed a job as a caretaker for the apartment building on University Avenue where Desiree, Amii, and Jeremy had met the patriot. It had been a good job up until Saturday when he had to help the cops knock on each door and provide them with tenant lists. Then he had to clean the blood and gore out of the elevator and patch the bullet holes once everyone left. *That* had been a real mess. He'd hoped the whole matter was over so he could get back to his daily routine. That hope went away when he opened the door and saw the two cops from Saturday smiling at him.

"Good morning, Mr. Garrity," the black cop said to him. "Pete Lincoln, from the Police Department. This is Detective McDowell. Do you remember us?"

"Ya, I remember." Garrity mumbled as he rubbed some feeling into his face. "What's the problem, what's the problem?" Garrity sometimes repeated himself due to residual brain damage from too many hard blows to the head, only some of which he received in the ring. He also had a stammer.

"When we spoke with you on Saturday you said that neither of the dead girls was a resident of this building. We learned that one of the girls named Desiree Blevins had listed this building, apartment 506 as her address two months ago when she was arrested in Dakota County."

"A l-l-lot of these kids come and go here," Garrity stammered. "It's a bunch of, bunch of, kids."

"How long have you been the caretaker, Mr. Garrity?" Lincoln asked.

"I-ah, b-b-been here two years. Two years is how long. I don't remember that name of that girl. I don't think she eh-eh-ever lived here."

"Who lives in 506?" McDowell asked.

"Ah, 506. Some boy I think, I think. Lemme get the list." Garrity shuffled to a desk and took out a book. "The owner, Mr. Polaski, he-he g-g-gave me this to keep track. I helped him a c-c-couple times and he hired me. 506? Ah, says his name is Jeremy Soderberg. Ya, he's the artist guy. He makes art stuff an-an-and stuff out of metal."

"Statues?" Lincoln asked.

"Ya, like that, like that."

"This Soderberg might be a friend of the girls. We'd like to talk to him," Lincoln said.

"Yeah, you could do-do that," Garrity said.

"We'd like you to come along with a passkey, just in case, okay?" McDowell asked.

"Lemme, lemme get some p-p-pants on," Garrity said, and walked off to do just that.

"Is this guy fried, or what?" McDowell asked Lincoln.

"Old boxer," Lincoln told him. "See his ears and the scar tissue over his eyes? His nose got in the way a couple times, too."

"A real Joe Palooka," McDowell said with a smile.

"Yeah, but be careful around them," Lincoln cautioned. "These guys can be pretty tough. I saw an old wino nail a partner of mine once when we were taking him to Detox. My partner was dissing him, called him a 'hound.' Never even saw the punch, and all of a sudden he was looking up at that old hound!"

"Ha!" McDowell chuckled. "I'll keep my guard up."

Garrity came back wearing an old tank top and some paint-stained polyester trousers. He jangled the ring of passkeys toward the detectives, and they followed him upstairs.

Once they reached apartment 506, Lincoln rapped purposefully on the door. Around the world, police have a certain knock. All street people know when The Man is knocking, and Garrity flinched when Lincoln did it. There was no answer, and Lincoln knocked again. He tried the knob and found the door wasn't locked. Lincoln eased the door open and called out, "Police! Mr. Soderberg? Hello?" The three men cautiously went inside and looked around at the living room.

"Do you smell something?" McDowell asked.

"No, I got a cold," Lincoln answered.

"I don't smell nothing, nothing," Garrity replied.

"Pete, I smell something," McDowell said. "Smells like a body. Smells like blood."

"Shit!" Garrity said. "More mess."

Lincoln and McDowell drew their handguns and asked Garrity to stay put. They moved from the living room to the work area around the corner. There, they saw the body of Jeremy Soderberg still clamped in the vise, partially covered by the sheet and resting in a pool of blood.

"Fuck!" Lincoln said. He moved to the body and tried to figure a way to look at the face, but decided the only way would be to crawl under through the pool of blood and look up into the vise. He decided he'd rather not do that. "So much for my cold, I smell him now. Let's call for help."

The three went back to the front door, where McDowell pointed out the broken chain. "You suppose this is new?" he asked.

"No way to tell." Lincoln said. "Mr. Garrity, somebody is dead in the next room. We're going to have to inconvenience you some more, I'm afraid."

"Dead?" Garrity asked. "Killed?"

"It looks that way," Lincoln answered.

"Is, is it a mess?"

"Yes, I'm afraid so," Lincoln said.

Garrity blew out a long breath. "N-n-nobody has heart attacks no more," he complained, shaking his head. "I never had such a m-m-mess-messy job!"

While Lincoln and McDowell were waiting for the crime lab team to arrive, Lincoln's cell phone rang.

"Pete? Mike Rawlings from BCA. How's it going?"

"Busy, Mike," Lincoln answered. "What can I do for you?"

"Pete, I'm wondering if you could come to a meeting this afternoon at my office. I think there are some links between that double shooting you worked Saturday and some other killings around the area. I think it's time for everyone to put their heads together."

"Mike, I'm strapped. We just discovered another murder in the same building as Saturday's double. Appears to be related to the girls, but this is a young guy. Looks like he's been here since Saturday, too."

Rawlings digested this information. "What's the link to the girls?"

"One of the victims from Saturday, Desiree Blevins, had listed this apartment as her address when she was in court in Dakota County a couple of months ago. We didn't find out until first thing this morning when we ran her background. My partner and I came out here and found out that the renter is a young guy. Our witness saw a young guy get off the elevator, so we went to talk with him and found him dead."

"Any other link? Anything to show he was involved with their animal rights activities?"

"Not yet. We just know his name, nothing more."

"How did he die, Pete?" Rawlings asked.

"Pretty grisly. Fucker got his head crushed in a vise. Then his throat was cut."

"Jesus!" Rawlings sighed. "Pete, I'm convinced we've got somebody running around the metro popping people. Nobody's put it together 'cause he's doing everybody different, but all the victims seem to be activists or liberals of one type or another. Listen, I know you're busy, but I have a couple investigators coming here at 1:00. Can I bring them to your scene? I really think we need to compare notes."

Lincoln didn't like the idea of being distracted while he was working a scene, but he'd known Rawlings for many years and knew he wasn't the "conspiracy-theory" type.

"Yeah, okay. We'll be here for a while, anyway. Come to 2510 University. We'll be on the fifth floor. Press hasn't gotten wind yet, so maybe we won't be too crowded."

"Thanks, Pete. See you in a while."

Lincoln disconnected and told McDowell that they would be having company on this one.

Mike Rawlings sat back in his office and scribbled on a pad. He wrote down the names:

1. Borgert
2. Ehrenberg
3. Berry

4. Blevins and Faust

5. Male in Apt.

All these murders had occurred in one week's time. *That* was very unusual for Minnesota. Rawlings knew that the Ehrenberg case had supposedly been cleared by the suicide of the chief suspect in the Goodhue County Jail, but he had persuaded the investigator who'd worked the case to come to the meeting anyway. Rawlings remembered it had taken some convincing, but Pappas had finally agreed. Poor Phil Deane of Edina and Gene Truman, the investigator from Burnsville on the Wallace Berry case, were more than happy to attend. Their murder cases with their high-profile victims had taken on a life of their own with the media. Both Deane and Truman were actively trying to avoid reporters, and were grasping at straws in an attempt to get any handle on a suspect. Both were being besieged not only by the media, but by their mayors, their chiefs, civil rights groups, community leaders, and family members, and by their own well-meaning co-workers, who kept asking, "Anything new yet?" Rawlings thought both Deane and Truman were about to weep from relief when he told them that he thought a serial killer was at work. It was nice to spread the blame and the investigative burden.

Rawlings then wrote out on the pad the way each victim had died:

1. Borgert—Shot by rifle in home.

2. Ehrenberg—Attacked in home, stabbed in ear, neck broken.

3. Berry—Attacked in home, stabbed in chest.

4. Blevins and Faust—Shot in elevator, friend's home.

5. New victim—Attacked in home, head crushed in vise, throat cut.

Rawlings sat back and looked at his notes. Assuming all the deaths were related—even though the Ehrenberg case had a good suspect—if there was one killer at work, he didn't appear to be married to one style of killing.

Next, Rawlings wrote out a list of traits shared by the victims, if, in fact, they were related. He excluded the new victim because he had no solid data on him yet.

Liberal. Very liberal.

Outspoken in their beliefs.

Actively defended their beliefs.

Have been identified in the press and received public criticism for their actions.

All had been in court recently in one capacity or another.

Champions of the underdog.

Rawlings then wrote out a list of people who would or might be hostile toward the victims.

Aryan Nation members.

Skinheads.

Ku Klux Klan (?).

Ultra religious right.

Crime victims.

Rawlings had put a question mark by Ku Klux Klan because he had no idea if any Klan chapters were active locally. He had put crime victims on the list because he thought it was possible someone might be nursing a grudge against a liberal court system and was trying to strike back.

It never occurred to him to put cops on the list.

Tony Bauer spent Monday like many other average homeowners. He mowed the lawn and used the electric weed-whacker to do the edging. At a local gardening shop, he bought some marigolds and petunias which he planted in a little area by his front door. After changing the oil in his truck, he cleaned the windows with glass cleaner and applied Armor-All to the dash. He chatted a little with his retired neighbor over the back fence. The neighbor, happy to have a deputy sheriff in the neighborhood, talked about how the world was so much better years ago, when people had pride in their country and criminals were put in jail where they belonged. Bauer agreed.

Unlike most other homeowners, however, he reflected on the people he'd killed in the previous week and thought about how things would escalate once his floppy disk had been read. He thought about how he could make tomorrow, his last day off, productive.

CHAPTER 18

▼

When Mike Rawlings, Phil Deane, John Pappas, and Gene Truman arrived at the apartment on University Avenue, a deputy coroner, Pete Lincoln, and Tom McDowell were leaning over the body of Jeremy Soderberg. The corpse was lying on its back on top of an open body bag. The body had stiffened from rigor mortis into the shape of a man who had died while crawling up a flight of stairs; lying face up, Jeremy's raised legs made him look sadly like a dog playing dead. The three wore surgical masks and had plugged their noses with Vicks to allow them to stand the smell. They were discussing the savage neck wound and the significance of the severed pinkie, which was on the bag next to the body.

Rawlings introduced everyone, and Lincoln suggested that they move into the bedroom. It had already been "cleared" by the crime lab, meaning they had finished collecting evidence there.

John Pappas was the last to follow. He lingered behind and stepped closer so he could get a better look at Soderberg. The duct tape and gag had been removed, and Pappas sucked in his breath when he looked at the wreckage that had been made of what had once been a handsome young boy. Both eyeballs were avulsed from their sockets and looked in different directions. Soderberg's mouth was open in a silent scream which seemed, to Pappas, as if it were accusing him. Pappas was living with the feeling of guilt for having pinned Sarah Ehrenberg's murder on an innocent man, and that this false accusation had driven that man to suicide. The idea that the real killer was still around, and killing so sadistically, almost seemed in a strange way as if it was his fault.

When a pale John Pappas joined everyone in the bedroom, Rawlings addressed the group.

"All right, I know that this isn't exactly the best place to hold a meeting, and I know that Pete and Tom have lots of work to do here. We all do, for that matter. We all seem to be working on cases lately that have a common thread, for all of the victims have recently been publicly proclaimed as liberally extreme. I think we should consider the possibility that these murders, and I think we all agree that there have been an unusually high number of them in the last week, may be the work of one person, or, very possibly, the work of a group of individuals, who may be following a political agenda."

"It's an interesting theory," Pete Lincoln replied, "but how do we go about proving it?"

"Do you think we should go off looking for a Republican version of The Terminator? What if we're wrong?" McDowell asked.

"This is just an educated guess at this point," Rawlings said, "and I'm not saying I know I'm right. I do know we have victims from very different worlds, from a judge and an attorney to an anti-nuke hippie and some PETA rejects. We also have differing murder methods. But what I think, and what I'd like you all to give me your opinion on, is whether we need to consider it as a possibility and if we may need to work together."

"Well, I'm open to anything," Deane said. "I've got the whole free world asking me who killed Judge Borgert and I don't have any answers."

"I hear you," Gene Truman said. "This morning a spokesperson from the ACLU was on the radio saying that we're deliberately tanking the Wallace Berry investigation because he was gay and hated by the police. Can you believe that shit?"

"Mike, I'm happy to share," Lincoln said. "I can't afford to spend a lot of time in meetings, though. If we get something concrete, I'll reconsider, but what is it that you're proposing right now?"

"I'd like to take all these files and send them to the FBI Behavioral Sciences people and ask them to run an analysis. I'd like to see if they agree that there may be a pattern here and, if so, if they would compile a psychological profile for us."

"You really think that'll get us anywhere?" Pappas asked. "Remember, my boss is satisfied that we've identified our killer and that our case is closed."

"Maybe so," Rawlings said, "but what if he's wrong?"

"We can play 'maybes' all day," Lincoln said, "but right now, Tom and I have to finish here. You want copies of the files on these killings, you got 'em. You want to send them off to Washington, okay by me. I'm open to anything, but we don't have shit right now other than suspicion, so let's stick to what we know works and do some police work."

By early Monday evening, Lincoln and McDowell had followed the crime lab team out of Jeremy Soderberg's apartment, leaving a frustrated Knuckles Garrity to clean up, not only the gore from his former tenant, but the mess from the fingerprint powder which now decorated almost every surface in the apartment. A re-canvas of the other residents of the fifth floor revealed nothing in the way of information to help solve the case. It seemed as if all of the neighbors preferred to pretend that they lived alone in the building and never interacted with anyone else.

Mike Rawlings had gone home to Lake Elmo after putting the materials the other detectives had given him into a new file entitled, "2002 Suspicious Deaths."

Phil Deane had met with Chief Roosevelt and told him about Rawlings's suspicions. He told Roosevelt that he was "cautiously optimistic" and hoped the case might get a jump start from the new perspective. Roosevelt told Deane that he hoped he was right and said that if he had to feed poor Captain Polaski, the press liaison, to the media sharks again, nothing of him would be of him left to retire in three months.

John Pappas drove back home to Red Wing and spent the evening watching his son play Little League baseball. Pappas usually loved nights spent at the field, but that night he kept seeing the deformed face of Jeremy Soderberg in his mind and was so bothered by it that he missed seeing his son hit a stand-up double.

Even more troubling to him was the growing certainty that Mike Rawlings's theory was right. As much as he'd like to soothe his conscience by telling himself over and over that Fast Horse was the killer of Sarah Ehrenberg, the mounting death toll was making it harder for him to do. Pappas was a good cop who recognized facts for what they were, and the little voice inside that had been telling him he'd been wrong was growing louder every day.

Pappas knew that Fast Horse's death could seriously impact both his career and the image of the sheriff's department, but what bothered him the most was that he may have driven an innocent man to suicide. Pappas's career as an investigator had mostly involved property crimes, such as burglary and stolen cars. There was the occasional beating and, very rarely, a murder. Suicides were fairly common, but Pappas wasn't usually as troubled by them because the dead person had made the decision to end their lives themselves. He didn't feel the need to avenge them that he did with a murder. He wasn't used to having the images of so many violent deaths in such a short period of time swirling around inside his head. Fast Horse's tear-streaked face merged with Soderberg's crushed head and then changed to Ehrenberg.

The crack of a bat brought him back to the game, but only for a few moments of peaceful distraction before the images came back again.

The friends and relatives of Wallace Berry held a memorial service at the ACLU office in downtown Minneapolis and said goodbye to their leader. Punch and appetizers were served, and the attendees comforted one another and spoke of how pissed off they were that the police had gotten nowhere with the investigation. There was talk of trying to bring the FBI into the case to force something to be done.

Arnie Knutsen was also pissed off. The new bookkeeper he'd hired hadn't bothered to show up for work that morning. Knutsen had endured a run of bad luck with bookkeepers lately and had hoped that this new fellow would be the answer to his problems. He'd had them steal from him, lie to him, screw up his accounts, everything. This latest guy had impressive schooling and was old enough that Knutsen figured that he would be competent and not call in sick when he was hung over or be unreliable because of family problems. Yes, he'd had great hopes, but then this guy didn't show, didn't call, nothing. He'd thought about calling him to see what the story was, but figured, hell, if the guy doesn't care enough to show up for his first day of work, maybe he's better forgotten. Knutsen had done a slow burn about it all day but had begun wondering if maybe there was a good excuse for his new employee's absence. Montgomery was an older man, after all, and didn't look to be in the best shape. What if he'd had a heart attack or a car accident on his way to work? Knutsen was a family man and a good Lutheran. He knew it wasn't very Christian to think only the worst of people. Besides, what would it hurt if he called the guy?

Knutsen took out Montgomery's phone number and dialed it. There was no answer. He wondered how far he should take it and considered calling the Shakopee Police. He debated whether that would be out of line, or worse, pointless. If he couldn't get an answer at Montgomery's house, why would the police? He put the number down, but then the image of Montgomery lying on the floor holding his chest rose up again in his mind. Well, there's no sin in good intentions, Knutsen thought. He leafed through the phone book, found the non-emergency number for the Shakopee Police, and called.

"Shakopee Police, how may I help you?" The dispatcher said as she answered.

"Yes, er," Knutsen began, unsure how to talk to the police. "I have a concern about employee of mine. He didn't show up for work today and, well, he's an older man and I was worried that something might have happened to him."

"What's his name?" The dispatcher asked.

"Peter Montgomery. He lives at 415 Apgar Street."

"You've tried calling him?"

"Yes, but there's no answer. As I said, he's older, and I'd feel terrible if something had happened to him."

"Yes, of course," the dispatcher agreed. "I'll send a car to check his address. Give me your name and phone number. I'll have an officer check the house, and he can call you if he has any more questions."

Knutsen provided his information and hung up, hoping that he hadn't just made a mistake, but felt somehow that he had.

"715?" The dispatcher's voice over the radio interrupted a conversation between Officer Curt Thompson and the intern who was riding with him for that shift.

"715," Thompson replied.

"715, welfare check. Go to 415 Apgar, check the welfare of a party who didn't show for work today. Subject is Peter Montgomery, age 55. RP info is on the way to your CAD."

"715 copy." Thompson heard his Computer Aided Dispatch laptop beep and saw that the reporting party was Montgomery's boss.

"Well," Thompson told the intern. "Guy didn't show for work. Maybe he had a better job offer." Thompson made a U-turn and headed toward Apgar Street.

Thompson cruised by the house and saw that the lights were on inside. According to the narrative sent over the computer by the dispatcher, the guy's boss had tried calling, but had gotten no answer. Thompson parked a house away from 415 out of habit. Cops know that pulling up right in front of a house, even on something as benign as a welfare check call, could be very hazardous to their health. Thompson and the intern got out, walked across the lawn, and approached 415 from an angle. Thompson checked the front window, and then climbed the front steps. He rang the bell, but no one answered. He tried the knob and found it was locked. He rang the bell again and then walked around the house. He was unable to see inside any windows as all of the blinds were closed. Thompson went to the side and found the door into the garage unlocked. He entered the garage and knocked on the door leading into the house. After not getting an answer, he tried the knob and found that this door was also unlocked.

Thompson cautiously opened the door and called out, "Police!" Hearing nothing, he and the intern stepped slowly inside. Thompson called out several times and put his hand on his handgun as he walked into the house. He motioned to the intern to keep back and then walked through a laundry room and into the kitchen. The kitchen opened up into a living room. Thompson wasn't looking down on the floor as he stepped through the archway. His boot kicked something yielding and he looked down to see that he'd just bumped the head of Peter Montgomery, which was rocking back and forth on the carpet. Montgomery's body was lying just to his right in a large pool of blood.

Thompson's heart skipped a beat, and he felt the coppery taste of fear rise in his mouth. He pulled his gun and willed his arm not to shake as he held it out in front of him. The intern, eager to see what was going on, came forward and saw the head. His mind didn't register what he was seeing until he saw the headless body for reference.

"Oh!" The intern said. "Oh, no! Oh, my God!"

"Shut up!" Thompson said as he struggled to control his own fear. "Stay put. Don't move!" he ordered as he moved forward. Thompson had never been in this type of situation and was doing everything he could to hold himself together. He checked the house and breathed a sigh of relief when he found no one else inside. He came back into the living room and looked at the headless figure on the floor.

"Let's get the fuck out of here and call for help," he said to the intern, who was beginning to think that police work just wasn't for him.

CHAPTER 19

▼

On Tuesday morning James Knox got out of bed feeling a little better than he had the day before. He'd been out to a bar the night before with a source who worked for the Ramsey County Attorney's office. The guy, who'd always provided Knox with solid leads in the past, had hinted that there was a corruption case being vetted for charges and prosecution and that there were some pretty high-up people who were about to be put on a spit for bribery and influence peddling. The guy wouldn't go so far as to name the suspects or the office they belonged to, but Knox was fairly certain they were Minneapolis city building officials. He'd learned recently from a couple of other sources that som businessmen had problems with code violations during inspections and that those violations had gone away when the right amount of money had changed hands. Minneapolis had just weathered a similar scandal involving a corrupt city council member, who had been using the building inspectors to lean on constituents. This appeared to be more of the same.

Knox knew that Minneapolis wasn't in Ramsey County, but it was normal procedure to turn a case involving city officials over to a neighboring agency to avoid any conflict of interest.

Knox didn't drink as much when he was in bars as he did at home because the liquor was so goddamned expensive. He did smoke in bars, though. An ex-smoker, he found that a bar filled with drinking and smoking people was too great a trigger. He'd smoked half a pack, and now his mouth tasted as if a group of Cub Scouts had lit their campfire inside it. After brushing his teeth and his tongue to get the ashes out, he fixed a strong pot of coffee. *Now, isn't it nicer to not be such a sad sack in the morning,* he asked himself. He knew the answer was yes, but he also knew from experience that, despite any good intentions, he'd overdo it again soon and find himself on the bathroom floor.

Jeeves the cat strolled into the kitchen and looked up at Knox with a strangely tortured expression on his face. Knox had never believed cats showed expressions, but Jeeves certainly did. This morning he looked about as bad as Knox had felt the day before.

"What's up, Jeeves?" Knox asked. As if in answer to the question, Jeeves said "OW!" loudly and plaintively, and then upchucked the guts of some animal he'd eaten onto the kitchen linoleum.

"Gross!" Knox yelled. Immediately he realized that was a mistake, as his raised voice caused Jeeves to run for cover behind the sofa. Knox heard the sound of more puking going on back there and wished he'd just have left Jeeves alone so he could do it all in one accessible spot.

Knox got some paper towels and scooped up the autopsy on the floor. It didn't even look as if Jeeves had chewed the organs, just eaten them whole. Knox felt bile rise in his throat and did his best to clean up without looking. Jeeves came out from behind the sofa, sat down and began licking his anus.

"Could you at least try to show a little class?" Knox asked him. Jeeves stopped for a moment, as if considering the request, and then resumed his task. Knox pulled the sofa away from the wall, removed more of whatever had been eaten, and sprayed some carpet cleaner on the stain.

On the way to work, Knox heard on the news that Israel was pounding the piss out of the Palestinians again because of another terrorist bomb blast. Knox shook his head at the dedication of the Islamic extremists. They send a suicide bomber in, kill two people, counting the bomber, all the while knowing Israel would respond by sending tanks and jets over the border to kill scores of Palestinians and flatten acres of city. Then they do it again and again and again. Knox thought of the quote from General George Patton who said "No one ever won a war by dying for his country. He wins by making the other poor son of a bitch die for *his* country." The cheerful news from the West Bank was followed by more when the newscaster told how India and Pakistan were lobbing shells at each other and testing guided rockets which could carry nuclear warheads. *Christ,* Knox thought, *the whole world is insane.* Like most Americans his age, Knox had grown up fearful of nuclear holocaust between the US and Russia. Now that Russia had thrown in the towel on Communism, joined NATO, and was trying to compete in the world markets, Knox had thought that the big danger had passed. Who'd have ever thought that people in countries like India and Pakistan would stop having twenty children each and plan to throw H-bombs at one another.

Knox walked into the newspaper office and plopped down in the chair at his desk. His in-box had the latest edition of both the Minneapolis and St. Paul papers, have to keep tabs on the opposition, right, and some mail. Knox flipped through the envelopes and stopped at a plain one with no return address. It was addressed to him and marked as personal. Knox opened it and found a floppy disk inside. *Okay, is this a joke,* he wondered. He looked around for any of the known office pranksters, but no one seemed to be paying him any attention. Knox booted up his computer and inserted the floppy. Sipping at his coffee mug, he opened the document and began reading. *This* has *to be a joke,* he thought as he read through the beginning of the manifesto. Either a joke, or it was written by a real crank. He scrolled down and saw the line which read, "On the morning of May 7 I killed the nuclear protester…" *What? What the fuck?* Knox asked himself. He backed up and read the letter again from the beginning slowly. His coffee grew cold as he read through the list of murders and how Knox could go about verifying the information. When he got to the end, he scrolled up and read it again.

Knox sat back in his chair and digested the confession he'd just read. He had been aware of the murders, hell, he'd even written some of the stories. Now there was some guy named Jeremy dead in a Dinkeytown apartment? That's right! Those two girls who'd been shot in the elevator. It must be the same building.

Knox printed the document and was about to start calling police departments to verify the information when his editor, Dave Joyner, called him and asked him to come in. Knox walked through the press room and into Joyner's small glass-fronted office.

"Jim," Joyner said. "a couple of murders were discovered last night and yesterday. One was in the same apartment building as…"

"I know," Knox said, cutting him off. "A guy named Jeremy. His head was crushed in a vise. I've just gotten a floppy disk in the mail from the killer, confessing to that and to a bunch of others! Look."

Joyner took the document from Knox and he read it.

"Christ, Jim!" Joyner breathed. "This is fantastic! This guy picked you! What an opportunity! You've got to get on this right away."

"Dave, where was the other murder?"

"Shakopee. The police got sent to a home last night to check on a guy who hadn't shown for work and found his head cut off. Not only that, but the victim was Peter Montgomery, the ex-priest who got accused of molestation, remember?"

"I remember him," Knox answered. "After we ran a story on him he got fired from a college. You say his head was cut off? Shit, that sounds like this guy. He said in the letter that he was going to go on. I guess he did."

Joyner picked up his phone and called the senior editor of the paper, Sam Graham, asking him to come down. He then called a couple of other reporters and the paper's attorney. In ten minutes the office was full. Joyner made copies of the patriot's confession and passed them around. He summarized how Knox had received the document and that, for now, they would treat it as genuine.

Graham, an old newshound, said, "Jim, this is the kind of story a reporter always dreams of, but it can get out of hand. You have to play this very carefully. The police are going to be very touchy about us having such explosive information without their knowledge, so we need to tread carefully."

"You're not suggesting we don't publish?" Joyner said.

"No," Graham answered, "but we'll need their cooperation and we'll give ours as well. After all, this guy has to be caught. We also don't want him fixating on Jim here and putting him in a body bag."

That's a nice thought, Knox thought to himself. He hadn't considered the possibility that the patriot might turn on *him.*

"My thought was to form a team," Joyner proposed. "I'd like to pull Keith and Larry here off the stories they're doing and put them in with Jim. Jim, you'll have the byline and Keith and Larry will get mentioned." Knox saw that Joyner was observing the protocols here. Knox was more senior than either of the other reporters, so the lion's share went to him. They would help gather the facts, but Knox would write the story, *hell, stories,* he thought, *this guy isn't done yet, and they would get credit.*

"Jim," Joyner continued, "get started verifying the information. Talk with the investigators working these cases, and tell them what you have. Guarantee full cooperation from our end, but demand a quid pro quo. We have some bartering power here." Graham nodded as Joyner outlined his plan. Larry and Keith took notes while he spoke and left for the crime scenes in Minneapolis and Shakopee for their background work.

Knox returned to his desk and wondered whom he should call first. Since the judge was the first victim, and one of the three who were high profile, he called the Edina Police. He told the dispatcher he'd like to speak to the investigator who was handling the Borgert case.

"That would be Detective Deane," The dispatcher said. "Is this a press inquiry?"

"Yes, I'm James Knox from the Trib."

"All press inquiries are being handled by Captain Polaski. I'll transfer."

"No, I don't want Polaski," Knox said. "I need to speak with Detective Deane. I have some information for him."

"Very well," the dispatcher said curtly. "Please hold."

After a moment, a tired voice came on the line. "Phil Deane."

"Detective Deane, I'm Jim Knox from the Trib. I received a floppy disk in the mail this morning containing what amounts to a confession written by a man who is claiming responsibility for the Judge Borgert murder."

"Yeah, we've had some of those, too," Deane sighed. "They've proven to be nutcases or weirdos wanting to publicize their cause."

"I imagine so," Knox said. "This guy claims that he not only killed Borgert, but several other people as well. An anti-nuclear protester in Prairie Island, Wallace Berry in Burnsville, and the two female animal rights people and their male friend in Minneapolis. The guy with his head crushed in a vise?"

Deane stopped breathing as his hand tightened on the phone. "Say that again? He specified that the victim's head was in a vise?"

"Not only that, the letter gives a lot of other detail as well. Tell me, was Judge Borgert wearing a light blue pullover shirt and eating Neapolitan ice cream at the time he was shot?"

Deane sat back in his chair. "Mr. Knox, I have to be very careful of what I tell you here. You know that certain details of a case under investigation *have* to remain confidential. I can't have you printing things that might hinder the investigation or, worse yet, help the offender escape."

"Detective, I'm not going to make you jump through hoops here, and I don't intend to print that Borgert ate Neapolitan ice cream. My bosses here are fully aware of this document and have asked me to assure you that we will cooperate fully with your wishes. However, this is a news story of enormous impact and we *will* be reporting on it. We can work together to each other's benefit or not at all. Remember, this suspect sought me out, for whatever reason, and said he would remain in touch. I would think that would be to your advantage."

Deane thought furiously. He would have to run it by Chief Roosevelt and get some suggestions for ground rules. He knew he needed to be squarely in line with his Chief's wishes here in order to cover his ass properly.

"Mr. Knox, could you e-mail or fax me a copy of that letter right away?"

"Not until we have an understanding about sharing, Detective. I have to make a living, too."

"Let me talk with my boss and call you back." Knox provided his phone number to Deane and hung up.

Deane hung up and called Mike Rawlings at his office. "Mike? Phil Deane. You were right."

CHAPTER 20

▼

While the press team was preparing for the biggest local story in many years, the police were forming a task force to meet The Patriot, as they now officially called their suspect, head on. First, though, they needed to play a little catch up. An agreement with the Tribune was put into place wherein the patriot's confession was provided to the police, and the press would be allowed to print the content of the confession without providing the details that had proved that the document was most likely written by the man responsible for the murders. The press team was happy with this as long as the police agreed to publicly verify to other media outlets that the facts of the story were true.

All the agencies involved agreed to assign the investigators already working the open murders to a task force commanded by Mike Rawlings. This agreement was put in place for one month, after which time the various police chiefs and sheriffs would determine what progress, if any, had been made. They would decide at that time to either prolong their commitment, or to abandon it for a different approach.

John Pappas had very mixed emotions about joining the task force. In a meeting with Sheriff Cooper, Pappas outlined how the murder of Sarah Ehrenberg would soon be revealed publicly to be the work of a man other than George Fast Horse. Not only that, but the suspect was still at large *and* still killing, *and* these facts had been brought forward by the news media rather than through police work. Cooper was less than pleased with the developments but, once he had been shown the confession with its details of Ehrenberg's killing that no one else could have known, he told Pappas that he would support him, and that he felt that Pappas had acted properly throughout the investigation.

Pappas knew that there would probably be a backlash from the Native American community and that the relatives of Fast Horse would be suing. He had seen a report that they had already retained an attorney for Fast Horse's in-custody suicide. The resulting lawsuit would undoubtedly become stronger and more expensive.

By afternoon, James Knox had confirmation from all of the police investigators that the details provided in the patriot's letter were factual. The story he was working up was already set to run on the front page of the late edition. Even though the letter had been sent to him personally, Knox decided to downplay his role in the story. He would stick to the facts and report the news. He had no proof as yet that Peter Montgomery had been killed by the patriot, but it had been decided that Montgomery's would be announced in the story anyway. Knox had plenty of quotes and facts for his story and knew he had a deadline to meet.

Mike Rawlings received permission from the BCA administration to set up the task force in a training room on the main floor of the BCA headquarters on University Avenue in St. Paul. All the members would gather their files and notes and meet for the first time as an official unit Wednesday at 8:00 a.m. Rawlings had also spoken with Sharon Bluhm, who was a member of the BCA's sex crime detail and a former intern in the FBI's Behavioral Science Unit in Quantico Virginia. Bluhm, age forty-two, had a Masters Degree in Abnormal Psychology after serving as both a police officer and as an investigator with the Minneapolis PD, she had won the opportunity to spend 10 months working with the FBI criminal profilers whose unit was made famous by the book and movie *Silence of the lambs.* Bluhm had enjoyed her time with the profilers and had learned a tremendous amount about serial murderers and their motivations, and how they give clues to their drives and fantasies in the way they commit their crimes. Bluhm had never been allowed to actually prepare a profile, but she had worked with profilers as they prepared them and her comments and thoughts had been considered very insightful. In fact, a very senior member of the section was so impressed with Bluhm's quick mind and innate ability to empathize that he strongly encouraged her to apply for the Bureau. She politely declined by explaining that she had family responsibilities in Minnesota and just couldn't relocate to Washington. Instead, she returned to her home, her husband Paul, and their autistic son, Steven.

Stevie was ten-years-old and had been considered "profoundly autistic" from the time he was three. Sharon had noticed it first when it seemed that Stevie's language skills just weren't progressing. He showed little affection for either Sharon or Paul and would not interact with other children. In fact, he often had fits of rage in which he would refuse to share a toy; this had made day-care options difficult, for Stevie was banned by one provider after another.

By the time his condition was confirmed, Sharon's career path was leading her out of the state toward more promising and challenging positions. The FBI job would have been priceless in terms of experience and job satisfaction, but the thought of trying to find good care for Stevie in an entirely new city was daunting. Plus, Paul had just gotten a promotion at the bank, and moving east just didn't seem fair to them. So, she found work in a hospital for the criminally insane and published several sterling articles on the subject in trade papers. She also found a very good therapist who suggested a school who could work with Stevie during the day and, though he would never be the bright, friendly boy she'd imagined he'd be, he had shown improvement.

She was approached in 1997 to head up the BCA's sex crimes unit and act as a general psychological consultant. Since then she had become a valued resource to all of the agency's investigators and applied much of the knowledge she'd gained about serial murder to her work. Sharon seemed to have a gift for getting inside the mind of complete strangers, and it had served her well, but the one mind she desperately wanted to peer into was closed to her. So instead, she would try to look into minds like the patriot's.

She told Rawlings that she would be happy to meet with his task force and provide whatever help she could in attempting to identify the killer.

Rawlings spent the remainder of the day setting up their work area and stocking it with the computers and supplies they would need to get started in the morning.

At 8:40 p.m. Tuesday, the patriot was in his Explorer heading north on Interstate 35E near the city of White Bear Lake, a nice suburb northeast of St. Paul. The city of White Bear Lake contains not only a lake with the same name, but also Otter Lake, Bald Eagle Lake, and Birch Lake. The patriot took the eastbound exit for Highway 96 and then drove north on US 61 for a few blocks before exiting onto Bald Eagle Avenue. His target, a well-kept two-story home, was owned by John Hughes, a sociology professor at Macalester College in St. Paul.

Hughes had made a name for himself recently after authoring a textbook called *A Study of Diversity*, which had been adopted by several high schools in Minnesota and four other states. Hughes's concepts of sociology in the text had recently stirred debate between the teachers who had issued the text to their students and the students' parents. The lesson plan outlined in the text taught that America was a nation divided by institutional racism, weakened by political corruption, and poisoned by its two-hundred-year history of imposing its will on other nations through military might and diplomatic pressure. Hughes felt that America's students spent their early school years being force-fed a pabulum of idealistic half-truths designed to instill patriotism and confidence, but lacking the concepts and perceptions felt by minority members of society.

Hughes believed that high school students needed to balance certain long-held beliefs with new ideas to inspire them to think independently. His text taught for instance, that while mainstream America celebrated Columbus Day, Native Americans perceived Columbus as a mass murderer who began the process of stripping them of their lands and their lifestyles. The text taught that America had long been a stronghold of white, Anglo-Saxon Christians and that this group had steadfastly ignored and subverted the beliefs and desires of minorities who differed from them, whether through race, religion, origin or sexual preference. Hughes wanted readers to put themselves into the shoes of people who felt disaffected and ignored.

The patriot saw Hughes's book as another example, albeit more venomous than most, of blooming communism in the public school system. He thought it was further evidence of the deliberate attempt to confuse and addle the brains of a generation of children who already received more class time in social studies, sex education, and computer technology than they did in reading, math, and science. He felt that the parents who had raised objections to Hughes's book were seeing only the tip of the iceberg and were beginning to recognize it for what it was. They needed to understand the whole picture; then, he hoped, they would turn off inane sitcoms long enough to take a hard look at the education, or lack thereof, that their children were really getting. The patriot felt that it was as important that this happen as it was for Hughes to be stopped.

He turned onto Hughes's street and drove slowly past the house. He knew that Hughes had a wife and two children and that the family spent a lot of time together, so it would be difficult to get close to him and get away clean. The patriot had not done as much reconnaissance here as he'd done with some of his other targets, and was using the time hoping an opportunity would present itself. This hope was dashed when he saw a large number of cars in Hughes's driveway and parked on both sides of the street in front. Obviously, a party was going on, and he would have to come back another time. He checked his road atlas, slowly drove down the tree-lined street, and headed back to Highway 61.

Andy Stoughten was flushed with excitement. The five-time convicted child molester who had been gratefully sentenced to the New Visions halfway house in Hastings was eagerly looking forward to tonight's activities. He was allowed to leave New Visions at 10:00 p.m. in order to go to his job at a local manufacturing plant. The rules stated that he had to be back in the home by 8:00 a.m. the following morning and that any absences from work were supposed to be immediately reported to the night staff at New Visions. Andy knew, however, that tonight his supervisor at the plant would be on vacation and that no one else knew about his past or about his rules. The plant had decided, when they took Stoughten on, that the fewer people who knew about his history, the easier it would be to prevent workplace harassment. He had figured a way to get loose for the first time in months, and he planned to make the most of it. Shortly after beginning his stay at New Visions, Stoughten had used his day passes to go to the Hastings Public Library. There, he would access his hotmail e-mail account and go into chat rooms with young males. These conversations with these boys gave him a certain amount of satisfaction, although not as much as he planned to get tonight. Stoughten thought it was amazing that, even though the press had reported in detail how Stoughten had used a computer and his hotmail username of "Andy123" to lure boys into sexual encounters, no one from law enforcement or the corrections system had ever placed any restrictions on his computer use, nor had they notified hotmail to invalidate his username! Stoughten had used this oversight to pick up his activities pretty much where he'd left off when he'd been arrested the last time. He was sure, as were the police and his probation officer, that he would be sent away to prison for a long time and was just as surprised as they were, although for different reasons, to be sure, when Judge Borgert had sent him to treatment. Stoughten never gave a moment's thought to altering his behavior. He was hard-wired to engage in sex with young males, and a psychologist would have as much success altering Stoughten's sexual desires as he would of convincing Hugh Hefner to give up huge-breasted models and start taking it in the ass from a longshoreman.

A short time after Stoughten logged back into cyberspace, he was contacted by another hotmail user, who signed himself "Jerry_USA1," who had e-mailed Stoughten and said that he had seen Stoughten's username in chat rooms and had enjoyed the conversations which he'd seen flying back and forth. He'd asked why Stoughten had been absent from the rooms for so long. Stoughten had e-mailed him back, and they had begun conversing regularly. It became plain to Stoughten that Jerry was a teenaged male who had discovered a developing homosexuality and was curious about experimenting. Stoughten had gotten very aroused by some of the messages he'd gotten from Jerry and had finally secured a promise that they would meet at 11:00 that night at Vermillion Falls Park.

Stoughten reported for work, as usual, but after half an hour complained of nausea and diarrhea to the man who was filling in for the vacationing supervisor. The fill-in told Stoughten that he should go home and that he hoped he would be feeling better soon. Stoughten agreed that he probably would. He left the plant, walked a few blocks to the park, and waited by the playground equipment, as he had promised Jerry he would. Because it was very quiet in the park, Stoughten planned to run into the brush if he saw any headlights in the area. He knew that being caught by the police late at night in a park when he was supposed to be at work would play hell with his probation. Stoughten found his fear stimulating because it made the forbidden encounter more exciting.

Jerry had described himself as six feet tall and thin, somewhat tall for Stoughten's tastes, but still acceptable in a pinch. Stoughten wandered among the swings in the quiet and tried to peer through the gloom to see his new friend. Suddenly, a voice from the picnic pavilion quietly asked, "Andy?" Stoughten's heart leaped as he moved toward the structure. He bumped his knee sharply on a picnic table as he rushed into the darkness.

"Jerry, its me! Its Andy!" He whispered. He could barely make out the figure against the back wall.

"Its me, its Jerry," the voice answered. Stoughten opened his arms to hug Jerry and was surprised when all the air was driven out of his lungs by a hard blow just below his breastbone. The blow was so unexpected and delivered with such force, that Stoughten could make no sound. He staggered backward and fell hard to a sitting position onto the cement floor, feeling as if his ribs were broken and he would never be able to breathe again. The patriot stepped forward out of the deep darkness of the back wall, and Stoughten saw that this wasn't the nervous teenager he'd expected. Stoughten had spent his whole adult life feeling intimidated by big men and repelled by women. Only when he was in the presence of boys did he feel any sense of confidence or empowerment. Stoughten gasped for breath and looked up at the large man who had now stepped behind him. There was a whistling sound as the patriot quickly looped a length of flexible wire around Stoughten's neck and pulled it taut. Stoughten fought back weakly against the terrible pressure that made it feel as if his head was being pinched off. Stoughten tried to beat his fists against the arms of the patriot and then tried to reach up and gouge at his face, but the patriot shook him like a dog shaking a bone, driving the wire deeper into Stoughten's neck. Blood began to run inside his shirt, and Stoughten drummed his heels on the ground as he felt the blood roaring in his ears from the pressure inside his head. His bowels and bladder let go as he made a last ditch effort to try to slip his fingers between his neck and the cutting wire, but it was in too deep. Scratching at the backs of the patriot's hands with his nails, Stoughten desperately tried to get his feet under himself, but he couldn't overcome the patriot's strength and leverage. As Stoughten's consciousness slipped away, his hands dropped to his sides, but the patriot kept twisting the wire tighter.

He held Stoughten for a full minute longer before letting him drop to the ground on his back. The patriot withdrew his Tanto knife from his boot and made a quick, savage puncture upward into Stoughten's chest just under the breastbone to ensure that the job was done. After withdrawing the knife, the patriot wiped the blood on Stoughten's sleeve and put it back in its sheath. He straightened and looked carefully around and listened for any sound, very much resembling a predatory animal at the scene of a fresh kill. He grabbed Stoughten's collar, dragged the body into the darkness of the picnic pavilion, and then walked casually toward the road. Avoiding lighted areas, he made his way six blocks to the shopping center where he had parked his car and drove home to tend to his bleeding hands, thinking that, although his night had been only half successful, it was not a total waste.

James Knox finished his news story with time to spare and submitted it for editing. He was pleased with the end result. He felt exhilarated and, somehow, young again at the prospect of being on the cutting edge of such an important story. He looked forward to going home and relaxing after his very full day, but for the first time in a long time, he didn't crave a drink. Knox thought he'd have no trouble sleeping tonight.

Police hunt for killer in metro area

Police investigators from several agencies are coming to grips today with the knowledge that a serial killer is on the loose and responsible for the deaths of at least six people in the last nine days. A confession to the murders of Judge Edward Borgert in Edina on May 5, Sarah Ehrenberg in rural Goodhue County on May 7, Wallace Berry on May 9, and the triple homicides of Desiree Blevins, Amii Faust, and Jeremy Soderberg in Minneapolis on May 11, was received in the mail at the offices of the *Minneapolis Star Tribune* early Tuesday morning. The letter contained details of each murder which were verified by police investigators working those cases.

The confession came as a bombshell to the police, who were operating under the belief that the murders had been unrelated due to the distances between the victims and their differing lifestyles and the fact that the victims had been murdered in very different ways. Now that the investigators know that the crimes are related, they hope that they will be better able to locate the man responsible and bring the violence to an end.

In his two-page confession, the killer, who calls himself as "a patriot," claims to be a man concerned with the degrading values of society and says that he is intent on removing people who, he feels, are "…threats to the great American way of life."

The article went on at length to again name each of the victims and how and where they were killed in grisly detail. Knox quoted Pete Lincoln, saying that the Soderberg murder was, "the single most brutal killing I've ever experienced" and Mike Rawlings saying that the confession was "a very substantial step toward solving these crimes."

Knox reported that the patriot's confession had absolved George Fast Horse and that his family was enraged that he had been incorrectly accused. Knox quoted Sheriff Cooper as saying that he was standing by the work that had been done by Pappas and that the entire matter was "a sad, tragic affair."

Dave Joyner spent little time editing Knox's story and sent it through to the printing department in time for the headline they'd been holding open. He sent Knox and his two assistants, Keith and Larry, home with instructions to get a good night's sleep and hit the story hard again first thing in the morning. Keith and Larry asked Knox how he felt about celebrating the scoop with a stop at his favorite watering hole.

"Well, okay," Knox answered. "I'm too keyed up to sleep anyway."

CHAPTER 21

▼

On Wednesday morning the patriot got up early and went straight to the morning paper, which was waiting for him on the front steps. The front page headline in bold type confirmed for him that his message had been taken seriously. He read through the article twice and was disappointed that Knox had written nothing of his plea for others to follow his lead. A popular movement was the reason he was doing this, after all. He was also disappointed to see his moniker capitalized as The Patriot. He didn't like that. He thought of himself as only one of many and realized fully that alone he couldn't bring about the sweeping changes that society needed. He knew it would require everyone out there who was angry, disillusioned, and fed up with what the nation had become would do their part. He thought that it couldn't be long before the national news services would pick up the story.

The patriot turned on CNN and then went online and checked various news sites, looking for his story. He checked Reuters, NBC, ABC, CBS, the Associated Press, and MSNBC but found nothing. He was finally rewarded when he turned on the local top-of-the-hour morning news. The anchorwoman shared a split screen with the words "Serial Killer" in red next to her head as she read the story.

"Good morning everyone, I'm Jennifer Connelly. Today, a multi-jurisdictional task force begins the hunt for a serial killer who sent a confession to reporter James Knox of the Minneapolis Star Tribune. The confession, sent in on a computer disk, comes from a man who refers to himself as 'a patriot.'"

Sitting at home, the patriot noted the heavy sarcasm in the woman's voice as she pronounced his pseudonym and he gave her image the finger. The anchor turned the story over to a male reporter, Gene Taylor, who was standing in front of BCA headquarters in St. Paul.

"Thank you, Jennifer. I'm here at the home of the Minnesota Bureau of Criminal Apprehension in St. Paul. This is where a task force made up of officers from several agencies will meet today to plan the strategy they will use to hunt down the man who has claimed responsibility for six murders in the last week and a half in the Twin Cities metro area.

"Yesterday, a computer disk arrived in the mail at the offices of the *Star Tribune* addressed to veteran reporter James Knox. Knox, who has written for the paper for fifteen years and who worked as an Associated Press reporter and correspondent for many years before that, was the person to whom the disk was addressed."

The story cut to an interview with Knox, which had been recorded outside of the Star Tribune office the previous night after he had filed his story. Knox looked disheveled and tired, but answered questions from Taylor.

"Mr. Knox, what was the substance of the letter you received?"

"Basically, it was a letter from a man who referred to himself as 'a patriot' and said that he is upset with what he feels are the decline of American society and values. He confessed to killing six people and provided sufficient details from each to confirm that he was, in fact, the person responsible."

"Why did he kill these people?"

"Well, he outlined his reasons for each killing and said, basically, that each victim was making America a worse place to live in."

"Could you give us a run down of the victims and explain why the patriot felt they needed to die?"

Knox consulted his notes, checking the list of victims and what the patriot had said about each of them.

"Mr. Knox, why did this man choose to send his confession to you?" Taylor asked.

"That wasn't made plain," Knox replied.

The interview ended, and they cut back to Taylor. "We are now joined live by Mike Rawlings, an investigator with the Minnesota BCA. Agent Rawlings will be heading up the task force which has been charged with the problem of catching the patriot. Agent Rawlings, do you have any leads?"

"At this time, we have several leads, we have a living witness, and we will be coordinating our efforts now that we know for certain that we're dealing with one man and not several."

"Agent Rawlings, do you believe that your suspect in these six murders is also responsible for the death of Peter Montgomery, the ex-priest who had been accused of sexual abuse?"

"That's going to be one of the things we'll be looking at today. Mr. Montgomery seems to fit the profile of victims, but we won't be jumping to any conclusions. I haven't yet had the opportunity to talk with the Shakopee Police in detail about the crime."

"Do you believe this man will strike again?" The reporter asked.

"Yes, I do."

"Why?"

"We know this man believes he's on a mission. He has an agenda and has been very active. I don't know of any serial killer who has killed so many people in such a short period of time. He's not what would be classed as a 'mass murderer'; those people kill many victims at one time in one place, such as the University of Texas sniper in the sixties or the man responsible for the McDonald's massacre in the seventies in San Diego. A serial killer stalks his victims and kills for a particular reason."

"Agent Rawlings, do you believe the killer has a target list that he's been working from?"

"That is a very likely scenario. I'm not going to get into any detail about what we know about how the killer is locating people who would ordinarily be hard to find, but I think it's plain from what we've seen, and what the killer himself wrote in his confession to Mr. Knox, that he does have a list, he's done his research on the victims, and is now carrying out the crimes."

"So, there could well be others killed?"

"That possibility is something we are going to be working very hard to avoid."

"Thank you." The camera moved in close to Taylor who wrapped up the story. "Jennifer, I was told by sources that these crimes were very brutal. Jeremy Soderberg was tortured prior to his death. He was beaten, a finger was cut off, and his head was crushed in a workbench vise before his throat was slit. Sarah Ehrenberg was killed by a tool similar to an ice pick being rammed in her ear and through her brain. Her neck was then broken by the killer for good measure. Clearly, this is a man totally without remorse and a very dangerous person."

The camera cut back to the anchorwoman who made a sour face at Taylor's wrap-up. "Ugh. Grisly. Thank you, Gene."

The patriot listened to the follow-up stories, which covered old ground and showed interviews with friends and family members of the victims. The patriot turned off the TV and mulled over the fact that his central message to Knox about encouraging an uprising hadn't been reported. He knew that the police would probably have encouraged Knox to avoid that angle in order to avoid copycat killings. The patriot felt he needed to lean on Knox some more. It was also the patriot's first chance to really get a good look at Rawlings. So, this is the hound in the hunt, he thought to himself. Rawlings didn't look like one of those administrative drones who were often found in high positions in big police agencies. He looked every bit like a street cop and the patriot knew he would want to keep tabs on this man. He trusted that the media would handle that task for him now that Rawlings had been publicly revealed as the man in charge.

The patriot donned another pair of rubber gloves and put a new floppy in his computer. Taking a fresh envelope out of the middle of the same box he'd used to send his last message, he used the computer to address the envelope to Knox and then set about typing another letter.

Mr. Knox,

Thank you for your article. Since it's obvious that I want everyone clear on what's going on, I thought I should bring you (and the police) up to speed. I haven't been resting on my laurels and have stayed quite busy. In answer to the question people are asking today, yes, I did kill the former Father Montgomery. He was scum and the worst type of criminal in the world. He used God and his religion to feed his own perverted desires and left who knows how many wrecked lives in his wake. I enjoyed kicking the shit out of him and dragging him around the living room like the dog he was with his bathrobe sash as a leash. I thought that it was generous of him to provide me with the Claymore I used to "take a little off the top" as the barber says. Nice weapon. I see why the Muslims use it to kill perverts and think we should follow their example.

I also killed another pervert named Andy Stoughten in a park in Hastings. Andy, as you may know, was another child molester and, therefore, the type of scum we are much better off without. It's Wednesday morning and Andy's body hasn't been found yet, but I suspect it will be before you get this. I strangled him with a piece of wire and stabbed him in Vermillion Falls Park in the picnic area.

Honestly, Mr. Knox, don't you agree that both of these men made the world around them a worse place? Aren't you tired of paying over 30% of your salary in taxes to feed and clothe these animals and to pay the police to try to catch them while having to use a ridiculous set of rules when the criminals operate by none? The deformed monster of our court system was created by lawyers in order to create work for other lawyers and thereby to ensure their own existence.

Our great nation is a living, breathing body, and it has an infection. Its virus is made up of deadbeats, perverts, and criminals, and the lawyers and liberal do-gooders are preventing the body from healing itself. Without action, the virus will kill its host, and the lawyers and liberals are too stupid and caught up in their own wants and desires to realize that they will die, too.

I happen to believe that America is too great and proud and valuable a thing to let waste away and die. I WILL do my best to stop it. I WILL fight on. and I encourage everyone who wants the same thing to join me.

a patriot

The patriot followed the same procedure as before in sealing the envelope, then he drove to St. Paul and mailed it. He then returned home and began to get ready for work.

While the patriot was writing his letter and describing the final resting place of Andy Stoughten, Bernice Flynn, a fifty-five-year-old retired librarian pulled into the parking area at Vermillion Falls Park. She got out of her car and opened the back door to hook up the leash on the collar of her golden lab Charlie. Charlie, eager to go for his morning walk in the park and smell all of the new smells that had been deposited the night before, jumped out and strained with all his might on the leash. Bernice hung on tightly and listened to Charlie gasp as the choker collar squeezed his neck. *Why the heck does he do that to himself?* she wondered. Bernice wasn't a strong woman and it wasn't long before being dragged around by Charlie from one smell to another made her arms tired.

"Oh, Charlie, give me a break, here," she said to the big dog as he went about his ritual of lifting his leg and sprinkling everything in sight. Bernice, a nervous woman, was afraid of letting Charlie run free to ease the strain on her arms. She knew he was a good dog and always came when she called, but she feared her husband's anger if she let him run away.

Charlie pulled her toward the playground equipment, but she didn't want to walk in the pea gravel and get it in her shoes. She tried to pull Charlie away, but evidently the smells left behind by the children who had last used the slides and swings were too much; Charlie would not be denied. In a burst of unaccustomed liberation, Bernice unsnapped Charlie's collar and let him run free. She plopped down on a bench near the playground and kept an eye on her dog, who took full advantage of his freedom to explore. Charlie trotted back and forth around the park sniffing and peeing, sniffing and peeing, pawing the pea gravel, tasting the remains of a sucker and gobbling a half of a cookie he had rooted out from under the slide.

Bernice relaxed in the morning sun as Charlie went about the serious business of being a dog. She reflected that it was so much easier this way rather than being dragged around like a plow. She knew she would have to corral Charlie if someone came into the park, but for the time being he seemed to be staying close by. He smelled every last smell available in the playground and moved off toward the picnic shelter. Bernice watched him sniff along the edge of the concrete walls of the pavilion and around the trash dumpster nearby. A lift of the leg and a quick sprinkle and Charlie moved off into the shelter entrance. As he trotted inside, Charlie froze for a second and the fur on his body stood on end. His big tail stopped swishing and stood straight out and Bernice wondered what he'd seen.

"Come here, Charlie," she called out. Charlie ignored her and walked slowly into the pavilion. *Probably saw a mouse, the big chicken,* Bernice thought. As she continued to let the sun warm her face, she slipped her sweater off and folded it across her lap. It was going to be a warm day, and she knew she should be home planting the flowers she'd bought at the nursery. Her husband thought she'd spent too much, but Bernice loved the burst of colors the flowers made around the house after winter's endless white.

"Charlie!" she called. "Come here, Charlie!" Bernice knew he hadn't left the pavilion. The bench was so comfortable that she hated to leave. She called the dog again, but he didn't appear. *Big dummy,* she thought. Bernice got up and laid her sweater down on the bench, thinking that it would be nice to sit back down for just a few minutes longer. The flowers could wait for a little while. She walked up to the pavilion and said, "Charlie, would you come…" The words choked off as Bernice came around the corner and saw Charlie standing next to the body of Andy Stoughten. The big dog was licking the bloody hole in Stoughten's chest, and he looked up at his mistress as his tongue lapped around his mouth and licked the blood off of his muzzle.

"Aaahhhh!" Bernice screamed as she ran from the pavilion and continued to scream as she ran to her car. Charlie, wondering what was wrong, ran after her. Bernice stumbled to the car and pushed Charlie away as he tried to get in with her. "NO! NO! FILTHY, FILTHY DOG!" she screamed. She fumbled with her keys and managed to start the car. She drove off leaving Charlie to lick the strange taste off of his chops, and wonder why he'd been left behind.

A short time later, the Hastings Police arrived and secured the scene. They'd tied up Charlie to the playground equipment, and a patrol officer was listening to Bernice Flynn say that she never wanted to see that dog again as long as she lived. Two detectives arrived, and the crime lab team had been alerted and was on the way. The police didn't need to look for ID on the body, for they immediately recognized Stoughten, despite the fact that his face had swollen and discolored during his strangulation. One of the detectives, Merle Anderson, a twenty-nine-year man who refused to retire despite urgings from his wife, said, "Well, well. Randy Andy bit the dust. I wonder if he got it from this patriot fella or if he grabbed the wrong crank here last night."

"Could have been either," Anderson's partner Vince Berger said as he looked closely at Stoughten's neck. "This doesn't look like any sissy killing to me, though. Somebody really cranked that wire tight on his neck. Is this hole a bullet or a knife wound in his chest?"

"Don't know," Anderson said. "I wonder which came first. Not a lot of blood, so he was probably strangled first." Anderson pulled Stoughten's shirt up and looked at the wound. "Hmm. Looks like a knife."

"Merle, lets not fuck around with him too much until the crime lab gets here," Berger said.

"Gotta see how he died, Junior," Anderson protested to the younger man. "Besides, do we *really* want to solve this one?" he said with a smile.

"I see your point," Berger replied. "Just don't let anybody hear you." Berger knew that Anderson was a hell of a cop in his day, but he looked at new ideas as worthless crap, and sometimes he would say the most embarrassing things. Berger had learned from him and admired him and even resented a little Anderson's grandfatherly gray hair and the way suspects seemed to hate to lie to him. Anderson had a way of getting things done, Berger knew, but you just couldn't joke around anymore like Anderson liked to. Cops were like politicians and preachers, everybody minded their business and loved to crow about it when they fucked up.

"Yes, Mother," Anderson said as he swatted Berger on the arm. They stepped out to let the department's photographer take pictures of the scene and then took a statement from Bernice Flynn before the crime lab arrived. Patrol officers, who had been detailed to hang yellow crime scene tape around the playground and the pavilion area, stood around and chatted while the crime lab began their chores. After more pictures, a technician looked at Stoughten's hands and called over the supervisor.

"Hey, boss, look at this guy's fingernails. Looks like debris and blood."

"Yeah, you're right. Bag 'em." The technician carefully placed paper lunch sacks over Stoughten's hands and secured them with tape to his wrists. That way, the flesh, hair, and blood that Stoughten had clawed from the back of the patriot's hands would be preserved for retrieval and DNA analysis. The task force had been given another piece of the puzzle.

The Patriot Task Force spent Wednesday getting their work areas sorted out and going over each others' case files. By afternoon, all of the investigators were as familiar with the other cases as they were with their own. Sharon Bluhm sat in for the first day and read the case files along with the others. Of all the investigators there, only Rawlings and Pete Lincoln knew Bluhm from having previously worked with her. She was wearing a black lightweight long-sleeve dress and her dark hair was pulled back in a loose bun. Bluhm, wearing reading glasses on a chain around the back of her neck, looked very much like a private school mistress or the private accountant to a wealthy corporation. She had a nervous habit of nibbling on the end of her pen and indulged in that habit while things got started. After a lunch of sandwiches brought in from a local deli, Mike Rawlings brought the team together and asked for preliminary thoughts and impressions. Pete Lincoln threw the first pitch.

"Well, we *know* our man didn't vote for Al Gore. Let's get voter records and eliminate all of the Democrats right away." The group all shared a laugh, and then Rawlings pressed on.

"Right, well, it may come to that. I don't have to tell any of you how hard it is to track a killer who has no ties to his victims except the ones inside his own damn head. Sharon, would you like to venture a viewpoint from what you've read so far?"

"Well," Bluhm said, "I've just started looking at the reports and I'd like to do some work-ups as well as call some people I know from Quantico, but I do have some first impressions.

"First of all, this man's letter shows me that he is very intelligent. His extremely orderly crime scenes show that he is neat and clean. We need to keep these traits in mind. He has wiped the blood off of his knife on his victims' clothing and seems to have draped the sheet over Jeremy Soderberg to keep from getting splattered with blood when he cut his throat. I can think of no other explanation for the sheet being there, for he's made no attempt in the past to hide his other victims. He *wants* them found, after all. I believe he's done a lot of recon on his victims, actively stalking them and setting up these killings for months. He moves in and out quickly and quietly, and he seems to be as comfortable with killing up close as he is from far away.

"He hasn't shown us a preference for working at night or during the day. Two of the six murders took place at night, the others during the day, so it seems that he adapts to his victim's schedules. He doesn't mind walking up to a house or crowded apartment buildings in broad daylight to commit his crimes. That means he's very confident. We aren't looking for a man who is the typical square peg in a round hole. I would believe he is employed, probably does well in his job, and can mix well in his circle of friends.

"Socially, I would think he is a loner, quiet, probably not a partygoer. I can't see him having a steady relationship without whatever issues he has boiling inside of him coming out and ruining it. He shows a sick sense of humor in his letter, for example his comment about Jeremy Soderberg having a 'narrow mind.' I think he is probably capable of using humor around his social circle and probably uses it as a bridge between his shy nature and his acquaintances.

"His driving force is his conviction that he must bring about change by killing the people he disagrees with. I believe that he also thinks he can start a popular revolution; that's why he contacted Knox. I don't think he's crowing about his crimes as much as he's looking for support, although there does seem to be an element of pride in his work.

"One thing I think is evident is that this man has experienced had some very traumatic experiences in his past. It's one thing to kill your enemy, but there is an element of overkill in some of these cases. He has taken the time and trouble to ensure his victims are truly dead in every case, except for the girls in the elevator, where he probably had too little time. I think that, if one of his victims happened to survive, our man would take that very badly, almost as an insult. This could be evidence of specialized military training. Most military-trained people are taught to inflict a casualty in battle, but there are some units, because of the nature of their mission, whose soldiers prefer to kill those they encounter, and they train specifically to ensure that this is done. He is comfortable with different types of weapons and appears skilled with them as well as with hand-to-hand combat. I would believe he is very physically fit and probably takes pride in his physique. We could check health clubs and gyms.

"Gentlemen, all of this is speculative, but based on solid theory. No one can point you to our man right now, but I think it's safe to consider these aspects of his personality as we begin to establish suspects."

"Sharon, do you think this guy will contact us again, maybe through Knox?" Phil Deane asked.

"I think it's a fair bet. He'll want to keep us informed as to which of the metro's homicides is his work. Plus, I really think he's looking for Knox to provide that popular support he thinks is out there."

"So, how can we control that?" Pete Lincoln asked. "All we need is this guy firing up a bunch of rednecks and skinheads and get them out blasting the neighbor kid for playing his stereo."

"That's not so far-fetched," Rawlings replied. "I think there's a very real threat of that here. I don't know if Knox and his editor will play ball with us on that or not, but they'll want to report everything, and if we don't come up with a suspect soon, they're going to be looking for new angles to write about. All we can do is make sure the paper understands the problem and hope they see it our way."

"If there is a follow-up letter from this man I'd look forward to seeing it," Bluhm said. "It would be revealing, I think, to see how he handles his new celebrity. I'd be willing to bet he might give us something about his goals."

"Goals?" John Pappas asked. "What goals? He's trying to kill as many people he disagrees with as possible before he's caught."

"No, the killing is incidental," Bluhm cautioned. "Don't be confused here, he's killing for a reason and that is to effect a kind of change which he sees as necessary. This man is very disturbed, yes, but he is far from insane. He knows he can't kill everyone in the country who has a view different from his. He's also lashing out, true, but he has a goal in mind. Whether it's a political revolution or what, I don't know."

"Could he be lured? Baited?" Rawlings asked.

"I don't want to go there," Bluhm answered. "There are people at Quantico who can direct you with that. It's a very iffy proposition and gets deeper into psychology than I'm willing to go. There's also the moral and ethical issue of pointing a dangerous weapon at someone and daring it to go off."

The intercom buzzed and Rawlings picked it up. He spoke quietly while the group tossed thoughts back and forth with each other. When he hung up, Rawlings said, "Well, we may have another case. Andy Stoughten, the child molester that Borgert set free, was found dead in a Hastings park this morning. He was strangled with wire and stabbed once in the chest."

"I know that turd," Gene Truman said. "I worked a case on him last year. We couldn't pin it on him, but I know he did it. The victim was just too young to take to court. He was supposed to be under some real restrictive supervision. How the hell did he wind up in a park with the patriot?"

"We'll soon find out," Rawlings answered. "Gene, why don't you go to Hastings and see what's up. See what they have for evidence and the whys and hows of

Stoughten's being out. Meantime, let's start hitting health clubs and gyms to see if anyone knows of a guy who might fit our profile. Ask about people with military experience, maybe combat experience."

"How do we know we aren't talking to the patriot?" Deane asked.

"Ask women who work at the clubs," Rawlings suggested. "Pete, did you guys get an artist's rendering of our man from your witness, the Russian?"

"No, he didn't get a very good look at his face."

"Okay, but that's something we may want to explore anyway. It could serve as a bone to throw at the press if this thing drags out. It might buy us some time before they start printing shit they think up themselves."

CHAPTER 22

▼

When Tony Bauer stopped into the office that afternoon to check his mail and read the information updates prior to going out onto patrol, his co-workers were discussing the recent rash of killings. Steve Bennington was reading aloud from the day's newspaper article and editorializing between the lines.

"It says here that a reward fund is being established. Are they going to give it to whoever turns this guy in, or will it go to the patriot as a Crime Stoppers reward?"

"Could go either way, I guess," replied Todd Erickson. "The guy's really getting around. I suppose he could use the money just for gas."

"Not just gas," Bennington said. "Ammunition isn't cheap, either, Buster. You suppose that's why he used a garrote on Randy Andy? Maybe he was cutting costs?"

"This is a sick line of conversation," Sergeant. Mike Fitz observed. "Be careful you keep this talk inside the building, and don't let the brass or the public hear you."

"The danger I see is that he might put us out of business," Bennington went on. "If he keeps killing criminals we might have to cut back on staff."

"Then what would you do if you couldn't rape the taxpayer?" Fitz asked.

"I think I'd make a fine District Court judge," Bennington replied. "We're short one at the present time. Listen to this: it says in the paper, 'the widow Borgert denounced the killing of her husband as a barbaric act and went on to say that she would be using part of her late husband's estate to establish a foundation to help disadvantaged kids.' Shit. By the time her liver gives out there'll only be enough left to send 37 cents to buy a kid in Africa an oxtail to use as a fly swatter."

"I was supposed to have a trial this week with Borgert on a crim sex case," Joe Burns said while typing a report on a word processor. "Now that His Honor is unavailable, they had to reschedule it. The poor suspect has to spend a little more time in jail while they set up with a new judge."

"That's a shame," Fitz agreed sarcastically. "Is that the guy who grabbed the jogger outside of Lakeville?"

"No, this was the guy who was going door-to-door saying he was a faith healer. Told the woman he could cure her asthma by laying on hands."

"And did he then lay on hands?" Bennington asked with a smirk.

"Yes he did. Hands and mouth. The woman didn't complain until her next asthma attack and only after she went to her pastor and asked if the healing hadn't worked because she hadn't been righteous."

"Amen, brother!" Erickson said. "Speak the good news!"

Ernie Engleman from the day shift strolled into the room wearing an enormous stained tank top, size 52 khaki shorts, and tennis shoes. He was carrying his four-and-a half-foot-long gun belt. "Afternoon, crime fighters," he announced to the group.

"Where have you been?" Mike Fitz asked.

"In-service training, gents," Engleman answered. "Today I was instructed in the proper methods of using my ASP." Engleman was referring to his new police weapon, an extendable steel baton made of three sections of pipe, which nest together into a length of about eight inches, and can be comfortably carried on the belt. When snapped open, the pipe sections lock into place to form a weapon about twenty-four inches long. The ASP replaced the old PR24 angled nightstick, which replaced the even older straight baton. The straight baton replaced the leather-covered, spring steel sap, which Engleman had used in the early days of his career, thirty years before.

"Ernie needs an ASP like I need the clap," Bennington said.

"Hey, I intend to put this to good use," Engleman said. He pulled the ASP out of its holder and snapped it open. He then pulled an eight inch length of tape off a roll, wadded it up, and stuck it on the knobby end of the ASP. He used his new creation to spear a piece of paper on the floor with the tape and lift it up without having to bend over. "It's a fucking beautiful thing," he said with an admiring smile as the others laughed.

Mike Fitz shook his head and turned to Bauer. "You're sure quiet today. Have some bad days off?"

"Couldn't be," Bennington interjected. "I saw Don Sundquist's sister-in-law giving Tony a tonsillectomy with her tongue at the party the other night. Was she a natural brunette?"

"All natural," Bauer replied with a smile. "Natural and healthy. I am a better man for having met her."

"I bet you are," Fitz said. "Tina used to babysit my kids when she was younger. She was fine then."

"Tony here may be big and strong, but Tina had him locked up tight at the party," Bennington said. "I thought she was going to throw you down on the floor and have her way with you by the can there.'

"She tried but I talked her out of it," Bauer smiled.

"What did you say?"

"I just told her that if we went to her place we wouldn't have you walking by us every five minutes to take a leak," Bauer smiled.

"I'm an older man," Bennington protested. "My bladder isn't what it once was."

"I understand completely," Bauer said. "In the words of our former Commander-in-Chief, 'I feel your pain.'"

The group laughed as Bauer imitated Clinton. Bauer was known to be a fairly good mimic and did Slick Willy very well.

Engleman grabbed hold of the back of Fitz's chair and released a growling fart. "Good afternoon, Sheriff," he said as deputies scrambled to get out of the area.

Bauer gathered up his papers and walked out to his car. The radio had sounded fairly quiet as he drove in and he hoped it would stay that way. He drove to the southern end of the county and spent an hour cruising Highway 3 and County Roads 86 and 47 looking for speeders. The area is agricultural and the roads are long, straight, and mostly flat. He clocked a Pontiac Bonneville at 76 in the 55 zone on County 47 near Hampton and pulled him over. The guy was very friendly and cooperative when he offered his license and insurance card to Bauer, but turned surly when Bauer returned with a ticket.

"This is bullshit! There were no other cars around. Can't you give me a warning?" the man complained.

"You've received and ignored quite a few warnings today," Bauer told him.

"What? What do you mean?" the speeder asked.

"All of these signs that the taxpayer paid to put along here that say 'Speed limit 55' are warnings. You ignored them."

"Great," the guy said. "A million cops and I get Joe Friday."

Bauer turned around and was headed toward Highway 52 when he got a call; "1130, medical."

"1130," Bauer answered.

"1130, a woman in labor. 21500 Darsow Ave. Be advised, ALF is 10-6 and unavailable, Northfield Ambulance will be responding but they are out of position. ETA is 25 minutes." Normally, an ambulance from ALF, which services the communities of Apple Valley, Lakeville and Farmington, would have been sent, but they were 10-6, which meant that they were busy. To make things worse, Bauer recognized the address as belonging to the trailer he'd been to the week before where he'd arrested the asshole who was beating his pregnant girlfriend.

"1130, is Cannon Falls Ambulance closer?" Bauer asked.

"Stand by," the dispatcher told him.

Bauer was just a couple of minutes from the address on Darsow and pulled in as the Dispatcher told him that he would have to wait because Cannon Falls Ambulance was also busy.

"Roll Randolph Rescue," Bauer said and then got out and went into a trailer home where a woman was lying on the couch moaning in pain. Bauer immediately smelled the booze on the girl's breath.

"Are you alone?" Bauer asked the girl.

"Yeah," she gasped as another contraction hit. "Jessie's at work."

"I take it you two are back together," Bauer said.

"I love him. He isn't so bad, he just gets angry when he's drinking," she slurred.

Yeah right, Bauer thought. *And I bet he's angry all the fucking time, too.*

"Is this your first baby?" Bauer asked.

"Yeah. It's not supposed to be due for another month. Should it hurt so much? It feels like its coming out!" Bauer looked at the skinny girl with the swollen belly and the stringy hair. She still had the bruises on her bare arms from the beating she'd taken from Jessie the previous week. *Just as likely they're from when he got home and pounded her for having been sent to jail,* he thought.

"What's your name again?" Bauer asked her.

"Corrine Steiger." She could barely speak, as her features were distorted in pain. "Oh, my God! Its coming out! Help me!"

Bauer was disgusted with her. Here she was, drunk at 4:30 in the afternoon and eight months pregnant. He smelled the cigarette smoke on her, too. *This is a mother-of-the-year candidate,* he thought. *Now she's gonna have a three-pound kid and the taxpayers will have to foot the million-dollar hospital bill, so this bitch will be able to bring it home and piss and moan about its crying.*

Bauer knelt down, pulled some rubber gloves out of his pocket, and put them on. He saw that the sofa was stained from Steiger's water breaking and he avoided leaning on the soggy cushion while he pushed up her nightgown and looked between her legs. He saw the crown of the baby's head pushing out and knew that she would be delivering at any moment.

"Take short, panting breaths," Bauer told her. He glanced around the trailer and saw dirty clothing lying in piles, beer and liquor bottles on the tables and floor, and ashtrays piled with cigarette butts. The air in the trailer reeked of booze, smoke, and cat urine, and Bauer began to feel his anger build at the thought of such worthless people having children and raising them to be the same way. He looked back at Steiger's exposed body and saw that she had a tattoo of a marijuana leaf high up on her inner left thigh. *This kid doesn't have a chance in hell,* Bauer thought and the idea formed in his head that it would be a good and right thing if the kid didn't make it. *This bitch doesn't want this kid. It'll cut into her partying,* he thought. *The father, worthless piece of shit that he is, will see the kid as competition for attention, and beat it like he did it's mother. The county would be better off not having to pay for its food stamps, pointless education, and its inevitable incarceration when it grows up to be a criminal, just like Mommy and Daddy.*

Bauer's mind ran quickly through his options. He knew the rescue squad would be arriving pretty soon and that he had very little time. He also knew that he would be running a huge risk if he did anything overt...but, still...

"Alright, listen to me," Bauer told Steiger. "Take a deep breath and push." Steiger whimpered and seemed to be near to passing out. "I need your help here!" Bauer told her firmly. "Push!" Steiger tried to rise up on her elbows, but collapsed. She took a breath and pushed, and the head of the baby popped out into his hands. Bauer had received first responder medical training on several occasions during his police career and had been trained in delivering babies. One thing that had been stressed was the importance of maintaining the baby's airway once the head was clear of the mother's body. He remembered that the baby took its first breath as soon as the head was clear and that it was critical to suction any mucus from the nose and mouth as quickly as possible.

Bauer looked at Steiger, who was lying there panting with her eyes closed and her arms limp at her sides. The baby was smeared with blood and mucus, and he saw little bubbles forming around the mouth and nose as the infant struggled to draw in air. Bauer knew that he should angle the baby downward to steer the shoulders out, but instead he used the fingers of his left hand to hold it in place. He used his right hand to raise the head up and pressed the baby's chin against its chest and held it there. Steiger seemed completely unaware of what was going on.

Bauer kept looking at her, thinking that he would pull the baby out if she opened her eyes, but she didn't. He heard Randolph Rescue Squad calling him on his portable radio.

"1130, this is Randolph Rescue. Do you have an update on the patient?" Bauer ignored them. Next, his dispatch repeated the call to him, but he ignored it. He looked down and saw that the child's face was getting darker and fewer bubbles were forming around its nose. Bauer heard the siren from the rescue truck growing louder in the distance and knew they'd be there very soon. He looked at Steiger and said, "Everything's going okay, here, Corrine," he told her, but she didn't respond. He continued to hold the baby in place until he heard gravel crunching when the rescue truck turned into the long driveway. He quickly angled the baby down and the small body popped out onto the couch. He saw that it was a girl.

"Corrine, you have a girl," he said loudly to Steiger, who stirred and moved her head a little. Bauer lifted the baby into his hands as the rescue volunteers ran into the living room.

"She just delivered," Bauer told them. "I don't have any suction." He handed the baby to the first rescue worker as others rummaged through their medical bag to find a rubber bulb syringe. Bauer stepped away and watched as the crew clamped the umbilical cord in two places and cut it. They moved the baby to a chair nearby, and one of the members used the syringe to remove some mucus from the mouth and nose.

"A lot of discharge here," he said as he worked. "Get a ventilation bag and the infant mask." Other crewmembers fitted a small air mask onto the blue plastic ventilation bag and handed it to the man with the baby.

"Baby's really small, I don't know if this mask will seal." He fitted the mask over the little face and tried to hold it in place while another squeezed the bag to force air into the baby's lungs.

"She wasn't due for another month yet," Bauer said. He walked into the kitchen, pulled some paper towels off of a roll, and wiped his arms. He then stripped off his rubber gloves, leaving them on the filthy counter as he used detergent to wash his hands. When he was finished, the ambulance arrived, and Mike Fitz pulled in behind it. A female paramedic and a male Emergency Medical Technician got out of the ambulance and trotted into the house, each carrying a bag. Bauer stood by in the living room as the rescue workers explained to the paramedic what was going on and what they'd done so far.

"We don't have a mask small enough for this baby," the rescue worker said. "She's a month premature and really small. Why the hell don't we have a preemie mask?" He asked angrily as he pawed through the rescue bag.

By now, Corrine Steiger had managed to roll onto her side on the couch. She appeared confused at all the strangers in her house and shook her head to try to clear it.

"What's going on?" She asked.

"My name is Joyce and I'm with Northfield Ambulance," the paramedic told her. "You've just delivered a baby. What's your name?"

"Huh?" Steiger asked. "Baby? My baby?"

"Yes, you've had a baby girl," Joyce told her. "What's your name?"

"Um, Corrine Steiger."

"Corrine, do you have any medical problems or allergies?"

"No. Where's my baby?"

"Your baby is right over there in that chair with my partner. Who is your doctor?"

"Let me see my baby," Steiger said.

"We will in a minute, Corrine. Who is your doctor?"

"Joyce, come here, please," The EMT said. Joyce moved over to the chair and her partner leaned in close to whisper to her. "She's unresponsive and cyanotic. We're going to have to intubate her." Seeing what was going on, a member of the rescue squad took over talking to Steiger to occupy her and prevent her from interfering.

Mike Fitz walked into the room and over to Bauer. "What's going on? You didn't answer dispatch."

"I was a little busy," Bauer told him. "There was no time and I had to deliver the baby. It came out just as the rescue squad pulled in."

"Well, congratulations. Boy or girl?" Fitz asked.

"Girl. Seems like there's a problem, though. She's a month premature and it looks like she isn't breathing."

"Shit," Fitz said.

Bauer and Fitz watched as the ambulance workers struggled to revive the baby. They inserted a tube into the baby's throat and used a portable suction pump to remove mucus from the little girl's airway and then tried to bag air into her lungs. They worked for a few minutes and Joyce listened to the baby's heart and lungs with a stethoscope.

"Call in," she told her partner, "and get a helicopter going. We need to ship her to Children's Hospital right away." The EMT ran to the ambulance and ordered the chopper. He came back and came over to Fitz and Bauer. "We're going to have a chopper put down here. Looks like the yard's pretty cluttered with junk, so let's use the road. Could you get on your statewide channel and direct them in?"

"Sure, we'll take care of it," Fitz told him. "How long?"

"Twenty minutes or so."

The ambulance and rescue crews kept bagging air into the baby. Steiger, now realizing that something was wrong, began crying and asking what was going on.

"Corrine, your baby isn't breathing on her own yet," Joyce told her. "We don't want to take any chances, so we're going to send her by helicopter to St. Paul Children's Hospital."

Steiger fell back onto the couch and cried harder. Mike Fitz looked at Bauer and pointed to the door. They went out and Fitz asked, "Are you okay?"

"Yeah, I'm fine," he replied. "Poor little thing's premature and her mom's drunk. Pisses you off, you know?"

"Yeah, what a sty," Fitz told him. "Have you ever delivered a baby?"

"No, first time."

"I've delivered a couple. You tend to get a little attached. Almost like they're yours, you know?" Fitz eyed Bauer carefully.

"Yeah. Maybe she'll pull through. Babies are tough."

"Yeah."

Bauer and Fitz turned their radios to the statewide emergency channel on their portable radios, and it wasn't long before they heard the pilot from Life Link Air calling. He told Fitz that he was following US 52 southbound and understood he would go west on County Road 47. Fitz told him to go north two miles from the church in Hampton, where he would see the squad cars and ambulance. The pilot acknowledged and said he would be landing in five minutes. They got in their cars and blocked off a section of Darsow Avenue.

Bauer sat in his squad car, thinking about what he'd done. While there was no way of knowing exactly how this child would have turned out, he had a pretty fair idea based on the parents and the conditions they lived in.

When he was young, Bauer remembered his father's campaign against the squirrels in their yard. Vern Bauer considered squirrels to be vermin, bushy-tailed rats that dug holes in the grass and raided the bird feeders of the seed that Vern religiously kept stocked to attract the prettiest of the songbirds. Every time Mr. Bauer looked out at his precious bird feeders, he would see the gray thieves scooping the seed onto the ground so they could more easily dine on the largess provided by the Bauers.

Vern purchased a live trap, which he stocked with the very best bird seed, and placed it strategically in the yard. Every day a new squirrel would blunder into the device, attracted by the irresistible smells coming from within and become trapped. Papa Bauer would clap his hands each time he saw a new victim and call young Tony to help him. Tony would follow his father out to the garage where a large barrel full of rainwater sat. Tony's father would explain each time how the squirrels were nothing but pests, flea-ridden nuisances who performed no useful purpose in the world. Then he would take the trap containing the frantic animal and slowly sink it in the rain barrel until it was totally under water. Tony would watch as the rodent would swim back and forth in panic, trying desperately to find a way out. After a few moments its mouth would open and close a few times and its eyes would bulge, and then it would stare fixedly ahead while its limbs would twitch a few times and then go still. Papa Bauer would leave the trap in the water a few minutes more for good measure and then remove the sodden corpse and throw it in the garbage can.

"There's one more we won't have to look at," Vern would say proudly to Tony and Tony would smile up at his father and be happy that his father was happy. It seemed to Tony that the problem which so aggravated his father was easily solved, and Tony knew that when Papa was happy, he was less likely to get angry with Tony or his mother, and that was a very good thing indeed.

The young boy learned that such a simple, effective thing as drowning the pests in the back yard rain barrel, could bring the peace and security that little Tony craved.

The blue Life Link chopper flew over the house, pivoted in the air and came to rest on the road, throwing out a huge cloud of gravel and dust. The two-person medical crew jumped out and carried their bags of equipment into the house. They emerged about ten minutes later, carrying everything they'd brought in and a small, blanket-wrapped bundle. Joyce was trotting alongside squeezing the ventilation bag as they made their way to the road and into the helicopter. As soon as everyone was aboard, the pilot fired up the engines and took off. Fitz and Bauer pulled back into the drive and saw the ambulance and rescue crews bring Corrine out of the house on a gurney. She was on her back with one arm over her eyes, and her shoulders shook as she sobbed. Joyce came over to the squad cars and wiped tears from her eyes with her forearm.

"We got a pretty thready heartbeat going, but I don't know. I think there's some health issues here that were working against us. Goddamn it!" Her voice broke as she choked back tears. "We're taking the mom into Northfield and she'll probably go to Children's unless the baby doesn't make it. Thanks for all of your help."

"No problem," Bauer said.

Fitz turned to Bauer as Joyce walked to the ambulance. "Tony, are you okay? If you need to, take the rest of the night off. We can cover the shift."

"Thanks, Mike. I think I'll take you up on that. That was a pretty intense roller coaster."

"Okay. Head home and take it easy."

"I will. Thanks." Bauer climbed into his car and headed for home. *It's only 5:35 p.m.* Bauer thought. *Nice night for a drive.*

CHAPTER 23

▼

The patriot used his unexpected time off constructively. He went home, changed, and gathered some items from his garage cubbyhole. He got in the Explorer and headed off to White Bear Lake to do a little more work on the problem of Mr. Hughes.

The sun was setting as he made his first pass by the house on Bald Eagle Avenue and saw Hughes's green Subaru Legacy in the driveway. There was no sign of the Honda Accord owned by Hughes's wife, Suzanne Baker-Hughes, a professor of Arts and Literature at the University of Minnesota. The patriot had read a review of John Hughes's diversity book which had stated, in part, that Hughes had credited his wife with many of the book's salient points, so the patriot had come to consider her almost as much of a menace as her husband. He had thought that a frontal assault in the night on them both might be a good plan, but balked at harming the Hughes's two children. The patriot didn't think it strange that he would hesitate to harm them after what he had done only a few hours earlier in the trailer. He thought that there was a possibility of redemption for the Hughes children. If they lost the influence of their father, they might one day learn the right way from someone new and follow the proper path. He knew that there was very little chance of that happening to the Steiger baby. That child had too many factors working against it, what with the mother's drinking and drug use during pregnancy and the bad genes from both worthless parents. Better that child never got a start. But the Hughes children still had a chance, but only if they had the opportunity to learn in a different environment.

The patriot drove around the next block and came down Bald Eagle Avenue from the other way. As he looked at Hughes's car in the drive he got an idea. He drove north on Bald Eagle Avenue until it intersected with Bald Eagle Boulevard. City planners weren't very inventive, I guess, he thought to himself as he turned right and followed the boulevard around the lake. The road connected to Highway 61 again and he soon found himself at Bald Eagle/Otter Lake Regional Park, where he pulled into a rest area. It was a nice evening and there were a few people gathering up picnic things and fishing poles as they prepared to leave. Two very attractive girls skated by on roller blades and the patriot eyed them appreciatively as they passed. He pulled into a parking space looking out over the lake away from most of the people and shut off the engine. He thought he would wait until full dark and then try to lure John Hughes from his home.

As he settled into his car to wait, the patriot thought of a day he'd spent at a lake long ago. He was six years old, and his family was vacationing at Lake Chetek in northern Wisconsin. Tony and his parents were sharing cabins with Tony's Uncle Harry, and Aunt Jackie, and their kids, Bud, Pete, and Jeannie. All of Tony's cousins were older and bigger than he was, and they spent most of the week tormenting him. Bud liked to put minnows in Tony's soda pop bottles, while Pete and Jeannie enjoyed terrifying the boy by telling him about the horrible monster that lived in the lake and ate children. Tony had tried complaining to his father earlier in the week but learned not to do that after getting a slap on his ear and a stern lesson about being a "sissy." Tony cried to himself and endured the treatment, all the while hoping the week would get over with quickly.

On one of the last days at the lake, Tony was swimming in the beach area with Bud and Pete. Jeannie had suffered a sunburn and was inside covered in lotion. Tony tried to join in the games made up by his cousins, but all of them seemed to have rules that required him to be dunked under water or splashed in the face, so he contented himself with playing around the dock pilings at the edge of the swimming area. He was dog-paddling around under the dock when Bud yelled, "Hey runt! Don't you know that the lake monster lives under there?" Tony had been having doubts about the existence of any lake monster but didn't want to become the object of Bud's attention by arguing with him. He thought it would be a good thing to ignore Bud and show that he was brave and not afraid of lake monsters. Tony paddled around under the dock and swam even further into the deeper regions to prove how bold he was.

"I hear that monster has 250 razor-sharp teeth," Bud observed to Pete.

"Really?" asked Pete, going along with his brother's tale.

"Yep. And huge lips that suck the blood right out of you after it bites. The guy at the store told me that it killed a kid last week."

"You don't say," Pete replied, very interested in the information.

"Yep. A kid from Michigan. Ate him up right under that very dock, there."

Tony was listening, even though he was pretending not to hear, and began to realize how dark and gloomy it was under the boards of the dock. Waves lapped against the wood, and he saw that there were some pretty ugly spiders clinging to the bottom of the dock. He knew that Bud and Pete would make fun of him if he swam out of there now, but his exploring was becoming less fun by the second. Bud continued to regale Pete with stories of lake mayhem and gore as Tony slowly made his way back into the shallows. Finally and mercifully, Tony's mother called out to him that lunch was ready. Tony, glad to finally have an excuse to get out of the lake, waded ashore. As he stepped out of the water he noticed what looked like leaves sticking to his legs and feet. He shook his leg but the leaves remained stuck. He tried to wipe them off, but they seemed to be glued to his skin. He tried to pull on one and his skin pulled painfully out from his leg and the object clung tenaciously. Tony tugged hard on it and the tail coiled around his finger.

"Aaaahhhh!" Tony screamed as he realized he was being eaten. "Bud, Pete! Help! The monster has me!!" Bud and Pete rushed to Tony and saw the leeches on his legs.

"Those are baby monsters, Tony," Bud told him. "They're sucking the blood out of you."

"Oh, no!" Tony cried. "Will I die?"

"Sure enough," Bud said, shaking his head. "They especially like little kids' blood. It's fresher."

"Help me, please!" Tony sobbed.

"We can't," Pete said, getting into the act. "If you hurt the babies, the mother monster comes and bites your head off."

"Noooo!" Tony cried.

"Yeah, and sometimes she bites your dink off!" Bud said.

Tony cried harder at his predicament. and soon his mother came walking from the cabin to see were he was.

"Tony, for God's sake, what is the matter?" she asked, seeing him crying and stamping his feet to try to dislodge the monsters.

"Mommy! I'm dying and these monsters are eating me, and the mother monster is going to come and bite my dink off!" Bud and Pete laughed uproariously at Tony's fear.

"Jesus!" Tony's mother muttered. "Bud, Pete, what have you been telling him?"

"Nothing," both boys said at the same time.

Tony's mother took him by the hand and led him to the cabin where she explained what leeches were while she covered them with table salt so they would let go and drop off his skin. Tony looked at the red circles left behind from the leeches' mouths and swore to himself that he would never swim in a lake again.

Later that evening, while the family was sitting around a campfire toasting marshmallows, Tony went into the cabin to use the bathroom. When he was through he sneaked out the front door and knelt by some rose bushes by the front steps of the cabin. He carefully broke off four sections of thorny branch, each about two inches in length. Tony carried them very gingerly, so as not to be impaled by the sharp points, into the cabin and placed one very carefully into each of Bud and Pete's tennis shoes, being sure to place them well up into the toes where they wouldn't be seen. The next day, Tony was beaten up by Bud and Pete for what he did, but he realized that getting his revenge had been worth it.

"Hey, nice car, *Ese*," a voice said, rousing the patriot from his thoughts. He looked around and saw that his car was surrounded by Latino teenagers. All of them wore blue bandannas either on their heads or around their wrists to indicate their affiliation with the Latin Locos street gang. Standing next to the driver's window was a kid who looked to be about sixteen as he smiled in and rested his right hand on the open window ledge. The patriot saw the star and crossed pitchforks tattooed in the webbing between the kid's thumb and forefinger with the letters "LL" underneath.

"Thank you," he replied.

"This is our park, *Ese*," the kid told him. "You don't belong here."

"I'm sorry, I thought this was a public park," the patriot replied, keeping his voice even.

"In the day, *Ese*, but at night, it's ours."

"Really? Well, I must have missed your sign. I'll have to be more careful in the future." The patriot knew that he was outnumbered and that gangs like this could get ugly fast, especially if they'd been drinking or smoking. He slowly slid his right hand into his jacket and quietly unsnapped the strap on the Hi Power's shoulder holster.

"I think you got to be real careful, *Ese*. I think you should give us something so we'll forgive you."

"Give you something? Hmmm. Like a fine, huh?"

"Yeah, just like a fine. You're trespassing. You need to pay your fine now, *Ese*," the kid said louder as the others laughed. The patriot knew he could pull out his badge and end this bullshit right away. These kids were punks and wouldn't have the balls to fuck around with him anymore if they found out he was a cop. He knew that it would be the smart play. It would allow him to go back to Hughes's house and do what he had come to do. But as the bangers laughed, he heard the sound of Bud and Pete laughing and it occurred to him that little criminals like this were part of the problem he was fighting. After all, he had another gang member on his list. It also occurred to him that if the local police's attention was drawn here, it would be easier for him to get at Hughes on the other side of town.

"Well, I think you should let me go with a warning, *Ese*," the patriot told the kid, mimicking his speech. "I think you should go find something constructive to do, *Ese*. Unless you've got a bigger set of *huevos* in there than I think you do, *you're* the one with the problem, *Ese*." The kid's jaw dropped open as he realized he was being called out by this *gringo*. Here he was, surrounded by his *vatos* and this *loco* was challenging him by himself?

A smarter person would have realized that anyone who was sitting alone in a car in a park after dark just might be dangerous. A smarter person might realize that anyone who smiled without fear at a group of bangers might have a secret. A smarter person might notice that the smiling *gringo* had one hand inside his coat and the other down by his the top of his left boot. But the kid wasn't smart. He was cocky. He was a little drunk and too excited by the prospect of beating the shit out of this *blanco loco* to see where this was heading.

"Fucking *Puto!*" the kid spat as he grabbed the Explorer's locked door handle. He rattled the door with both hands and groped around for the lock. As he reached inside the car, the patriot slit open the back of the kid's right forearm with his Tanto knife. The knife was so sharp that the kid didn't even feel the pain and by the time he realized the guy inside was pointing a gun at his face, it was too late. Two loud cracks sounded inside the car and the kid fell back onto the tar with a neat hole on each side of is nose and most of the back of his head missing. The patriot stepped quickly out of the car and waded into the group of six stunned teenagers. He fired once into each kid as they started backing away. He dropped four before they knew what was happening and then shot the last two as they turned, too late, to run. As they were hit, three of the gang dropped knives they had pulled in anticipation while their leader was taunting the *gringo*.

"Shouldn't bring knives to a gunfight, kids," the patriot told them as he stood among the fallen, wounded bangers. The Hi Power held fifteen rounds and the patriot moved swiftly among the bodies, firing one more round into each head before he wiped the blood off of the Tanto on one of the kid's shirts, climbed into his truck, and sped out of the park.

He drove north on 61 and then turned right onto 120th Street. He pulled over and consulted with his map book before taking off again. He followed the road around until he was once again moving south and took it back to County Road 96. It wasn't long before he was back near the Hughes home on Bald Eagle. He parked around the corner and was walking in the darkness toward the Hughes home when he heard the first sirens. The patriot rightly figured that all of the resources of the White Bear Lake Police Department would be heading toward the regional park once it was discovered that seven people had been shot there. He made his way onto Hughes's street and cut through a neighbor's yard into Hughes's backyard. He walked quickly and quietly to a back window and looked into the living room. The Hughes children were sitting at a coffee table doing homework and their father was sitting at a desk, working at a computer. The patriot breathed hard while he considered his situation. He was full of adrenaline from his confrontation and wanted to have the chance to calm down. Still, Hughes had proven hard to corner, and he was eager to cross the professor off the list.

"Hey, you! Get away from there!" a voice yelled from behind, startling the patriot. A neighbor of Hughes's had evidently seen him looking in the window and taken him for a pervert. The patriot growled in frustration and ran around to the driveway on the side of the house. He looked into Hughes's Subaru and saw a checkbook and cell phone on the seat. The door was unlocked, so he quickly took the items for later use and ran back up the street.

By the time he made it back to his car, the patriot was very frustrated. He was happy to have tangled with the gangbangers but would have liked to have been done with Hughes. He drove back onto the highway and made his way home, where he intended to lift weights and burn off some of his frustration.

John Hughes heard a knock on his door and opened it to see a man he vaguely recognized.

"Hi," the man said. "I'm Ken Richey, I live in the brown house behind you?"

"Oh, sure," Hughes said. "I'm John Hughes. What can I do for you?"

"I just saw someone peeking in your back window."

"What? Just now?" Hughes was amazed.

"Yeah, I saw him standing by your bushes looking in your big window back there."

"Where did he go?"

"Well, I yelled at him and he ran around the side by your driveway. I thought I'd better tell you."

"Yes, I'm glad you did," Hughes told him. "This has never happened to us. Is this the sort of thing we should call the police about?"

"I would," Richey said. "Maybe they can catch him if he's still around."

"Well, I'm sure he's run off," Hughes said. "I'd better look around, though." He got a flashlight from under the kitchen sink and went out with Richey to check the yard.

"He ran right around here, by your car," Richey told Hughes. Hughes shone his light around the driveway and in some bushes near the car. He opened the car door, looked in, and said, "It appears that my cell phone is missing." Hughes's wife joined the two men outside and asked what was going on.

"This is our neighbor, Ken Richey. He saw someone looking in our back window and now it seems that my cell phone has been stolen from the car."

"You're kidding!" Suzanne said.

"Yes, I suppose it's my own fault. I left my phone in here with the doors unlocked."

"Well, if you're going to call the police, they may want to talk to me," Richey told him. "I'll be up for about a half-hour yet if they need to stop by." Richey walked home.

"Dear, is anything else missing besides the phone?" Suzanne asked.

Hughes took another look around inside the car and said, "Did I bring my checkbook in?"

"I don't remember seeing it," she answered. Hughes went back in the house and looked around the kitchen were he kept his wallet and keys.

"I'm afraid I left the checkbook out there, too. It seems to be gone."

"Well, you'd better call the police," his wife told him.

Hughes looked through the phone book's blue government pages and found the non-emergency number for the White Bear Lake Police. He dialed and was surprised that it took nine rings before someone answered and immediately asked him to hold. He stood there for a full minute before the dispatcher came back on the line.

"White Bear Police, can I help you?"

"Yes, er, my name is John Hughes, and it appears as if someone stole my checkbook and cell phone out of my car."

"Mr. Hughes we have an emergency on our hands, and I have no one available to send to your house. Can you call back in the morning?"

"Yes, er, I suppose I can." Hughes hung up feeling rebuked and somewhat annoyed. What could be so important that every cop in town was tied up? Hughes thought. Probably a fire at the doughnut shop.

CHAPTER 24

▼

On Thursday morning, the Patriot Task Force office was alive with activity. The investigators hadn't had time to sort out all the details of their open cases of deaths admitted by the patriot when they were confronted by the death of Andy Stoughten and now were learning of the White Bear Lake Park shootings. Representatives of both the Hastings and the White Bear Lake Police forces had issued statements about their cases which, without declaring it to be fact, strongly hinted that they were prepared to believe that those crimes had been committed by the patriot.

The task force was learning about the park shootings the same way the public was that morning, by reading the account in the paper and watching the most up-to-the-minute news on the morning TV.

"Police are hunting for the person responsible for the violence which erupted last night in Bald Eagle and Otter Lake Regional Parks here in White Bear Lake," the reporter said, gesturing to an area of the parking lot roped off with yellow crime scene tape. "Police were called here at about 10:30 last night when gunshots were heard in the public access boat landing area. When they arrived they found seven youths either dead or severely wounded. Rescue and ambulance units from White Bear Lake and two other neighboring communities were called in to assist with the victims, all of whom had suffered gunshot wounds. Police initially believed the shootings were gang-related, as all of the victims, according to police, were known members of the Latin Locos street gang, and all had extensive juvenile records. However, a witness to the violence, a man who was in the park walking his dog, told them a different story." The picture cut to an interview with a man whose face was blacked out for anonymity.

"I seen this group of kids standing around a dark colored truck," the witness told the reporter. "I thought, gee, that looks kind of fishy. I've seen these groups of kids in this park at night and I don't mind telling you, I give 'em a wide swath. They're always drinkin' and fightin' and carryin' on. Suddenly, I hear one kid yell, and then I hear a couple of bangs. The kid next to the car falls back, and I see this guy get out of the car. Real calm and businesslike, he walks right into this group and starts shooting them. Well, I jumped behind a big tree, and this guy shoots for a real short time, then stops. I looked back around and he's looking at them laying there, like he's seeing if they were alive. Then he, quick like, shoots a couple more times and then takes off."

"Could you see the man who did the shooting?" The reporter asked.

"I couldn't really see his face, it being dark and he moved so fast. I was moving fast, too, I don't mind saying."

"I bet he moved fast," Pete Lincoln said, watching the interview on the office TV. "I bet he filled his Dockers, too."

The news then ran an interview with the White Bear Lake police chief.

"We have not as yet had the opportunity to speak to either of the two victims who survived the shooting rampage," the chief said. "Both are critically injured and we don't have a good prognosis for them. At this time we have identified only one witness who was in the area. He has been very helpful to us but could not provide a good description of the suspect or details about the truck he was driving. It is speculation at this time, but we believe that this incident is the work of one man working alone, it's quite possibly related to the vigilante-type killings which have been going on in the metro area recently."

"The patriot should go to Vegas, the luck he has," John Pappas said to the group watching the interview as the reporter wrapped up the story.

"A spokesperson for Regions Hospital in St. Paul, where the two living shooting victims were taken, told us off-camera that one victim, Hector Zuniga, is believed to have suffered irreversible brain damage and is not expected to recover. The other, who has not been identified, pending notification of relatives, is said to be in a coma and his recovery is, 'doubtful'. We will bring you more at 5:00 p.m. on what may be the latest in a string of related killings."

"This guy is gonna make us chase our tails," Mike Rawlings said disgustedly as he turned down the TV. "I think it's time to do something proactive here."

"Such as?" Gene Truman asked.

"We know the types of targets our boy has been going after, right? High-profile anti-establishment types, ultra-liberal or criminal types. He seems to slant toward child molesters, that sort of thing. How could we go about trying to identify future targets? Who would be considered at-risk?"

"Doesn't a newspaper office have cross-referenced material for stories?" Phil Deane wondered. "For instance, if a reporter is writing about arsons, can't they find cross references for other arson stories? I wonder if our friend Mr. Knox would help us with that."

"That seems as good a place to start as any," Lincoln said. "Besides, it might keep him from writing too many long stories about how our killer wants to form a club."

"Right," agreed Rawlings. "Phil, why don't you go see Knox today and see if the two of you can come up with some names who've been in the paper recently. We know that our man reads the Tribune, maybe they can point us somewhere."

"And if they do," asked Tom McDowell, "do we go to those people and suggest they go on an extended vacation?"

"No," Rawlings answered. "We tell them why we're concerned and question them about any strangers they've met recently. Have they noticed a phone company repairman at their door? Have they seen dark trucks hanging around? Anyone noticed if their garbage has been gone through? We need to find out how this guy operates. And, if it makes potential victims start looking over their shoulders, maybe it will help them to avoid a situation where they might end up on a slab. We can run after this guy from killing to killing and hope he slips up and gets caught, but I'm for trying to get out in front of him. Sure would be nice to have him reacting to us for a change."

Thursday morning the patriot devoted his pre-work time to working out. His hectic schedule as of late had made him eat at off hours and ignore his regular exercise routine. He spent almost two hours lifting weights and working out on the stair-climber in his basement. After showering and dressing, he ate an early lunch of chicken breasts, rice, and salad. While he logged onto the Internet and browsed through news websites, happy to see that he was now front page news on *USA Today* and CNN. He munched on his salad and read through accounts of the murders and what the police in Minnesota had to say about them. He then logged into a website devoted to gun owners and browsed through the discussion forums. He frequented one forum which was supposed to be dedicated to gun owners and saw that there had been a posting on the site already this morning from a person in Texas who used the name "Texshooter." Texshooter related the fact that someone in Minnesota, of all places, was trying to take back the country from the socialists. "Killed himself a judge, four activists, an ACLU snake and now they're saying maybe he killed two child abusers and some Mexican gangsters? Whooee! Send that man some ammo on me, and tell him to keep up the fine work!" The patriot was tempted to answer him but knew better.

Another posting in response to Texshooter was from someone in Maryland called "TRO437." He wrote, "Dude, I'm all for crime control, but some of the people this guy's killed are just kids."

A person called "BIGBALLS1" had this to say to TRO437: "Kids? Wake the fuck up and smell the coffee, *dude*. I don't care if a person is 16 or 60. They can be a hard-core, dangerous criminal and they should be treated that way. Isn't everyone out there sick of the system coddling psychopaths because they're 'young' or 'retarded' or 'abused' or 'poor.' A criminal is just that, nothing more, and we have got way too many of them around and more every day. I'm not saying we need to open fire on everybody, but stop feeling sorry for the bad guys here, *dude* or go and be fitted for your new vagina!"

The patriot got a kick out of that.

Tina Sullivan sat at her workstation at Blue Cross in Eagan, and her mind wandered for the twentieth time that day. It was a beautiful day outside, she could see from her cubicle out a window, and she hated to be cooped up. Part of it was because she was bored with explaining to people for the eight-hundredth time that, yes, you need a referral from your personal physician before you can go to the eye doctor/marriage counselor/sports medicine clinic/psychiatrist, etc. Part of it was her asshole boss who kept staring at her tits whenever he talked to her, part was because she hadn't heard from Jerry, her now ex-boyfriend, and part was because her mind kept wandering to Tony Bauer and the night they'd spent together. She knew that it was a good thing to be done with Jerry; he was an asshole, really. But she thought he would have at least called her once after she moved out, if for no other reason than to let her hang up on him. She thought that having lived with someone for six months would at least require a man to call when his girlfriend moves out after she comes home early and catches him in the shower with a waitress.

But, he hadn't and she was frustrated. Frustrated and more than a little horny. Her mind wandered back to the night with Tony, and she smiled as she remembered how strong he was and how easily he lifted her off the floor and held her to him.

Her sister had warned her that she'd never get close to Tony, that he was too much of a loner and had been hurt by his ex pretty badly. She wished he'd have called her after their night together, but, in fairness, she had left it pretty open when they parted. Telling him that the night was just what she needed kind of sent a message that she had only been interested in a one-night stand, didn't it? She hadn't hinted around with "See you?" or "Let's get together again?" She wondered if it would be okay to call Don and get Tony's number. She could just call him up, make some conversation, and see what developed, right? No strings attached. Would he think she was being too forward, or slutty? Well, she wouldn't be any further behind then, would she?

Just then her line rang, and an older woman asked, "What benefits does my policy provide for exorcism?" Jesus Christ, Tina thought, appropriately.

Phil Deane and James Knox met at Knox's office and Deane laid out the concerns of the task force. "Basically, Mr. Knox, I'm asking if you and your paper would help us screen recent news articles and try to identify potential targets of the patriot."

"Well, Officer, er, Detective…" Knox hesitated and then said, "look, if we're going to work together at all, it would be simpler if you called me Jim."

"I'm Phil," Deane smiled.

"Great. Look, Phil, I have to clear this with my boss. No one, but no one, goes into the morgue here without permission."

"Morgue?" Deane asked.

"Yeah, we call the room where we keep all of our old articles and information 'The Morgue.' All newspapers do. Kind of functions like a real morgue, when you think about it."

"True. Okay, I don't want you getting into any trouble, but if it cuts any ice with your boss, tell him that it's in everyone's best interest that this so-called patriot gets caught soon."

"He knows that, Phil. We report the news but we're human and even though these stories sell papers, we'd prefer to be able to report that the killer's been caught. I'm sure that either I or one of the other guys who are working on this story will be able to help you."

"The paper has other reporters assigned?" Deane asked, somewhat surprised.

"Thought you were the only ones with a task force, didn't you?" Knox answered with a wink.

A few minutes later, Knox returned and said, "I can help you for a couple of hours since my column is finished for today. If you need help tomorrow, come back and ask for Keith Kruse, okay?" Deane nodded and followed Knox down to the building's basement, where Knox used a key card to enter a room filled with rows of shelves, computers, microfiche machines, and marked boxes.

"Wow," Deane commented. "You must have the entire history of the planet stored down here."

"Well, not really," said Knox, "but a good portion of it. Let's see what we can find that's cross referenced with PETA, ACLU, American Communist Party, Socialism and Education. We should also check the police beat for crime stories about sex abuse and activism. Those seem to be our man's hot-button topics, right?"

"Right," Deane answered. "From the looks of this place we'll have our work cut out. I'll be here for weeks."

"It's not as bad as you think," Knox said. "We don't need to read everything. You get a feeling for these files once you start on them, and you don't have to read every word. Scan the page for names you don't know, and note anything that grabs you. I've done some work on this already getting background for my stories, and I've been on the crime beat a long time. We're not totally in the dark." Knox took Deane to a computer terminal and had him pull up a chair. Knox booted the computer up to a search screen and began entering data in the boxed fields. Soon, the computer was listing topics, names, dates, places, and tidbits from articles on file. Knox printed out several pages and showed it to Deane.

"See?" He asked with a smile. "This is where we start."

Both men divided up the work and Knox showed Deane how to pull up items on CD ROM's. They decided not to worry about stories more than five years old since the people who had been selected by the patriot had been the subject of relatively recent news accounts. Both men took off their jackets, Deane loosened his tie, and they got to work.

At 3:30 p.m., Knox and Deane compared notes. They had agreed that Knox would be informed of the names of all the people whom the task force considered to be at risk. He agreed not to publish their names, but the knowledge would certainly give him a leg up on any other reporter in town.

"So, what did you come up with?" Deane asked.

"Well, I started with the crime beat 'cause that's easiest and what I'm most familiar with," Knox answered. "Here's a list of people who were arrested but were found not guilty or were released for lack of evidence. I put the file numbers next to each in case you want to go back for more details." He offered Deane another group of pages stapled together. "Here's a list of names from stories about environmental and political activists and their brushes with the law. I included stories about the victims we already know about. I thought you might need them in your case files."

"Yes, thank you, I appreciate that." Deane said.

"Okay, here's something else I found that looked interesting." He handed an article to Deane and waited until he'd read it through. "I wonder, do you think he would have the balls to go after this guy?"

"Jim," Deane said, "I think he's capable of most anything."

"It occurred to me while I was going through these that we in the media have really done a lot of the patriot's work for him. We've put people on display, announced their names, even said where they lived in some cases. Which reminds me, do you know how he found some of these people? I couldn't find any reference to the Minneapolis address for those kids killed near the University."

"No, not yet," Deane answered. "We were able to locate some of the victims through Internet searches even if they were unlisted in the phone book, but he has some source of information that we haven't tracked down yet."

"What did you find?" Knox asked.

"I've got a list of people identified with PETA, here." Deane gave Knox a copy of the list. "I also have the names of some of the World Trade activists who were involved in the confrontation in Minneapolis not long ago. I also discovered that Ruth Schoen-Williams will be autographing her book at Bookends book store in Minnetonka next week. She's the one who wrote the book about child sexuality that made waves in the national media. I think our man would object to her views. Also, remember this guy?" He pointed to a name on the list.

"Hughes," Knox read. "Oh, the Macalester professor who wrote the diversity textbook. Yeah, he made waves. Even in the national media."

"Well, this is as good a starting point as any. I'll run these by my associates and get back to you," Deane said.

"Phil, remember, I have to have something to take back to my boss, or he'll think we're trading off good information for no return."

"Jim, I haven't hidden anything from you. Off the record?" Knox nodded. "We're totally in the dark now. This?" He gestured around at the work they'd done. "This is grasping at straws. The fact is, we need this guy to mess up. That, or we need a real breakthrough, such as how he finds these people, or if someone he's confided in comes forward. Until that happens we're just trying to make up lost ground."

"Do you think he'll confide in someone or mess up?"

"We know he wants others to follow him. He's proven pretty cagey so far, but I think he'll feel the need for acceptance or validation to bolster his belief in his cause. Let's hope he tries to recruit someone who sees him for what he is."

A short time later at the Task Force office, Deane shared his and Knox's findings with the rest of the group. They discussed some of the names and their potential as targets for the patriot. They all agreed that it would be wise to interview the subjects, if possible. Some of the names on the list belonged to people who didn't make a habit of chatting with the police. Deane showed them the one name that Knox had thought stood out.

"He'll be coming here in two weeks," Deane said.

"Now *THAT* would require some major balls," Pete Lincoln commented. "Does the article get into more detail about where and when he'll be speaking?"

"Minneapolis Hilton, June 1st, 8:00 p.m.," Deane answered. "Nothing about security, mostly who's sponsoring the dinner and the cost. Do these guys travel with Secret Service protection or what? I guess I've really never heard."

"We need to find out," Rawlings said. "I'll call in the morning. Let's divide up the list and get going first thing tomorrow. Did Knox pump you at all?"

"I was up front with him. I told him, off the record, that we were stumped and waiting for a break. He won't print that. I think he's an up-front guy."

"He's also a reporter," Gene Truman said.

"I told him that we thought that sooner or later the patriot would need validation or acceptance and would have to confide in somebody. Hopefully, that person will come to us."

"Oh, yeah," Tom McDowell said. "You weren't here earlier. I was doing some Internet searches looking for gossip or stories about the patriot. Look at these." He handed Deane a handful of printed sheets from web pages he'd been looking through. "You say he'll need validation?" Deane leafed through the pages and shook his head in disgust.

"My God," Deane muttered as he looked through dozens of comments praising the patriot for jobs well done. "Page after page."

"Yeah, and those are just the ones I found. There are almost as many discussion and chat pages devoted to politics as there are to titties. If our man has Internet access he's found his audience."

CHAPTER 25

▼

On Friday morning James Knox woke up and, after disposing of a critically injured chipmunk left proudly on the hood of his car by Jeeves, drove to work. As he walked in the press room, he saw Dave Joyner frantically waving for him to come into the editor's office.

"Jim, you got another blank envelope with a floppy inside. It's in my safe. I've called the police, and they'll be here in 15 minutes." The newspaper had agreed to handle any further suspected letters from the patriot as little as possible and allow them to be fingerprinted by the police before the contents were read. Since the envelopes were addressed to Knox, the task force had agreed to allow Knox to open them, and he had promised to give them copies immediately.

After about half an hour, Mike Rawlings arrived with a fingerprint technician he'd picked up at the Hennepin Sheriff's Crime Lab, which was based only a few blocks from the newspaper building. Knox joined them and Sam Graham in Joyner's office. Joyner opened the safe, and the technician donned a pair of rubber gloves before removing the envelope. He slit the side of the envelope with a knife and let the floppy slide out onto Joyner's desk.

"I assume you have no need for this," he asked, holding up the envelope. "I'd like to take it back and try to get DNA off of the seal and then Ninhydrin it for prints." The lab tech explained that Ninhydrin is a chemical spray which, when sprayed onto a paper surface, will reveal fingerprints.

"We don't want the envelope, just the floppy," Joyner answered. The technician then opened his case and carefully ran a light brush with powder over both sides of the floppy.

"Nothing at all here," he said. "Looks like a glove smudge in the corner."

"I'd be surprised if he didn't wear gloves," Rawlings said. "He's going to the extreme of sending floppies."

"Why floppies?" Graham asked Rawlings. "Why not just a letter composed on a computer?"

"Floppies are untraceable. If you use a typewriter, the machine will leave tiny marks which can then be compared to that machine when you find your suspect later. Similarly, a computer printer can leave identifying marks from its flaws and imperfections. We'll keep the envelope to make comparisons in case we find his printer. Also, printing ink can be analyzed to tell us the brand of the printer used. A new, unused floppy bears no imprint or identifying characteristics from being put inside a computer."

The technician declared the floppy worthless from a forensic standpoint and cleaned the powder off so it could be viewed. Joyner popped it into his computer and opened the single document it contained. Everyone crowded around the monitor and read the letter as Joyner slowly scrolled through.

"Well, this confirms his involvement in the Montgomery and Stoughten murders," Rawlings said.

"I assume you'll be taking over those cases?" Knox asked.

"That's right," Rawlings answered.

"What do you think about the White Bear Lake shootings? Patriot, copycat or someone else?"

"Could be any of the above. It hasn't really fit the patriot's pattern of selecting and stalking his victims over time. On the other hand, the businesslike manner in which the suspect carried out the crime is consistent with what we've seen from the patriot in the past, including this habit of wiping his knife clean on the victims' clothing. I'd find it hard to believe there is more than one person in the metro area right now as brutal and calculating and as efficient a killer as the patriot," Rawlings said.

"In this letter, the patriot ends with an encouragement to others to follow his lead. Are you concerned about copycats?"

"Very. It's the last thing we need now."

"Detective Rawlings, are you aware that the patriot has become something of a celebrity on the Internet? Many right-wing groups are hailing him as a hero. Saying he's handing out long-overdue justice."

"I am aware of that," Rawlings answered. "And I think it's a sad commentary on our times that a man would be called a hero who brutally kills people with whom he disagrees. Several of the victims weren't criminals, just people who held opinions different from the patriot. I can't understand the justice in killing them."

"Do you have any thoughts on the opinions the patriot expressed in this letter concerning lawyers and the nation being infected with a virus?"

"Just that it shows me that he is very disturbed. Look, America isn't perfect, and there are problems I wish would be fixed. I might even go so far as to agree with the patriot on a couple of his points. But when you're looking for reasons why this guy does what he does, you always have to return to the central fact that he is using these reasons to justify murder. I hope that, if people are concerned for their country and really want to effect change, they will do so without violence. You can't use political differences as a license to commit murder."

That night at work, Tony Bauer met Mike Fitz at a little restaurant called Little Oscar's. After ordering two coffees, Mike said, "I didn't get a chance to talk with you yesterday. I got involved in a real cluster-fuck with Social Services over a family living in a garbage house. It's funny how they always want us to make a decision for them but then complain that we didn't do enough."

"Yeah," Bauer agreed. "They can save the world as long as someone stands next to them holding the manual."

"I wanted to ask you if you called Children's Hospital," Fitz said.

"No. Why would I do that?"

"I figured you might be curious about how the Steiger baby was doing."

"She lived?"

"No, they pulled the plug on her a little while ago. The parents were reluctant, but the doctors told them there was no hope."

"These aren't rocket scientists, Mike. You remember I booked that guy for beating the shit out of the girl just a couple weeks ago."

"I remember. Still, it's gotta be a hard decision for them. Pulling the cord on your only child."

"Probably want sympathy," Bauer said. "Hope that everyone will feel sorry for them and give them special treatment."

"Oh, I think that's a little strong. They must be pretty overwhelmed. Someday you'll have a child and know how close you get to it."

Bauer felt a flash of anger and pain at Fitz's comment. He knew that Fitz didn't know about Amber's abortion and wouldn't have said that if he had, but he flashed to the dream and the needle sliding into the soft spot on his son's head.

"I was a little concerned about you, though," Fitz went on. "I delivered two babies and I still send them birthday cards. You get a sense of responsibility for them." Fitz eyed Bauer carefully. "I thought you might have gotten a little down when you found out about this."

"Well, I kind of figured that was going on when they flew her out," Bauer said. "I knew that it didn't look good."

"Yeah, it made me sad to see that girl crying like that. Probably doesn't have much right going on in her life anyway and now has to deal with losing her baby."

Bauer made a disgusted face and said, "Her problems are her own making. If she really cared about that baby she wouldn't have smoked and drunk and done meth. Now she can go on partying to her heart's content. The only thing that bothers me is that she'll probably have a bunch more kids and that she'll have the chance to really fuck the next ones up by trying to raise them."

"Well, maybe I'm a softie. I just thought you might be upset, is all."

"Well, thanks, Mike, but I'm not. Not in the least."

Mike Rawlings sat in the Task Force office long after the others had gone home for the night. The rest of the crew hadn't been thrilled when he'd returned from the newspaper office with the news that the patriot had confessed to killing two more. The case was out of control, and they all knew they were no closer to finding their man than they were the night Judge Borgert was killed.

Rawlings paged through the cases searching for something that had been overlooked. He thought that the answer was in there, somewhere. Sharon Bluhm stopped by on her way out to the parking lot and looked in at Rawlings. She shook her head and said, "Mike, don't let this case drive you nuts. He'll make a mistake. He's too driven, too disturbed, to go on much longer."

"Well he's gone on for quite a while, hasn't he?"

"Not really. It took years to catch Bundy and some others. The patriot hasn't been active long, he's just been *very* active."

"Sharon, how do we catch this guy? The public, the press, even the police departments are calling asking what's going on. I'm no cherry, but I've never done one like this before."

"You know the answer to that, Mike. Slow and steady wins the race. Keep the faith and do what you do best. He'll make a mistake." Rawlings winked at Bluhm as she walked out the door.

Rawlings thought about the killer. He has an equal hatred of government figures and criminals. He claims he'll keep on with his "campaign" so we can assume he has a list he's working through. He hit two child molesters in what we can assume is the early stage of his "campaign," so maybe he's a victim of molestation. Maybe he's worked with kids. Could he be a social worker? Hard to believe; they're pretty soft. He picked a judge first. Who hates judges? Skinheads? How about the Posse Commitatus folks who were running around a few years ago? Any of them left? They hated the government. Any militia-types around? Rawlings made a note to call the FBI in the morning with those questions. There has to be some history here...he's too brutal. Lopping off Montgomery's head with a fucking sword! Crushing Soderberg's head in a vise, for Christ's sake? Did he stand fast against that group of bangers in the park? Pretty ballsy. Knows how to talk to intimidating people, at least long enough to shoot them one by one, like fish in a barrel. Reminds me of Jerry Brown, he way he could wade into a group of legitimate bad guys and stroll out dragging his suspect behind. Rawlings smiled when he thought of Brown, who had been his first partner on the street, a cop who was afraid of no man on earth, and who had taught Rawlings everything he needed to know about what it meant to be The Man. Jerry hated child molesters, too. Said there was a special corner of Hell reserved just for them. Jerry was a good cop who genuinely cared about people, but he wasn't what was known today as *politically correct*. For example, when they were walking a foot beat at the Winter Carnival, a teenage boy kept saying "Oink, oink" every time they walked past. After the third pass, Jerry had grabbed the kid by the collar and yanked him to a standing position. "I hear one more oink," Jerry told him, looking him squarely in the eye, "and you'll be picking your teeth out of your ass."

Just then, Rawlings's thoughts were interrupted by the ringing of his cell phone.

"Mike Rawlings."

"Yeah, is this the Patriot Task Force?" a female voice asked.

"Yes."

"This is Sergeant Lori Stiles of the Minneapolis PD. We have a suspect in custody who might be your man."

"I'm on my way. Where are you?"

"Second Precinct."

"I'll be right there."

Rawlings pulled into a space in front of the Minneapolis Police's Second Precinct office. The precinct covered the north side of the city, which was known as the toughest part of town. It had more violent crime within its confines than all the other five precincts put together. Rawlings walked in, showed his ID to the desk sergeant, and asked for Sergeant Stiles. A short time later, a tall muscular woman, dressed in the light blue uniform of a Minneapolis Police sergeant, came out and offered her hand.

"Agent Rawlings? I'm Lori Stiles."

"Pleasure to meet you," Rawlings said as he admired her firm handshake. "What do you have?"

"One of our patrol units was doing a field interview on a suspected flasher at the corner of Broadway and Emerson when they heard shots. They heard tires squeal and then saw a pickup come barreling around the corner from Dupont. The truck loses it and smashes through a store front right in front of them, and the driver tries to bail. They drew down on him and find a 9mm pistol on the floor near his feet. The car reeks of gun smoke, and they throw cuffs on him. Then they hear yelling, and a guy comes running around the corner screaming that the guy had just shot at him. Turns out that there's a Muslim mosque on Dupont, and the faithful were standing around outside getting ready to go inside, when this guy in the truck cruises by twice and then opens fire. He hit an old guy, who'll probably be okay, and a young guy, who just got a flesh wound out of it. When the arresting officers asked him why he did it, he told them that he was, quote, 'A patriot who is concerned about America.' We held off on questioning him any further, thinking that you would have bigger issues to discuss with him."

"Have you assigned an investigator?" Rawlings asked.

"No, for this type of thing we'd just put him on a Probable Cause hold at the jail and let the day investigators have him, but we figured we should call you."

"Yeah, I'm glad you did. Is he talkative?"

"Too much so. Keeps rattling on about the government, criminals, all that."

"What's his name?"

"Gary Benson. Lives in Brooklyn Center," Stiles answered.

"All right. Where is he?"

Stiles led Rawlings down a hall to a locked interview room. Rawlings had pictured in his mind what it would be like when he finally came face to face with the patriot, and he had a mental image of an intricate war of wills and intellects in which he would have to be in top form in order to wrangle a confession out of his quarry. Stiles opened the door and Rawlings saw a fat, balding man in a stained softball jersey and jeans. Benson was handcuffed to the table and the odor of alcohol was pronounced in the small room.

"Mr. Stiles? My name is Mike Rawlings. I'm with the Minnesota Bureau of Criminal Apprehension. I'd like to talk with you if that's okay with you."

"Sure," Benson slurred.

Rawlings turned on a tape recorder he'd brought with him and said, "The date is Friday, May 17, 2002. The time is 7:45 p.m. and I am Mike Rawlings from the Minnesota BCA. I'm in the Minneapolis PD Second Precinct office. With me is Gary Benson. Mr. Benson, I'd like to tell you that you are currently under arrest. You have the right to remain silent. Anything you say can and will be used against you in a court of law. You have the right to an attorney, and, if you can't afford an attorney, one will be appointed to represent you, if you wish. You can decide at any time to exercise these rights and not answer any questions or make any statements. Do you understand?"

"Yeah."

"Would you agree to give me a statement?"

"Definitely. Let's get this shit out in the open," Stiles slurred, and Rawlings began to have misgivings that he was finally face-to-face with the patriot.

Rawlings ran through some preliminary questions and then asked Benson why he had shot up the men on the corner by the mosque.

"They are the people who are responsible for what happened on September Eleventh! Those camel-fuckers! Rag heads come to this country and ruin our way of life with their refusing to learn the language and bringing different ideas and shit. I need to let the people know that these foreigners need to be run off! The country will be better for it." Benson waved his arms dramatically while he spoke.

"Mr. Benson, how much have you had to drink tonight?"

"Jus' a couple of beers."

"Mr. Benson, you are aware that a number of murders have been committed by a person who calls himself 'a patriot,' correct?"

"Tha's right. A fuckin' patriot. Tha's what I am."

"Mr. Benson, do you ask me to believe that you are responsible for these previous crimes?"

"I am a patriot. I'm sick of all these perverts and foreigners coming here, taking our jobs and dressing funny. I shot at those guys on the corner, and I'm an American, through and through!"

"Mr. Benson, have you ever been to the Prairie Island Indian Community?"

"I heard about it. It's by the casino, right?"

"I asked if you'd ever been there," Rawlings repeated.

"I've been there," Benson said.

"Did you kill a person in that community?"

"Damn straight. A real pain-in-the-ass foreigner."

"What was the name of the person?" Rawlings asked, certain now that his time was being wasted.

"You're so smart, you tell me!" Benson answered pugnaciously.

"Mr. Benson, I'm a very busy man. If you expect me to believe that you are the man responsible for all these murders, you have to give me some proof. How did you kill Wallace Berry?"

"Who?"

"Wallace Berry. The head of the Royal Canadian Orchestra. He was a small man, always wore a red football helmet?"

"Fuckin' bastard. I shot him!" Benson said.

"I see. Thank you." Rawlings got up and left the room. He went out and was met in the hall by Sergeant Stiles.

"I'm really sorry to waste your time," Stiles said with a meek look on her face.

"No. Don't apologize," Rawlings said as he shook his head, thinking about Benson. "These things happen. It looked good for a minute there, anyway."

"Are you any closer to catching the real guy?" Stiles asked.

"Well, let's put it this way, if he and I were the last people on earth, I'd be 100 percent sure I had the right man."

CHAPTER 26

▼

On Saturday morning, Mike Rawlings, Phil Deane, and Pete Lincoln gathered in the Task Force office. They had agreed that the force would work weekends, at least for a while, and that the group would split up into two, one working on Saturday and the other on Sunday, so they could maintain some semblance of a life outside of the investigation. Working nonstop with no opportunity to go home and maintain perspective was unhealthy. The investigators would become distracted thinking about things that needed to be addressed in their private lives, and their work would suffer eventually.

The three watched the top-of-the hour news on CNN, where the patriot killings were the lead story. The news giant had flown two of their best reporters, Peter Sciaccio and Tori Bellows, to the Twin Cities, and Sciaccio led off the first story while standing in front of the pavilion at Vermillion Falls Park where Andy Stoughten had been killed.

"Police in Minnesota are hunting for a man who has admitted to killing eight people in what he has termed as an effort to rid society of criminals and those he feels are a threat to American values," Sciaccio said. "The man, who refers to himself only as 'a patriot' is also a suspect in the mass shooting of seven young men in a park late Wednesday evening.

"The suspect has sent two letters to a local reporter admitting to the crimes, the latest being the murder of Peter Montgomery, a former Catholic priest and accused child molester, and Andrew Stoughten, a five-time convicted child molester. Stoughten's murder occurred in this park Tuesday night," Sciaccio said as he gestured to the pavilion. A couple of kids on bikes could be seen in the background smirking at the camera and waving. "CNN has learned that last night Minneapolis police arrested a man named Gary Benson who they believe was involved in a copycat crime when he fired into a group of Muslim men standing outside a mosque in that city. Two men were wounded, but both are expected to recover fully. The suspect was interviewed by a member of the joint law enforcement task force which has been formed to try to locate the killer. A spokesperson for the police would not reveal any details of the interrogation other than to say that it had been determined that Benson was not responsible for the other 'patriot' crimes.

"This is Peter Sciaccio, reporting for CNN."

The anchorwoman said, "Police across the nation are bracing for the possibility of other violence related to the events unfolding in Minnesota. In Texas, a man claiming to be a tax protester was arrested after he was caught firing seven shots into the courthouse in Lubbock, and another man was shot and wounded by police in Fairfax, Virginia, after he opened fire on a county jail work crew, who were cleaning ditches along a busy stretch of Highway 50. None of the workers were hit, but county officials have suspended the use of prisoner work crews for the time being. The suspect, identified as Albert Topp, was pursued by police after the incident and was seriously injured after he fired shots at officers.

"CNN reporter Tori Bellows also spoke with Dr. Sharon Bluhm, a criminal psychologist with the Minnesota BCA and a consultant to the task force about the recent violence."

The picture switched to Bluhm sitting in office against a backdrop of books in the background.

"Dr. Bluhm," Bellows began, "what is your assessment of the events that are unfolding in Minnesota?"

"Ever since the terrorist attacks of September Eleventh, we've noted a growing sense of dissatisfaction with the government's ability to protect us and a resurgence of distrust toward people of foreign birth around us," Bluhm answered. "I believe that a segment of the population harbors a positive image of vigilante justice but their desire for swift retaliation for the attacks has been somewhat stifled. Osama bin Laden was quickly offered up to Americans as the mastermind behind the attacks and, as yet, no one seems to know where he is. The American public wants very much to see him caught and punished so they can feel safe again. I believe that some people, such as this man who calls himself 'a patriot,' think that they can do something the government hasn't been able to do, which is to make themselves feel safe."

"Do you think this vigilante mind-set will spread? If so, how bad will it be?" Bellows asked.

"I can give you only my opinion," Bluhm smiled. "I think this vigilante mind-set will be a very large problem until this man, this so-called 'patriot' is caught. Those personalities who choose to emulate his actions identify strongly with him, but, when he is caught, that sense of identity will evaporate."

"Great," Pete Lincoln said to the TV. "I can see it now. A whole bunch of rednecks around the country blastin' away at chain gangs, black folk, powwows, faggots holding hands and what-all, and cops everywhere sayin' 'Don't look at us; tell those dumb bastards in Minneapolis to catch the guy.'"

Rawlings and Deane laughed despite their growing unease. "Well, the national spotlight is on us now for sure," Deane said. "I read James Knox's column in today's paper. He tried to balance out the story with some tough quotes from you, Mike, and a U of M sociologist, but it still reads like a call to arms for revolution."

"Yeah," Rawlings said. "I was afraid of this. Let's see if we can do some containment and maybe eliminate a few targets. I'm going to head up to White Bear Lake and try to talk to that professor Hughes. Pete, can you hit a few of those on the list who were publicized as getting off on their charges, and, Phil, try to interview some of the PETA and activist types. Whoever we can't reach we'll leave for Tom, Gene, and John tomorrow."

"Sure," Lincoln said. "You go to White Bear to talk to a teacher, and we get to check under rocks like that Australian snake guy."

Rawlings smiled and said, "I'll trade. My next interview is Fred Corly, the guy who got caught with 300 stolen pairs of women's underwear in his apartment, and who liked to masturbate in front of a girls' gym class in St. Paul. He's out of St. Peter State Hospital now."

"No thanks," Lincoln said. "Guys like that make me wanna walk naked through the touchless car wash."

As Mike Rawlings was driving north toward White Bear Lake, the patriot was also northbound on Interstate 35E. It was 9:15 a.m., and both men had the same destination. The patriot had altered his disguise, thinking that the ball cap and handlebar moustache had been seen too often. He had gotten his hair cut shorter than usual and was wearing a blond wig which just covered the tops of his ears. He wore a tweed snap-brim cap, and his tan windbreaker to cover his shoulder holster. He moved his tongue around and felt that his false goatee had not shifted and seemed to be secure. Because it was a hot morning, he had the air conditioning on, so he wouldn't sweat and dissolve the glue.

John Hughes's cell phone and checkbook were in his glove box. The patriot hoped to be able to finally scratch this name off his list.

John Hughes was in his garage preparing to mow his lawn when he saw the stranger pull into his driveway. Hughes wasn't much of a socializer and kept a pretty routine schedule. Rarely did someone to visit him unannounced, especially on a Saturday morning. He wiped his hands with a rag to remove the gasoline he had accidentally splashed on them and walked out to the car in his drive. A man got out and said, "John Hughes?"

"Yes, I'm Hughes, and you are?"

The man pulled a wallet out of his pocket and said, "Mike Rawlings, Minnesota Bureau of Criminal Apprehension. Could I have a few minutes of your time?"

"What's this about?" Hughes asked.

"I have a concern for your safety, Mr. Hughes. Could we go inside and talk?"

"Well, my wife and children are inside. I'd rather not upset them. Let's talk out here."

Hughes led Rawlings to a patio around the back, where they sat down on metal patio chairs.

"Could I offer you some coffee?" Hughes asked.

"No, thank you very much," Rawlings answered. "I won't take up very much of your time. It looks like you're getting ready to do some yard work."

"Yes, I like to mow before it gets too hot. Am I in some sort of trouble?"

"No, not at all. Mr. Hughes, I assume you've been following the news recently and know about the killings attributed to a man who calls himself 'a patriot'?"

"Yes, I've heard of them. We don't watch a lot of television, so I may not be very well informed. He's been killing activists, isn't that right?"

Amazing, Rawlings thought. *This guy writes textbooks for school kids, but knows so little about what's going on in the world around him.*

"Yes, activists, people he thinks are warping American values, and criminals he believes haven't been punished for their crimes. He has been very active. He's killed eight people that we know of and he may be responsible for the seven youths shot here in your city the other night."

"Yes, I heard about that. Five dead?"

"Six, now. The seventh is expected to recover. I'm heading up the task force which has been formed to try to locate and stop this man. We know that he has a list of future victims and that he's been working his way through the list. We haven't confirmed yet that the shootings in the park here were really his work. It may have been that he just took advantage of an opportunity while he was doing something else, or it may have been the work of someone else altogether. We don't know right now."

"I see," Hughes said, "but does this relate to me?"

"My colleagues and I have identified a pattern in the patriot's selection of his victims. All of them have received media attention recently in which they were involved in something controversial. Two, a judge and an attorney, had been portrayed in the media as extremely liberal. Two victims made the news when they were accused of molestation. Others had been involved in animal rights and anti-nuclear power causes. We think that the patriot is attempting to rid the world of people whom he sees as having anti-American values."

"Well, the right to protest and disagree is an American value."

"I agree. The problem is, the patriot does not. He has been in contact with a local reporter and has expressed exactly the sentiments I mentioned. This reporter and one of our investigators have gone through last year's news articles and assembled a list of people in this area who may be potential targets for the patriot. Your name is on that list because of the controversy which surrounded your diversity textbook a short time ago."

"This is incredible. You think someone would want to kill me because I wrote a book?"

"Not just any book, Professor. You did know about the strong criticism from parents about your book, didn't you?"

"Of course, but I think that the idea that someone would feel so threatened by it that they would try to kill me is silly."

"Professor, I hope that we're wrong and you are right. Unfortunately, you do share some similarities with the type of person the patriot has told us he intends to kill."

"Nonsense."

"Professor, please read these two letters we've received from the patriot. He is quite outspoken about educators. Here." Rawlings handed Hughes the letters, who read through them, grimacing at the callous references to the murders.

"He's obviously insane." Hughes said.

"He may be," Rawlings agreed. "However, he is very skilled at killing and leaving no evidence behind to incriminate himself. We don't have any suspects at this time that we could follow, so, until we do, we're trying to caution some people we think might be at risk."

"And you think I'm at risk?" Hughes asked.

"Yes, you among others. The patriot hasn't provided us with any other information, so we're casting a large net and trying to educate as many people as possible."

"In what? What am I supposed to do? Leave the state? Not teach my classes?"

"No. What I'm asking you to do is to be aware of any situation where you may be lured somewhere alone or approached by a stranger. This man is cunning and, as you have read, prides himself on his ability to talk his way into his victim's homes. If you are contacted by a stranger, especially a white male with a muscular build, please try to not be alone with him."

"Detective, I'm a college professor," Hughes smiled. "I'm alone with muscular young men all the time."

"I understand," Rawlings said. "I have a moral and ethical responsibility to warn you that I believe you might be in danger. How you choose to address that is your business."

Inside, the phone rang. Hughes said, "It's all right, my wife will get it. This sounds like extreme paranoia to me. You do realize that you've made a list of potential victims using your own criteria. You don't really know what criteria this patriot might be using. The disturbed mind usually doesn't follow logical thought patterns."

"Professor, you're right. However, we've assembled a pretty good group of experienced investigators and are consulting with premier criminal psychologists in an effort to try to get inside this man's mind."

The patio door opened, and Hughes's wife stepped out holding a cordless phone, "Oh, hello," she said. "I didn't realize you had company, John. It's the police,"

"How did you know he was from the police?" Hughes asked her.

"What? No, on the phone. It's the police on the phone."

"Oh." Hughes took the phone and said, "Hello?...Yes...Yes, I am...No. Where?...Well, is it necessary for me to come there?...I see...Okay, I'll be along directly." Hughes hung up and said to Rawlings, "Well, it appears to be my day for talking to the police. That was the White Bear Lake Police. They've found my stolen checkbook and cell phone. They want me to come over to claim it."

"Were your phone and checkbook stolen?" Rawlings asked.

"Yes, from my car the other night. An officer has them and I have to leave to pick them up. Do we need to discuss anything further? I shouldn't be long. You're welcome to stay."

"Thank you, but I think we've covered what I wanted to discuss with you. Here's my card." Rawlings handed Hughes his card, and Hughes stuck it in his pants pocket. "Call me if you have any questions or concerns."

"Thank you, but I'm certain I'll be fine."

"John, what's this about?" Hughes' wife asked.

"Suzanne, this is Detective Rawlings from…what agency was it?"

"The BCA," Rawlings said. "Pleased to meet you." He and Suzanne shook hands.

"Mr. Rawlings is concerned that someone may be out to get me for writing my diversity textbook," Hughes said with a smile.

"Who?"

"Well, I don't think it's really that much to be concerned about. I have to go, I told the officer I would come straight away. Mr. Rawlings, thank you for your concern and good luck in your investigation." Hughes shook Rawlings's hand and walked to the garage. Rawlings got in his car and saw the look of concern on Suzanne's face as he backed out. He decided to go around the block and return after Hughes had left. If Hughes wouldn't look out for his own safety, maybe his wife could convince him to do so. Rawlings drove slowly until he saw Hughes's car pull out and he circled the block. Suzanne was still in the drive when Rawlings returned.

"Ma'am, I think I may have left a notebook here," Rawlings lied. "Could I see if it's still on the patio?"

"Of course," Mrs. Hughes led the way back to the patio and said, "No, I'm sorry, it doesn't appear to be here."

"Well, I wonder where I could have left it."

"Detective, is my husband in some sort of danger?" she asked.

"Well, I don't know that for sure. I told him that I was working with a task force to catch the man who's been killing activists and people in the area whose views he disagrees with."

"Oh, that 'patriot' man. I was reading about him in the paper."

"Yes. We've taken what we've learned about him so far and tried to come up with a list of people we think might be at risk from him. The killer is fixated on people who, he thinks, are trying to change America. He's very conservative and views such things as your husband's textbook as threatening American values. We may be way off-base, but we think your husband might be the type of person the patriot might target. I just asked your husband to be very careful about meeting with strangers and to be wary of unusual situations that he may find himself in— particularly strangers who want to come into your house."

"I can imagine that John wasn't very keen on your advice," Mrs. Hughes said. "He is the classic professor, I'm afraid. I'm usually the one who worries about potential problems. John is very much a man who refuses to worry about things in the abstract."

"Well, I hope I'm wrong. The patriot is very cunning and seems to have a knack for finding people's weak points and then taking advantage of them."

"How many people are on your list?" Mrs. Hughes asked.

"I hope more than are on the patriot's," Rawlings answered. He returned to his car and was just getting in when Suzanne Hughes came walking back down the driveway.

"Mr. Rawlings, is it normal for the police to ask someone to go and get property that's been found? They wouldn't just bring it to you?"

"Not necessarily. Usually you have to go to the police station and claim your property."

"Well, it's odd, then, that John went the way he did. The police department is the other way. If he was in a hurry, he should have gone south, but he went north."

"When were the phone and checkbook stolen?" Rawlings asked.

"Wednesday night."

"The same night as the park shootings. What time?"

"I don't recall. After 10, I think."

Right after the park shootings. Could they have been a diversion? Rawlings thought.

"Mrs. Hughes, what exactly happened Wednesday night?"

"Well, our neighbor in back saw a man looking in our window and yelled at him to go away. The man ran around the side of the house, and the neighbor came and told us. John looked in his car and saw that his phone and checkbook were missing. Since the man ran right by there, we assumed he must have taken it."

"Did you call the police?"

"John tried, but the police said they were too busy, and they asked him to call back the next morning."

"And did he?" Rawlings asked.

"No, he went to class. Come to think of it, he never did call back, said it was a waste of time."

"So the police have no record that those items were stolen. That seems odd."

"Why?" Mrs. Hughes asked.

"Well, if the police found a checkbook, they would call the owner to see if it was missing. Since the police had no record of the items having been stolen, it seems to me that whichever officer called your husband would have made inquiries about when the items were stolen and from where and if a report had been made. Police are very particular about keeping records straight. That was a pretty short conversation your husband had on the phone."

"It could be that they would get all that when he came down, though, right?"

"Possibly." Rawlings pulled out his cell phone and dialed information. He got the number for the White Bear Lake PD and called.

"Hi, this is Agent Mike Rawlings of the BCA. Can you tell me if one of your officers is dealing with a found property matter right now? Are they all accounted for? I see. Can I speak to your on duty supervisor right away? Yes, it's an emergency."

"What's wrong?" Mrs. Hughes asked.

"Maybe nothing, I just want to be sure," Rawlings told her. "Hello, what was your name?"

"This is Sergeant Pressman, how can I help you?"

"Sergeant, I'm Mike Rawlings with the BCA."

"Oh, I've met you before," Pressman said. "We met a few years ago on a death investigation."

"That's right. Ken, isn't it?" Rawlings asked.

"Kent."

"Kent, sorry. Listen Kent, I'm in your city at the home of John Hughes, 4819 Bald Eagle Avenue. While I was talking to him, someone claiming to be from your department called saying that they had recovered Hughes's missing cell phone and checkbook and asked him to come and claim it. The odd thing is, Hughes left going the opposite direction from your PD, and the items were never reported as stolen."

"Is Hughes a suspect in something?" Pressman asked.

"No, I'm working the patriot investigation and we think Hughes might be at risk because of his notoriety from that diversity text. I'm concerned he may have been lured out."

"Oh my God!" said Suzanne, covering her face with her hands.

"Hold on a second, Mike," Pressman said. "I'll make sure no one's dealing with this." Pressman put Rawlings on hold.

"Mrs. Hughes, please don't get alarmed. This all may be explained in a minute here." After a couple of minutes, Pressman came back on the line.

"Mike, we've got six people on right now, and no one's working any found phone or checkbook."

"I see. Can you get some squads and head to this area? Let's work north looking for a green Subaru Legacy. Mrs. Hughes, is the Legacy in your husband's name?"

"Both of our names," she answered.

"Kent, I'm going to give you John Hughes's middle name and DOB. Can you get your dispatch to run a check and get the plate number?"

"Sure."

"Mrs. Hughes, what is your husband's middle name?" Rawlings asked her.

"His middle name is Daniel. What else do you need?"

"His birth date."

"May 14, 1963." Rawlings relayed the information to Pressman, and they agreed to meet at the Hughes home. Rawlings also gave Pressman his cell phone number. He hung up and turned to Mrs. Hughes.

"Suzanne, listen to me, no one from the police called here."

"Oh, my God!" she cried. "Oh, no!"

"Suzanne, listen. The police are on their way and we're going to find him. I don't think he's too far away, or he would have said that they wanted him to drive a long way. We'll check public areas just north of here and then work our way out from there." The two small Hughes children came out, hearing the sound of their mother crying.

"I'm coming, too," Suzanne cried.

"No. Please stay here. We need to know where you are. Besides, you have children here to take care of."

Rawlings sent her back into the house and saw her standing inside looking out a picture window with the children held close to her side. He turned when a squad car, driven by a young Latino female officer, pulled up. "Are you Agent Rawlings?" the officer asked.

"Right," Rawlings said as he walked over to her window.

"I'm Janice Lazaro. The sarge said you're looking for a green Subaru?"

"Right. A Legacy. Being driven by white male, age thirty-nine, dark hair, beard. I think he was lured out of the house by a false phone call from a person claiming to be from your PD. Did your dispatch get a plate number yet?"

"Yeah, GHT274." Rawlings wrote the number down in his notebook. Just then, another car pulled up with Kent Pressman inside. Rawlings hopped in with him and said that they should start with any public areas in the northern part of the city and then work in different directions.

"Mike, is this for real?" Pressman asked. "I can free up some other guys, but only if we've got something substantial here."

"Kent, I think we need to worry. Something very odd is going on."

Pressman called another officer on his cell phone and explained the situation. He asked him to get over to the area by the lake right away.

"On a nice Saturday, those parks are going to be filled," he warned Rawlings.

"We can only do what we can do."

As they sped up Bald Eagle Avenue, Rawlings fought down a wave of nausea. Here you come to warn the guy to be careful, he thought, but then you shake his hand as he drives off to slaughter. Rawlings knew that he couldn't have put all the pieces together in time to stop Hughes, but the timing was just incredible.

Just as Pressman pulled into a strip mall, the radio gave out the three short beeps of a "hotshot" call.

"2300 units, report of a shooting, Four Seasons Park, in the public parking area. Getting more info now."

"Shit!" Rawlings and Pressman said in unison. Pressman hit the lights and siren and tore out of the mall, headed to Four Seasons. They covered the short distance in under two minutes and saw people clustered in the lot as they pulled in. One woman was holding a boy who was about four years old and a girl who was about seven. All of them were shrieking. A man ran up to Pressman and said, "A guy just shot a guy over there! He took off across the grass that way!" He pointed to the back of the lot, and Rawlings saw Hughes's Legacy parked at the far end, farthest from everyone. He ran through the lot with his gun drawn and came up to the car from the rear. When Rawlings came around the side and looked into the open driver's window, he felt sick. John Hughes was slumped over the center column with his hands limp in his lap. Recognizing the danger too late, in death he still appeared to be trying to turn away from it. Blood was everywhere inside the car, and Rawlings didn't have to look too closely to see that he man he had so recently been chatting pleasantly with had been shot several times in the face and head.

"Goddamn you!" Rawlings said to the sky as he jammed his pistol back in his holster. "God*damn you!*" He heard sirens wailing and heard Pressman come up behind him, but he couldn't speak. Unfamiliar tears choked his throat as he thought of Suzanne and the two confused children she'd been holding close to her as he left. What the hell can I say to them now?

CHAPTER 27

▼

It was a drained Mike Rawlings who finally returned to the BCA office later that afternoon. The rest of the team members had been called in and were aware of what had happened in Four Seasons Park on what had been a sunny, warm, cheery Saturday morning. Now, it was hot, humid, and overcast. A tornado watch had been issued, and the mood in the task force office matched the change in weather.

Usually a cop will respond to a call of a crime of violence committed upon a stranger and will have the luxury of emotional distance so he can work the case without personal attachments taxing his mind. Most cops have been on calls where someone has died, and the circumstances caused them to form some sort of bond with the victim. Usually it happens in the death of children. Maybe the officer has a child that same age, or maybe the child resembles one they know. Sometimes the bond forms because the person has died in such a horrible, disfiguring way that the very sight makes the officer think of his own mortality. Sometimes it forms because the person just looks so peaceful, as in the case of a crib death, that it seems that they should just be able to wake up. When the bond forms, for whatever reason, it makes working the scene a little more difficult. It makes asking the necessary questions of the loved ones seem a little more intrusive, and it makes the officer die, just a little, inside.

Some of the team members had been unlucky enough to have had to have been present at the deaths of friends. Both Pete Lincoln and Mike Rawlings had been there when fellow officers had died. Gene Truman had had to go to the suicide death of the wife of a fellow officer. John Pappas and Phil Deane had both been to the death scenes of acquaintances, both accidental and deliberate. Tom

McDowell, for all of his nine years in police work in Minnesota's largest city, had been fortunate enough never to have been present at the death of someone he knew. He'd lost friends, of course, but through some quirk of fate, had never had to look into the dreamy, sightless eyes of someone with whom he'd laughed and shared a piece of himself. He counted himself very lucky and wondered how long it could last.

Rawlings tiredly told the others about his conversation with Hughes and how he had become aware that something was wrong with the call Hughes had taken. Then he went over what the witnesses had said.

"We had several different accounts from the witnesses, of course," Rawlings said, "but what seems evident is that Hughes drove into the parking lot and straight to the back of the lot. A witness said that a man who had been waiting at a picnic table got up when he saw Hughes pull in. Our witness was a woman who was close by with her two kids, waiting for her husband to bring a picnic basket from the car. She said that our suspect was wearing a coat and cap, and she thought it was odd to be dressed that way on such a warm day. She said he had blond hair and a beard."

"Disguise," Pete Lincoln said. "Must have been. Our man's been described as dark-haired."

"Right," Phil Deane said, "but which is the disguise? Is he blond-or dark-haired?"

"I think we need to assume he's been in disguise each time he's been seen and not rely on those descriptions," Rawlings said.

"And he was on foot?" Truman asked.

"At first," Rawlings said. "The witness said the guy was at a table watching the lot until Hughes pulled in. She said that Hughes pulled up to the end of the lot, and, by that time, our suspect was walking toward him. She said he gave Hughes a little wave and walked up to the driver's window. She couldn't hear any conversation but said that there couldn't have been very much, because she said he pulled the gun from his coat, maybe from a shoulder holster, and open fire right away. She said she pulled her kids down and didn't know what exactly he did then, but another witness said that he saw a man run to a dark SUV and drive out of the lot over the grass to the road, probably so he wouldn't pass any of the people standing around near the entrance."

"So, no one got a plate, then?" McDowell asked.

"Nope," Rawlings answered. "It was all pretty quick and over before most people knew what was happening. The driver got back onto the road and took off toward Highway 61. The shell casings found at the scene were 9mm, and the same brand of ammo as those in the elevator killings. We also found a partial tire print on the verge of the grass which they were going to try to cast. It's been pretty dry so they didn't know how good it would turn out."

"Does this seem a little desperate to you?" Pete Lincoln asked. "I mean, he's been so careful to confront his victims alone and in private. Why would he set something up in front of so many people, in such a busy place? Is he getting cocky? Can we hope he's getting careless?"

"I've been thinking about that," Rawlings answered. "We don't know for sure that the park shootings of the gang kids in White Bear were the patriot, but it seems awfully likely now. The dark SUV matches, too. Just after the shootings, less than half an hour, a man was seen looking into the Hughes's back window by a neighbor. We know it was the patriot, because when he ran off, he stole Hughes's checkbook and cell phone from the car in the drive and used them to lure him to Four Seasons Park. Mrs. Hughes told me that her husband wasn't very sociable and preferred to stay at home. I think the patriot couldn't figure a way to get him alone and had to gamble on a meet."

"I think we know now how he's getting inside these houses, too. He's claiming to be a cop," Deane said. "That's going to open a can of worms."

"Right," Lincoln said. "None of us will be able to knock on a door once this gets out."

"Does it have to get out?" Truman asked.

"Yeah," Rawlings sighed. "We agreed that we needed to forewarn our potential victims, if possible. Nothing's changed."

"We can encourage the press to tell people to be sure to demand proper ID from anyone claiming to be a cop," Pappas said.

"Right," said Rawlings. "Another in a long line of ideas we've had that'll make no fucking difference whatsoever."

Pete Lincoln noticed how down Rawlings was and guessed the reason. "Mike, you can't blame yourself. You went there and discussed what we all agreed was a remote possibility. We can't guard all of these people twenty-four hours a day."

"I know," Rawlings said, rubbing his face with his hand. "I just wish I'd listened to the advice I'd just given him."

"Mike, any one of us would have done it the same way. It's says something about your instincts that you went back and talked more with the wife. I think a lot of cops would have just delivered the message and left."

"That's right," Phil Deane said. "It was the second conversation with the wife that gave you the only solid info you had that he was in real danger."

"What you need is some sleep," Lincoln said. "And you need some distance. We all need you to hold this three-ring circus together."

Rawlings knew Lincoln was right. And he knew deep down that he wasn't responsible for Hughes's death. But when Rawlings had gone back to the house, talked to Suzanne and then saw her holding her children, the bond had formed. And then when he had to go back again to break the news and to break her heart, a little piece of him died.

At 7:30 p.m. that Saturday, the patriot was in the garage at his house working on a project. It was hot and stuffy inside and he wished that he could open the garage door, but he didn't want any nosy neighbors walking by and looking in. Outside, the humid night had been absolutely still until about half an hour before, when a stiff breeze had kicked up. Through the propped-open window, the patriot could hear the rumbling of distant thunder, promising that rain would soon come. So much the better, he thought.

Maybe cool things off a little. He was involved in a task that was more time-consuming than mentally taxing. The heat and humidity added to the boredom of the repetitive task and he longed for a distraction.

The patriot was building what was known as a Hedgehog. Also known as a sparkler bomb, the simple device was a favorite among teens who built them for amusement when they partied in the rural areas where the patriot patrolled. He had often found the remains of them in fields the day after, surrounded by beer cans and food wrappers, and had the process explained to him once by a helpful teen who enjoyed impressing the big deputy with his knowledge.

Simply stated, a Hedgehog is a large bundle of sparklers bound together with wire, with a sparkler sticking out of the top to act as a fuse. The larger the bundle, the larger the display when the fusing sparkler burns down to ignite the rest. When the Hedgehog goes off, it is best to be a good distance away, because the fireball that erupts is larger than what might be expected by those who have never experienced one before. The patriot had been told by his teenaged informant that some people combine the bundles around containers of gasoline or aerosol cans of carburetor cleaner to enlarge the blast. He had taken the lesson to heart and was building his Hedgehog around a series of plastic water bottles arranged in a honeycomb pattern. In two weeks, when he was ready to put the finishing touches on the device, he would be adding something other than water to the bottles.

To ensure a truly memorable display, he had purchased 1000 sparklers from various stores and fireworks vendors in the area. The Minnesota Legislature had made his task easier by legalizing sparklers and other less dangerous fireworks earlier that year. He carefully unwrapped package after package of the wire sparklers and tightly bound them to the central octagon-shaped frame. This frame was made of heavier gauge wire that was wrapped around the bottles and attached to a chicken wire base. The finished product would be about two feet in diameter and ten inches high. The whole structure would be covered by a thin plastic dome that had once been the cover for a large meat, cheese, and vegetable tray at a department party. When the time came, the patriot intended to cover the dome with another substance that would complete the surprise.

The patriot sweated as he worked the stiff wires together. He had tried wearing leather work gloves to protect his skin but found that they were too bulky for the fine work, so he had to put up with the wire ends occasionally jabbing his fingers and palms. He was thinking to himself that it was time for a break when he heard the phone inside ringing. He entered the air conditioned comfort of his kitchen and caught the phone on the fourth ring.

"Hello?"

"Oh, hi. I thought I'd missed you," a vaguely familiar female voice said. "This is Tina Sullivan."

"Hi, Tina." *What now?* he thought.

"Am I calling at a bad time?" Tina asked, wondering if he was with another woman.

"No, I was just working on something in the garage."

"I got your number from Don, I hope you're not mad."

"No. What's up?"

"Well, I guess I just wanted to call and, well, see how you are. I really had a nice time with you at the party and, um, I guess I thought that if you weren't busy, um, we might see each other some time."

"Well, I didn't know that night if you were looking for just something casual or something else. I guess we just kind of left it open the next day." *I really don't need someone hanging around my house! Looking in cabinets, wondering where I'm going!*

"Yeah, I was kind of coming off a breakup and just pissed off and needed some support. You were great, just what I needed. I just, well, I've been thinking about you, wondering what kind of place you're in." *How can I ask you if I can see you and keep my dignity if you say no?*

"Well, I'm, well, I'm kind of a loner I guess. I told you I had a bad divorce, and I guess I kind of got used to doing my own things. I'm not against seeing someone. I guess, though, when we met, everything happened so fast, I wasn't sure what to make of it."

"They sure did!" Tina giggled.

The patriot let his mind flicker over the memory of the night he'd spent with Tina, her soft brown hair lying against his belly, her small brown nipples in his mouth. Then he thought of the Hedgehog and its thousand sharp points waiting on the workbench. He had until June 1; the Hedgehog could wait.

"Well, I'm not promising anything, but I'm not busy tonight. Would you like to meet somewhere?"

"Yes, I'd like that."

"How about Bogart's in Apple Valley? Ever been there?"

"Sure, I love it. What time should we meet?"

"Eight-thirty sound okay?"

"Sounds fine. I'll meet you then! Bye!"

The patriot hung up and wondered if he was making a mistake. It really wasn't fair to use her. He couldn't let her know what he was doing, but he felt a longing inside. Part of it was sexual, he knew. Hell, maybe most of it. But even soldiers take furloughs sometime.

After stowing the Hedgehog in the garage attic and showering, Bauer drove through the bright, constant lightning to Apple Valley and found Tina already there near the bar, nursing a wine cooler. He kissed her quickly on the cheek and ordered a beer for himself. Bogart's, a dance bar, was one of the few places in the Twin Cities which featured live bands anymore. The music was deafening, and the place was packed, despite the heat. Some people were dancing, and others were standing around in clusters drinking.

"Good band!" Bauer shouted.

"Yeah, I like good rock!" Tina replied.

"Let's move over here," Bauer said, pointing to an area of the bar furthest from the stage. They walked to an area occupied by pool tables, where they could talk without having to shout in each other's ears.

"So, how have you been?" Bauer asked.

"Okay. Just working, you know? Doing the nine-to-five thing."

Bauer could tell she'd had a couple and figured rightly that she had felt the need for them in order to get her courage up.

"Blue Cross, isn't that where you work?" he asked.

"Yeah, sitting on the phone all day. It's boring. Not like what you do. Don's always told me cool cop stories. I bet you never get bored at work."

"Well, sometimes. It's not like TV. We do a lot of nonsense, too. Overall, though, it's not boring."

"I bet. Tell me some cop stories." She asked and moved closer to him.

Wow, Bauer thought. *She must be pretty tanked. Either that or pretty horny.*

"Well, not long ago I stopped this woman for going 54 mph in a 30 zone and she told me that the reason she was speeding was because she was distracted. I asked by what and she said that she was concentrating on putting her seatbelt on."

"Ha! Do you get a lot of excuses like that?"

"Yeah. One guy told me he was speeding because he'd come from the theater where he'd seen the movie *Grand Theft Auto* and was all keyed up. Another time a woman told me she had to rush her dog to the vet because she had discovered the vet had operated on the dog's wrong ear."

"Did you believe her?"

"Yeah, she had the dog in the back seat with a bandage on its ear!"

Tina giggled and pressed her hip against Bauer's leg. "So, do you ever get calls about women who're having wild sex, and the neighbors think she's being attacked?"

"I haven't, no, but I know it happens," Bauer said as he reached around her and rubbed her back.

"Do other cops tell each other about stories like that?"

"Sure. They make the job more fun."

"Do you drive around horny the rest of the night, then?"

"That depends. If the woman was pretty hot, I might, but if she was a real mutt I guess I'd try to forget about it and think about something else."

"A mutt!" Tina cried and gave him a playful slap on his chest. "That's mean! A mutt! I hope you wouldn't call me a mutt!"

"Never!"

"So, if you're all horny, and there're only mutts around, what do you do?" She wrapped her lower leg around Bauer's and rubbed his flat stomach with her hand.

"Then it's cold shower time. I don't think I could get my soldier to stand at attention for someone who looks like Janet Reno."

"Your soldier! And how is your soldier?"

"Right now?" Bauer asked.

"Yep, right now," Tina answered and let her hand slide down to brush Bauer's fly.

"He's finding things a lot tighter in there than they were a little while ago." Bauer brought his hand around and brushed the side of Tina's breast with his index finger.

"I guess I'm not a mutt, then," Tina said, looking into his eyes.

"Definitely not. Let's go."

Back at Tina's apartment, she eagerly freed Bauer's soldier from his tight confines and sent him into action. The thunder and lightning that crashed against the bedroom window acted as special effects for their wild lovemaking. Bauer happily discovered that Tina enjoyed being on top, and he enjoyed the freedom of running his hands over her body while she moved smoothly and liquidly on him. His exploring hands found sensitive, tender nipples, and she moved more quickly as he caressed them. Her moans increased when he ran his hand down to where they were joined, and his thumb pressed against her tender flesh. Soon, Tina was thrashing so wildly on him that it began to hurt a little, but still, they came together with the storm outside adding a counterpoint to their cries. Bauer rolled her over and continued to move inside her more and more slowly until he withdrew and lay next to her.

"Wow!" Tina said after catching her breath.

"Wow," Bauer agreed.

Tina put her head on Bauer's chest and traced a line in his chest hair with her fingernail. "I hope you don't think I'm a slut for calling you like I did."

"I don't think that at all" Bauer told her.

"It's hard to ask a guy out, even when you know him. I just missed you, and, well, I was a little horny."

"A little horny!" Bauer laughed. "I'd hate to see you really horny! You could kill me!"

Tina giggled and reached down and shook Bauer's penis. "Is he dead?"

"No, just taking a rest."

"Roll over," she ordered. Bauer did as he was told, while she grabbed a bottle of lotion off the bedside table and sat astride his hips.

"What are you doing?"

"I'm going to give you a back rub. Hopefully, it will relax you, and your soldier will wake up."

"Yes, ma'am."

That night, Mike Rawlings found sleep difficult. He tossed and turned until 2:00 a.m., finally getting out of bed when his wife sleepily complained that he should lie still. He went to his living room and poured himself a generous shot of brandy. He sat down and looked out across the lake as the rain pounded against the window. The lightning and thunder were moving off to the east, and the sky still flickered like the distant artillery he remembered from rainy hot nights in Vietnam when he was a young Marine.

What had happened to John Hughes that day reminded him of fellow soldiers whom he'd spoken to and then lost minutes later. Somehow, this was harsher, though. In war, you expect to be shot at. It was one thing to sit on a patio in the morning sunshine and listen to the sounds of children playing nearby and lawn mowers humming; it was another thing to be on patrol in a jungle, moving your M-16 from side to side, waiting for the explosion of gunfire and hoping it wouldn't happen.

Rawlings kept picturing Hughes lying in the car, turned away from his killer. He'd known within minutes of talking to Hughes that he wouldn't, couldn't, take a threat to his life seriously. Hughes was a man who lived in a safe, comfortable, theoretical, academic world. It was one thing to read about violence in the paper, but it was always happening to someone else. John Hughes was a man who felt that, through better understanding, people could leave behind their differences and quarrels and create a more peaceful society. The idea that people struggle with ancient, often prehistoric, drives that compel both men and women to do things that even they can't really, thoroughly understand, was ridiculous to him. Hughes had written his book so races and cultures could try to see the world through each other's eyes, and it had cost him his life. He was certain that his insights would bring harmony, but he didn't have the capacity to understand that his views could feel threatening to those who preferred the status quo.

Rawlings sipped at his brandy and thought of the time he'd spent with Suzanne Hughes when he'd returned to the house after an officer had told her of the murder of her husband. She seemed so confused by it all. She couldn't understand the motives of the patriot and couldn't see the anger and primal emotion some people felt when they thought that their beliefs and the things they held dear were being threatened. Rawlings remembered a case he'd worked in St. Paul once when a forty-year-old man had argued with his forty-six-year-old brother over who would get the last pork chop in the pan. The forty-year-old gave up his claim on the meat by forcing it down his brother's throat, tearing his esophagus and killing him. The strange thing was, the killer showed no remorse. He felt that his brother was intruding on his rightful property. The man wasn't insane; he didn't even have much of a criminal record. He just saw that last pork chop as something so valuable that it was worth killing for.

The bond that had formed between him and Suzanne Hughes that day caused him to share in her loss. He felt some of her loss—a fraction, to be sure—but his heart ached for her. All of her plans had changed; all of her routine had been stripped away. Her sunny Saturday morning had ended in loss and confusion in the same way as the weather had changed from pleasant to stormy. Rawlings knew it would change back for her, over time. She would cry less each day and eventually put the death of her husband behind her. She might love again and find her smile returning along with sunny Saturdays when she could count on things happening according to plan.

For Rawlings, though, the bond was there and would never go away. Each time he went over his time with her in his mind, he would feel her sadness and see her tears falling onto the hair of the children she held close to her. He would remember the smells inside the house that day and again he would die, just a little, inside.

CHAPTER 28

▼

On Sunday morning, Tom McDowell, Gene Truman, and John Pappas gathered at the Task Force office amid a horde of TV, radio, and print reporters. After the killing of John Hughes, what had already been the area's top news story turned into a feeding frenzy. Photos and biographies of each task force member had been created and put out, friends, associates, and family members of each of the victims had been located and interviewed, many several times. Reporters eager to scoop their competitors dug for any possible piece of information that hadn't been found before in an effort to hype their stories.

Each investigator had to force his way past the assembled mob out front with terse "No comment" answers as microphones were thrust in their faces. The reporters were frustrated by the rebuffs they received and formulated their own opinions to tell the public why the investigators weren't saying anything.

The cops, finally inside in relative peace, watched the morning news and discussed their plans for the day. Each saw that their hopes of conducting their investigation in cooperation with the press had gone out the window. The story was international news now, and, to the reporters, it was every man for himself. The investigators saw that the media would now be their biggest obstacle to maintaining any integrity in the investigation at all. A couple of people, who had been interviewed the day before by Pete Lincoln and Phil Deane and who were on the potential target list, had gone straight from their meetings with the police to a handy reporter and discussed, in detail, that they might be the next victim. In so doing, they revealed a part of the task force's strategy in trying to catch up with the patriot, who remained at least a step ahead.

"I guess I can't blame them for doing that," Truman said. "If I were a target, I think I'd be more comfortable if a lot of people knew about it. Maybe it would make the patriot think twice about coming after me."

"Could be," McDowell said, "but what if you weren't on *his* list before you ran to the press. A person could just be waving his arms yelling, 'Hey, what about me!'"

"True. Either way it's going to be really tough to work now. Tom, you're heading to White Bear?"

"Right, I'm going to help their police department with witnesses that might have been missed yesterday and hang out for a while in the park looking for others. You guys doing follow-ups on the target list?"

"Right," said Pappas. "Gene, there's a couple of people on this list that I don't mind saying I'd be more comfortable if you came along. Like this so-called 'youth leader'—the one who was tried for murder in Chicago and who's been arrested 34 times."

"Yeah, it isn't prudent to go flashing badges in certain neighborhoods without some muscle," McDowell chuckled.

"No problem, John," Truman said. "Tell you what, let's do a couple each from our lists and then meet around lunch time and head into the projects."

"Pete Lincoln would pay to see that," McDowell laughed. "Two cops from Burnsville and Goodhue County banging on doors in North Minneapolis!"

Tony Bauer woke up from a restless sleep feeling very unrested. Tina had kept him up most of the night, but then he'd had the dream again. All in all, he figured he'd only slept about three hours. He eased his way out of bed and went to the bathroom, where he sat on the toilet and considered his situation. He felt that it would have been better if he'd made an excuse and not seen Tina last night, that lust had overcome his will power, and that he'd traded unnecessary complications for a night of sex. He wanted to get out and go about his day, but knew he'd be obligated to spend some time with her today. He had today and tomorrow off before returning to work on Tuesday, and he had to complete the Hedgehog for sure. He also intended to visit a certain fellow who lived out in the boondocks of Chisago County north of the Twin Cities. Bauer had driven there before and knew it would take a couple hours of his night.

He washed his hands and face as quietly as he could and slipped into the bedroom, intending to go out to the living room. He stopped when he saw Tina lying in bed smiling at him.

"Good morning!" she said. "Get enough sleep?"

"A little," Bauer returned with a grin.

"Come snuggle with me?" she asked.

Bauer climbed back into bed, and Tina curled up alongside him like a big cat. She rubbed his chest hair and said, "What would you like to do today?"

I'd like to finish my bomb and then go strangle a guy who raped and murdered a four-year-old girl, he thought. Aloud, he said, "Well, I have some stuff I've got to finish around the house, but I thought first I'd take you out for breakfast. Would you like that?"

"Sure," Tina said. "How about we work up an appetite, first?" She said as she moved her hand lower down his torso.

God, he thought. *This girl's going to kill me.*

Vladislaw Peschola spent Sunday working alone at his remote home five miles northwest of the town of Almelund. His battered trailer house was set up on five acres of wooded land, and he hoped to one day earn enough money to replace it with something larger. He knew that getting his business off the ground would be more important than a nice home and that he had a lot of work to do.

Peschola was born outside of Krakow, Poland, in 1959 and was one of the few Poles who were allowed to migrate to the United States by the former Communist government in 1980. Perhaps one reason the state was willing to let him go was because Peschola was the typical square peg amongst round holes in a society which frowned on individuality. The conservative streak which ran through most Poles by nature and which was reinforced by decades of harsh Communist rule, didn't run in Peschola. He didn't get along well with others and was moved from one job to another until his twenty-first birthday, when his request to emigrate was granted. The police also suspected Peschola of numerous misdeeds but were unable to pin anything on him, because Peschola, despite his faults, was a very bright young man.

In America, Peschola enjoyed his newfound freedom and found that a smart person who was willing to work hard, as Peschola certainly was, could enjoy a very comfortable lifestyle. He settled in Ohio and soon was making a good deal of money as a landscaper and nurseryman. Once growing communities around Columbus eagerly contracted with Peschola to beautify their grounds, he had a very successful business built up by 1994, when another aspect of his personality became apparent.

Peschola had an affection for very, very young girls. A psychiatrist hired by the state of Ohio later said that it stemmed from an unusual upbringing in which he was made to sleep in the same bed as his two sisters who were sexually molested by their father, often while little Vladislaw pretended to be asleep. As a result, Peschola's sexual fantasies involved girls who were younger than school age and, because acting out theses fantasies is illegal in civilized areas, both in Krakow and in Columbus, he was forced to indulge his tastes surreptitiously.

He set up a day-care service for his employees and had built a very elaborate play area complete with a small scale, but still impressive, version of Cinderella's castle for the children to play in. The parents thought the service was wonderful and that Peschola was a great boss to go to such lengths for his employees. Peschola often visited the play area and liked to romp with the smaller children in the castle. After a while, some of the little girls told their parents that Mr. Peschola touched them "there" and that he kissed them. Because they were so young, it was very difficult to get their stories straight, and consequently many parents chose to remove their children from the day-care rather than make embarrassing accusations.

In June of 1997, Peschola's world collapsed when he was caught inside the play area by the enraged father of a three-year-old girl. The father had come to get his daughter earlier than usual due to a family emergency. He looked for the woman who supervised the day-care for Peschola and found that she was on a break. He went looking for his little girl himself and found her on the lap of his wife's employer. Peschola had removed her diaper and was rubbing her vulva while masturbating. The father, a powerful cement worker, removed his daughter from Peschola's lap, set her aside, and then began beating the living shit out of the surprised Pole, who was soon lying unconscious with his penis still protruding from his fly. A scandal ensued, and Peschola was run out of business. Charges were brought, but later dropped when the family of the girl refused to cooperate with police, citing concern for their daughter and because the beating Peschola had taken had cost him the use of his left eye and his livelihood; that was enough for them.

Peschola sold off his assets and relocated to Wisconsin, where he was soon in trouble with the law again. This time, the four-year-old daughter of a neighbor disappeared. A thorough search was conducted, and the girl's bloodstained jumper was found on Peschola's property. Brought in for questioning, he found himself being interrogated by a deputy who, it turned out, was the missing girl's uncle. Such are the dangers of living in a small town. The beating Peschola took that time cost him one testicle and the feeling in three fingers of his left hand. After being treated at the local hospital, Peschola called an attorney and discussed plans to sue, but after a visit from the county sheriff, a very well-liked local law enforcement official, Peschola decided not to. The sheriff had unrolled a map of the county, pointed out several remote areas where no one even hunted, and assured Peschola that his body would never be found in any of them, should he decide to continue to make Wisconsin his home. Peschola agreed and moved to Minnesota, where he put what few dollars he had left into five acres and a trailer and purchased equipment and nursery stock to open another landscaping business.

A local newspaper had somehow discovered Peschola's past and had printed a story several months earlier, which was reprinted in the St. Paul paper in an article about the difficulties in tracking sexual offenders. Peschola hoped the article wouldn't be too well-remembered by his neighbors and damage his business. He had been grateful at the time that the story hadn't been carried by the Minneapolis paper with its larger circulation. He didn't know that since the story hadn't been tracked by the *Minneapolis Star Tribune*, his name didn't appear in their morgue during the dates searched by James Knox and Phil Deane. What he also didn't know was that it had been read by the patriot, who made the first of three trips to Peschola's house the very next day.

While Tom McDowell spent the morning speaking to those who were present at Four Seasons Park the day before (the local police had taken a lot of names, but very few complete statements), Gene Truman and John Pappas put on a lot of miles trying to find the people on their lists. Some weren't at home, and others had moved, leaving no forwarding address. They each managed to locate a total of three of the people from their two lists and none of the three were very happy to see them. One was a woman who led a group of people opposed to the American military action in the Middle East. She became very indignant with Gene Truman, telling him she was offended that the task force would consider her a target and, thereby, had put her in jeopardy from other "gun-toting nutcases" out there who wanted to emulate the patriot. Gene tried to explain that the task force list was private, but the woman would have none of it. Another man Truman talked to had been in the paper after being acquitted of drug-smuggling charges. Truman spent fifteen minutes in a fruitless conversation trying to get the guy, who was completely stoned on pot, to focus on the topic. Finally, he left his card and told the guy to call him when he was well enough to dial a phone. Pappas's single success of the morning was with a pink-haired, 250-pound lesbian who had sued a local department store for refusing to hire her to model their clothing. The woman sat through her meeting with Pappas, cracking her knuckles and saying that she hoped the patriot would come after her.

They met for lunch at the Ground Round Restaurant in Burnsville and then headed into North Minneapolis in search of Diondre Simmons, a man who called himself a "youth leader," but who the Minneapolis Police knew was a former member of the El Ruiken drug gang in Chicago and who, they suspected, hadn't completely abandoned his former line of work.

Pappas and Truman found Simmons on the front porch of his house at Lowry and Dupont Avenues. Everyone in the neighborhood recognized their dark blue Chevrolet Impala for what it was when it pulled up to the curb. Simmons pointed at the car as they pulled up, and two men who had been talking with him stood and went immediately into the house. The investigators knew they were in very unfamiliar (and unfriendly) territory, but both had been cops long enough to know that showing fear was the best way to lose any edge they had. Both took their time walking up the walk to the porch as Simmons glared at them.

"Mr. Simmons, I'm Gene Truman and this is John Pappas. We're police officers."

"No shit," one of the men on the porch replied.

"We're on assignment to the Minnesota BCA. We're investigating the patriot murders, and we'd like to speak with you if you have a moment."

"Don't know nothin' 'bout no murders. Sorry," Simmons said, making a point of looking past them out onto the street.

"We don't suspect you of any involvement, Mr. Simmons," Pappas said. "We're here because we think that the recent publicity you've received may be putting you in danger."

"Oh? How's that?" Simmons asked.

"The man who calls himself 'the patriot' has been killing people who have been publicized for speaking out about things like civil rights, animal rights, nuclear power. He's killed those who've been called unpunished criminals by the press. We're trying to stop him, and we're talking to people who, we think, might be future targets of this man."

"So, this redneck is killin' folks who complain 'bout they rights, huh?" Simmons turned to another associate and said, "Shee-it, sound like the PO-lice to me!" The others laughed. Simmons turned back to Pappas and said, "So, you-all are here to tell me what?"

"We want you to be aware of the danger and take precautions. Don't allow yourself to be alone with anyone you don't know. We know this man is white, so start from there. He has also impersonated a police officer, so be sure to ask for proper ID from anyone not in a uniform who claims to be a police officer."

The men around Simmons broke up laughing. "Where you from, man?" Simmons asked Pappas.

"I'm an investigator from the Goodhue County Sheriff's Office, on assignment," Pappas answered to more laughter.

"Goodhue-what? Where's that?" a man asked.

"Red Wing. It's just south of here."

"Damn south!" Simmons laughed. "Sho 'nuff south! Listen, Officer, you tell the Minneapolis PO-lice to be sure to bring they ID cards round here when they come, and I'll ask to see 'em."

"Only the white ones!" someone added from the back.

"We have two members of the Minneapolis PD on our team..." Truman began.

"Where are they today?" Simmons asked.

"One is on a day off, another is on another matter."

"So they sent you."

"Yep," Pappas answered.

Simmons laughed again. "This is funny as hell. Go back and tell them what you just told us, okay? Tell 'em you don't want us goin' anywhere with them, tell 'em to bring they ID's when they come! I bet they'll laugh, too."

"Mr. Simmons, we're only trying to warn you about the danger. This man is a stone-cold killer. If he has you on his list, he won't hesitate to try to kill you."

"Okay, Officer," Simmons said. "I'll watch for the bogeyman. But do me a favor, okay?"

"What's that?"

"When you tell them local cops what you said here today, be sure to tell 'em with a straight face. Makes it funnier!"

Pappas and Truman walked back to their car to the sound of laughter from the porch.

"Well, that went well," Truman said.

Bauer took Tina to a nearby Perkins Restaurant for a late breakfast. He stayed cordial, but told her he had to get some things done around the house when he took her home. Promising to call her, he dropped her off and then headed home. After a shower and a short nap, he returned to his garage and resumed work on the Hedgehog. It was more than half finished and he hoped to get it at least three quarters of the way finished before evening. His mind wandered as he worked, both remembering the night with Tina and also contemplating his plans for tonight. The two thoughts clashed in his mind, and he shook his head to try to focus. He didn't need distractions like Tina, but there was something about her that drew him. He knew he could fall for her, but his mind assured him that she wouldn't understand what he was doing or why. He'd come too far to give up and try to live normally again. Something about that idea appealed to him, but he considered it unrealistic. He'd tried that path with Amber, and it had ended in heartache and the murder of his son. He'd just have to turn Tina away.

At about 8:00 p.m., the patriot donned a T-shirt, a bulletproof vest, and his shoulder holster and hung an open plain blue button-down shirt over the top. He made sure his boot knife was secure and pulled the leg of his jeans down. He climbed into his Explorer and set out to the north. He followed Highway 61 through St. Paul and took it to Forest Lake, where he turned off toward Almelund about an hour after leaving home.

The previous night's storm had taken the humidity out of the air and the sky was a cheery orange as he turned onto the county road that led through the woods to the nearly half-mile-long gravel drive marked with Peschola's brown aluminum mailbox. There was no name on the box, just a number, but the patriot knew he was at the right place. He bounced over ruts in the gravel and pulled off onto a wide spot on the side of the drive about halfway to the house. As he got out, he heard the sound of a chain saw buzzing far off ahead of him.

The patriot walked quickly and quietly along the edge of the woods toward the house, wishing he'd thought to bring some Deep Woods Off with him. The rain had brought out mosquitoes by the thousands, which swarmed around his face as he walked. The drive twisted and turned around some low hills. As he neared the trailer, the rising and falling sound of the chain saw grew louder. He came to a steel gate attached to poles strung with barbed wire, so he crawled between the strands and followed the sound of the saw to the rear of the trailer.

As he stepped cautiously to the side of the trailer, the sound of the saw stopped. He stood still in the dark shadow of the wall, smelling fresh-cut lumber, and peeked around the corner to see Peschola, illuminated by a large farm light on a pole, working on a large pile of brush. He was cutting the limbs down to sections about five feet long and a large chipper/shredder stood waiting nearby, evidently to convert the limbs into mulch for Peschola's new landscaping business.

As the patriot watched, Peschola pulled some more limbs off the pile, spread them out in front of him, started the saw again, and began cutting. The patriot studied the yard and saw that Peschola had brought a great number of new items onto the property since the last time he'd been there. Balled trees and shrubs stood crookedly, and bags of peat moss and fertilizer were stacked against a shed on the other side of the limb pile.

As Peschola worked, the patriot studied him from the back. He wasn't a large man, only about five-foot-nine inches tall and lean, but his shoulders and arms were solid from his work. The tank top Peschola wore stuck to him with sweat, and the muscles in his back flexed as he wielded the saw. The patriot decided it would be prudent not to approach Peschola while he was able to defend himself with something as serious as a chain saw. He considered shooting Peschola, but wasn't sure how far off the neighbors to the north were. He looked at the yard light and saw that the power supply to it came from the trailer. He walked back and followed the cord to an outlet on the other side.

The patriot found an axe handle propped conveniently against the side of the trailer. He hefted it and figured it would do nicely. He loosened the plug from the outlet, just until the power went out, and then, when the yard went dark, he quickly moved around the corner of the trailer. The saw stopped, and the patriot heard Peschola flick the switch on the pole a few times. The patriot heard Peschola make an incomprehensible comment and heard him walk toward the side of the trailer. He waited until Peschola pushed the plug back in and then stepped around the corner behind him.

Peschola had just turned back to the limb pile when he heard a noise behind him. He turned and, with his one good eye, caught a faint glimpse of a moving figure before his face exploded in light. Peschola hit the ground immediately, and the patriot stood over him looking at what had been the Pole's face. The axe handle had struck just below Peschola's nose and had reduced his mouth and cheeks to a red, bleeding mess. Most of Peschola's teeth were blasted out of his upper jaw, his nose had disintegrated, and flesh had fallen into the void. Peschola was helpless, but, surprisingly conscious, as the patriot quickly searched him for weapons.

"Evening, Vladislaw," the patriot said. "Thought I'd help you tonight." He took hold of Peschola's belt and dragged him to the limb pile. Peschola moaned as his body bumped over the grass, and he struggled to breathe through his ruined face.

The patriot pulled a Flex Cuff from his pocket and used it to bind Peschola's hands behind his back.

"Looks like you've been a busy boy," the patriot said as he stood over Peschola's body. "With all this work, I don't see where you found time to bother any little girls." Peschola struggled against the flex cuffs and chilled as he suddenly realized that this was retribution for the past.

"Maybe, if you had some help, you'd have more spare time," the patriot told him. He picked up the chain saw and pulled the cord. Peschola twisted on the ground and tried to move away. The patriot held the buzzing saw over Peschola and brought the spinning chain down in front of his eyes. Peschola squeezed his eyes shut and was amazed when the saw sputtered and quit.

"Fuck," the patriot muttered. "Damn thing." He tried to pull the cord again but the saw wouldn't turn over.

The patriot tossed the saw aside and looked around the work area. His eyes fell on the chipper that Peschola had been using to make mulch. It was a huge industrial model that was capable of chewing up limbs nearly six inches in diameter and that had a conveyor-belt-fed opening nearly three feet wide. He looked down at the terrified Pole with a wide smile, and Peschola knew his fate. He cried aloud and struggled vainly to break free of the plastic band holding his hands, while the patriot primed the engine. Then the mechanical monstrosity roared to life. Their eyes locked one last time as the patriot turned to him and said, "Come on, Vladislaw."

As he drove home, the patriot decided that another letter to Knox was in order. After all, the pervert had lived alone, and, once the raccoons and crows got into the mulch pile, no one would know for sure whatever had really happened to Vladislaw Peschola.

CHAPTER 29

▼

On Monday morning, the members of the Patriot Task Force convened at the BCA office. The local and national press affiliates who were camped out on the story were requesting (and some nearly demanding) a press conference to address the death of John Hughes and any new developments in the case. The team members decided that Mike Rawlings would speak for the group in order to allow the others to work, and also to avoid the spectacle they knew would occur.

The first order of business was a call made by Rawlings to Charles Dodd, the head of the Minneapolis office of the United States Secret Service. Dodd referred Rawlings to Agent Vincent Cushing in Washington, D.C. Cushing was in charge of the protective detail of agents who were assigned to the task of keeping George Ernest Hudson and his eight colleagues alive.

Hudson was the most junior member of the United States Supreme Court. Appointed by Bill Clinton during his second term, Hudson was a very liberal justice on what was mostly a conservative panel. Hudson had cut his legal teeth during the Civil Rights battles of the sixties and had gotten a reputation by defending people who were using the nation's upheaval to try to push their own ideas of change. Hudson rigorously defended Black Panthers, members of the Students for a Democratic Society, a Jewish Defense Leaguer and others. During the seventies and eighties, Hudson concentrated on death penalty and civil rights cases. He managed to avoid gaining the notorious media reputations of such attorneys as Melvin Belli, Allen Ginsberg, and F. Lee Bailey. Such reputations in the legal profession make for lucrative practices and large bank accounts, but virtually guarantee that those attorneys would never survive the Senate confirmation hearings, should an appointment to a high court open.

Hudson quietly went about climbing the legal ladder by first being appointed a judge by the governor of Massachusetts and, three years later, in 1991, he rose to that state's Court of Appeals. He was known to be a friend and confidant of Hillary Clinton and was nominated for an opening on the U.S. Supreme Court during her husband's presidency. The legal wheels turned and thrashed, but Hudson survived the confirmation process through the usual combination of political arm twisting and backslapping, and joined the court in 1998. Since then, he had been a very outspoken member of a traditionally low profile group. He authored many opinions (mostly dissenting ones) and made many public appearances in support of causes. He'd been publicly critical of gun ownership, the death penalty, corporate perks, religious causes, and any legislation designed to broaden the scope of law enforcement. Because of all of this, he had been excoriated by organizations from the NRA to the National Chiefs of Police Association. He'd become a public lightning rod and, it was rumored, privately considered by his fellow justices to be a nuisance.

Members of the highest court in the land have historically been extremely private individuals. A recent poll showed that over 95% of people interviewed on the street could not name more than one or two sitting justices. "The Supremes," as they are known in the legal community, appreciate their privacy and enjoy the freedom of being able to move about in their private lives in relative anonymity. They usually are unrecognized in all but the innermost Washington circles. When they do make appearances, they are provided protection by members of the U.S. Secret Service, and it was Agent Vincent Cushing's job to arrange for their safety.

Cushing was an eighteen-year veteran of the Secret Service and had protected three U.S. presidents and so many foreign kings, queens, ministers, rajahs, sheiks, and presidents that he'd lost count. He enjoyed his most recent assignment to the Justices because it was mostly administrative and allowed him to remain in his home in Virginia. Also, because so few people knew or cared who the justices were, his job was made so much easier. The more recognizable people are, the harder it is to fend off the people who would like to hurt them. The appointment of G.E. Hudson had complicated his life to the extent that Hudson was younger than the other justices, he insisted on more traveling and public appearances, and his political leanings brought him into disfavor with a large segment of the population. Aside from the usual number of mentally ill people who would attempt to kill any government figure for whatever reason happened to be in their minds at the time, Hudson was despised by people who were becoming fed up with the state of the nation. One such person was the subject of Rawlings's call.

"Agent Cushing, I'm Mike Rawlings, a major crimes investigator with the Minnesota Bureau of Criminal Apprehension."

"Good morning, Mike. Call me Vince. What can I do for you today?"

"Vince, I'm heading up a task force investigating the patriot murders here in the Twin Cities. I'm assuming you're aware of these cases."

"Yep, I've seen the national news. Kind of hard not to, especially the last three days or so."

"Well, the reason I'm calling is that my associates and I have, in addition to pursuing leads on the case, assembled a possible target list in an attempt to identify possible future targets of the patriot. As you may know, the patriot has targeted criminals—child molesters in particular—as well as activists and those with very liberal leanings."

"That was my understanding from the news," Cushing said. "Do you have any good leads?"

"Well, nothing yet to point to a name. We've discovered that he has impersonated a police officer to access some of his victims, and we actually did have one victim on our list who was then targeted by the patriot. Unfortunately, he got to the guy anyway."

"The professor, right? The one who wrote the book?"

"John Hughes, yes." Rawlings didn't want to go into Hughes's death again if he didn't have to. "He was killed on Saturday. We have another name on our list, a person you look after."

"Let me guess," Cushing said. "Justice Hudson, right?"

"Right, we understand he's speaking to the graduating class of the University of Minnesota Law School on June 1 in Minneapolis."

"That's correct. And, not to sound cocky, I *have* had my doubts about bringing Judge Hudson into your patriot's back yard."

"Actually, I'm glad you're thinking along the same lines as we are. We like to hope we're on the right track and not just running around cleaning up the bodies later." Rawlings said.

"No, I think you've got a valid concern. Hudson gets ten times the hate mail as the other justices combined. He requires full-time protection and insists on going around to his appearances despite any advice we give him."

"So you don't think he could be dissuaded from making the Minneapolis trip?"

"I doubt it. We've had direct threats toward him before from people whose whereabouts we couldn't pin down, but he's gone anyway, over our objections and recommendations. Don't get me wrong, I intend to strongly recommend he not go on this trip, but I'm expecting he'll ignore me."

"Would it be possible to get together with whoever is going to be in charge of the protection detail on this trip? I'd like to compare what we have with any correspondence you guys may have picked up from our suspect."

"Not a problem Mike, in fact, we'll be wanting to know everything you do, too. What's this guy's body count up to now? I'd like to tell Hudson when I ask him to reconsider his trip."

"Fourteen and counting. We think he's working off a list because he's striking so quickly and knows the movements of his victims."

"Now, you've had some communications from him, right?" Cushing asked.

"He's sent two letters on floppy disks to a local reporter. He wants to make sure we know whom he's killed," Rawlings said sarcastically. "He also wants people to rise up and overthrow the government."

"I see from the news that he's inspired some people. Every day more copycat crimes are attributed to him."

"Yeah, over the weekend I heard of six across the country."

"Well, this is the reason why we're keeping up with the news. This is a real concern to us. Government officials are targets anyway, and now we've got a whole bunch of people who were just waiting for somebody else to make the first move. We may need to hire a lot more agents. Mike, give me your number, and I'll be in touch as soon as possible. I intend to talk with Hudson this morning."

Rawlings gave Cushing his cell number and hung up. He joined the other task force members and related what Cushing had said. "Sounds like the judge will be coming regardless of what's happening here."

"Shit, he may as well come here," Pete Lincoln said, pointing to the TV news.

"What's going on?" Rawlings asked.

"Copycat crime in Florida. A guy claiming to be a patriot opened fire on a Cuban street dance last night. Killed twelve people, injured nine. The previous story was the bombing of a Somali community center in Pennsylvania this morning. Haven't counted all the body parts yet, but sounds like at least six dead. They think the bomb went off too early, like before a good crowd could have been there."

"Shit."

"Yeah, add that to the mugger who got beaten to death by the mob in New York and the guy who popped the sixteen-year-old in Arizona for selling dope to his daughter, and you got the makings of a real rodeo here."

The patriot had watched the morning news as well, but with considerably more satisfaction than the task force team. Some of the people who were being targeted around the nation weren't people he would have considered proper and worthy, but he was very happy that people were taking notice of his actions and joining the fight. His forays into the Internet were even more gratifying. Conservative chat sites and gun owner sites were buzzing with debate, mostly pro-patriot. Even the President had issued a statement condemning the patriot's actions and urging people to calm down and follow the law.

That morning, Bauer dropped his next floppy in the mail to James Knox and prepared for an evening drive.

At 8:10 that evening, the patriot's Explorer turned onto the narrow winding streets near the Eagle Valley Golf Course in Woodbury, a wealthy community just east of St. Paul. The patriot was concerned about being in such a heavily populated area with narrow, winding streets, which would make a clean getaway difficult, but he had taken precautions that he hoped would give him an edge. He turned onto a circular road and passed the home of Terrence Busch, a Minnesota State Senator and member of the Senate Tax Committee. The patriot was very concerned about taxes and the ways in which they were levied and enforced. He had said as much in the letter that he'd mailed that morning to James Knox. He also mentioned Busch in his letter and was glad to see him and another man outside in his driveway, washing his car. With them was a little girl of about seven, whom the patriot recognized as Busch's daughter from campaign ads Busch had run in the past.

The patriot went around the block hoping the other man would leave, but when he came back the two were in a very involved conversation. Shit, the patriot thought to himself, well, they can't all be easy. He considered coming back another day, but he had another stop to make tonight, and he had rashly mentioned Busch in the already-mailed letter. *Goddamn it!* he thought as he went around the block again and rolled down his passenger side window. As he drove, he removed a loaded Remington 870 12-gauge shotgun from the back-seat floor and set the muzzle on the passenger's armrest. A .00 buckshot shell was loaded in the chamber, and five more were in the extended magazine. Busch noticed the truck slowing and sliding up to the curb behind his car and, ever the politician, walked up to the passenger side to see who this might be.

"Can I help you?" Busch smiled and the patriot answered by raising the shotgun with his right hand and firing point blank into Busch's throat.

On television people who are shot fly backward ten feet or more, usually in slow motion. This is a physical impossibility, of course. Any weapon whose blast is capable of lifting a 175-pound man and throwing him that distance would also cause a recoil equal in force and make it impossible for anyone to fire such a gun. However, on television, when a person is shot at close range with a shotgun he also usually dies; that is true in real life as well. A shotgun is a devastating weapon at close range, and Busch never knew what hit him. The patriot hit the gas before Busch even had time to fall, and he heard Busch's daughter screaming "Dad-yyyyyy!!!" as he tore off down the street. One of Busch's neighbors, a seventeen-year-old boy named Curt McDonald had just pulled into his drive when he saw the black Ford pull over to the Busch driveway and heard the shotgun blast. McDonald hunted ducks and knew right away what the sound was. He hesitated for only a moment before throwing his car into reverse and setting out after the Explorer.

The patriot had gone only a block before he saw the red Mitsubishi Eclipse skid around the corner behind him and knew he was being followed. He also knew that his Explorer was no match for a sports car on these goddamned winding streets. The Eclipse quickly made up the gap between them, and the patriot turned down another street and then quickly onto another until he neared a gas station. Throwing the shotgun onto the back seat, he clawed on the floor behind him for his Mini-14 rifle, which he had loaded with a 20-round magazine. The patriot's police drivers training had been top notch. He also had the advantage of years of high speed police driving behind him, which he used to his full advantage.

The gas station was empty when the patriot roared into the lot and threw the truck into a skidding turn. He ended up broadside to the entrance and raised the rifle up to his left shoulder, sighting in on the Eclipse's windshield. The Mini-14 is a semiautomatic weapon, which means that only one round will fire each time the trigger is depressed. The rifle has a very efficient mechanism to eject the spent shell and reload the next one in a fraction of a second, so it can be fired very quickly.

McDonald didn't really know what he'd do if he caught up with the truck; he hadn't thought that far ahead. He only knew that someone had just shot his neighbor and that he had to do something. He saw the Explorer skid and stop and saw that the truck's passenger window was down when flickering lights like camera flashes began going off inside the truck's cab. His windshield starred in several places immediately, and he hit the brakes. The patriot poured 15 rounds into the windshield and front grille of the Eclipse before hitting the gas and taking off again. McDonald was remarkably untouched. He had glass in his hair and on his lap, and his shirt had been nicked in several places around his shoulders. His engine was steaming from the coolant escaping from his radiator, which had been turned into Swiss cheese by the .223 caliber rounds. He suddenly realized that doing what he'd done was very stupid, and he began to shake from the delayed stress reaction people, even very brave people, sometimes have when they've come very close to being killed.

Forty minutes after the shooting of Terrence Busch, and ten minutes after Mike Rawlings's beeper had gone off, interrupting a rare romantic session between him and his wife, the patriot cruised down Lowry Avenue in North Minneapolis at sunset. Diondre Simmons, who normally would have been entertaining friends and associates on his front porch on a nice evening like this, had been finding reasons why he should stay inside for a change. He would never have admitted it, but the visit from the two cops had shaken him up. Simmons considered himself a brave man. He had been in more fights than he could count and had even survived a couple of shootouts, earning a scar on his shoulder, which he enjoyed showing off. But the idea of a totally unknown killer stalking him disturbed him greatly, especially when the killer was frightening enough to make two cops venture into the ghetto just to tell him to be extra careful.

Simmons was drinking a beer with some friends and waiting for a woman he knew to stop by with the bag of crack cocaine rocks that he sold in order to enjoy his lifestyle. Simmons had told his friends that it was better to wait inside tonight, claiming that the cops who'd come by the other day were really narcs who wanted to look him over close up and try to scare him. He said that they probably had the house under surveillance, so they should do the deals inside for a while. The old house they were in wasn't air conditioned, however, and it was stifling inside.

"Yo, Dee, man, let's go outside. It's like an oven in here, man," one of Simmons friends complained.

"Shut up," Simmons said. "I told you why we're in here."

"Yeah but Aaron keeps fartin', man. And it's hot."

"Aaron, stop fartin'," Simmons told one of the others. "It ain't that hot anyhow. What a bunch of pussies."

"Dee, you always sit on the porch, man," Aaron said. "Folks'll start wondering why you hidin' all the time now."

Simmons jumped to his feet and grabbed the now terrified Aaron by the shirt. "I ain't scared, motherfucker!! You hear me? I stayed out of the joint a long time by bein' smart, and I ain't gonna get dumb now 'cause you-all are fuckin' hot!"

"Dee, I ain't sayin' you scared, man!" Aaron cried. "I'm sayin' that's what people are sayin', that's all."

"What people, fool?"

"Some. You know how people talk."

"Fuck 'em," Simmons said as he sat down. "Get me another beer," he said to one of the women nearby. Simmons drank in silence for a few minutes and looked around to see the others wiping the sweat off of their foreheads and putting the cool cans of beer up to their faces. He was disgusted. Then he smelled it.

"Goddamn you!" he yelled at Aaron. "Smell like you died, man." Simmons got up and strode to the front door and threw it open. "You-all are some kinda pussy, that's all I think." He looked out and saw the dark truck parked across the street. "Monte," he said to one of the others, "who you know in a dark Explorer?" Before Monte could answer, Simmons's face blossomed in blood, and he fell back into the house. He collapsed into a sitting position against a closet door, and four more quick shots struck him in the chest and neck before he toppled over onto his side. Everyone heard the sound of a big engine and tires roar off down the street, and guns were pulled from various places in the home as the braver of the men ventured outside to see what could be seen. Only gun smoke remained as the patriot had turned the first corner and was gone. The men looked back at Simmons and Monte summed it up by saying, "Damn, Aaron. You shoulda held that last fart, man."

CHAPTER 30

▼

The next morning, a ragged Mike Rawlings came into the Task Force office. He'd been up most of the night at the scenes of both killings and had gotten only two hours sleep. Despite his exhaustion, he had a spring in his step that had been missing for a while. He strode to the unit's TV/VCR and triumphantly held up a cassette for all to see.

"Gentlemen, we may finally have the break we've been waiting for." The other investigators knew the basics of the two killings which had occurred the previous night, but it was Rawlings alone who had been to both scenes. He inserted the tape and pushed play. The black and white image of the outside of the gas station in Woodbury appeared as seen through the lens of the business's security video camera. "Last night we recovered this from the Holiday station where the patriot shot up the car of the teenager who was chasing him." The tape showed a couple of customers pumping gas and then coming in to pay and then leaving. The lot was empty, and they could see cars going by on the adjacent roadway.

"Right about here," Rawlings said, and then they saw an Explorer bounce into the lot and skid around sideways. The picture was a little grainy, but they could see the sports car following and then see its front end dip as McDonald slammed on the brakes. Because there was no audio, they couldn't hear the shots, but it was possible to make out McDonald's windshield and grille breaking up as they were hit by bullets. The whole thing only took about 15 seconds, and then the Explorer took off in the other direction. The tape played out, showing an employee of the gas station coming out to check on McDonald and then squad cars speeding in and officers running around with guns drawn while they sorted out who was in the Eclipse. Rawlings stopped the tape and rewound it to where he'd begun.

"Well, it's good, but how is this a break?" McDowell asked. "You can't see the patriot, and we know what kind of car he drives already."

"Oh, ye of little faith and less observation skills," Rawlings said with a smile. "What you *can* see is the license plate of the Explorer as it slides around and comes to a stop."

"What?" several of the others asked at once.

"Yep, I'll play it again. Pay more attention, now," he grinned to McDowell. Rawlings started the tape again and, sure enough, the front license plate was briefly visible when the truck approached the building before it spun around sideways.

"Not only is the plate there, but this also gives us a chance to narrow down the year Explorer he's driving, and it shows us something else, too. This guy can drive. SUVs are notoriously hard to handle at high speeds, but he spun that beast around like a pro. I've watched it over and over; this guy's been trained."

"Wait a minute," Pappas said. "I hate to rain on your parade here, Mike, but the picture's pretty grainy. I couldn't make out the plate either time you showed it. It all goes by too fast and the tape is worn."

"I know," Rawlings said. "The tape, like all security tapes, has been used over and over again. But, I think it can be slowed and enhanced and maybe become a lot clearer. We have pretty good equipment here, but I know who has better."

Just then there was a knock on the door and Agent Olivetti from the FBI stuck his head in the room.

"Hi, there!" Rawlings said with a wide smile. "I was just talking about you."

The team members all sat down to go over the entire case from the beginning. Agent Olivetti sat in after promising to jet the tape to the FBI lab in Virginia so their technical experts could have a go at it. Sharon Bluhm sat in as well, and they went over the case, their activities to date, and what should be done now.

"While we've made some progress, we need to stay aware of the fact that we still don't have a solid suspect," Pete Lincoln said. "This tape may be a breakthrough, but then again it might not. Evidence usually doesn't solve murders, talking does, and we need to do a lot more of that."

"The problem has been finding the time," Gene Truman pointed out. "We haven't had the time to catch our breath here because these murders are happening so quickly."

"That's something I'd like Sharon to address," Rawlings said. "Sharon, we've talked in the past about serial killers and the inherent difficulties in catching them. The only link they have to their victims are ones that exist in their own minds. We have the same thing here. What are your thoughts?"

"Well, I think we can classify the patriot as a serial killer. He isn't killing to act out a sexual fantasy, which is the normal motivation, but he is killing according to a pattern. Maybe 'pattern killer' would be more accurate, but it really doesn't matter. When I was working with the profilers in Virginia, we followed up leads on serial killings that had happened months and even years apart. The need to kill builds in these suspects over time until they feel compelled to release it. In this case, we have a man who's acting according to a plan he created to rid the country of people whom he considers undesirable and threatening. The other problem is that serial killers often have trouble fitting into society and often get pointed out by their acquaintances. Ted Bundy was an exception because he was so skilled at subverting his dark side behind a handsome, friendly exterior. I think we have another Bundy here, only he's driven to do what he does by something else."

"You made some assumptions about the patriot when we first formed this task force," Rawlings said. "Would you care to change any or add some?"

"Well, I'll stand by my observation that he's intelligent and fits into his environment. I think it will be a big surprise to his friends and co-workers when he is eventually caught. I thought at the time that he had military training and, while that's still possible, I think I'm leaning more toward police training. He tried to prevent us from knowing that he was impersonating an officer, remember? In his letter to Knox he said that he used means he wasn't going to reveal in order to get into Wallace Berry's apartment and Sarah Ehrenberg's house. Now, we know he used a police cover to get John Hughes to come out to the park, and, although this may have been a different ploy from the one he used on Berry and Ehrenberg, most people use the tools that have worked for them in the past. He was very comfortable playing the cop to Hughes, enough so that he was immediately believable over the phone. It's an assumption, but an educated one at this point, I think.

"He's good with weapons and his hands, and we know now that he can drive well. The military does have such training for certain specialty assignments, but I think it's safe to say that there are more people out there who have been police-trained in these areas, correct?" She looked around the table where most heads were nodding in agreement. "Now, the next question is whether we are dealing with a current or former officer." She noticed the others shift uncomfortably in their seats. "I know no one likes to think about the idea of investigating another officer. I'm not an officer, but I know it's considered a touchy subject, right?"

"Yeah," Pete Lincoln said. "In most departments, working Internal Affairs makes you a pariah. People who were your friends won't associate with you anymore."

"Isn't it desirable to weed out officers who are corrupt or incompetent?" Bluhm asked.

"Of course," McDowell said, "but the thing is, cops know they have to trust each other with their lives. They have to know, for a fact, that the people they're with out there with can be trusted 100% of the time. To be investigated means you're not trusted and it causes bitterness. Every cop can tell you that they know it would be fair if they got punished for doing certain things or fired for doing other things. But where the line should be drawn between being punished and being fired varies from cop to cop, and the internal investigator is caught in the middle."

"Not only that," Rawlings said, "but there is, I think, a certain reluctance to open that can of worms. The papers make such an issue out of a cop who gets in trouble that it makes every cop out there a little embarrassed. To the public, it implies that we're all bad."

"I can understand that," Bluhm said. "Police are given a great deal of power and authority by society because we realize it's necessary. At the same time, we resent people who hold power over us, and there is a tendency to crow when something bad happens to those we resent."

"Kind of a vicious circle," Phil Deane said. "People expect us to know everything about what's going on in order to solve crime, but yet want us totally out of their business."

"Correct," Bluhm said. "Even criminals don't want to be the victim of a crime. They just rationalize the things they do others."

"So, where does this leave us?" Rawlings asked. "We can't go on TV and say we think we're hunting a cop."

"That's your call," Bluhm answered. "I'm just here to give advice on his personality. We can draw some other conclusions here. He isn't poor; we know this from his access to weapons and the vehicle he drives. That tells me he has a job. Another thing that leads me there is that he hasn't been very mobile. He's stayed in a fairly small area. I'm sure there are people he'd like to kill in, say, South Dakota or Wisconsin. If he's trying to start a nationwide movement, why not move around the country?

"I think it's possible that he may be an active-duty officer, a former officer, or someone who's working security somewhere. There was some speculation early on as to how he located the homes of people who were unlisted or in hiding, like the animal rights people; maybe through his work he can access confidential information. Perhaps he can access court records or even state driver's license files."

"Of course!" Deane groaned. "How is it we didn't see that before?"

"It's understandable when you consider that you people haven't had the time to sort out one crime from another," Olivetti put in. "This is a nightmare scenario, fourteen victims that we know about in a little over two weeks. We've had mass murders in this country with more victims, but they all happened at one particular time. No police agency, to my knowledge, has ever dealt with one man killing so many unrelated victims in such a short period of time. It strains your resources, and traditional methods of investigation can't cope."

"So what do we do?" Pappas asked.

"More people," Olivetti said. "Simple as that. When the Klan was tearing up the south in the sixties, we sent in an army of agents and overwhelmed them. My supervisors have gotten word from the Justice Department in Washington that this situation is in danger of getting out of control. We have scattered crimes being committed all over in response to what's going on here now, and there is a very real danger that like-minded people will go to the next step and organize. I don't have to tell you how frightening that prospect is."

"True," Truman said, "but it's also true that the FBI didn't exactly follow the letter of the law when they dealt with the Klan in the sixties. And the letter of the law was considerably different then as opposed to now. Police had a lot more freedom and scope then. Can we realistically use forty-year-old tactics to deal with this?"

"We wouldn't be using forty-year-old tactics. We'd be using more people to do what's being done right now," Olivetti answered.

"Does this mean we're being replaced?" Lincoln asked. "Is this a matter of 'Okay, the Feds are here, you fellows go back to writing parking tickets now'?"

"I have no directive to take over the investigation, *at this point*," Olivetti said, letting the last three words hang in the air for a second, "just to tell you that the federal government is going to be more involved now. A judge and a state senator have been killed. The patriot has advocated open rebellion against the government and it appears that his actions have gained a following. I want to work with you, but I won't mislead you; very powerful people are watching this closely. The landscape of this investigation has changed."

After the meeting, Mike Rawlings's secretary told him he had a message to call Agent Cushing of the Secret Service. He returned the call and Cushing greeted him regretfully.

"Well, Mike, it's what I suspected. Hudson isn't going to cancel. I could approach him again this morning and see if what you had happen last night would change his mind, but I doubt it would."

"Yeah, we're not getting much rest here. The patriot's going full out to cross names off his list."

That night at work, Tony Bauer spent a good deal of his evening patrolling his beat and listening to talk radio. His actions were the hot topic of the evening, and people were stacked up on the call-in lines to get on the air with their opinions. The give and take was so spirited and became so heady for Bauer he had to turn it off. Things were going better than he could have hoped! Earlier that day a bomb had gone off in a county courthouse in Nebraska, killing three employees in the tax assessor's office. An unknown man in Indianapolis was being sought in connection with the street corner shooting deaths of two men who were known to be drug dealers. The stories went on and Bauer laughed and drummed his fist on the squad car's dashboard as he listened. The people were rising!

While the patriot was on patrol, Mike Rawlings settled into his favorite chair at home and hoped to find something distracting on TV. He flipped through the channels, looking for a light comedy or maybe an old movie—anything to take his mind off of the investigation. He hit MSNBC's channel, where a debate was going on between Stuart Davies, one of their anchors, and a man who was identified as Arthur Birmingham, President of the American Morality League. Rawlings was going to pass it by, but stopped when he heard Davies say, "Mr. Birmingham, you don't mean to tell me that your organization is supporting the actions of Minnesota's 'patriot,' do you?"

"No, I don't," Birmingham replied in a syrupy southern accent, "but we *are* completely in support of many of the arguments he's made."

"Such as?"

"We wholeheartedly agree that there has been a critical breakdown in American morality and ideals in the last twenty to thirty years in this country. America was founded on principals of freedom, hard work, protection from overzealous government, Christianity, free trade…"

"What about the principals of tolerance, non-violence, and law and order?" Davies interrupted.

"Of course," Birmingham replied with a smile. "Those are treasured American values, and I would never minimize them. However, our forefathers, the framers of the American Revolution and that great document, the Constitution, understood that there may come a time when change is required. We believe that the landscape of American life has changed to such a degree that those same forefathers would completely support efforts to bring the nation back on track and headed correctly into the twenty-first century."

Disgusted, Rawlings turned the TV off and pondered his role in what was becoming much, much more than any police investigation. He felt that the nation was looking to him and his group as their salvation. And yet, another portion of America seemed to be rooting for the patriot and hoping he would be able to stay free just long enough to ensure that the snowball was truly rolling down the mountain. He would never have admitted it, but he knew he believed that the patriot was right about some things. And *damn it,* he did sound a lot like a cop in what he'd written. Rawlings had never heard any cop he knew proposing armed rebellion; that was contrary to everything they stood for. Cops were about civil order and right and wrong. Hell, most cops only asked for a quiet shift when they came on so they wouldn't have to cope with the types of things that wore them down, like misery and hatred and pain. Rawlings wondered if the patriot could be a cop, after all. He'd heard what Sharon Bluhm had said and knew she had a sharp mind. Sharon could get inside someone's head and crawl around better than anyone Rawlings had ever seen. Yet, it was so goddamned, well, *uncomfortable,* to think they were hunting a fellow officer. And to think that anyone with a badge would be capable of the things the patriot had done. The image of Jeremy Soderberg and his crushed skull flashed through Rawlings' mind.

Rawlings had never investigated another officer. He'd never been in Internal Affairs during his time in St. Paul's investigations unit. If the patriot was a cop, he asked himself, how would he feel about those of us who were trying to stop him? What if it came down to his having to murder another officer in order to stay free? Would he hesitate? How would I feel, faced with the prospect of having to shoot him, if it came down to that? Rawlings wondered.

Rawlings got up and poured himself some brandy over ice. His idea of getting away from the case for the night hadn't panned out too well. He went out on his deck and sipped his drink while he looked out over the lake at the lights on the other side. Cop or not, I've got to try to stop him, Rawlings thought. I can't look at another Jeremy Soderberg and know that I haven't done my best. The only question was, would Rawlings's badge buy him an instant's hesitation if he did come face to face with the patriot?

CHAPTER 31

▼

On Tuesday morning, James Knox had planned to sleep in. He'd been living the patriot story more so than any other media person, and he was exhausted. He'd given almost as many interviews to reporters curious to know, and write about, why he'd been the one sought out, as had the officers who were working the case. Learning firsthand what it was like to be a "media darling" had been heady and exciting at first, but he'd found it difficult to keep up with the demands of his editor, fill his column, and still be approachable to his fellow reporters. A publishing company had sent a representative to Knox in order to discuss a possible book deal, and a Hollywood screen writer had sent him an e-mail to sound him out about making a TV movie once the patriot was finally corralled. It was all new to Knox, this sudden upheaval of his ordered world, and this morning he'd decided to forget about it for a while.

Jeeves the cat, surprised to find his roommate home for a change, celebrated the event by jumping onto Knox's dresser and doing his impersonation of a ten-pound furry bulldozer. He'd learned that he could get his lazy human out of bed by pushing everything, including a glass coin jar, off the top onto the floor. Knox waited him out until he heard the heavy jar being inched to the edge when he gave in and got up.

"Why is it you can sleep 22 hours a day, but I have to get up when you want to go out?" Knox asked the cat, who responded with a glare.

Knox started a pot of coffee and considered getting the paper off the front steps, but decided it could wait. He felt a surge of domesticity and had started mixing up some scrambled eggs when the phone rang. It was Dave Joyner, and the editor was ready to breath fire.

"Jim! Where the fuck are you?" He almost yelled into the phone.

"Well, I guess I'm at home, since you called me here," Knox replied.

"Don't be a smartass! Get down here right now! You have another letter from the patriot. That Agent Rawlings is on the way!"

"Shit," Knox said under his breath. "All right. I'll be right there." Knox hung up and sadly dumped the eggs into the disposal as he resigned himself to another hectic day.

Dear Mr. Knox,

Time to check in and separate fact from fiction. I've been eagerly watching the progress of the news story since my last letter, and I'm encouraged. It seems that there are others out there who think, as I do, that the country needs restructuring. Just breeze through the daily paper and see the rot out there. Stifled justice, rampant government corruption, street crime, lawyers making a mockery of the system—it's all in there. EVERY DAMN DAY! What's worse is reading about our elected leaders acting like children and bickering over how much to raise our taxes in order to pay for those who choose to make living off others a way of life.

And reading right along with me is the common man, the taxpayer, who, like the victim of a swindler, continues to pay out more and more of his hard-earned money while having no say whatsoever about how it is spent. He's become apathetic and has withdrawn from his duty to make these politicians answer to their constituents, but that's all about to change.

People are sick of street crime and seeing illiterate, immoral and unworthy psychopaths strut around selling drugs and living off the misery of others. They've hidden in their homes and moved farther out to the suburbs to try to get away, but the wave of crime has followed. They've listened to politicians and do-gooders say that they should feel sorry for this filth and that, if only more money was spent, they would clean up and become hard working members of society. Well, the people are beginning to realize that this has all been a huge lie and that human behavior isn't all that much different from animal behavior. There are sheep, and there are wolves, and there are shepherds who keep them apart. We need more shepherds.

I stopped a pack of wolves from picking on the sheep in Four Seasons Park in White Bear Lake. I was minding my own business and a bunch of little guys who thought they were tough tried to tell me that the park belonged to them. They wanted me to pay a fee or they would "fine" me. I fined them. It cost me some 9mm ammunition, but it was worth it. I doubt the one kid's mother was happy with me, shooting him in the face like that, but the way I see it, she shouldn't have raised such a piece of shit.

Professor John Hughes had to go, too. People like him are more dangerous than street gangs because they pretend to be something that they aren't. They go around pretending to be educators and teachers, but they're really devoted to subverting America's youth. They want our kids to believe that everyone in the world is equal and that people will really learn to recognize that if they only read it in a textbook. Well, the truth is, humans are NOT all equal. There are those who are faster, stronger, smarter, taller, more talented and more able than others. The Russians learned that humans won't work for nothing and gave up on communism, why are we trying to tell our kids that it can work here? The harder you try to achieve something, the better at it you become, and the more you will be rewarded. It's the only system that makes sense, because it follows human nature.

You already know that I lured Hughes out of his house pretending to be a policeman after having borrowed his cell phone and checkbook while on a reconnaissance mission, which brings me to another point. Why was that policeman at Hughes's house that day? It said in the paper that he was there on an "unspecified matter". That's pretty coincidental. Or was he there trying to warn Hughes that I might be coming? When you show this to the police, ask them if they have a list of their own. And if they do, how did they get it? Did they write down the names of people who are criminals running around free? Or maybe the names of radicals and activists who want to turn America into their own perverted idea of what a country should be? Pretty smart...that's exactly what I did.

By the way, no one's found the body of a pervert named Vladislaw Peschola, whom I killed last Sunday night up in Chisago County. Near Almelund, to be specific. This guy liked very little girls and was hounded out of one place after another because of his sickness. He came to liberal Minnesota and was going to open a business, for God's sake! He should have gone into calligraphy instead of landscaping, though, because the tools aren't as dangerous. I found him alone at home and sent him through his chipper-shredder. Dangerous tool, but it sure made short work of him. There may not be very much left now that the skunks and squirrels have nibbled on him, but I suspect you may find enough teeth to get an ID.

I hope people see that this mission I'm on is a long overdue taking-out of the trash. I'm gratified that more people have taken up the fight. I would encourage them to do a little more planning, however. It's better to get away clean to fight another day. And don't forget that the root of all of this is to change the government. We need our 'leaders' to understand that THEY WORK FOR US! Not for Exxon, not for General Electric, not for Ford, but for us. We DO have a say in how our tax money is spent. We've let them run loose for too long and they need to change. Find out who controls your taxation and demand an accounting. Here in Minnesota, Terrence Busch has done a piss-poor job of managing taxes, and he needs to go.

If we cause enough concern in the government, it WILL change. We can take advantage of that time to get some needed things done to make our nation strong again. We need a constitutional amendment declaring English the national language. There is too much wasted motion until this gets done. We need to reinstitute the free market economy and stop apologizing for it—it works. Very well. You work, you earn, you spend, and this makes companies strong. They pay workers, who earn and spend, and the cycle continues. It works. Look what we've accomplished here. We need to stop paying for those who are too lazy to work. Either they'll adapt or they'll die. It doesn't matter which, as the strong will go on.

A time of change is near. It could be dangerous, or it could be a great opportunity. Be strong, DO YOUR PART, and we can have another 200 years of strength, pride, and success.

a patriot

"Jesus Christ," Knox breathed as the text was read in his crowded office. "Welcome to Civics 101."

"Mr. Joyner," Mike Rawlings said to Knox's editor, "I appeal to you. *Please* don't print this verbatim. We've got too many copycat crimes now. If you run this, this, call-to-arms, here, the gutters will be running blood."

"I'm sorry, Detective," Joyner replied, "it's not my call anymore. My bosses have said we will run any correspondence from the patriot verbatim from now on. We'd be considered negligent later if we didn't. We *have* to report the news completely."

"Don't you see what's going on here?" Rawlings said. "You're being used by a madman! He's using your paper to incite others to kill! How is *that* not negligent?"

"I'm sorry, the decision has been made," Joyner said as he walked out of the office.

"Jim," Rawlings appealed to Knox, "do something, please. This is strong stuff. There are people out there who've been following this thing just waiting and hoping for the time to be ripe. This may push them over the edge, and then it'll grow totally out of control. Can't you see that?"

Knox rubbed his hand over his face and shook his head. "Mike, I hear you and I'm afraid you're right. But this story is *THE* story right now, all over, and it belongs to this paper. Believe me, even if we held back, the other media outlets have powerful resources, and the story would get out, probably within a couple of days. This building has too many eyes and ears in it, and everyone is trying to climb the media ladder. Any number of budding reporters here would trade this information to CNN or any of the other biggies for a job in a heartbeat."

"Too tempting to pass up if you're 23 years old and stuck writing the obituaries, huh?" Rawlings asked sarcastically.

"Yeah, that's the news biz. Although I, for one, don't like being a pawn. I'm supposed to report the news without bias and I've done that all of my adult life. I don't know why this guy chose me, but I don't like being used. I *have* to write the piece, Mike. I don't have any choice. But if I can, I intend to tell everyone exactly what I think of it."

Knox pitched his idea to Joyner, who denied his request. Then, Knox said that he would give an interview to one of the numerous TV crews roaming the city looking for 'patriot' material and tell them exactly how he felt about the paper. Joyner was angry, but knew that Knox had him over a barrel. Knox had become a celebrity, the closest thing to the patriot that was available, and was in a position to make demands he couldn't have made two weeks ago. They compromised: It was decided that Knox would run the story to form and then be allowed an opinion piece in the editorial section. Knox knew he was getting a good deal and took it.

Feeling Unclean
by James Knox

On Tuesday May 14, I walked into my office and opened my mail to find a floppy disk written by a madman who had killed a bunch of people and who now informed me that I would have the privilege of telling the world why he had done it. I did the right thing and told my boss. We called the police, who told us that the details provided in the letter showed it had been written by the man responsible. They asked us to report only the context of the letter and not the actual wording in an effort to keep those who might be "a few bricks short of a full load" from getting excited and opening fire.

Well, that letter was followed by more killings. Then another letter arrived, and again the police came. Then, the story became a stop-the-presses saga, and it seemed that every reporter from radio, TV, and print came to Minneapolis and they all wanted to know why I was the Chosen One. "I don't know," I said truthfully, but I basked for a time in the notion that I was, for the first time in my long and somewhat sullied life, a big shot. I gave interviews and issued my theories on why this nut was running around sticking people's heads in vises and ramming ice picks in their ears. I tried to stay humble, but I have to admit, it got a little intoxicating. I always considered myself a good reporter. I tried to be thorough and unbiased. When I promised a source something, I always followed through and appreciated that they chose to speak through me. I protected those who wanted to remain anonymous and never, *ever*, revealed a name.

So, I was tearing through this story, looking for sidelines and people who could add something to it, I wrote some terrific stories (if I may be so bold), and my stock in the news business rose. I've been around long enough to know that once the madness was over, I'd go back to being the graying, rumpled old curmudgeon way in the back of the newsroom, but I'm sad to say I actually *enjoyed* the illusion that I was, for a time, important.

It is said that every good thing must come to an end. My illusion of importance crashed to the ground today when I received my third letter from the man who gave it to me in the first place. I've always considered myself a bright fellow. I don't design computer systems or cure disease, but I always thought I was pretty savvy and had too many miles on my odometer to be fooled in the business of reporting the news. Boy, was I wrong!

One of the investigators on the case, a fellow I've come to know and respect, begged us not to print The Patriot's latest ramble. He pointed out the copycat crimes that had already occurred and said that this story would only encourage more. "Hell, we know that!" we answered. We'd been doing our job and reporting those incidents, too. Everyone wanted to know about them, and they'd buy our paper to find out. If we didn't do it, another paper or TV station would, and we might as well report corn and hog shares from then on. He asked me whether I realized I was being used, and it hit me like a bright shaft of light. By golly, we were! Somewhere out there, a guy sat down, made up a list of people he didn't like, stocked his tool chest full of weapons, and started killing. And then, maybe to justify the slaughter, he decided it would be nice if others joined in and, in a very short period of time, got the *worldwide* media to publish his propaganda.

The decision was made, the story was written and there, on page one, you can read for yourself that The Patriot hates teachers, politicians, and criminals. He hates them enough to ram them into wood-chippers and would ask everyone, if they could find the time, to please find someone they don't like and rip them apart, too. No bother, really. It's good for the country! The good old US of A! That car salesman told you your new hatchback would get 40 miles per gallon and it only gets 35? Shoot him! Your neighbor's kids play loud rap music? Kill them with your trusty chainsaw. Didn't win the Powerball? Take it out on the clerk who sold you the losing ticket.

I'm not blaming my paper for their decision. There's no way we could keep the letter quiet, considering the value that's been placed on any little part of this story. If Mr. Patriot wants, he can always send his floppies to another desk in another building, and the story will get out anyway. I even saw a national newspaper ad directed at The Patriot, offering to pay him for any communications he might send them! These are the times that I get embarrassed about my profession.

We live in the Information Age, and the public has a right to know. A free press is vital to democracy. I believe all of that, but there's an upside and a downside to everything. Information can be dangerous, too. Today, a lot of people will read what The Patriot had to say and, thankfully, most will see it for what it is—the distorted ideas of a lunatic. Sadly, some will see truth in it and use it as an excuse to take life.

Well, news is my profession, and I'll go on reporting it as long as I'm able. I'm paid to be a messenger, and I guess I'll keep doing it because it's all I know. But right now, I feel dirty. I'm going home and take a shower.

That night at work, the patriot sat in his parked squad car and read the evening edition of the paper with Knox's front page account of the latest letter and the deaths of Peschola and Hughes. As expected, the police had gone straight to Peschola's property near Almelund and found blood on the chipper and scattered pieces of bone around the mulch pile, which they intended to try to DNA match to Peschola. Since there was no reason to believe otherwise, Peschola's disappearance was officially classed as a homicide.

The paper had run a couple of side pieces in which family members of the patriot's other victims were contacted and asked to comment on the latest developments, and they responded to form, saying that the patriot was little more than an animal and that the police needed to redouble their efforts to stop him.

The patriot leafed through the paper and passed by the editorial page. He rarely read letters to the editor or opinion pieces as they didn't interest him. The Minneapolis paper was so liberal and read by so many like-minded people that the letters gagged him, more often than not. He went back to the front page story and finished reading it, then saw a tag line at the bottom which directed readers to the back page for a follow-up article by James Knox. He turned to it and began reading Knox's "Feeling Unclean" article. He had figured in the beginning that Knox wouldn't approve of what he was doing, but would, like a good little reporter, enjoy the exclusive insight he'd been given and run with it. As he read on he became offended by Knox's use of the words *propaganda* and *ramblings*. And for Knox to *trivialize* what he was trying to do by saying people should shoot car salesmen and store clerks when you don't get your way! He was missing the point entirely! The patriot threw down the paper and struck the dash with his fist. *Knox is a fucking reporter,* he thought. *He's paid to report, not to run off at the mouth about things he didn't understand!* It was almost as if he was trying to sabotage the patriot's efforts to assemble the people he needed to get the job done. He knew that many out there felt the same way he did, but they were just hesitant, and someone needed to show the way. *That goddamned pencil pusher!* the patriot raged. *Who the fuck does he think he is? What's a reporter anyway except someone who writes about the actions of others! A nobody who tells people the actions of great men, men who change history!*

"1130," the police radio said.

Bauer took a breath and shook his head to clear it. Was that the radio?

"1130," the radio repeated.

"1130," Bauer replied.

"1130, go to 27215 Grenada Ave, in Eureka Township. A female at that residence is requesting to see a deputy about a child endangerment issue."

"Copy."

The address was in the western part of Bauer's patrol area and, of course, he was east, but traffic was light, and he made it there in about 20 minutes. While on the way he read on his MDC screen that the complainant was a woman named Jennifer Kruger. The dispatcher had added a comment that she "sounded 10-57," meaning intoxicated. He pulled into the drive of a little rambler and walked up to the door. Before he could knock, the door was yanked open by a skinny woman in her twenties with dark straggly hair. Bauer could tell she was blowing off 100 proof through the screen door.

"What the fuck took you so long?" She demanded as she let him in.

"I got here as quick as I could," Bauer said. "What's the problem?"

"My fuckin' boyfriend took my son and I wan' him back, tha's what's wrong," Kruger slurred.

"Okay, how old is your son?"

"Eighteen months. I come home and that worthless fuck's gone and took my son. He's at his girlfriend's place and they're prob'ly doin' meth."

"All right, slow down," Bauer told her. "Who is your boyfriend?"

"He's not my boyfriend! Well, he used to be, and we had a kid together. Now he lives with this other slut, and he thinks he can take my kid!"

"Okay, just so I understand, you and your ex-boyfriend had a child, now you've broken up, and he lives with someone else, and he took the child over there. What's this guy's name?"

"Andy Hudson. He lives in Lakeville with that bitch. Go an' get my son!" Kruger demanded.

Bauer was getting fed up with this drunk. "Do you have a restraining order or any custody agreement with Andy?"

"No, he just moved out a couple weeks ago. But I'm the boy's mother!"

"So, you have nothing from a court saying when Andy can take the boy and when he can't?"

"No. But he can't just come in here and take him!"

"Is he the child's father?" Bauer asked.

"'Course! What, you think I sleep around?" Kruger asked.

"I didn't say that. I want to make sure he is the boy's father."

"Well, he is. And I'm his mother, and I want him back!"

"How is it that he could take the child without you being here? Who was babysitting the kid while you were gone?"

"He was!"

"Andy was babysitting? You invited him in here to watch his son, and he left with the boy before you came home?"

"Yes!" Kruger said, exasperated. "When I go out, Andy…watches…the…baby!" She said each word slowly as it was obvious to her that she was talking to an idiot.

"So, how do you know he took the kid to his girlfriend's? Maybe he went to the store."

"Duh! I called her apartment, and he's there, and he told me he isn't bringing Justin back."

"Did he say why?"

"'Cause he's an asshole! He knows this will piss me off, and tha's what he want's to do! Now you go get my son back!"

"Give me the number for the apartment," Bauer told her. Kruger staggered off to the kitchen and came back with a piece of paper with a Lakeville number on it. "Wait here," he instructed and went out to his car. He called the apartment and spoke with Andy, who told him that he had taken Justin because he knew that Kruger would be coming home drunk. He said he didn't want to leave the baby with her in that condition and that he was working with a lawyer to try to get custody of the boy. Bauer got the address and asked for a Lakeville car to check the child's welfare in order to counter Kruger's claim that Hudson and his girlfriend were doing drugs there. A Lakeville unit stopped by and found the apartment cluttered with some evidence of alcohol usage, but no drugs. The child seemed healthy and well cared for.

Bauer went back into Kruger's house. "Well, here's the deal," he told her. "You don't have any custodial rights in writing from a judge, so the child is as much Andy's as yours. I had a Lakeville officer check on him and was told the baby is fine. Considering the fact that *you've* been drinking, I don't think the child should come back here tonight. Sleep it off and call Andy in the morning."

"NO!" Kruger yelled. "THAT BABY IS MINE, AND YOU GO GET HIM NOW!!"

"Nope," Bauer told her. "And you stay away from there. If you go over there and cause a problem you're getting popped for DWI and child endangerment."

"YOU FUCKING ASSHOLE!!" Kruger screamed.

"If you want to complain, you can call the sergeant, but that child stays where he is tonight."

"I'll call the fuckin' sergeant!" Kruger hissed. "I'll tell him what an asshole you are! I'll have your job, you big fuck! I suppose you hate women, too, tha's why you agree with Andy! Isn't your wife giving you any? Is that it? You're not getting any pussy, so you go to work and be an asshole to women, right?"

"You're sweet," Bauer said. "Now go to sleep." He turned to go and an ashtray sailed past his ear and hit the door frame.

"Why don't you hit me, huh?" Kruger yelled. "You want to! Big, pussy-whipped asshole. You know, if you had a bigger cock, your wife would want it, but she's happy to get it somewhere else!"

Bauer felt the blood running in his head. He clenched his fists and held back. *Oh, how sweet it would be to throw her through a wall!* he thought.

"Lady, I'm leaving now and you better settle down. You throw anything else at me and you're going to jail."

"Wha's the matter? Get mad?" Kruger sneered. "Can't stand the truth? Big guy with a little cock! Your wife's out fucking niggers and you hate it! All you guys eat shit! Cops are pigs!"

Bauer had had enough. He felt his blood go cold just as it did when he was the patriot. He had come to like the feeling more and more as he experienced it. His mind cleared, his body felt so alive and strong! It felt as if all of his senses were clear and sharp!

"I can sure see why Andy traded you in for somebody better," Bauer told her coldly. "If that nasty old hole of yours smells as bad as your breath, he probably *ran* the fuck out of here!"

Kruger gaped at Bauer and he smiled as he reached for the door knob. Just as he turned, Kruger screamed, "MOTHERFUCKER!!" and launched herself at his back, just as he knew she would. Bauer spun around and slammed his palm into

Kruger's chest, sending her flying onto the couch. She bounced back up and ran at him again, trying to claw his face. A couple of months before, Bauer would have easily spun this drunken 110-pound skank around and cuffed her, but the deputy sheriff that he'd been was gone for good. He found he enjoyed her attempts to hurt him and toyed with her like a cat playing with an injured mouse. He held her at arm's length while she swung her arms and kicked at him to no avail. She tried to grab a couch cushion to hit him with, but he knocked it out of her hand with a chuckle. She launched herself at him again and this time, she managed to slap his face. Bauer pulled back and she kicked him in the crotch. The blow wasn't very strong, and Bauer wasn't hurt, but he'd grown tired of the game. It was time to show her who he was. He crossed the four feet between them in an instant and grabbed Kruger by the throat with his right hand, lifting her off of the floor in one smooth motion. He slammed her against the wall and held her there. When he put his face up to hers, Kruger's booze-soaked brain finally registered that she was really in trouble.

"You like pain, baby?" Bauer hissed into her face. "So do I! I'll show you more pain than you knew existed on this fucking planet!"

"Let me go!" Kruger sputtered.

"You started this dance, bitch! It ain't over until I say it is!" Bauer pulled her away from the wall and grunted as he tossed her like a rag doll onto a coffee table, breaking it.

"Ow! Ow!" Kruger cried.

Bauer yanked her to her feet and spun her around so he was behind her. He grabbed her left arm with his left hand and dug the fingers of his right hand into the trapezius muscle on the right side of her neck and bore down. Kruger screamed and sank to the floor in agony. He maintained pressure until she stopped struggling and then flopped her onto her stomach. He handcuffed her and straightened up.

"1130," he called on his portable radio.

"1130."

"I need assistance at this address. I've been attacked by the complainant and have her restrained at this time. Send a supervisor, please, and a unit to transport."

"Copy."

Bauer looked down on the sobbing woman at his feet and felt the rage ebb out of him. It would have been so easy to kill her, Bauer thought. He was glad that he'd gotten control of himself before that had happened because he knew it would have been dicey for him to get out of that one. Besides, a weak, drunken slut like this wasn't worth his getting into trouble. If only he hadn't been reading that bullshit in the paper before he'd come here! *That FUCKING Knox!*

Bauer looked at the red marks around her neck and shoulders. He would be easily able to explain them by saying, truthfully, that she attacked him from behind and he had to fight her off. He would tell Mike Fitz how she'd kicked him in the balls and that he had to use a pressure point hold on her neck muscle to get the cuffs on. The broken table could be accounted for in the struggle. It was pretty flimsy, after all. She could say whatever she wanted, but who would believe a drunken bitch like this? Hell, Andy's lawyer would probably turn cartwheels when he found out about the brawling behavior of his client's ex. His case just got a lot easier.

CHAPTER 32

▼

Wednesday would have been Bauer's last day of his workweek, but he did something he'd rarely done since he started in police work: he called in sick. He didn't believe in cheating his employer. After all, returning America to its roots of hard work and fair play was what he was trying so hard to do. *I hadn't really been lying when I called in,* he thought. He'd had a hard time sleeping when he'd gotten off work the night before after his fight with the drunk. As he tossed and turned, he kept remembering the pleasure he'd felt when he saw the look in the woman's eyes at the moment she saw what she had in *his* eyes, when she realized that this wasn't some TV cop whom she could trash talk. Bauer had found that the feeling that swelled inside him when he was carrying out the work of the patriot was almost intoxicating. It was a rush that he'd never had before. There were times, like when he'd strangled Andy Stoughten, standing out in the night with danger all around, that he felt like a pure creature, like a wolf or a panther—something that existed to kill, but yet something more. He felt that he was carrying out a purification. He struggled to form the most exact way to describe in his mind how it was. There was a sense that, if he wanted to, *at that exact moment,* he could stretch out his arms and stop time!

Something inside of him knew that the idea was silly. He cautioned himself, knowing that he had to remain vigilant. He could still lose this battle that he'd fought so hard to win. He knew it was foolish to allow his mind to dwell on ideas like that, but *Oh, God* did it feel good! He lay there wondering if it would be possible to bring on the feeling by concentrating, but it wasn't the same. He needed the reality of being near someone. He had felt the rush for the first time when he'd shot Judge Borgert, but it had been tinged with something else that night.

He was nervous then, and still not fully committed to his mission. He remembered how he lay in the bushes that night and debated going on, but once it was over, he'd felt free! He'd crossed the threshold, and his path was clear, and nothing could stand in his way.

He thought of Sarah Ehrenberg and how powerful he'd felt when she struggled against his grip as he pressed the tool into her ear. There was an almost sexual element that sent a chill through him as he remembered. He'd hated that woman so much! He thought of the times he'd seen her on TV and how she would chant or scream slogans. A fire had smoldered inside of him then, thinking what it would be like to see her paralyzed with fear and finally quiet.

He had also laid awake thinking of Knox and how he'd been betrayed. All he asked was for Knox to tell people why all of this was happening and why it was so important and that *bastard* had the audacity to write what he did! As far as Bauer could tell, the story only ran locally, and there didn't seem to be much in the way of fallout from it. Too many such stories could slow support for the cause and perhaps even stall the movement entirely.

This morning's news had a story about a vocal activist for illegal immigrants' rights being found shot to death in El Paso, Texas. The police had no suspects, but believed the woman's death was similar to the murder two days before of a local civil rights attorney. A police spokesman said that it was too early to say if the two crimes were related, but the national media seemed to be gearing up to proclaim that a second vigilante killer was on the prowl there. More significantly, a Michigan militia cell announced the night before that several of their members had left the group intending to take up active violence against the state. The parent group's commander said, in a statement, that his organization was severing ties with these former members, and intended to remain "loyal to the United States Constitution." An FBI spokesman in Michigan told the press that they knew the names of some of the defecting members, and said that the FBI feared the newly formed group may begin robbing banks to finance their campaign.

All of this was good news to the patriot. He had launched his battle only hoping that he could remain free long enough to make people see that the country had to be changed. He had accomplished more than he thought he could in a very short period of time and that fact had brought him a new dilemma: he had nearly exhausted his target list. He had initially made a list of potential targets, then narrowed it to those he was able to locate through motor vehicle or court files. He then conducted his preliminary scouting trips and, only after doing that, made his final list. When he shot the drug dealer, Simmons, he was left with only two good names. The plans he'd made for June 1 were still on, but that had been thrown together just a few weeks ago when he'd learned of the opportunity in the news. That was ten days away, and he needed to keep the police task force busy so they would have a hard time making up any ground on him.

The patriot decided to send off another letter to Knox, both to warn him not to make any more stupid comments, and to lay a false trail for the police to follow for a while. He needed to buy time and to repair any damage that Knox's opinion piece may have caused. He had done some research on Knox before picking him to write his story, and he thought he might know a way to get his point across.

That morning, Mike Rawlings was gathering case notes from the massive amount of data that had so far been collected in the patriot case, and was organizing them for his meeting the next morning with Vince Cushing of the Secret Service. Pete Lincoln had attended the autopsies of both Busch and Simmons the day before, and recovered the slugs and shotgun pellets that had killed them. The other task force members spent their time interviewing witnesses to both killings, and found that the acquaintances of Simmons were much less cooperative than those who had been with Busch.

It seemed that the men who had socialized with Diondre Simmons, and who were there when he was killed, carried no real grief at his passing. Theirs was more of a business relationship with Simmons, and he had ruled his associates with an iron fist, employing threats and intimidation. His death opened doors for some of the men who were in the house that night, and they were pleased to pass through them over the body of the man they had called their friend. That didn't mean, however, that they had any intention of helping the police find the man who killed him. There are certain neighborhoods in America where the police are not viewed in a positive light, and Simmons's neighborhood was one of those. To these men talking to the police, for any reason, just wasn't done. The investigators' questions were answered with a lot of shrugs, mumbles, and the intensive scrutiny of fingernails.

The detectives who spoke with the neighbors of Terrence Busch faced a different problem: people didn't know when to shut up. It seemed as if everyone on the block had lined up to be interviewed, saying that they wanted to help find the bastard who killed their favorite neighbor, but, unfortunately, most had very little of importance to add. The investigators were pleased to know that Busch was so popular, but they burned through a lot of notebook paper with little to show for it. The most solid information came from young Curt McDonald who, after recovering from his close call, was able to give a good account of what had happened. He hadn't been able to read the Explorer's license number during the chase, but said he had gotten a glimpse of the driver just before he opened fire on McDonald's car. The two clerks on duty in the gas station were too shocked by the incident to remember any valuable details, and there were no customers around. A man walking his dog nearby told police that he saw the Explorer roar by him just before pulling into the lot, and that he thought the driver had dark hair and a moustache, but hadn't gotten a good look. It seemed to the investigators that the patriot led a charmed life, pulling off all of these killings, many in broad daylight, without anyone ever really getting a good look at him. Names, addresses and phone numbers were taken down, and the patriot file grew another couple of inches thick.

Rawlings was wondering how much of this Cushing would really need to see in order to do his job, when there was a knock on his door. He looked up to see Agent Olivetti along with a thin, sandy haired man who looked to be about twenty-years-old.

"Can we come in?" Olivetti asked. Rawlings cleared some files off two chairs and invited them to sit.

"This is Bill Shire," Olivetti said, introducing the man to Rawlings. Rawlings shook the man's hand and thought he might break it, Shire's grip was so light. "Bill is a police artist who's been working with the Bureau for a little while now. He's also done a lot of work with police agencies in New York state, and with many of the major agencies along the eastern seaboard. I thought it might be a good idea to have him sit down with your witnesses, and see if he can come up with a rendering of your suspect."

"Well, that might be a little premature," Rawlings said. "To date, only one man has really had a look at the patriot's face and he was about 50 feet away. Plus, we think he was in disguise."

"I understand," Olivetti said, "but Bill has a knack for getting details from witnesses like no one else I've ever known. Plus, we have the people from the park shootings and the one in Woodbury, right?"

"Well, yes, but all of those people were too far off to see much, or the patriot was moving too fast. I'm not against the idea, you understand, I just wonder about the value at this point. I've been involved with cases where an inaccurate sketch came out, and the defense made a big deal out of it in court later."

"Yes, and I don't want that to happen either," Olivetti said with a smile. "When I say Bill has a knack for getting details, I mean to say he...well...he has a *sense* for people. It's hard to put into words, but Bill has a way of reaching into your mind, and taking out what's there."

"Okay," Rawlings said. *Shit, is this what the FBI's into now, psychics?* he thought.

"Mr. Rawlings," Shire said in a soft, even voice, "I think Agent Olivetti may be misrepresenting me. I just talk with people, and help them remember things in ways that policemen don't use, that's all."

Rawlings found that it was impossible to look away·from Shire when he was speaking. There was something about Shire's voice that was almost hypnotic, and his eyes were a soft-brown and huge. They seemed to look right through you, and into your soul. Rawlings thought, strangely, that he'd like to talk to Shire all day.

"How long have you been doing this?" Rawlings asked.

"I've been drawing all of my life," Shire answered in an even, gentle voice that seemed to draw Rawlings in. "I did my first police sketch for the Albany Police in 1990. It was of a rapist, and we were able to catch him a little while after that."

"1990?" Rawlings asked. "What, were you nine-years-old?"

"No," Shire answered with a gentle smile, "I was twenty and in college. I'm thirty-two-years old."

"Geez, you sure look young. I'd never have thought you were more than twenty-one. I bet you get carded a lot," Rawlings said with a chuckle.

"No, never," Shire answered. He didn't offer anything more, and Rawlings decided to let it drop.

"Well, as I said, I have no objections to trying. You just whistled this young fellow up?" Rawlings asked Olivetti.

"I've known of him for years, and thought he might be of help. I called and, luckily, Bill was free, so we flew him out here on the red-eye."

"Well, fine. I'm gathering the files here for a meeting I have tomorrow with the Secret Service. They're concerned that the patriot might try to assassinate that Supreme Court Justice whose coming for the University of Minnesota Law School graduation on June 1."

"That seems pretty ambitious," Olivetti said. "I think he'd have a hard time getting through the screen they put up around those justices."

"Maybe. But they're concerned, and I said I'd meet with the guy. This Justice Hudson is pretty liberal, and the Secret Service agent in charge said they get a lot of threats against him. I wouldn't put it past our man to make a play when he's here."

Olivetti chuckled. "I doubt it. He's not the type to trade his life for a target. That's the only hope he'd ever have of getting Hudson."

"I hope you're right," Rawlings said. "In the meantime, I'll have my secretary get the most updated list of witness names, and you can set Bill up wherever is most convenient."

"Thank you," Shire said quietly. "I'd like to speak to them one at a time, but to be able to bring them all together at the end, so they'll have to wait for a while. It should take about one hour per witness."

"Well, let's set you up downstairs in our conference room. That way, the witnesses can come in at staggered times, and use the commissary while they wait afterwards."

"Thank you," Shire almost whispered.

Rawlings made the arrangements and went back to his work, but was distracted. Shire had given him the creeps. Rawlings felt like the guy knew his bank balance, his locker combination from high school, and his wife's bra size, just from the few words they'd exchanged. *I bet there was a UFO sighting the day he was born,* Rawlings thought.

At two o'clock that afternoon, the patriot parked two blocks away from James Knox's house on a side street in Golden Valley. He was wearing jeans, and a work shirt with the symbol of a local power company on the breast. He had on a baseball cap, with the same company logo, over his shaggy blonde wig. He pulled a clipboard from his truck, and began walking through the neighborhood, going to the back of each house, and looking at the meters. He made notes at each house, and unassumingly made his way to the rear of Knox's rambler.

The patriot had gambled that Knox wouldn't be home during the day and was pleased to see that the garage was empty, as he looked in the windows while he walked by. He'd read Knox's biography some time before, and knew that he was divorced, and that he had a grown daughter, named Trisha, at school in Tempe, Arizona. The patriot had intended to leave a floppy disk for Knox outside the house, but when he found the backyard to be overgrown with shrubs and trees, and very private, it gave him an idea.

He went around the house, and found a back door leading into the garage. It was locked, but with an ancient knob, and not with a deadbolt. It was a simple task for the patriot to turn the knob very hard and break the mechanism inside. He wiped the knob with a handkerchief, and donned a pair of surgical gloves before he walked inside. He found the door leading into the house unlocked. Knox often came home bleary-eyed, and found unlocking doors a time-consuming nuisance. The patriot walked into the kitchen and pulled a pistol from his waistband. He quickly checked the house, and was startled when Jeeves streaked by him, surprised at the appearance of this stranger in his world.

The patriot took a minute to look at some of the photos Knox had framed on his walls. There were pictures of Knox at various ages, and in different locations. In one, he was standing outside of a tent, wearing jungle fatigues. In another, he was standing in front of Buckingham Palace. Four others held photos of a pretty young woman, and in one, she was wearing a sweater with "Sun Devils" on the front. *That would be young Ms. Knox in Tempe,* the patriot thought. He carefully removed that picture from its frame, and put it in his pocket. He re-hung the empty frame in its previous location, and then pulled an envelope containing the floppy from his pocket. He nailed it to the sheetrock wall inside the frame, using his Tanto knife as a hanger. He thought that leaving the weapon that he'd used to kill three of his victims with would be a nice touch, and would go a long way toward convincing Knox to play by the rules. He left the house the way he'd come, and walked the neighborhood for the rest of the block before returning to his truck. He didn't want anyone wondering about a meter reader stopping in mid-block. Besides, it was good to know the area in case he had to come back in the future.

At work that afternoon, Mike Fitz got a message from the dispatcher to call Tina Sullivan at her home. Mike knew Tina through Don Sundquist, and she'd babysat for Mike's kids when she was a teenager. He suspected that the call might be about Bauer. Those who had been to Don's graduation party had eagerly recounted how Bauer and Tina had been coiled around each other in the hallway that night. Cops make their living being involved in the intimate details of people's lives, and are quite comfortable prying. This nosiness makes them habitual gossips, and Fitz wasn't surprised that the tale, juicy as it was, and coupled with the fact that Tina had a really sporty body, would spread around the department like the Ebola virus.

Fitz called Tina's number, and she answered on the first ring. Shit, she must really have it bad for him, Fitz thought.

"Tina? It's Mike, what can I help you with?"

"Hi, Mike. I'm sorry to bother you at work, but, well, I guess I need some advice."

"Okay, what's up?"

"Well, you know that Tony and I are, kind of, seeing each other. And, it seems like maybe he wants to see me, but then something gets in the way. It's hard to explain, but it seems like we really have a nice time when we're together, but then he gets scared of me or something."

"Well, Tina, this really isn't any of my business," Fitz said, hoping she'd leave it at that. Fitz believed that he was a better friend and supervisor than some other sergeants, because he tried to stay out of the guys' personal lives. Sometimes that wasn't possible, but Fitz tried to avoid it whenever he could.

"I know, but you know him best, I guess. What I want to know is, am I wasting my time? Should I try harder? I mean, I know he had a bad marriage and maybe I can help him get over it, but I don't want to push him too much, you know?"

"Yeah, I know. Tina, I know he really took it in the gut from his ex. I don't really know everything that happened, because Tony is pretty close-mouthed, and, frankly, I've been a little worried about him. He's a private guy, but lately he seems to be…I don't know…different, I guess. Maybe he does need someone to bring him out of his shell, and help him see the good side of life again. On the other hand, if you push too hard he's the type to shut you out. I guess I don't know what to say. Maybe women are better at giving this type of advice," he chuckled. "My wife claims to know more about men…well, me anyway."

"Mike, I'd like to send Tony a letter. Maybe it would be better that way. I could explain everything I feel, and then let him read it without any pressure, and then, he can call me or not, depending on whether he wants to."

"I think that's a good idea Tina," Fitz said

"One last favor," Tina said. "I don't have Tony's address. Could you give it to me?"

"Sure. I don't think he'd mind. Just a second." Fitz looked through his briefcase and found his department roster. "Here we go, 1009 Pine Street. in Hastings."

"Thanks so much, Mike. I really appreciate your help."

"No problem Tina. Good luck and I hope everything works out okay for you."

Fitz hung up, and wondered if he'd just done something good, or something stupid. It would be ten days before he got his answer.

At 7:30 p.m. the patriot was just leaving Enterprise Rental at the Minneapolis/ St. Paul International Airport complex. He had decided after the Busch killing, that his Explorer was too easily identifiable, and it would be prudent to drive something else for a while. His dark hairpiece and false handlebar moustache were in place, as he steered the white Chevy Tahoe out onto Interstate 494 and headed east. His Explorer was parked in the short term lot, and he'd ridden in an enterprise Rental shuttle to the rental office.

When he was in the early days of his mission planning, the patriot had come to the conclusion that he may need a couple of false identities at some point. He had driven to a large cemetery in St. Paul, and walked through until he found the grave of a boy named Joseph Albert Wicks, who had been born a year earlier than he, and had died at age two. The headstone of Wicks's parents lay alongside with the names Albert and Harriet Wicks, with a blank space where the dates of their deaths would go. The patriot assumed that both of them were therefore still alive, and probably still living in the area. He found their listing in the phone book, showing that they lived in South St. Paul. A trip to the St. Paul Public Library allowed him to browse the obituaries for the date listed on Joseph's headstone, and he found the notice, which read that young Joseph had died tragically in an auto accident. The helpful obituary told the patriot that Joseph had been born in St. Paul, so his next destination was the Ramsey County Records Office where he requested, and obtained, for a small fee, a certified copy of Joseph's birth certificate.

From there, the patriot drove across the state border to the neighboring community of Hudson, Wisconsin, and to the Post Office located on Myrtle Street, where he paid for a post office box. He then drove to the St. Croix County Government Center, where he used the birth certificate to obtain a Wisconsin Driver's license, listing the post office box as his mailing address. After passing the test, and having his picture taken, the patriot had photographic proof that he was Joseph Albert Wicks, of PO Box 248, Hudson, WI.

At the Enterprise Rental counter, the harried clerk barely looked at the Wisconsin license, as she quickly filled out the forms. She gave the patriot a map of the Twin Cities, and sent him on his way. He stopped back at his car to retrieve a few items which he decided might be frowned upon if discovered in an airport these days and headed out.

As he drove, the patriot thought of the luck he'd had so far and wondered how long it could hold. His advance planning had served him well, and his knowledge of police procedures certainly didn't hurt either. He knew how time-consuming a major crime investigation could be and how much pressure there was on investigators to be certain to cover all the bases. One little screw up, and the investigators would get reamed by judges, attorneys, prosecutors, supervisors, and the media. Each piece of evidence had to be handled perfectly, each statement had to be precise, each crime scene had be thoroughly photographed, and no small detail could be overlooked. Investigators were encouraged to take their time and do it right, but the patriot knew that the people chasing him were drowning in procedure. That fact had been mentioned in news stories about the task force, and the patriot was glad to know that his planning was paying off. He'd handed them too many bodies in too short a period of time, and it had bought him time, and space in which to maneuver. Now, he had to buy some more.

Gordon E. Holmes was a Congressman in the district surrounding Hudson, Wisconsin, and neighboring communities. The area was quickly becoming a burgeoning suburb of the Twin Cities area, and attracted people with its natural beauty and reasonable tax structure. Minnesota is a relatively highly-taxed state, and some of its residents found the living better and cheaper across the Mississippi River, and, like the restaurant ad said, made a run for the border.

Wisconsin is a mostly rural state, excluding the Madison and Milwaukee metro areas in the east, and is best known for hunting, fishing, beer, and cheese, not necessarily in that order, depending on your value system. It is known as a conservative state, and the residents don't worship at the altar of political-correctness quite as much as their neighbors to the west. Several years ago, the state was forced by a federal judge to honor an ancient treaty made with the Indians, which allowed them unrestricted fishing rights, including the right to take fish with gill nets. Many of the state's sportsmen were enraged by this decision, and vowed to fight it by any means, including violence. The local FBI discovered that someone was printing and selling bumper stickers in the northern part of the state which read, "Save a fish, kill an Indian," and they made efforts to curtail the sale of these stickers, which were appearing on pickups all over the state. The state's Department of Natural Resources was viewed by its resident sportsmen as a collection of idiots, and it seemed that the only thing that stood between peace and total anarchy, was whatever native goodwill that existed in the Lutheran/Scandinavian population.

The area around the westernmost point of the state was occupied by transplanted Minnesotans, who brought their sense of right and wrong and concern for the feelings of the downtrodden with them. They were pretty liberal, wrote letters to the editor about things that bothered them, voted for the most Democratic candidate available, and they were proudly represented by their man, Gordon E. Holmes.

Holmes was the only child of two college professors, and was raised in an intellectual environment. He was discouraged from participating in sports, and encouraged in academic studies, at which he excelled. He grew up in the era following Vietnam, and came to believe that the military-industrial complex was standing in the way of true progress in America. He despised big business, considered labor unions to the saving grace of the worker, and befriended every cause that supported the working man. He considered the Army and Navy to be relics of a bygone era, and regularly used exaggerated stories of ridiculous military spending to prove the point that the Pentagon had to be reined in.

Holmes ran for a congressional seat in western Wisconsin, and won by default when his opponent suffered a debilitating stroke one month before the election. Since taking office, he'd sponsored many bills, most of which were shot down, and had gained a reputation as a firebrand, who enjoyed bringing debate and controversy to the house floor. He was considered a hero by his left-leaning constituents, an embarrassment by the right-leaning, and a pain in the ass by his congressional associates, and it was widely believed that he would be a one-term legislator. His attempts to lobby for a bill which would restructure the state tax system, creating a heavy burden on corporations functioning in Wisconsin, made him hated by businessmen, loved by the poor, and had landed him on two lists: one compiled by a police task force in Minnesota, and one which was inside the garage wall of the patriot.

The patriot pulled into Hudson at 8:05 p.m. The sun was going down on a cloudy, cool day, and the shadows were longer than usual for this time of year. The heavy woods enhanced the effect, and most of the cars on the road had their lights on. He turned off Interstate 94 on 11 th Street and took back roads to Coons Hill Park, in the center of town. A short street called Hunter Hill Road ringed the eastern edge of the park, and one of the older homes along that road was the residence of Gordon E. Holmes and his wife, Melissa. The patriot stopped near the park, and waited for darkness to fall. It had rained earlier and there was no one using the little park's playground or picnic facilities. A few cars drove by, but no one seemed to take special note of the Tahoe sitting in the parking area.

The patriot was unhappy with this location because was surrounded by homes. He would have preferred a more unremarkable location to wait, but the Holmes's liked having people around them. He passed the time by reading a book for 45 minutes until it was fully dark. He pulled out from the park, drove a block away, and parked on a side street in front of a dark house. He adjusted the ride of the items inside his windbreaker and walked back into the park.

He followed a tree-shrouded path which led around the edge of the area, and toward the rear of Holmes's house. The patriot wore dark clothing, and counted on the dreary weather to keep people from noticing him as he made his way through the park. He found the row of shrubs, which marked the border between Holmes's backyard and the park, and crouched down inside them. He had been in the yard before and watched his prey through brightly lit kitchen windows. The legislature was not currently in session, and the patriot could see Holmes busily washing dishes in the bright window. He couldn't see anyone else moving in the house but assumed that Mrs. Holmes was somewhere inside, and he prepared to carry out his plan.

The patriot made his way to the backyard, and then to the rear door leading into the garage. It was unlocked, and he slipped inside quietly. From inside the house he heard classical music playing, and the sound of water running in the kitchen, just on the other side of the wall. He intended to lure Holmes into the garage while he waited in the dark, and immobilize him with a stun baton just as he had done with Wallace Berry. The door leading into the house had a screen door outside of a heavy metal fire door. The patriot eased open the screen as quietly as he could, and very slowly turned the knob of the interior door until the latch opened. He crouched outside the door frame and softly pressed his fingers against the door until it slid open an inch.

In the kitchen, Gordon Holmes was just finishing up with the dinner dishes when he looked to his right and noticed that the door to the garage was open. *Did I leave that open?* he asked himself. He thought he'd shut the door firmly when he'd come in from the garage. *I better make sure it's closed so Max doesn't get out.*

Holmes and his wife were dog-sitting for Melissa's brother, Carl, while he was in the hospital. The Holmes's weren't pet people, but had agreed to watch Max, only because his owners were in a real bind. Carl was at St. Mary's Hospital in Rochester, Minnesota, two hours away, with his wife spending each day at his side. The Holmes's agreed to take in the Chesapeake Bay Retriever for the time being, even though they found the presence of such a big dog in the house a nuisance. Chesapeake males tend to be big and heavy, and Max was no exception. He stood nearly a yard high at the shoulder, and weighed 94 pounds. Max, like the majority of his breed, was a one-owner dog and missed Carl terribly. He tolerated the new people whom he'd been left with but longed for his own home with its own smells and familiar surroundings.

Max was lying in the living room with his head between his front paws, thinking of Carl, when he saw Holmes leave the sink and slam the garage door shut. Max cocked his ears in curiosity.

The patriot jumped when the door slammed shut next to his head. He gripped the stun baton and his muscles tensed as the now familiar wave of combat slipped through him, but then he realized that Holmes wasn't coming out. He heard the water turn on again in the sink, and heard the clink of glasses. He slowly turned the knob again.

Holmes rinsed the last glass and then noticed that the door had opened again. He froze by the sink and reassured himself that he had closed the door. Holmes had been on edge since the weekend before, when he'd been visited by the investigators from Minnesota. He'd listened to their story when they told him that he needed to be on guard against the lunatic who'd been killing people across the river, and he'd responded to them with his best bravado. He'd had trouble sleeping that night, and, quietly, he'd changed some of his patterns, as the police had suggested. He could never publicly admit that he was afraid of such a threat, but he'd watched the evening news closely, and a chill had coursed down his spine as each murder was recounted in gory detail.

Holmes stood frozen and stared at the open door. *There must be an explanation,* he assured himself. Maybe the damp weather warped the door. Holmes quickly shut the door again, and rattled it to make sure it was latched. He stepped back and stared at the knob for a few moments, waiting for it to turn. Reason finally took hold of him, and he shook his head and took a deep breath. *God, I'm really spooked!* he thought. He laughed at his paranoia, and began wiping the wet dishes with a dish towel.

The patriot sat sweating and frustrated in the humid, stuffy garage, and wondered if he should try something else. He had another boot knife and his trusty Browning nestled in his shoulder holster, but he wanted to take Holmes quietly, so none of the neighbors would hear. He could hear Holmes on the other side of the door putting things away in cupboards, and had an idea. He looked around in the garage and saw that Holmes had some garden stakes piled on the workbench. They would support the summer tomato vines that Melissa had just planted in the back. They were three feet long and would do just fine. He brought one to the door, and again eased open the screen. He gently turned the knob, and slid the door open ever so slowly. This time, he slid one end of a stake into the gap at the bottom of the door, and secured the other end to the floor with the heel of his boot.

Holmes put the last pan away, and draped the towel over the oven door handle. He walked toward the living room and cast a glance at the garage door before he shut off the light. "What the hell?" he demanded aloud, and, angry that he had been so frightened, strode back to the door.

Max, hearing Holmes using the alarmed tone, raised his head and watched Holmes walk quickly back into the kitchen. He sensed the fear that Holmes's body was giving off, and came instantly alert.

Holmes tried to slam the door, but it bounced off something. He looked down and saw an obstruction of some kind in the jamb, and a wave of relief swept over him. Something stuck in the door, he chuckled. He tried to push the door closed, but the obstruction wouldn't give. He opened the door, and pushed the screen open into the dark garage to see what was going on. Holmes's eyes were used to the bright kitchen light, and he couldn't see the man dressed in dark clothes, kneeling by the side of the door. Holmes started to step out, and felt rather than saw, the blur move toward his stomach. He lunged backward, just as the patriot triggered the stun baton, and Holmes saw a blue electrical charge arc across in front of him, as the electrodes missed him by a fraction of an inch.

Holmes fell back into the kitchen onto the tile floor, and the patriot rushed in after him. The patriot dropped the baton, pulled out his boot knife in one smooth motion, and jumped on top of Holmes, who was frantically trying to crawl backward into the kitchen. The patriot brought the knife down hard into Holmes's chest and Holmes yelled, "NO!!" The knife sunk into his left shoulder, and Holmes's arm went numb, as both his brachial nerve and artery were severed. The patriot yanked the knife out, and swept it across Holmes's throat, but, because Holmes was struggling so wildly, only delivered a flesh wound. The patriot reversed his grip on the handle, and pinned Holmes to the floor with his left hand, intending to open Holmes's belly, when a big red shape descend on him with a roar.

Max wasn't trained as an attack dog, but he knew that something was very wrong. Deep in his canine brain, an ancient instinct was triggered as soon as he smelled the blood that was spurting from Holmes's open artery. He charged around the corner and launched himself at the stranger, who was hurting his master's friend. Max sunk his teeth into the patriot's right shoulder, and shook him like a doll. The patriot growled, swung his arms at the dog, and managed to dislodge him. Max spun and bit down on the patriot's right forearm. The knife fell from his gloved hand, and he saw stars as the dog's strong jaws ground his forearm bones together. The patriot grabbed Max by the upper jaw with his free hand, pressed the dog's lips against his teeth, and squeezed hard. Max yelped and let go of his grip. The patriot held the dog's jaw, and punched hard between the dog's eyes, causing Max to fall back. The patriot picked up the knife as Max leapt again. He brought the knife up into the dog's ribs as it fell on him, and they collapsed on top of Holmes, who still had only uttered a single word during the ordeal. Max yelped as the knife cut into him, and he crawled away in pain, leaving a trail of blood.

Holmes had lost a lot of blood from his shoulder wound, and was going into shock. The patriot was bleeding from his shoulder and arm, and, from upstairs, they heard Melissa call out, "Gordon?"

Holmes, knowing now who had attacked him, considered his position. He considered yelling to Melissa to run, but realized that the patriot would kill his wife if she came to the kitchen instead. He offered a trade.

"Please don't hurt my wife," Holmes said to the patriot in an even voice. "I don't care what you do to me."

"Tell her you're okay," the patriot hissed. "Say you were playing with the dog."

"I'm all right, honey!" Holmes called out, his voice breaking. "Just having fun with Max. Go back to your reading."

The patriot respected that Holmes had decided to act like a man and protect his wife. It was with some regret that he pulled the blade across Holmes's throat, and then left the way he'd come.

That night, James Knox came home after downing a few cocktails with a buddy. He walked in, and had just tossed his keys on the table, when he noticed a knife sticking out of the wall. His blood ran cold when he realized that his daughter's picture was missing. He considered running out and calling the police, but an inner voice told him that the patriot was responsible, and Knox knew that if the patriot had wanted him dead, he would already be. He removed the knife, and pulled the floppy disk from the envelope. He felt very old and tired as he sat down, and turned on his computer.

Mr. Knox,

I thought we had an understanding. I made the news and you reported it. Now I see that you've decided to pass judgement on my cause and my methods. So be it.

I don't need you. I can find someone else to tell my story. What bothers me is that you've developed something of a following yourself in the national media, and I can't afford to have you running your mouth, taking attention away from the important work I am trying to do.

We had a simple deal: you sit at your desk, report the news, accept the acclaim, and keep your fucking personal opinions to yourself.

I could threaten your life, but let's face it, you're an old, washed-up drunk who doesn't have much of a life anyway. I could tell you that the next time we meet I'll snap your back and leave you in a wheelchair pissing into a bag, but that might not convince you either."

The next passage made Knox feel like someone had dunked his testicles in ice water, and a shaft of fear rammed through his body and into his head.

So here's what I'll do: keep your end of the bargain, and I won't go to Tempe and visit Trisha at the little apartment she's in at 2337 Maynard St. I won't wait until she comes home some evening, and pull her into the bushes, and tear her pretty face to pieces. Keep your end of the bargain, and Trisha won't require craniofacial surgery so strangers won't look at her from then on and say, "It's a shame. She used to be so pretty."

It's your choice.

Knox sat for a long time staring at the screen, frozen by the thought of his little girl, the only person in the world who mattered to him, the only person who cared about him, being hurt so badly. Finally, he stood up shakily, and poured himself a tumbler of whiskey. He stood in the dark room forcing down the burning liquor, and felt hot tears burn their way down his cheeks.

C H A P T E R   33

▼

On Thursday morning at 10:35, Agent Vince Cushing of the U.S. Secret Service arrived at Minneapolis-St. Paul International Airport. A veteran traveler, Cushing had only a carry-on bag and walked straight from the plane to the airport concierge desk, where he was met by Janet Luce, a trim, forty-two-year-old agent from the local office, and they drove straight to BCA headquarters. Cushing was forty-nine-years-old, and had been described as movie-star-handsome in his youth. He still maintained a fit appearance, and the gray that was just forming at his temples added a touch of life experience to the easygoing manner he exuded when he wasn't discussing business.

Cushing had seen the CNN broadcast before he left Washington and knew that the patriot had struck again. Gordon Holmes's death had set the press across the Wisconsin border like locusts after a ripe new field, and, even though the killing couldn't yet be officially pinned on the patriot, they were in a journalistic feeding-frenzy.

Cushing and Luce walked into the Investigations office at BCA headquarters and asked for Mike Rawlings. The secretary was expecting them, and told them that Rawlings was on his way back, and had left the case file for them to read until he returned. She got them some coffee while they settled in Rawlings office, and they began to page through the massive file.

Just before noon, Rawlings arrived, along with Pete Lincoln and Phil Deane. Rawlings made introductions, and told the agents that the other members of the team would be arriving shortly. He suggested they move to the meeting room, so they would have space for everyone. They gathered up the files and moved to a large room with a massive oak table surrounded by padded office chairs. Cushing loosened his tie and motioned to the file saying, "Quite an investigation you're faced with, here. You guys have really had your hands full."

"We haven't had a chance to catch our breath, much less make up any time on this case," Rawlings answered. "I think we're on to something, though, if we could just get the digging time we need."

"What's your theory?" Cushing asked.

"We think our man has been police-trained, and could be either a current or former officer."

"Based on…?"

"Based on the fact that we know he's impersonated a cop at least once," Rawlings said, "and he feels comfortable enough doing it to completely fool his victims. We know he tried to hide the fact that he did that when he wrote his letter to James Knox. He obviously has had hand-to-hand combat training, and is able to immobilize his victims quickly and quietly. He drives like a cop, we know that, and, just yesterday, Gene Truman went to Dakota County Court, and discovered that Desiree Blevins, one of the victims who was killed in the elevator in Minneapolis, had listed Jeremy Soderberg's apartment as her residence when she appeared in court there on a criminal charge. As far as we can determine, that was the only time she'd ever used that place as her own address. We've been trying to figure out what drew the patriot to Soderberg's apartment looking for Blevins, and that may be why."

"Pretty good police work," Cushing said. "You're looking onto the backgrounds of your victims now to find common threads."

"Right," Rawlings said. "Somehow, the patriot got private information on these people. The first victim, Judge Borgert, wasn't listed in phone information, and we couldn't find him through Internet searches. Now, it's possible the patriot just followed him home from work one day, but, if he *is* a cop, he could have easily found all of these people through drivers license files, and court records."

"So, Blevins listed her address as Soderberg's apartment only the one time, and that was in Dakota County court?" Luce asked.

"As far as we can tell, yes," Lincoln answered.

"So, if the suspect is an officer, he's probably in Dakota County somewhere?"

"Not necessarily," Lincoln answered. "Any cop can pick up a phone, and say, 'Hi, I'm Officer Jones, of the Podunk PD, and I'm wondering if you have an address for a woman I'm looking for?' Adult records are public documents, and court clerks take calls like that all day."

"Well, it sounds like you gentlemen have come a long way, and you still have a long way yet to go," Cushing said. "My concern is for a pain-in-the-ass Supreme Court Justice who insists on coming into your suspect's front yard on June 1. Realistically, how much of threat *is* he?"

"Hudson will be very tempting, no question about that," Rawlings answered. "He's everything the patriot hates the most. He's liberal as hell, he's a judge, he's a representative of the government, and he's said publicly that he's not afraid to come to Minneapolis—I don't think we should wonder *if* the patriot will try, I think we should assume he *will* try, and then attempt to figure out what method he might use."

"We'll have Hudson, his car, the airport, and the hotel covered thoroughly," Cushing said. "This is not for public consumption, but Hudson intends to stay overnight at the Hilton, and leave the next morning. Local police will not be allowed within 100 feet of him because of your suspicions, and that's going to require us to use a lot more agents. The problem with this is, we have a presidential trip that same week, and, with all of the unrest going on around the country, due to your man here, its going to make it tough to gather enough agents to do the job right. We can short-staff some field offices, but I need to figure out just how big a circle I need to put around this judge. The patriot has demonstrated proficiency with a rifle, so we need to cover arrivals and departures. Janet, what's the front of the Hilton like?"

"Busy street, big overhang and parking area," Luce answered. "If we shut down the street, and pull him up right to the door, it'd be tough for anyone to snipe him from any location along the block. We've got a plan for the Hilton filed at our office—we've had numerous VIP visits there in the past. Securing the inside shouldn't be hard due to the layout."

"I need to review that plan," Cushing said. "Now, Hudson may want to go for a walk in the morning. He's insistent about this shit, and we've managed to keep this habit out of the press. Luckily, no one really cares about Supreme Court Justices. I don't really want to shut down downtown Minneapolis during a workday morning, so maybe I can get him to abandon the walk by threatening to do just that. Maybe he'll feel guilty, and listen to us for once."

"Can't you just tell him it's too dangerous, and refuse to let him go at all?" Lincoln asked.

"Unfortunately, we work for him. He'd go without us if he could, but we have standing presidential orders to protect the court, so we have to do as he says. So far, the patriot hasn't done anything with explosives. I wonder if he has expertise there," Cushing wondered.

"Hard to say," Rawlings answered. "The patriot likes to be sure his victims are dead, so he attacks them up close, and often cuts them to finish them off. He shot Borgert in the face after hitting him twice in the chest, and he shot Simmons several times after he was down. The coroner told us that Andy Stoughten was dead from strangulation before the patriot stabbed him in the chest."

"Not to mention cutting Jeremy Soderberg's throat after crushing his head in a vise," Lincoln added, as Luce winced.

"Yeah, lots of overkill here," Cushing said. "The problem with bombs is, will they go off? Will they go off near your target? Will they kill your target, or just make him crap his pants? Also, we'll have bomb-sniffing dogs and Army ordinance people there, and I believe the patriot will assume that. It'd be tough to get a bomb in there."

"Also, bombs kill with flying shrapnel when the bomb's case splinters. We'll have metal detectors all over, so it would be hard to get anything through that has a metal casing." Luce added.

There was a knock on the door, and the rest of the task force investigators filed in. Rawlings made introductions all around, and the men settled into chairs.

"Do you think he'd sacrifice himself for Hudson?" Cushing asked. "Would he come in close, strike, and be willing to be arrested?"

"Well, let's get our psychologist in here for that one," Rawlings said, picking up the phone and calling for Sharon Bluhm. Bluhm was in her office down the hall, and joined them right away. After introducing her to the newcomers, Rawlings asked, "Sharon, Agent Cushing is wondering if the patriot might be willing to trade his life, or his freedom, in order to kill a very tempting target."

"Am I allowed to know who the target is?" she asked. Everyone looked at Cushing, wondering how secret the Secret Service man's mission was.

"Sure, I want your professional opinion," Cushing replied with a smile. "You've been working on this case, and I'm not going to play games keeping anyone who can help in the dark. Its Justice Hudson from the Supreme Court. He's coming on June 1 to address the graduating class of the University of Minnesota Law School. We're thinking we can limit his access to Hudson to the extent that, he would be unable to kill him, and still have a good chance of escape. However, anyone who's willing to trade his life for someone else's, is very hard to stop. Do you think the patriot would do a John Hinkley or a Sirhan Sirhan? Would he rush up and start shooting?"

"Well, that's a good question. My initial reaction is to say no. He's been very cautious, planning his crimes, and reconnoitering the places beforehand. He does his homework, and he's a list-maker. He has an agenda, and that means he's thinking far ahead. When was this judge's visit announced publicly?"

"Just a couple of weeks ago," Cushing answered.

"Okay, we know the patriot was well into his planning stages at that time—very far into it, in fact. If he's tempted to try to get this judge, then he'd have to adjust his other plans to accommodate it. No, I don't think he'd be inclined to give himself up. On the other hand, we don't know how many targets he has yet to go on his list, or what he intends to do if, and when, he gets through them all. We know he's enjoying the media attention, so there's a possibility he might just be willing to go out with a bang, or be caught, and become a jailed celebrity."

"Wonderful," Cushing said.

"Well, it's possible, but not probable," Bluhm said. "My opinion is, this judge would be a very tempting target, and the patriot would certainly think hard about how to get to him. Keep this in mind—the patriot is a *very* intelligent man. He's quite resourceful, and if he is police-trained, as I think, he knows what you men know. If there's a chink in your armor, he'll find it. But I still don't think he would sacrifice himself. It's too short-notice, and wouldn't have been part of his original plan. The patriot is an organized person—he's tidy—he wipes his knife off after he kills, and he makes sure his victims are truly dead before he leaves. His major motivation is insuring a national uprising, and I don't think he'd want to give up until that happened."

Rawlings's secretary stuck her head into the room, and said, "Mike, the FBI is here."

"Let them in," Rawlings said.

Agents Olivetti and Loomis walked in, along with Stuart Carrington, who was the Special Agent in Charge (or SAC), of the Minneapolis Field Office of the FBI. Introductions were made, and Carrington, a tall, thin, dour, and business-like man in his early fifties, who had a look on his face that seemed to Rawlings as if he'd just caught a whiff of cat piss, asked about the team's progress. Rawlings repeated what they'd learned at Holmes's house, when they'd been contacted by the Hudson Police the night before. He explained why Cushing and Luce were there, and the psychological assessment Sharon Bluhm had just offered. Carrington nodded, and cleared his throat.

"Yes, you've all done good work here. I'm sure that, given the time, you'd see this through to the end, and make an arrest. Unfortunately, I've received instructions this morning from the FBI Director. It says that, by the order of the US Attorney General, the FBI will now take over the hunt for the patriot." The task force members all exhaled at the same time, and a couple of them cursed.

"Shit" Lincoln said. "All this work, and now we get handed a cookie, and sent home! Thanks, fellas, the FBI will get your man for you."

"Mr. Carrington," Rawlings said, "this team has worked day and night, and each member has busted his ass on this case. Surely you see the unfairness in what you're proposing."

"I don't mean to minimize anything you people have done here," Carrington said. "I have great respect for each of you, and I have no doubts you would make an arrest very soon."

"Which is why they want in now," McDowell said. "We've done the legwork, now they can get the credit when he's caught."

"I know that, in the past, the FBI has taken credit for work done by local police," Carrington said, holding up his palms. "But I don't intend to allow that to happen here. You will all receive proper credit, when the case is solved."

"So, what happens to us now?" John Pappas asked.

"That's up to each of your superiors," Rawlings answered. "You were assigned by them to this task force, and, now that the task force evidently no longer exists, its up to them what you do."

"Bunch of crap," Phil Deane complained. "I've been on this from the very beginning."

"I'm sorry," Carrington said. "You must understand—the patriot has crossed a state line now, and killed another government official. He's declared war on the government, and the entire nation is suffering from a wave of violence that this man created. The White House cannot stand by and not take forceful, public action."

"What the White House needs to understand, is that we *were* taking forceful action!" Truman said, angrily. "We were busting our butts to catch this guy. What can you do that we can't?"

"Besides that," Phil Deane said, "we don't know for sure that Holmes was even killed by the patriot. It's just speculation."

"True," Carrington replied. "But, its the public's perception that he *is* responsible, and that's what matters now."

"We have a lot more people," Olivetti told them all reasonably. "We can put a hundred men on this. You guys have been overwhelmed just trying to document one scene after another. We have many more resources, and, hopefully, we can do the work you would need two weeks to accomplish in half that time."

"Yeah, a hundred guys all doing an investigation," Truman said. "How is that gonna work? This is one guy you're after, not the Ku Klux Klan, or the Mafia."

"We know how to conduct a manhunt," Carrington said crisply.

"Right, the FBI did such a fine job on those terrorists," Lincoln said sarcastically.

"Pete," Rawlings said, "don't make this personal. They've got orders, let's just keep in mind that their goal is the same as ours."

"It *is* personal, Mike," Lincoln replied angrily. "We gotta go back to our agencies with our tails between our legs! What a slap in the face!"

"I agree, but what can we do?" Rawlings answered with a tired smile. The investigators filed out of the meeting room, and went about gathering up their things to take back to their departments, and their routines. Each had the bitter taste of failure in their mouths, and would carry it for a long time. It was Tom McDowell who came up with the idea of a liquid lunch at O'Gara's, an Irish pub not far from the BCA.

"Gentlemen, I think we all need to have one after today. Call it a 'calmative.'" There was total agreement from the others, and Lincoln called Rawlings's office to invite him along. Mike came down the hall and addressed the group.

"Get started without me, guys. I've been instructed to participate in a press conference at 1:30 today to announce the changeover to the media. If you're still there afterward, I'll join up with you. In any event, I want to have all of you out to the lake this summer for a barbecue, and a boat ride. It's been my privilege to have worked with each of you, and my only regret is, we couldn't have seen it through to the end. You guys are pros—don't forget that."

With that said, the detectives who had the best feel for the patriot's actions, thoughts, and intentions, the men who had knelt by his victims, stared into their sightless eyes, snorted the smell of their blood from their noses, and listened to the sobs of their families, went back to solving forgeries and robberies. They turned the case over to a new group of people, who would, in some ways, be starting almost from scratch.

The press conference was just as miserable as Mike Rawlings knew it would be. The one thing he knew he wouldn't miss in the least when he retired as a police investigator, was standing in front of bright TV lights, and answering inane questions geared more toward getting a nifty sound byte, than telling the public what was really going on. Besides having to answer dumb questions, Rawlings had to make it sound like he was really in favor of the idea of the FBI sending him, and his team, packing.

Rawlings stood by while Carrington made the opening statement, and broke the news that his agency had been, "regrettably", called in to take over from the police task force. He said that he had the highest regard for the men who'd worked the case to that point, but left the point that they still hadn't gotten the job done, unsaid. The implication hung in the air, and stung Rawlings.

When it was time for questions, one reporter referred to the killing of Gordon Holmes and his dog, and asked if the FBI considered the patriot to be responsible.

"We are looking into that," Carrington answered. "It certainly has the earmarks of his work, but we won't know until our investigators have had the opportunity to review all of the evidence."

You won't know until the patriot writes another letter to James Knox, you mean, Rawlings thought, shaking his head.

The conference went on, but nothing was said of real substance. The reporters went out, and recorded their own conclusions as to whether the arrival of the FBI was a positive thing, or not. National events had cast a dim view on the country's most famous law enforcement agency, and it seemed that each news agency had their own opinion of them. One viewer, sitting in his living room in Hastings with an ice pack on his swollen forearm, had *his* own opinion. The patriot knew that the change meant that there would be more people hunting him, but he also knew that it wasn't as personal for the FBI as it was for the other cops.

He watched Mike Rawlings with interest while the conference was going on. He could see just by looking at him, that losing his place in the hunt was aggravating as hell to Rawlings, and the patriot was glad to see him go. He was happy to have a fresh start and be hunted by the FBI.

There is a saying among police officers that the initials FBI stand for "Famous, But Incompetent." This sentiment isn't fair, considering the successes the agency has had in the past. It is true, however, that the agency has known some monumental failures, and the patriot considered the fact that he was now being tracked by accountants and attorneys, instead of street cops, a blessing.

After the press conference, Olivetti pulled Rawlings aside. "Mike, I'm extending an invitation, hell, it's a plea, for you to work with us to the end on this one."

"Does *he* know you're asking me this?" Rawlings asked, jerking his head toward Carrington.

"Yeah. Look, Carrington's a cold fish, but he's capable, and he lets us run our investigations without a lot of quarterbacking. Mike, we'll need you to walk us through this case file mostly, but you *know* this fucker better than any of us. You've been on it from the beginning, and you know your job. You won't be taking a backseat to anybody and, if you're half the cop I think you are, you still want to nail this guy, right?"

Rawlings rubbed his temples and looked Olivetti in the eye. "Yeah. Yeah I do."

"Okay. Carrington will smooth the way through the politics with your boss—he's good at that. We're going to move our headquarters to the airport this afternoon. Take the afternoon off and have a drink with your guys."

"The airport?" Rawlings asked.

"Yeah. We have a hanger there we use for a lot of stuff. It's roomy, there's lots of parking, and best of all, we can keep the press away. The materials we'll need are almost all there, and the rest will be in by tomorrow."

"Tell me the truth, Frank—how long ago was this decision made?"

"It was in the works when Busch got killed," Olivetti answered. "I tried to warn you the last time we talked."

"I remember. Okay, where do I go tomorrow to find this super-secret hanger?"

"Go to the main terminal, and have one of the airport cops direct you to the 'Domestic Ports Building.' You'll have to badge him, or he'll play dumb."

"Domestic Ports. I'll be there."

"Right. Have a couple cocktails, and we'll get started fresh in the morning."

"I wonder how many times I'm going to have to get started with this case before it's over," Rawlings muttered.

While the members of the former Patriot Task Force were calling for their fifth pitcher of beer, and telling each other how all of this bullshit really sucked, an elderly, nervous woman, in Hudson, Wisconsin, was trying to find someone who would listen to her story. Agnes Torkelson lived across the park toward the rear of the late Gordon Holmes's house, and she was just *mortified* when she'd heard about how that terrible man had snuck into a house so close by, and stabbed that poor man and his dog! Of course, she hadn't cared for Holmes's politics—she thought he was a rabble rouser, and maybe even a Communist—but *land sakes!* Someone being murdered so close by her house!

Ever since Agnes's husband, Rusty, had died, she felt very uncomfortable in her big house all alone. Her children had urged her to sell the place and get an apartment, but the house was paid for, and it still held memories of Rusty that she knew wouldn't be found in any apartment. So, she carefully locked the doors, and peeked out the window at the slightest noise.

The night before, Agnes had heard a car door slam out front, and she looked out the window just in time to see a man in dark clothes walking from a white truck into the park. With the weather so drizzly and damp, it didn't seem normal that a man would go for a walk in the park at that hour, with no dog, or any other reason to make him. She watched the man disappear into the park, and she considered calling the police, but she knew that they'd just tell her it was a public street, and anyone could park there if they wanted to. She'd called the police many times when she was frightened, and they all knew her by name. She got her binoculars from the end table, and carefully copied down the truck's license number on a piece of paper. It was a Minnesota license, but that wasn't unusual, since Hudson was a border town.

When she'd heard the next day what had happened, Agnes had recalled that she'd heard the truck leave a short time after the crime, and that it seemed to speed off in a hurry. When it occurred to her that the stranger had walked straight toward Holmes's house, well, she thought that someone ought to know. She'd called her local police, and told the dispatcher that she thought she'd better report a strange man whom she'd seen the night before. The dispatcher, who'd been around a while, rolled her eyes when she took the call from old Agnes, and passed her on to one of the patrol officers, who had been unfortunate enough to have been called out on several of Agnes's wild-goose-chases. He remembered the time she'd reported hearing someone on the roof, but it turned out to be walnuts falling out of her tree. He decided to handle this one over the phone, since Agnes could be hard to get away from, once you were in her house. After she explained what she'd seen, the cop was convinced she'd had a good look at some guy who was going door-to-door, or maybe poking someone's wife. He knew the patriot drove a black Explorer, not a white one. He also didn't like the idea of writing a report, filing it, and then getting shit from his colleagues later, when they found he'd gotten a hot tip from Agnes Torkelson. He told Agnes that it was probably very important, indeed, and suggested she go right to the top.

The Hudson PD chief of police was doing everything but lighting candles down at the church in hopes that the killing would be proven to be a patriot crime, so someone else would investigate it. He had strongly encouraged all of his men to pass along any relevant information about the case to that BCA guy who was heading up the task force. The cop found Rawlings's name and number, recited it carefully to Agnes, and told her to be sure to call over to St. Paul, so they could get right on this. Agnes called the number, but got a secretary, who said that there was no such task force anymore, and that the case had been turned over to the FBI. She gave Agnes a number for the FBI in St. Paul. Agnes called there, and asked for Agent Rawlings, just like the Hudson cop had told her to, but was told that there was no one by that name in that office.

Agnes hung up, wondering what she should do next. She didn't want to be a bother, but she wished she could tell someone about the strange man.

CHAPTER 34

▼

The next morning, quite a few people who were linked by their association to the patriot case were nursing hangovers. Hangovers are always unpleasant, but Friday morning hangovers are the worst. There are those who would argue that a Monday hangover was the nastiest, because the sufferer has the entire week ahead of him. But, if you are suffering on Monday, you probably have a raging drinking problem, and one day is pretty much like the next. Friday hangovers are usually experienced by ordinary social drinkers, who had some extraordinary reason to get lit up on a Thursday night. They are then forced to get through their last work day feeling like they had a Metallica concert going on inside their heads.

The patriot spent Thursday night in front of the TV, drinking brandy, and nursing his damaged arm. His shoulder hurt from Max's first bite, but the big Chesapeake had really gotten a grip on the patriot's forearm. The bleeding had stopped, but the patriot's whole right arm throbbed, and his hand was swollen. He had swabbed the bite thoroughly with hydrogen peroxide immediately after returning home, and was fairly certain that the wound wasn't infected, but he was having difficulty closing his fist. The patriot hadn't even considered going to a doctor, as he would have had to explain the injury. He knew that the press had reported that Gordon Holmes had been defended to the end by his brother-in-law's brave dog, and there was speculation that the killer might have been bitten. Area hospitals and clinics, who routinely reported dog bites to the police anyway, were asked to do so with extra urgency.

James Knox had spent Thursday night at home. He'd gotten so falling-down drunk on Wednesday night after reading the patriot's threat, that he had been unable to go to work the next day. His editor had called to tell him about the press conference, but Knox told him that he was too sick to attend, and to send someone else instead.

He called Trisha that evening, and they talked about mundane subjects, while Knox gathered his nerve to tell her about how badly the biggest news story in his life had turned on him, and why she would need to start looking over her shoulder. Finally, he just let it pour out, and the guilt he felt for putting her in harm's way caused him to break down. Trisha was worried, but assured her father that she would take extra care, and that she would be all right.

Knox had never considered himself a good father to his little girl, though he loved her deeply. He'd been away too much to be the kind of dad he thought a girl needed, and the guilt he bore had caused him many a sleepless night, in which he'd turned to a bottle for relief. After hanging up, he almost ran to the kitchen cupboard where his demons awaited him, and guzzled bourbon until he'd gotten himself under control. He'd slept as he always did, waking several times during the night, when his blood sugar dropped, and his fears arose.

The members of the former Patriot Task Force returned to their old desks Friday morning feeling mixtures of anger, sadness, frustration, and resignation. They swallowed antacid tablets, drank black coffee, and told their tale of woe to their co-workers, who shook their heads, spoke palliatives, and suggested going out after work to celebrate their returns. These offers were kindly, but firmly, turned down.

Mike Rawlings drove to the International Airport and cringed at the sounds of heavy jets taking off as he pulled in front of the main terminal. He found an air-port cop, showed his ID, and asked to be directed to the Domestic Ports Building. The cop gave him a map, and circled where the building was on it. He said that Rawlings would have to pass through a guarded gate, and that the FBI would get him a key card so he could drive through in the future without all the hassle.

Rawlings parked in a small lot in front, which contained a small airport bus and about 15 cars. Frank Olivetti greeted him when Rawlings came in, and handed him a key card with no markings on it. Rawlings tucked it away in his wallet, and was given a short tour of the building, which was basically a big room on the main floor containing numerous desks separated by partitions, a couple of large private offices, a couple of conference rooms, and two restrooms. A staircase led to an upper floor, which held more offices, a lunch room, and a ready-room containing weapons, flak vests, ammunition, and other law enforcement equipment.

Olivetti led Rawlings to the desk he'd be using and told him there would be a planning meeting in half an hour in Conference Room A.

"In the meantime," Olivetti said with a sly smile, "take a look into Conference Room B. Bill Shire's working with one of the witnesses. You might be interested in watching him work."

Rawlings went into the room, and saw Shire, who was sitting at the far end of a big table, with a drawing pad in front of him. Alexander Shermentov, who was sitting across from Shire, was wearing baggy corduroys, and a blue button-down shirt. Shermentov was talking about the Ukraine and his life there when Shire invited Rawlings to join them.

Rawlings sat down, and Shire went back to work.

"Alex, tell me about your mother," he said in his soft, curious voice.

"My mother was called Petra," Shermentov said. "She was from Minsk, and met my father when they worked together at a factory."

"What color was her hair?" Shire asked.

"She had blonde hair. You would call dark blonde, maybe."

"What things did she enjoy doing? Did she like music, or dancing?" Shire asked, tilting his head, and smiled softly.

"Yes, Ukrainians are great lovers of music," Shermentov answered, smiling at the memory. "My mother would sing to me, and I remember her songs as she worked in her garden."

Shire went on in this vein, and Rawlings realized that he was putting Shermentov completely at ease. Shermentov's body relaxed, and he, too, leaned forward, so he could look into Shire's placid eyes. It wasn't long before they were laughing together, like old friends. As he spoke, Shire sketched on his pad the outline of a man's face. His hand swept softly over the paper, as he filled in details.

"Alex, I like you," Shire said. "You seem like a kind man, and someday I'd like to see your Ukraine, the things you've seen."

"It is beautiful, Bill (which Shermentov pronounced 'Beel'), and I would love to show it to you."

"I love to draw, Alex," Shire said. "I always have. I love to sit outside on a warm day with some tea, and draw rivers, and lakes, and city scenes. Would I find nice scenes to draw in Kiev?"

"Oh, yes!" Shermentov agreed, nodding his head. "So many! It is beautiful city! Wonderful buildings and parks. People skating in winter, and lying in flowers in summer. You would like it very much."

Shire smiled and nodded, as he continued to draw. Shermentov looked at Shire's drawing, and said, "You have much talent, Bill. I cannot draw so well as that."

"Thank you," Shire said, smiling. Shermentov hesitated a moment, watching Shire draw, and said,

"His face was not quite so wide."

"Like this?" Shire said, as he quickly erased one side, and drew in another line.

"Yes, and his jaw was more square."

"Yes, I see. Like this?" More fast movements on the pad.

Shire and his new friend alternately discussed subjects that Shermentov clearly enjoyed, and, alternately, the man he'd seen coming off of the elevator. It was clear to Rawlings that Shermentov had none of the fear talking to Shire that he must have felt the day of the killings, when he spoke with McDowell.

It wasn't long before Shermentov told Shire that the drawing looked very much like the man he'd seen.

"It is him, Bill," he said. "I wish I could have seen him better so I could help you more. I've seen all the news, and I am afraid for your people. So much killing, so much anger."

"I'm afraid, too, Alex," Shire answered.

Shire walked Shermentov to the break room, and shook his hand warmly. He asked him to wait awhile, so he could spend some time with the other witnesses, and Shermentov gladly agreed. Rawlings went to the next conference room and found Olivetti sorting papers.

"That guy's something," he said. "I've never seen someone put people at ease like that."

"Yeah, he's a real find," Olivetti agreed. "He'll get drawings from the others, and then come up with a master. He can tell by talking to the witnesses what their strengths and weaknesses are, and it isn't long before he knows which one got the best look. He uses that drawing as the main one, and applies whatever details might be known to the police. Usually, he comes pretty close."

"I look forward to seeing it," Rawlings said.

"Now, though, we need to plan. Grab some coffee if you want. You'll be doing most of the talking, so get comfy."

"Thanks for the warning. What am I supposed to say?" Rawlings said, somewhat crossly.

"You're the expert here," Olivetti told him with a smile. "You know the file, and you have the names, places, and dates, in your mind. We need them. You also have theories, hunches, and doubts. We need those, too. Just relax, and tell us a story, Daddy."

Rawlings chuckled. "How about The Three Bears?"

"More like, The Big Bad Wolf."

The conference went well. Rawlings addressed a room full of FBI agents, and told them the unabridged version of the past two-and-one-half weeks. It was hard to believe that 18 deaths were attributed to one man in such a short period of time. If the speculation was right, the correct figure was 19, in as many days, and that made the men and women assembled in the room shift uneasily in their seats.

Rawlings went over the steps taken by the previous task force, and led them through each crime scene and each witness statement. When he was through, he went over Sharon Bluhm's ideas, and ended with a summation based on his own thoughts and opinion.

"Right," Carrington said. "Good job. Now, we have our own profilers doing a work up and they are going to expedite it. The tape from the convenience store has been undergoing tests at the lab in Quantico, and we should have word very soon concerning its value. Bill Shire should have a rendering for us soon, and I want it to go out to the news broadcasts as soon as possible. I understand there's a lot of evidence scattered between crime labs, coroner's offices, police agencies, etc. I want that all accounted for by day's end, and I want it documented and here by day's end tomorrow. Mr. Rawlings, are all relevant photos in this file?"

"Yes. Everything taken by us or by the crime lab. Copies are on file with each original agency and the crime lab."

"Good. I want files on each killing cross-referenced to a master file. I want all serious witnesses, and by that I mean those with something important to say, to be re-interviewed. Mr. Rawlings will you draw up a list of those today?" he asked, looking at Rawlings.

"You got it," Rawlings answered.

"I want Hudson, Wisconsin hit hard, starting this afternoon. I want a door-to-door done, and I want you to talk to everyone in a four block radius. We will NOT make the assumption publicly that the Holmes killing was a patriot crime, and I do not want to hear any sources within the Bureau quoted saying that. We are looking for the killer of a congressman, and will arrest the person responsible, whether it is the patriot or not.

"Now, Mr. Rawlings…our link to the patriot has been this reporter, Knox. How well do you get along with him?"

"I know him a little," Rawlings answered. "He seems like a pro, and he's been willing to help us from the beginning."

"Well, find him and see what he's up to. We need to keep our lanes of communication open with him, and it won't hurt to have a reporter playing ball with us."

"Right."

"Frank Olivetti will give each of you your assignments. Why are you still here?" Carrington said, with a reasonable facsimile of a smile. The agents stood, Olivetti gave them each their tasks, and they filed out one by one to begin. Rawlings had respect for Carrington's ability to organize, but wondered how well he might take a differing opinion raised by one of these agents, or especially by Rawlings himself.

After finishing with the witness list, Rawlings put in a call to James Knox. A secretary at the paper told him that Knox was out on an assignment, and she couldn't say when he would be back. Rawlings left a message that he wanted to speak to Knox at his earliest convenience.

James Knox was, in fact, sitting at the darkened bar inside Lucky's Saloon in downtown Minneapolis. It wasn't one of Knox's regular hangouts, but he'd been driving by in the hot sun, and the prospect of one short, cold beer attracted him. He had his story for the day in his head, and could pound it out in 15 minutes once he got back to his desk. The beer had soothed his aching head, and the next one removed the sandpaper from his throat. He switched to vodka gimlets once the thirst issue was conquered, and after the third one of those, he found it easier to think about the patriot.

Every time Knox closed his eyes, he saw the image of the knife sticking out of the empty frame of his daughter's picture. It was stark and obscene, almost sexual in a way. The phallic knife jutting out, and his beloved little girl, so far away— her picture, like her, missing. The thought of the patriot stalking her, hurting her, filled him with dread. He'd spoken to one of the technicians at the coroner's office after the bodies of Jeremy Soderberg, Amii Faust, and Desiree Blevins had been autopsied. He'd offered to buy the guy a drink after work, and it turned into several as the man, a two-year veteran of the office, tossed them back, trying to get the image of Soderberg's ripped throat, and crushed head out of his mind.

Knox had been to many crime scenes, not to mention the time he'd spent in Vietnam. He'd seen two Vietnamese, who had been shredded by a Claymore mine in 1969, and had thrown up for two days afterward. After that, he handled gore pretty well, and had never lost his lunch at a homicide scene once. He'd learned not to bond with the victims, and the practice had served him well.

But now, every time he thought of the patriot, he thought of Trisha, and then Soderberg, who was her same age. Knox had spent an afternoon with Jeremy's parents, and they'd shown him pictures of their boy when he was little. In the photo, Jeremy had a cowlick in his blonde hair, and a wide smile when he was in grade school. He reminded Knox of Jay North, as Dennis the Menace. The Soderbergs had tried to talk to Knox about happier times, and then, for an instant, a smile at a memory would cross their faces. But then, the smile would falter, and their voices would crack as reality crept back. The heavy weight of how Jeremy had died hung in the air like an anvil, and the conversation was filled with pauses, interrupted thoughts, and never-too-far-away tears.

As a younger man, Knox could have built a wall in his mind between the patriot, Soderberg, and Trisha, but now he was old, tired and defeated. It was easy to let his mind wander, and just too hard to control where it went. It was easier to turn to the release and solace of alcohol, than to deal with the problem head-on. Knox had long ago given up on causes, fights, and crusades as fool's errands. Today, everyone had a cause, whether it was the elimination of land mines, animal rights, or AIDs research. Everyone wore ribbons or buttons, as if doing so could bring about the changes they desired. Knox had grown weary of covering marches and pickets, and thought that the people who participated in these activities were naïve. Nations wouldn't throw away their bombs and mines, and tear up the instructions on how to build them, because 15 women stood in the rain in St. Paul wearing purple ribbons.

He looked at his watch, and realized he'd better get back. He paid the tab, slipped off the stool, and, surprisingly, found himself on the floor when his legs gave out from under him.

"You okay, buddy?" the bored bartender asked.

"Yeah. Sure." Knox got up and steadied his legs before trying for the door again. *Christ, I better be careful,* he thought. Knox made it to his car, and it took three tries before he could get the key in the ignition the correct way. He fired up the engine, and rubbed his face, finding his lips, nose, and cheeks numb. Had he only had three gimlets? He couldn't remember. He pulled into the thickening afternoon traffic, and pointed himself toward the office.

The four lanes of cars on the one way street blurred into six, and even seven, as Knox made his way toward the *Tribune*. He straddled the divider as he moved through one of the construction zones, which seemed to be a perpetual plague in downtown Minneapolis. It seemed that the street department just moved the orange barrels and cones from one intersection to another every few months, just to confuse the commuters, or possibly to keep them from getting bored.

Knox picked up his cell phone and dialed his voice mail to see if Trisha had called and, as he did so, weaved across two lanes of traffic, causing four cars to slam on their brakes. Then, he ran a red light in front of a Minneapolis PD traffic officer, who was just coming on duty. Knox saw the red lights in his rearview mirror, and pulled over across from the Hubert Humphrey Metrodome.

"May I see your drivers license, and proof of insurance?" the cop asked. He watched as Knox fumbled through his wallet, passing the license twice, as the cop smelled the booze. "Step out of the car," the cop said, and Knox realized he probably wouldn't get to his column today.

Mike Rawlings was having a conversation with Frank Olivetti when he was paged to the phone.

"Mr. Rawlings? This is Jean Graham. I work with Jim Knox at the *Tribune*?"

"Yes, of course."

"You were looking for Jim earlier. Well, he's in some trouble. I'm afraid he got in some, well, legal trouble…you see, he was arrested."

"Arrested?" Rawlings said. "For what?"

"I'm afraid he was driving, and got stopped by the police. They arrested him for drunk driving."

"Oh, no," Rawlings sighed. "Where did this happen?"

"Near here. By the dome."

"Okay. I'll see what I can do." Rawlings called the Hennepin County Jail, and asked for the duty sergeant. He explained who he was, and asked what the terms of Knox's arrest were.

"Well, looks like he just came in from Minneapolis Chem Testing." the sergeant told him. "Charged with DWI, nothing else. We have to book him, and then we'll probably cut him loose. You need him held?"

"No, but I'll pick him up. When will he be processed?"

"Give us an hour," the sergeant said.

Mike Rawlings waited outside the jail in the front lobby as Knox was given his appearance ticket, and paid his bail. He looked disheveled as he walked out of the steel door, and over to one of the couches, collapsing on the first one.

"Jesus, how fucked up is this?" Knox asked no one in particular. Rawlings shook his head and patted Knox on the shoulder.

"Come on, Jim, I'll give you a ride. Let's go." They walked out, and Rawlings made sure Knox was fully inside his state-issued car before taking off.

"Where to?" Rawlings asked.

"A bar?" Knox asked hopefully.

"I think that's a bad idea," Rawlings chuckled. "Where do you live?"

They pulled into Knox's drive and went inside. Rawlings went into the kitchen, and began making coffee, as Knox fell into a recliner.

"Did you ever get the feeling that your whole life, everything you've done, was a huge, fucking waste of time?" Knox asked.

"I think every cop has had that thought," Rawlings answered. "We both have jobs that involve human behavior, and people always find new ways to disappoint you."

"Disappointed, yeah," Knox nodded. "You know, there was a day when I was really a hot reporter. People really wanted to know what I had to say. Young reporters came to me and asked my advice. My stories always got lots of mail, and comments. Thanks," he said, as Rawlings handed him a cup. "I always thought that the people's right to know was so important. The news, and freedom of the press, was an American value—even mentioned in the Constitution. I went all over, and told so many stories: crime, human interest, politics, everything."

Rawlings thought that Knox needed to ramble, so he settled into the couch, sipping at his coffee.

"Spent a lot of time getting tips from informants," Knox went on. "Lot of time in bars, alleys, cars. Some wanted to be paid, most just wanted their stories told. They all thought their story was the most important one ever, and none of those stories, *none,* ever amounted to anything in the whole grand scheme of things. I wrote about the war, and the people who fought against it, and it didn't end until the government couldn't squeeze any more interest out of it from the public. I've written about crime for decades, and it only gets worse. I thought that if the public knew what was going on, they'd take steps. Haul their children aside, and threaten to beat the shit out of them if they ever got in trouble, but nothing changes. I wrote about drug addicts—how they can wind up losing everything and living in a box, but nothing stops people from snorting it up.

"Then, along comes this guy—the almighty patriot. Tells me to tell his story and, just like a pup, I fall for it, and jump on board the train. Interviews, book offers, TV deals, the young reporters looking at me with *that look* again. You know, a mixture of envy, and hate? And, I follow along like a rube, writing the words, telling the story, and selling the papers. By the time I realized I was being used, it was too late. So, to ease my conscience, I storm into my editor's office, and tell him I want to write an opinion piece about the whole thing. 'No,' he says. 'Do your job, tell the stories, sell the papers,' but I can't do that. I have to stand for something. So I write about how I hate being used, and how I think the patriot's butter has slipped off his noodles, and then I come home, feeling strong, feeling noble, and I find this." Knox got up and brought the floppy and a printed copy of the patriot's message to Rawlings. "Stuck in a wall with this," he said, handing the Tanto knife over. "Right inside the picture frame where my daughter's face used to be." Knox quietly sat down, and sipped at his coffee while Rawlings read the letter. Knox went on: "So, what has all of this brought me? How has it impacted my life? Not for the better, that's for damn sure. All of my *opportunities*, Vietnam, the riots, scandals, murders, bribes, payoffs, and misery, the things that held the promise of *success,* have given me *nothing.*"

"Jim, why didn't you tell us about this?" Rawlings asked.

"So you could do what?" Knox sighed. "Catch him? Stop him? Maybe he will start his war. His *revolution.* Maybe his way is right, and I should wave his flag for him some more. Hear ye! Hear ye! All able body Americans are hereby called upon to eliminate pests, nuisances, and all manner of scoundrels! Bounties to be paid to the man who kills the most perverts, intellectuals, and nineteen-year-old artists!" Knox shouted, waving his arms, and then falling back onto the chair.

"Well," Rawlings said. "I guess you've really been feeling sorry for yourself. It's gotta be scary, having your daughter threatened like that, but still, you surprise me."

"How's that?" Knox asked.

"All this drama—the self-righteousness. You thought you could change the world by writing about things, just like a lot of young cops think they can change the world if they just catch enough bad guys. Anyone who thinks that ends up deep in the dumps, at the bottom of a bottle, or chewing on the barrel of a gun. Here's a news flash for you, Mr. Reporter: you can't change the world. You are one of six *billion* people in the world, and unless you're somebody very special, you're not going to make that much of an impression while you're here. It's sad to say, but the fact is that the best most people can hope for, is to live a long and happy life, raise their families, and die in their sleep. Sound miserable? Well, it really isn't so bad at all. In the whole grand scheme of things, each of us is passing through like a gnat. In all of the lives that have come and gone in history, only a few have had enough of an impact to even rate a mention in a book that school children are forced to read.

"You got caught up with the excitement of this story? So what? Somebody would have told it. Did you ever write anything that was a lie? Anything that went against your principals?"

"No," Knox grumbled.

"Okay, then. What's the big goddamned deal? You're a reporter, and you reported. You didn't make the news, the patriot did. All of those nuts who loaded their guns, and went out to copy him made the news, not you. You talk about liking the way the young reporters looked at you again? How will they look at you if you fuck up your life with booze, and waste it all away? Do you want them to look back years from now and say, 'I remember old Jim Knox—he was a good reporter, but, Christ, what a boozer.'

"Who knows what's going to happen?" Rawlings asked. "Maybe there *will* be a revolution. Maybe we'll end up with marshal law, or complete anarchy. Maybe we're living through a defining moment in history, just like the average people in 1776, who read newspaper accounts of change and death, and wondered what the hell was going on. Or maybe the patriot will get captured tomorrow, and in five years we'll look back, and laugh at ourselves for ever wondering if a single man could overthrow the United States government. Either way, we have to be content to live out own lives our own way, and be content in the knowledge that we had more good days than bad, had a few laughs, shed some tears, and were able to be happy that we didn't waste it all by spending quality time feeling sorry for ourselves!"

CHAPTER 35

▼

Saturday and Sunday passed quickly. The new FBI manhunt, still in its infancy, made little progress. Stuart Carrington had been summoned to Washington, D.C. for a late Friday afternoon meeting with the Bureau Director and the Attorney General to plan strategy. Frank Olivetti had to leave right after the Friday morning meeting to testify in federal court on a bank robbery that he'd investigated. Carrington had left a skeleton staff of four agents on the patriot case for the weekend, being careful not to make too many decisions until he'd run everything by his superiors.

The four agents who had been left to work were given instructions to canvas the neighborhood around Gordon Holmes's house in Hudson. That they did, working from 9:00 a.m. until 5:00 p.m. They spoke with a number of neighbors, but concentrated on those houses which were to either side, and in front, of Holmes's. Because of that, they never made it to Agnes Torkelson's house, and it wouldn't have mattered if they had, since she spent the weekend with her son, Robert, in Forest Lake, Minnesota, telling her dubious boy a story about a tall man in a white truck, who she'd seen the night her neighbor was murdered, and who, she was sure, was the killer. Her son tried to reason with her, and explain why the killer *couldn't* really have been the patriot, but ended up promising to find a cop who would listen to her story first thing Monday morning.

Mike Rawlings spent the weekend catching up on lost time with his wife, Mary. His police career had cost him a lot of missed moments with her and their children, and while she'd always been supportive, lately she'd brought up the prospect of Mike's retirement. Never in a pushy way...that wasn't her style. Mary would leave brochures of vacation hideaways, and other interesting places, around the house where Mike was sure to see them. She'd commented on a Lake Superior fishing package she'd found in the paper, and how fun it looked. Mike knew Mary couldn't care less about fishing. He knew her underlying motive, and loved her all the more for it. The prospect of retirement frightened him a little because he'd known so many ex-cops who turned in their badges, and then died soon after. Police have a poor life expectancy after retirement; on the average, they die within five years. Mike thought it was a combination of thirty years of stress, irregular eating, irregular hours, and the weight of responsibility that shortened their lives. He thought it was ironic that the same desire for responsibility which drew young men and women into the field, would be the same thing that put them into an early grave.

This case may put me in an early grave, he thought. Every day brought national news programs which opened each broadcast with announcements such as, "Upheaval in America: The Winds of Change," or "America Trembles: The Second Civil War?" The local news ran a countdown each day, "Patriot Siege, Day 21," and another had "Manhunt Continues" at the start of each broadcast. Rawlings felt that he and his team should have been allowed to continue, but at the same time he felt that they'd been getting nowhere. He wondered if the patriot was really a cop, and, if so, if somehow he and his team had subconsciously overlooked something.

Getting another cop in trouble was considered an onerous violation of "The Thin Blue Line," and most cops worth their salt wouldn't consider it. Trust among officers is a mighty force, and there isn't a good cop alive who wouldn't rather face an armed suspect than be involved in an internal investigation any day of the week. Street cops everywhere feel that they can't depend on their administration, the courts, or the public for True Justice, but they can depend on each other. That's the reason why cops often lose the friends they had outside of police work after they'd been on the job for a while. It's comforting to socialize with people who truly understand how you think, and have seen the things you've seen.

Mike had socialized many times with non-police, usually friends and associates of Mary's, and had enjoyed good times with them. But there is a discomfort that a cop feels when he's around outsiders that adds something of an edge to those situations. He feels that people are just a little uncomfortable around him; maybe they like to light up a joint at night before bed, or maybe they weren't quite as honest with the IRS on their last return and, somehow, the cop at the party might find out, and come for them someday. Every cop has been at gatherings where he's introduced, and someone will "assume the position" against a wall, or throw up their hands, and say, "I didn't do it!" and laugh. And every cop has been at parties when someone will single him out, and tell him about the speeding ticket he got five years ago, or ask him to critique how some other cop handled his son's drug arrest last year. After a few such encounters, cops come to dread non-police functions, and start answering people evasively when they ask, "So, what do you do?"

"I work for the city."

The truth was, Rawlings enjoyed what he did, and who he did it with, and the idea of giving it up was dreadful. Yet, the same sense of responsibility which drew him into the job, and held him so tight, told him that he owed something to Mary for the years she'd done without. On Sunday night, he took her out to dinner to Mancini's, their favorite restaurant in St. Paul, and he told her that, as soon as the patriot was gone, he would be, too. She took his hand in hers, and smiled her quiet smile, and told him that she was happy. But, happy though she was, Mary had a sense that stopping the patriot would be the most dangerous thing her husband had ever done.

The patriot spent his weekend getting ready. He'd been a cop long enough to know that his run would be coming to an end soon. He'd done a good job of covering his tracks, but the Saturday evening news reported that sources within the FBI manhunt had told the press that their focus was on someone either in the police, or security field in the Twin Cities, and that the agency was working with witnesses to try to assemble a possible sketch of the suspect. It was also reported that Rueben Gonzalez, the only survivor of the Four Seasons Park Massacre, as the press was calling it, had come out of his coma, and was under a twenty-four-hour guard. The patriot knew that Gonzalez had gotten a good look at his face, but didn't know how much the kid would remember after being unconscious for so long.

The patriot had planned for this stage of the game, and was ready to move at the first sign he was under suspicion. He was expected back to work on Monday, and had to work through Thursday. Saturday would be June 1, and he was hoping to stay in the clear until then, so he could make his loudest statement yet. He'd mailed a new floppy on Friday, hoping to buy some more time and space. That one had gone directly to Mike Rawlings. Knox had outlived his usefulness, and, besides, proved a disappointment. He assumed that the FBI would be releasing fewer details than the police had, and also that Knox might be too scared to be of further use. He'd sent another floppy to a reporter from the St. Paul paper containing the same information as the one he'd sent to Rawlings. He hoped that doing that would enhance the believability of the content, insure its being made public, and buy him the week he needed.

The patriot went through the items in his garage cubbyhole, and made sure everything was cleaned, oiled, and ready. He went into his garage attic, checked on the Hedgehog, and found it was fine. He wondered if the heat of the attic would be a problem, but felt that it wouldn't be bad enough to combust the magnesium sparklers. To be on the safe side, he ran an extension cord unobtrusively up a 2 X 4 into the attic, and set a small fan to oscillate there during the day on a timer.

The patriot planned one more mission before the week was out to eliminate the last name on his original list. He then intended to lie low until next Saturday. His target was a self-described Eco-Terrorist, named Phillip Brummel, who lived in the city of Coon Rapids, just north of Minneapolis.

Brummel had made the press when he presented himself as the spokesman for a group calling themselves, "Earthwatch." They had been making a nuisance of themselves combating what they termed as the "rape of the planet and its natural resources." They began by going to the lumbering regions of northern Minnesota and Wisconsin, and engaging in an act known as "tree spiking." This involves pounding long steel spikes into the trunks of trees, so that when they are harvested for lumber or paper, the spikes will foul the chainsaws of the lumberjacks, and the cutting blades of the equipment at the mills. The fact that this practice had caused numerous serious injuries to people in that industry was counted as a measure of pride by the members of Earthwatch. In fact, the group stepped-up their activities to include setting fire to vehicles owned by paper companies, and they had firebombed a warehouse in St. Paul, which was owned by a large lumber outlet.

Phillip Brummel had stepped forward in the media, and said that, while he personally was not guilty of any of the acts committed by Earthwatch, or have any foreknowledge of future acts the group planned to carry out, he was totally sympathetic to their cause, and would act as the "press liaison." Clad in the ridiculously oversized clothing and stocking cap favored by Generation X rebels, skateboarders, and white rappers, Brummel smugly took responsibility for the group each time a crime was carried out in the name of saving the planet. He had been brought in for questioning on several occasions by the police, but always had an alibi for his whereabouts whenever the group did something. The fact that each alibi involved Brummel being so obviously in a public place, making certain that many people, including police, knew that he was there at *just* the same time that something burst into flame, didn't go unnoticed by the FBI, who were assembling the probable cause needed to charge the loudmouth with a RICO violation.

To prove that Brummel was guilty of a "Racketeer-Influenced and Corrupt Organizations" crime, the federal government would have to show that the group was a criminal organization, that Brummel had knowledge of the group's activities, and that he profited from it. A team of agents from the FBI, ATF, IRS, and the Forest Service had been assembling data for over nine months, but had been unable to get solid information on any other members of Earthwatch. They hoped to file charges against Brummel, and squeeze him to give up other cell members in exchange for leniency.

The patriot had other plans for Brummel. He didn't know that the government had gone to great lengths and expense to get close to Brummel in an effort to expose the other, more virulent members of the group. He didn't know that an undercover federal agent had wormed his way into Brummel's confidence, and had become his almost-constant companion. All he knew was that he was very tired of seeing the snotty little fuck on TV wearing that stupid goddamned stocking cap, and hooded sweatshirt in 80 degree weather, and crowing about how it was a good thing for the Earth when a night watchman was burned over 40 percent of his body trying to get out of a paper mill that had been set aflame by the "ecologically conscious" members of Earthwatch. The patriot intended to do his part for the planet by reducing Phillip Brummel into fertilizer.

On Sunday night, Phillip Brummel took it easy. His friends at Earthwatch had nothing going, so it wasn't important that he be noticeably visible. He'd hung out at Perk Up!, which was his favorite coffee house in downtown Minneapolis, then gotten a ride back from a buddy, named Tom, to the garage attic-apartment he rented in Coon Rapids. Brummel had considered moving to the inner city recently to be closer to the people and things he liked to be around, but the apartment was cheap, and owned by a seventy-two-year-old woman, who was nearly deaf, and provided a great alibi in a pinch. Sometimes it was boring having to sit with her when he couldn't find a better place to be while something somewhere was exploding, but a dude did what a dude had to do.

Brummel affected an inner-city-rebel persona, walking with the exaggerated rocking gait of a rapper, and carefully culturing a black-speaking voice to cover his white Minnesota vowels. He butchered his grammar and syntax whenever he spoke publicly, but not out of ignorance. Brummel had attended St. Cloud State for two years, and received high grades, before leaving to follow his cause.

Brummel chatted with Tom on the drive home, while the stereo blasted Eminem and Insane Clown Posse. Tom Kessler was an old acquaintance from St. Cloud State when Brummel went there, and they'd recently hooked up again when Kessler wandered into Perk Up! for a cup of coffee. They hadn't been close at school, only sharing a few classes, but they recognized each other, and started talking. It seemed that Kessler had been bouncing around from one odd job to another since college, and mentioned the fact that he'd been fired more than once for pissing off his bosses. Brummel liked that, and told Kessler that it was a good thing to keep the establishment off-balance. Nothing could be worse than to waste your life on the 9-to-5 hamster wheel.

Kessler agreed and they began hanging out together. After a week or so, Brummel and Kessler were watching a news broadcast about an affluent neighborhood in Wayzata whose residents were calling on the Department of Natural Resources to relocate a group of beavers who had moved into the area, and were busily dropping expensive trees around a pond, which was surrounded by half-million-dollar homes in order to make a dam. The residents were pissed off at the big rodents, and in a hurry to replace their Maples and Mountain Ashes as quickly as possible. Kessler had surprised Brummel by becoming very upset at the homeowners in the story, calling them "rich assholes," and saying that the beavers were only doing what was natural, and that the world would be a better place if people let the animals show them how to get along with nature. Brummel agreed and shared some of his philosophies with Kessler about the decline of the rainforest, and the rape of the land being committed by the mining industry. He spoke about the slaughter of wildlife by so-called sportsmen, who fooled themselves into thinking that they were living like mountain men, while using telescopic sights and fish finders, and how they polluted the air and water with SUVs and 200-horse-power motors.

Kessler agreed whole-heartedly, but Brummel didn't fully disclose how far he was willing to go to save the planet. The friendship was too new, after all, and he couldn't trust Kessler with everything yet. Recently he'd brought up Earthwatch to Kessler to sound out how he felt about such an organization. Kessler told him that he thought the group's motives were good, and he had no problems with anyone who took action to back up their beliefs. Brummel had let the matter drop, thinking it would be best to open up to Kessler a little at a time.

Kessler's Honda pulled into the driveway, and alongside the garage at 10:30 p.m. The lights were off in the big house since old Millie went to bed at 9:30 sharp every night. Brummel and Kessler went up to the attic apartment, and opened a couple of bottles of beer. Brummel offered to share a bowl of good hash that he had in the bedroom, but Kessler declined, citing his asthma, which made it hard for him to stay too long in the coffee house, and for which he blamed on the black, oily smoke that had belched out of the manufacturing plant near the town he'd grown up in. Brummel agreed that anything that came out of a plant's smokestack was bad for you, and then proceeded to fire up the hash, which he'd bought from a Salvadoran named Bennie, who had smuggled it into the U.S. inside a dog's rectum.

Tom Kessler sat sipping his beer and laughing, while Brummel got stoned and found hilarity in watching his fingers wave in the air in front of him. Kessler had seen Brummel on hash before, and knew that his mood would swing from hilarity to paranoia, and then he would start talking about the Earth. It was a pain in the ass to sit through the process, but getting Brummel to talk about the Earth was why he was there.

Tom Kessler had left St. Cloud State and finished his education at Boston College, where he'd been recruited into the Bureau of Alcohol, Tobacco, and Firearms. His youthful appearance and naturally adaptive personality made him a fine undercover operative, and once his superiors found that he had actually known Phillip Brummel from the old days, he was immediately tapped to try to get close to him.

Inserting himself into Brummel's life hadn't been hard. Brummel had very few close friends, and he seemed to enjoy someone who could talk with him about life before Earthwatch. Kessler thought that Brummel secretly wondered if the members of the group were using him and if they really respected him. Kessler felt that Brummel was a very sad, mixed-up person, who was clinging to a cause to give his own shallow life meaning. Brummel had played the whole Earthwatch topic very close to the vest, and it was frustrating to have to sit through so many empty sessions like this—but that was the nature of undercover work. Sometimes your targets spoke volumes, sometimes they spoke shit. Kessler just had to bide his time.

The two sat in the apartment watching late night TV and drinking beer. Kessler choked on the acrid hash smoke, and sat on the sofa next to an open window on the other side of the little room to try to get away from it. He was starting to get a contact-high from the smoke, and was feeling a little dizzy. Brummel sat giggling at the TV program which featured a re-run of *Saturday Night Live* with John Belushi dressed as a bumblebee.

Suddenly, Brummel sat up and, fumbled with the mute button on the remote, saying, "What was that?"

"What was what, man?" Kessler replied.

"I heard a noise. Sounded like the stairs." Brummel looked around warily.

"It's the hash, dude," Kessler told him. "You're getting paranoid."

"I *heard* something!"

"Maybe you farted," Kessler laughed.

"Did I?" Brummel looked around, confused.

"You should lay off of the hash, Phil, and stick to beer. You get too squirrelly."

"Look at this!" Brummel said, turning his attention back to the TV as quickly as he'd left it. Belushi was waving a sword around dressed as a Japanese Samurai. The two laughed at the old skit until a commercial came on, and Kessler decided to try to pry some conversation out of Brummel before he got sleepy.

"You know Phil, you brought up that group Earthwatch. I wish that I could really *do* something positive, you know? Really take steps. Those guys are really doing something positive, and I admire them. I'd like to do something to hurt these fucking companies, too, but I don't know what I'm doing. I need some advice, some training."

"You wanna be a eco-terrorist, huh?" Brummel asked, smiling.

"I wanna *do* something instead of just bitching. But if I went off half-cocked, it'd be worse than not doing something at all, right?"

"Sounds like you wanna join Earthwatch, but, what can you do for them?" Brummel asked.

"That's what I don't know. I wanna help them, but I don't even know how to let them know I'm alive."

"Well, my friend, there are ways to…" Brummel was interrupted by a sharp pounding on the door. It was a loud and purposeful knock; a cop's knock. Brummel had heard knocks like that before, and immediately stuffed the hash bowl under his chair. He took the remainder of the hash, which was wrapped in aluminum foil, and stuffed it under the couch cushion.

Again, the knocking shook the door, and Brummel leaned close to Kessler, whispering, "Don't say anything! Let me do the talking!" Kessler nodded and watched Brummel walk to the door.

"Who is it?" Brummel asked.

"Police!" came the reply. "I have a search warrant. Open the door immediately!"

"Fuck!" Brummel muttered. He turned to Kessler again and said, "I'll handle this. Just shut up!"

Kessler wondered what the hell was going on. He knew that there was no local investigation into Earthwatch. The Justice and Treasury Departments had this one solo. No one should be busting in like this with a search warrant. It wasn't until Brummel slid the chain off and turned the deadbolt, that Kessler thought about the patriot.

The door swung open and Kessler had a fleeting glimpse of a man taller than Brummel and much wider, wearing a dark colored coverall, framed in the dark hallway. Kessler started to stand when he saw Brummel rise up on his toes, and his arms fling out to his sides, gasping in agony. The man stepped into the doorway, and Kessler saw that he had clamped his left hand down on Brummel's shoulder, and had just used a very sharp knife to rip open Brummel's stomach from his left hip, angling up to just under the ribcage on his right side. Kessler stood stunned as Brummel's intestines slithered out of the wound and uncoiled their way to the floor. In a split second, the patriot reversed his grip on the knife, and drew it forcefully across to the ribs on Brummel's left side, severing the aorta just under his heart. Blood poured from Brummel as if from a waterfall, and he sagged to the floor, gasping. He feebly tried to gather up his fallen insides in order to get them off of the dirty floor, as he took his last breaths.

The patriot stepped quickly into the room over Brummel's prostrate form, and grabbed Kessler by the hair, lifting him into the air. Kessler gasped at the pain, and yelled, "Federal agent! I'm a federal agent!"

"Right," the patriot said, as he rammed the knife into Kessler's stomach. Kessler cried out as the steel blade cut through his spleen, and across into his liver.

"I am!" Kessler cried. "I'm ATF…" he sobbed as he fell to the floor. "I have ID…I was undercover…"

The patriot stared into Kessler's eyes for a moment, and then let him fall to the floor. He quickly wiped his knife off on Kessler's shirt sleeve, and, after dropping something small onto Brummel's body, walked out, leaving the young agent writhing on the floor, sobbing, and trying to crawl for help as his strength ebbed away.

Outside, the patriot quickly stripped off his bloody coverall, and stuffed it into a plastic leaf bag. When he got back to his truck, he changed his shoes for another clean pair from the back, and threw the bloody ones into the bag, along with the latex gloves he'd been wearing. The bag went into the back of the rented Explorer, and the patriot drove off through the quiet neighborhood. His head pounded from a headache brought on by uncertainty. *Shit!* he thought. *Had the guy been telling the truth about being ATF? He seemed too young.*

Tom Kessler summoned all of his strength and rolled onto his back. He used his legs to push himself into the kitchen on his back, and pulled a towel off the back of a chair to use as a compress. The effort nearly exhausted him, but he knew that he would need to get help fast if he had any hope of survival. He pressed the towel tightly against his wound, and panted until he was able to get his breathing under control. He gathered himself again, and pushed his body across the room to the phone. The room seemed to grow in size as he made his way, and Kessler fought off nausea as the shock of blood loss gripped him. He pulled the phone off of the end table by the cord, and grabbed for the receiver as it fell next to him. He dialed 911, but heard only the sound of silence, because the patriot had cut the line outside prior to entering the house.

Kessler cried out in frustration and pain, as he desperately tried to think of how to call the police. He tried to pull himself to a kneeling position, but immediately returned to his back, as he felt his insides moving around inside the gaping wound in his abdomen. He had a cell phone in his car, but wondered if he had the strength to get down the flight of stairs. He tried to think of his options, but none came to him. He pushed himself to the door, going around the dead form of Phillip Brummel. Kessler grasped the handrail with his left hand, while holding the towel on his stomach with his right, as he agonizingly lowered himself head-first down the stairs, one at a time.

Kessler was twenty-four-years-old, and in prime condition. The fact that he survived the trip down the stairs, and then managed to pull himself out onto the lawn, was a testimony to his grit and determination. Kessler used the last of his energy to open his car door, and groped under the driver's seat to get his cell phone. He turned it on, and dialed 911, which put him in touch with a State Patrol dispatcher, who heard a weak voice say that an ambulance was needed at 10105 Olive St. North, in Coon Rapids. The dispatcher immediately contacted the Coon Rapids Police, and squad cars, rescue units, and an ambulance were on their way in minutes.

When the first officer arrived on the scene, she found Kessler lying on his back, clutching the cell phone and a blood-soaked towel. She couldn't find a pulse, and began artificial respiration as the paramedics arrived. Tom Kessler's clothing was cut from his body, as two large-bore IV's were inserted into his arms, and saline was forced into his veins. An artificial airway was put in his throat so a medic could breathe for him by squeezing an attached bag. His legs and hips were fitted with MAST (Military Anti Shock Trousers) trousers, which are similar to snow pants with air bladders in them. A paramedic used a pump to inflate the bladders, and squeeze Kessler's legs, so that any blood which remained in his lower torso could be forced up into his organs and brain where it was desperately needed. They continued CPR as Kessler's body was put onto a cot, and put into the back of the ambulance. Each thrust to Kessler's chest caused blood to seep from the massive wound, but keeping his circulation going was critical as the ambulance sped toward North Memorial Hospital in Robbinsdale, the closest Level 1 Trauma Center. The ambulance driver called the hospital on the radio, and told the ER team that they were bringing in a "Code Red," so the staff could be prepared to deal with someone who was bleeding to death.

Kessler was wheeled into the Emergency Room ten minutes later, and doctors and nurses quickly added O-negative blood to his IVs while his blood was typed and cross matched; they then began transfusing the young man, who lay pale and unresponsive on the table under the glaring lights. He was hooked up to a cardiac pacemaker and monitor, which showed that his heart was faintly quivering from diminishing electrical activity. A defibrillator administered shocks to try to get his heart back into a normal rhythm, while a trauma surgeon worked to locate and clamp off the bleeding vessels inside him. Other staff workers injected Kessler with the drugs Epinephrine and Dopamine, to try to restore his pulse.

Tom Kessler had a strong heart and a strong will to live, but he'd used up all of the strength he needed to live by pulling himself down the stairs. The head of the trauma team finally called a halt to the efforts, and noted the time of death at 0113 hours on Monday, May 27.

CHAPTER 36

▼

At 8:30 a.m. on Monday morning, Mike Rawlings stepped into a madhouse when he entered the airport office of the FBI task force. Agents and secretaries were bustling about, phones were ringing, and all of the conference rooms were occupied. Rawlings asked one of the secretaries where Frank Olivetti was, and she jerked her head toward the first office along the rear wall, which had been dubbed, "The Command Center."

Rawlings knocked on the closed door, and found the room occupied by Stuart Carrington, Frank Olivetti, and Bill Shire. There with them was Brady O'Gorman, a man Rawlings had known for years as the head of the local office of the Bureau of Alcohol, Tobacco, and Firearms. O'Gorman was a local legend in law enforcement, and he and Rawlings had worked together many times. O'Gorman was a big, brawling Irishman, whose salt-and-pepper hair was as messy as his clothing was right then, and his red eyes told Rawlings that he'd been up all night. Rawlings greeted O'Gorman, and Carrington directed Rawlings's attention to another man, who was standing behind the open office door. "Mike, this is Jacob Corliss. He's a prosecutor with the U.S. Attorney General's Office." Rawlings shook hands with Corliss, and closed the door. "Mr. Corliss has been assigned as our legal counsel on this case." Carrington went on. "He'll answer any questions we may have, and provide direction, so that we have a solid case once we locate our suspect."

"Mike," Olivetti said, "we're not sure, but it looks like the patriot struck again last night."

"Shit," Rawlings said, shaking his head. "I caught the news this morning, but I didn't hear anything. What happened?"

"We're keeping it under wraps for right now," Carrington said. "Last night someone knifed Phillip Brummel, a spokesman for an eco-terrorist group called Earthwatch, in his apartment in Coon Rapids. With Brummel in the apartment, was an undercover AFT agent named Tom Kessler, who was trying to get into Brummel's inner circle. The suspect killed Brummel, and knifed Kessler for good measure. Brummel died at the scene, and Kessler died on the table at North Memorial Hospital a short time later."

"Goddamn it!" Rawlings swore. "Brady, I don't know what to say. I'm sorry." O'Gorman patted Rawlings on the arm.

"Because of Brummel's background, we're treating this as a patriot killing." Carrington went on. "We have no other suspects at this time, and the reports that Kessler had filed on Brummel up to last night said nothing about his being in danger from anyone else, right Brady?"

"Right," O'Gorman said tiredly. "As near as Tom could figure out, Brummel was just a hanger-on with Earthwatch. He liked the exposure more than anything. Brummel was basically an asshole, who liked to play the part of the big anti-establishment hero without ever really getting his own hands dirty. There was nothing to indicate that the group would want to take him out, nor are there any other real suspects. Brummel was a doper, but not a dealer, so the killing probably wasn't drug-related. We have nothing that would suggest a love triangle, so jealousy isn't likely. This one came out of the blue."

"Brummel was on our target list," Rawlings said. "Our guys tried to meet with him, but he refused."

"I wish he had," O'Gorman said. "Maybe Tom would have had some warning."

"I've seen things like this happen when two different agencies are investigating different matters, and they overlap," Carrington said. "There's just no way to prevent it. Criminals often have their hands into many different activities, and two uncoordinated offices find themselves getting tangled up. No blame to be found, it's just bad luck."

"Bad luck for a really nice young kid," O'Gorman said. "And bad luck for this patriot, because when I find him, I'm gonna plant him."

O'Gorman was a very able administrator, and had run a successful team out of the Twin Cities for 10 years. He was also an ex-Chicago cop, and known far and wide as a "hard guy." Suspects who went along with him peacefully had nothing to fear from the big Irishman, but those who fought carried the scars to their graves. O'Gorman had killed two men in the line of duty, and in neither case was he unjustified. But people knew that when he said something, he meant it, and everyone in the office that morning knew that Brady O'Gorman hadn't just made a threat; it was a promise.

"Bill," Carrington said, "how's the sketch coming?"

"Well, I've finished with the witnesses," the artist said in his even voice. "I'm going to call the hospital this morning, to see when I can meet with the gang kid, Rueben Gonzalez. He's had the best look at the patriot, and I'm hoping he remembers something. After that, I'll be ready to give you a finished picture within a day."

"Okay, get going. Frank and Mike, review the reports from last night, and head up to the scene. See if you can shake something loose."

"Brady," Rawlings said to O'Gorman, "we're going to get this bastard. No question."

"I know, Mike," O'Gorman answered. "He's had his run, but it's at an end. I just hope I'm there when the curtain drops."

When Rawlings came out of the office, one of the secretaries called him over to a phone, telling him that he had an urgent call from the BCA office.

"Rawlings."

"Mike, it's Sarah," his secretary said. "You have an envelope here with no return address. It feels like it's got a floppy inside."

"Get it to the lab now, without handling it anymore. Have them do the floppy, and the envelope while I head over."

"Okay."

"Frank, we need to make a stop on the way to Coon Rapids. I think I've got a fan letter."

Dear Agent Rawlings,

I thought it was time that I sent you a letter personally. I've watched you on TV, and I must say that you've impressed me as a tireless investigator. Bustling from one place to another, looking for clues, fielding inane questions from the press. I've kept you very busy the last couple of weeks, haven't I?

You've crisscrossed the state, and worked morning, noon, and night. For your efforts, the government gives you your pink slip and turns all of your hard work over to the varsity team: the FBI.

Our paths crossed back in White Bear Lake, when I took Professor Hughes away from you. I bet that pissed you off. You were so close that morning, but I got him. I've given a lot of thought to that day, as I'm sure you have. It's amazing that two men would go out looking for a similar type of individual among millions of others, (for different reasons, to be sure) and locate the same man on the same day. I don't think that this is just a coincidence. I think that you and I are participants in, and what people will one day look back on, as the end of one historical era and the beginning of another.

Throughout history, ordinary people have found themselves caught up in extraordinary events, simply because of where they lived or something they'd done. Consider the security guard who walked in on the Watergate burglary, or Lincoln's bodyguard, who got sick, and left his post at Ford's Theater. Two men, who thought they were living through an ordinary day, found themselves inadvertently making history. One became a hero, the other a goat. Life is funny, isn't it?

I believe you are an intelligent man and, as a lifelong police officer, you've seen first-hand how our nation has declined. You've seen the rampant crime, the upswing in senseless violence, and the decay of our moral values which lead to crime. And I'll bet you've seen the decline of the fabric of our culture. You've seen perversions, and mental illnesses reclassified as, "alternative life styles" or "personal preference choices." Our nation was formed on principals and values, which forced us to work together as a team, but now we embrace principals that pull us apart. We don't even have to speak the same language.

That is why I chose to eliminate Gordon Holmes. He was elected to represent the needs of his constituents, and he chose to represent his own views, and the views of those like him. He sought to cripple our nation's military, and the very businesses which provide jobs, and wages to the residents of his district.

It's easy to find the people responsible for this. All you and I had to do, was look in the paper, or on the news. Each of us looked and saw these people for who they were. The only difference between us is that I sought them out intending to stop them from hurting the country any more. I hoped to make others see the dangers I saw, and join me in the fight.

I know you've seen these things. The only thing that keeps you from joining me, is your stubborn adherence to a rule that says it's wrong to kill. I agree that in general it IS wrong to kill, but our culture has made exceptions to that rule, hasn't it? It's fine for a soldier to go off to a foreign land, and kill someone over a dispute our nation has with another. It's perfectly all right to put someone to death who has committed a capital crime. It's also acceptable for someone to kill in self-defense. You might argue that the first two incidences require government sanction, but the last one is the kicker, isn't it? You face an immediate threat, you fear for your life, or the life of others, and you act.

Well, I say to you that we face the same threat that the patriots of 1776 faced. Oppressive government, unwanted taxes, and rule by a master who doesn't give a rat's ass about the people are exactly what our forefathers fought against in 1776.

I'm going after just such a person this weekend. He likes to brag about the criminal acts of others, and justifies destroying legitimate businesses in the name of saving the planet. I won't say his name, as I haven't visited him yet, but you'll know him later. He has a very high opinion of himself, likes to talk, and I intend to let some of the hot air out of him. I'll leave an American flag pin with him, so you'll know it was me. It's certainly not something he'd buy for himself.

I also have plans for the next weekend that may interest you. I'll have to drive a little way for this one, but I feel the time spent will be well worth it. I'm going to be a little cagey about giving hints about this one, but you'll know my work when I'm through, I'm sure. I'm sick of outsiders who come here to stir up our young people, and teach them that being strong is wrong. The events of September Eleventh should have taught all of us that Americans need to protect themselves, but some people just don't get it. They whine about the immorality of war, when war has already been waged on their own people! If the next generation understands nothing, it MUST know that violence from outside our borders cannot be tolerated. Turning the other cheek is NOT an option.

In closing, I'll say that I'm enjoying the hunt. You've been a fine adversary, but you'll understand if I don't wish you good luck. It's too bad that you don't have the capacity to see the good in what I'm doing, but I hope that someday you will. I had thought that James Knox would, but it seems I latched onto nothing but an old drunk. Tell him not to worry about me being too angry with him; he can crawl back into his bottle until his liver rots.

I look forward to matching wits with the FBI. I caught the press conference, by the way. That Stuart Carrington looks constipated; recommend a good laxative, would you?

a patriot

Rawlings and Olivetti called Carrington immediately after reading the letter, and read him its contents. He asked that they fax him a copy, and bring the floppy back in with them, to be booked as evidence. Carrington said he was going to call an emergency meeting for 2:00 p.m. that afternoon to discuss how to deal with the new information. In the meantime, he asked them to check the newspaper morgue to try to find who the patriot might have been referring to when he spoke of his "weekend plans".

The mood at the *Tribune* newsroom was subdued. Dave Joyner, the news editor, had been upset over the fact that his paper had lost its inside track on the patriot story. With Knox on the outs with the patriot, and the police moving their task force into an impregnable office inside the airport security perimeter, they were back to scrabbling for hard facts to print, just like the other media outlets.

Joyner was reluctant to allow Olivetti and Rawlings into the morgue without a quid pro quo, so the FBI man had to promise the *Tribune* a one-hour head start on the story, once the patriot was captured. Joyner wanted more, but Olivetti reminded him that he had access to the Library of Congress in Washington, which maintained a very complete collection of all U.S. regional press information. He also promised Joyner that any delays in capturing the patriot would be blamed on the *Tribune*'s unwillingness to cooperate. Joyner surrendered, and Olivetti and Rawlings were soon browsing news accounts from outlying areas of the Twin Cities.

They decided that, in order to save time, they would check news and events notices within a four-hour driving time from Minneapolis. Rawlings took north and west, and Olivetti took east and south. At 12:45 p.m. Rawlings said, "Frank, look at this."

Olivetti took the clipping from the *Duluth News Tribune*. It announced that Beverly Geary, Hollywood actress, and renowned activist against the war in Afghanistan, was to speak at the University of Minnesota's Duluth campus on June 1. Geary had taken up the plight of the Afghan children as he cause, and had been on every news program, and talk show touting her latest movie, and her political views. The article, written two weeks before, said that Geary would be speaking at the college's Montague Hall at 7:30 p.m. on June 1.

"I saw this woman on *The Tonight Show* just the other night," Olivetti said. "She gets pretty worked up about the war over there. Says we're acting like the neighborhood bully, beating up everyone who gets in our way."

"She thinks we shouldn't have responded to the attacks?" Rawlings asked.

"Nope. Says the attacks only happened because Americans are such assholes that the whole world hates us, and we shouldn't be surprised when they fight back."

"Jesus," Rawlings said, shaking his head.

"Yeah. Says we can't interfere with anyone else's government, and that all we're accomplishing over there, is killing the children of the people we did wrong in the first place."

"And people come to hear her speak," Rawlings said. "What the hell? Well, I think she falls into the category of someone who'd draw the patriot. Her talk is the same night as Justice Hudson's though. I think that he's still a more attractive target than this nitwit actress."

"Well, Carrington believes that the Secret Service have Hudson wrapped up tight, and we should focus elsewhere. After seeing this, I have to agree."

"Frank, the patriot is trying to effect what he sees as real change. Don't you think he'd be drawn more by an outspokenly liberal Supreme Court Justice, than by a fruitcake Hollywood actress?"

"Sure, but I think he's also smart enough to know when he's overmatched. He won't be able to get within 100 yards of Hudson, and he knows it. Besides, how has he effected real change with his other victims? He's killed more obscure people than a Hollywood actress."

Rawlings knew that Olivetti was right, but his gut instinct told him that Hudson was the more desirable target.

"I don't know, Frank. What you say makes sense, but I still think he'll try for Hudson."

"Well, it isn't our call any way you look at it. The patriot will pick his target, and Carrington will decide which one we'll focus on. Hey, we have another 45 minutes before we need to head back. Let's look some more to make sure we haven't missed anything."

Rawlings and Olivetti arrived five minutes late for the 2:00 p.m. meeting due to heavy traffic. Stuart Carrington and Jacob Corliss were waiting, along with Vince Cushing of the Secret Service. Everyone had had a chance to read the patriot's message to Rawlings, and was eager to put the new information to good use.

"Gentlemen," Carrington began, "did you come up with anything?"

"Well, Stu," Olivetti said, "we searched news and entertainment clippings for all of outstate Minnesota and western Wisconsin. We tried to stay within a four-hour driving radius because we didn't have much time. I'd strongly suggest someone do a more thorough search, just because we may well have missed something. Also, we can't safely assume that the patriot wouldn't go further than 4-hours away, so it would be smart, I think, to expand the circle."

"Noted," Carrington answered. "Go on."

"We found that Beverly Geary, the actress, and anti-military activist, is speaking on June 1 at U of M in Duluth. She's giving a lecture against the military action in Afghanistan." Olivetti handed out copies of the clipping announcing Geary's visit. "As you can imagine, there wasn't much else in the papers relating to activists, and anti-anythings in the last two weeks. They seem to have been lying pretty low."

"Understandably," Cushing put in.

Jacob Corliss cleared his throat, and said, "Um, I realize that I'm new to this investigation, but has anyone else noticed that the patriot seems to be selecting targets almost in a representative manner? By that I mean, there are a lot of liberal judges, but he only went after Borgert. There are a lot of eco-terrorists, but he only went after Brummel. He got a teacher, an anti-nuke protester. Does it seem like he's trying to cover a lot of bases?"

"He killed two legislators," Carrington pointed out, "three child molesters, three PETA people."

"Agreed, but it seems to me that he's really making an effort to spread it around. Hit all the bases, as it were. Maybe an actress would be right up his alley," Corliss said.

"Of course he's selecting a wide variety of victims," Rawlings answered, remembering Sharon Bluhm's admonition that, to the patriot, the actual killings were incidental. He kills, not to eliminate that particular victim, as much as he means to spur others to do the same. He's marking a trail for others to follow."

"So, can we apply that theory to who he'll be after next?" Carrington asked. "His letter would seem to point toward the Geary woman."

"I think that is exactly what the patriot wants us to think," Rawlings said.

"You think he'll be after Hudson?" Cushing asked.

"That's my bet. He's used distraction when he needed to in order to get the police away from Hughes. He probably could have talked his way out of that confrontation with the gang-bangers in the park. Instead, he took a huge risk by shooting seven people in a public park, in full view of witnesses."

"And you feel that he took such a risk to divert the police from Hughes's house?" Carrington scoffed. "That seems pretty thin. Isn't it more likely that he was in the park, biding his time until dark, so he could go after Hughes, and found himself presented with an opportunity to eliminate a *bunch* of people he didn't like? He's no fan of street criminals, either."

"Mike," Vince Cushing said, "we're going to have Hudson in and out of there fast this Saturday. The joint will be locked down. No one, and I mean *no one*, will be able to get within a half mile of Hudson, without my knowing everything about him."

"I still believe that Hudson is the target," Rawlings said stubbornly. "The patriot's movement, as he sees it, is starting to roll along. There's more vigilante crime everyday across the country. He needs something big to kick it into high…"

"And a famous actress can provide that," Carrington interjected with some exasperation. "Maybe better than a Supreme Court Justice can. People *worship* Hollywood types. Look at all of the TV programs, and magazines out there that report every little detail of stars' lives. When was the last time you saw a Justice on *Entertainment Tonight*, or the *Tonight Show*?"

Rawlings rubbed his face. "I won't disagree with anything you've said," he told Carrington, "but my gut tells me otherwise. He wants a revolution, right? A popular front to rise up, and throw out the old regime. The only thing his "movement" is lacking, is a central core. All revolutions and civil wars require a leader—someone to rally the people, and get them behind the cause. I think that the patriot either hoped that someone would step forward by now to claim the role, or he plans on doing it himself, even from jail."

"A Nelson Mandela?" Corliss asked.

"Right. Keep in mind, he's thought this out for how long, we don't know. He's not stupid. In this last letter, he seems pretty confident, appealing directly to the police. He's been using us, and the press all along to get to whatever goal he has in mind."

"Mike," Carrington said, "the danger in this type of case is reading too much into your suspect. This guy is pissed off, and thinks he's doing the world a favor by killing people. I disagree with your observation that he's way ahead of us. He's nutty enough to imagine that he can overthrow the entire United States government with a killing spree in Minnesota. He's out of his mind, and he *will* make a mistake because of it. This letter is dripping with confidence—you're right about that—but it's because he thinks he's invincible. He mailed his last letter naming Busch as his victim before he killed him, and he just did it again. He's getting very confident, and it will be his downfall."

"So, we're focusing on Geary?" Olivetti asked.

"It's the safe bet," Carrington replied. "Vince and his people will look after Hudson, and we will look after Ms. Geary."

"You going to tell her of the danger?" Rawlings asked Carrington, as the Agent In Charge was gathering up his papers.

"No," Carrington said simply, without looking up.

"So, you're going to use her as bait, and she won't even know it, right?" Carrington didn't answer. He quietly snapped his briefcase closed, and walked out.

"Frank, don't you have a problem with this?" Rawlings asked a clearly uncomfortable Olivetti.

"Carrington has his orders, Mike. He's under more pressure from Washington than you can imagine. If Geary gets spooked, and cancels, the patriot will go off in another direction, and then where the fuck will we be? This might be our best chance to be at the same place he is at the same time."

"And what if he gets her anyway, and it gets out that we didn't warn her? Whether we catch him or not, we're the assholes."

"Shitstorm," Olivetti agreed, nodding his head. "But we're gonna do everything we can to see it doesn't happen."

CHAPTER 37

▼

On Tuesday morning, James Knox managed to make it in to work. Through supreme force of will, he'd managed to get through the weekend without drinking and, although Monday had been a washout and his sleep was still restless from withdrawal, he felt mostly human. Rawlings had struck a chord when he asked Knox how he wanted to be remembered, and the question had bothered him since then. He'd found strength by spending a lot of time on the phone with Trisha, and the two had finally talked about things that were years overdue. Overall, Knox felt as if he'd been run through a wringer, but something told him he would come out the other side.

He sat at his desk, contemplating where to go from there. He knew that the patriot had, in all likelihood, abandoned him as his mouthpiece, and with him had gone his standing with his superiors. He was still the *Tribune's* main crime reporter, though, and the patriot story was unfinished. He decided to go back to doing journalism the way he always had: legwork, informants, bribes, and the gift of gab he'd always counted on before the patriot had spoon-fed him his stories.

At 9:30 he was getting ready to head out when the phone rang. The newsroom secretary told him that there was a man named Robert Torkelson on the line, who said that he had some information for him about the patriot.

"Hello, this is James Knox."

"Mr. Knox, I hope I'm not wasting your time, but, well, I have a mother who lives in Hudson, near where Gordon Holmes was killed?"

Torkelson related his mother's story about the tall man in the street outside of her house the night of the murder, and how he'd been unable to find this "Agent Rawlings" the Hudson cop had told her about.

"Mr. Torkelson, I think I might be able to help you, and your mother. What was her name and address again?" Five minutes later, James Knox was in his Mustang, headed to Wisconsin, and back at what he did best.

It was also on Tuesday morning that Bill Shire was able to get permission to visit Rueben Gonzalez from doctors at Hennepin County Medical Center. Gonzalez was still in the Critical Care Unit, but his condition had been upgraded from critical to serious since he came out of his coma.

Gonzalez had been shot twice by the patriot that evening in Four Seasons Park. The first bullet had struck him in the chest, and the second in the head, but it was the first that had caused the most serious damage.

Many people mistakenly believe that a bullet to the head is almost uniformly fatal, but this is not true. Nationwide statistics show that only about 15% of people who suffer a gunshot wound to the head die. The skull is a very hard, oblique mass of smooth bone. Bullets tend to glance off of it, leaving nothing more than a flesh wound to the scalp. If a bullet does happen to penetrate the skull, it may have spent all of its penetrating power on the bone, and not cause very much brain injury, or it may strike an area of the brain which does not contain densely-packed blood vessels. In this case, the victim may suffer some loss of memory, or motor function, but is entirely capable of survival.

Gonzalez's coma was caused by a loss of blood he suffered from the chest wound. The first bullet fired into him by the patriot hit him in the ribcage, and splintered into several pieces. One shard rattled around in his chest cavity, nicking his lung, liver, and pericardium, which is the protective sack surrounding the heart. Another shard glanced off his rib, and made a small hole in his left pulmonary artery, the main source of blood flow to the lung. Gonzalez's chest cavity began to fill with blood, as did his pericardium, which began to compress his heart and interfere with its ability to pump blood. This interference resulted in an interruption of the blood flow to his brain, and caused the coma.

Rueben Gonzalez was fortunate in several respects. He was lucky to have been the first victim to receive emergency care by the first paramedics on the scene. It was only their skill, and speed of treatment that prevented his bleeding to death on the grass that night. He was also lucky in that, when he fell, he landed on his side, so when the patriot tried to insure he was dead by firing a second shot into Gonzalez's head, the small 9mm bullet stuck just above his right ear, flattened out against his skull, passed between the scalp and skull, and exited into the grass, leaving his brain intact.

Even though he'd lost over half of his body's blood volume by the time he reached the operating room at Hennepin County Medical Center, Rueben Gonzalez had been able to be one of the lucky number of people who could say that they were once shot in the chest and the head, and lived to tell about it.

So, it was a very lucky sixteen-year-old who sat in his bed that morning telling Bill Shire what he remembered about that night in Four Seasons Park.

"I remember the guy," Gonzalez said in a very raspy voice, which was caused by the tube that had been in his throat until two days before. "Rico was just fucking with him a little. He was just trying to scare him a little, you know?"

"Yes, I know," Shire answered. The doctors had only allowed him half an hour with Gonzalez, and he had to get what he needed without using his usual approach.

"The dude didn't get scared, though," Gonzalez said quietly. "He got, like, calm. It was like he was having a bad day, and Rico just made it better, you know?"

"Yes."

"There was something about the guy that scared me. I know it scared Angel, too because he looked at me funny when the guy was talking back to Rico like he was, all calm." Gonzalez asked Shire for some ice chips from a bedside glass, and Shire helped him swallow some.

"Thanks. Rico had a bad temper, and grabbed at the guy through his window, but the guy cut him, real quick, like he was ready for it. Then he shot him in the face, and came out of the truck fast, like an animal. He was smooth, like he'd done that a million times, man. He walked around shooting us like he was shooting dogs, man. Bang, bang, bang." Gonzalez motioned the shots with his forefinger. "I felt myself get shot, and I thought I should play dead. I saw Angel get shot and try to crawl away, but the dude just put the gun to his head and blew him away. I felt him shoot me in the head, and that's the last thing I knew. I was sure I was dead," Gonzalez said the last part very quietly.

"Rueben, can you help me catch the man who killed your friends?" Shire asked.

"I'll try."

Together, they worked on a sketch. Shire had a working knowledge already from the other witnesses about the patriot's general appearance, but he was careful not to steer Gonzalez. Shire knew that this was the person who'd had the best look at the mystery man. When they were finished, Gonzalez nodded at the drawing Shire had made.

"Yeah. That's him."

At 11:30 in the morning, Rawlings's cell phone rang.

"Mike, it's Jim Knox."

"Jim, how's it going?"

"Much better Mike. I'm calling from Hudson, Wisconsin. I'm at the home of a lady I think you'd probably like to talk to. Her name is Agnes."

As Shire made his way back to the airport office, Frank Olivetti called him on his cell phone.

"Bill, am I interrupting?"

"No, I'm finished, and on my way back. What's up?"

"We have another witness. An old lady named Agnes Torkelson is being brought in by a couple of agents from Hudson. They think she saw the patriot park his car, and go into the park behind Holmes's house."

"I'm on my way."

Agnes Torkelson was the center of attention in the big conference room when she was brought in. She'd provided the license number she'd written down to the first set of agents who visited her, and a different team of agents was on their way to the Enterprise Rental office to look up the rental records from the night of Holmes's murder.

Agnes was intimidated by all of the investigators sitting around her asking questions. She'd seen a couple of them on the TV, and she hoped that her son wasn't right when he told her it was a wild goose chase.

"Mrs. Torkelson, are you sure the truck was white?" Rawlings asked.

"Yes. It was white. It could have been cream or even pale yellow, I suppose…the light was poor."

"Did it look like any of these models of truck?" Rawlings provided her with a handful of pictures of SUVs.

"Oh, I don't know cars so well," she protested. "It was big, like this one." She pointed to a picture of a Ford Explorer.

"The registration lists to a white Explorer," Olivetti said to Rawlings.

"Mrs. Torkelson, how good a look did you get of the man's face?" Shire asked.

"Well, as I said, the light was poor, and he was walking quickly."

"Would you recognize him if you saw him again?" Shire asked her.

"I think I might."

The other agents filed out, knowing that they'd gotten all they could out of the old lady. It was up to Shire to use his unique style to remove the image of the patriot that was locked away in Agnes Torkelson's brain.

An hour later, Shire had gotten as far with Agnes as he thought he could. He had a drawing that was fairly similar to the others, and now he had to meld them in his mind into one, consistent image. He told Olivetti that he wanted to grab some lunch, return to the peace of his hotel room, clear his head, and that he should have a finished product first thing in the morning.

At the Enterprise office, two agents retrieved the records of the rental of the Ford Explorer on the afternoon of the 22nd. They brought a copy in, and turned it over to Olivetti and Rawlings, who immediately instituted a computer search for Joseph Albert Wicks, date of birth March 12, 1969. They found a valid Wisconsin driver's license, but nothing else.

"No Social Security number on file for him, though," Olivetti said. "It's an alias, I bet. He probably got the name off of a headstone."

"Shit," Rawlings said. "Well, our man is a creature of habit. If he's comfortable at Enterprise he may rent there again. Let's ask them to flag the name in their computer, and call us if he shows again." Rental car companies, due to their attractiveness to criminals of all types, the drug trade in particular, have established guidelines for flagging names and alerting police. Counter agents are trained in that and, depending on their experience, most are fairly good at calling for help while appearing to be going through normal procedures.

"May as well call all of the big rental outfits, and give them this name, too." Olivetti said, picking up the phone.

"Are you sure you don't want to run that by Carrington?" Rawlings asked. "You know the tradeoff by doing that."

"Yeah, it might leak out. But we have to let somebody know what name to look for, right?"

On Wednesday morning Stuart Carrington met with Frank Olivetti, Mike Rawlings, Bill Shire, and Brady O'Gorman. They'd discovered that the patriot had assumed the identity of a two-year-old named Joseph Wicks, long dead from a car accident, and buried in a public cemetery in St. Paul. Shire had worked most of the previous night, and looked drawn and tired, but had completed the task he'd been brought in for. The final draft of his suspect sketch looked more like a photograph than the usual line drawings that appeared in newspapers. Shire had drawn the patriot in profile as well as full face, and his rendering surprised even the agents who'd worked with him before. He was congratulated, and offered the chance to stay on in Minneapolis in case another witness was found, or to return home to New York. Shire chose to stay. He wanted to look the patriot in the eye when he was caught to try to see what lived inside of him.

Carrington told them that he would be calling a press conference for 1:30 that afternoon to bring the media up to date on what had been done, and to release the drawing. He wanted Olivetti and Rawlings to finish up with any lines of inquiry they'd begun, and to go to Duluth on Friday morning to prepare for Beverly Geary's speech.

"At what point do we tell Geary why we're there?" Rawlings asked, still annoyed at what Carrington was trying to do.

"You don't," Carrington said. "You will meet with the campus police, who will help you cover the preliminaries quietly. Make them believe that this is a routine precaution, and that we have no direct threat to Geary. You will learn that auditorium inside and out and tell college officials only that you are conducting a routine security check. On Saturday, I'll arrive with a team of agents, you two will give us the layout of the place, and we will all work up a plan to cover it during the speech. These agents will be from the FBI Hostage-Rescue SWAT team, and we will all be in plain clothes that night. I want you to find out where and when Geary is arriving, how she's getting to the campus, and what the plan is for afterward. We need to be around her at all times, blend in, and not be blatantly obvious."

"You don't want to scare off the patriot," Rawlings said, matter-of-factly.

"That's right. I know you disapprove, but frankly I couldn't care less. We are no closer at this moment to solving this case than we were a week ago, so we need to push it a little. Live bait works the best."

"Even if we get an innocent person killed?" Rawlings asked.

"Twenty-one innocent people have been killed," Carrington said crisply, "including a federal agent. If you have a suggestion that's proactive instead of reactive, I'll listen."

"We're not covering the Hudson visit at all then?"

"That task will ably handled by the Secret Service. Our presence there would be unnecessary."

At the afternoon press conference, Carrington, Olivetti, Shire, and Rawlings stood in front of a podium at a meeting room in the main terminal of the airport. A large group of local and national press had shown for the event, because reportable tidbits had become hard to come by since the FBI took over the case, and moved inside their protected area. The news programs had taken to re-reporting old developments, re-interviewing old witnesses and survivors, and indulging in endless speculation about who the patriot might be. Experts of every kind had been sought out, and their opinions recorded, and played, and replayed. Anything new was pounced upon and torn to pieces by the reporters, who were tired of their editors telling them, "Find something worthwhile, or else!"

Carrington went over the most recent events in the case, and with a flourish entirely out of character with his personality, unveiled Shire's drawing of the patriot. Copies were provided for each of the attendees, and they eagerly left the room to report the latest facts on the biggest story of the year.

That night at work, Tony Bauer took his calls, and excused himself from meeting Erickson and Fitz for coffee. He had the front page of the *Tribune* on the seat next to him, and kept looking over at Shire's picture, which held a peculiar fascination for him. The picture was a very good likeness, and it meant that the hounds were closer now, but it was still a two-dimensional image, and there were differences. He went over in his mind his plans for Saturday, and the things he needed to accomplish before then.

CHAPTER 38

▼

On Thursday morning, Tony Bauer woke early and spent an hour on his weights. He'd let his regimen slip somewhat recently, and he knew that he would need everything working well this weekend, most of all. The damage done by the dog bite was healing nicely, and the swelling was gone.

As he sweated his way though his exercise routine, the local news opened their broadcast with a breaking news story, and the anchor turned the story over to a female reporter, who was standing outside the International Airport Terminal.

"Thank you, Tom," she said into the camera, as the wind pushed her long blonde hair into her eyes. "I'm here at the Minneapolis—St. Paul Airport, where we have learned from a source who works for an auto rental firm, that the FBI has asked the major auto rental companies here to flag a name in their computer, and that the request was made by the Patriot Task Force. We have been told that the FBI believes that the patriot rented a vehicle at least once, and that they were asked to watch for that name again.

"We received this information last night, and have been following up on it. Now, we would not have reported this matter at all if we thought that doing so would help the patriot evade capture, but we discovered that the name the patriot used, Joseph Albert Wicks, was an alias. The real Joseph Wicks died in 1971 after an auto accident, and he is buried in a cemetery in St. Paul. We've learned that adopting the name of a deceased child is a fairly common means of obtaining the necessary documents to set up a false identity. The suspect obtained, and used, a Wisconsin driver's license to rent the auto, and here is the picture from that license." The screen switched to a blurry image of the patriot in disguise. "As you can see, it is very different from the police drawing we saw yesterday, but we can assume that the suspect was in disguise when he had this license photo taken. Sources tell us that it is doubtful that the suspect would use the same name again, and it is certain that authorities could have no way of knowing exactly how many other false identities he may have obtained."

"Thank you!" the patriot said to the TV screen as he did his exercises. He had another Wisconsin license ready to go, but it was nice to be told that the Wicks identity had been burned.

"We located the parents of Joseph Wicks," the reporter went on, "who are still living in the area, and asked them how they felt about this development."

The camera cut to a man and woman, who appeared to be in their early sixties. Under their image were the words, Eugene and Elizabeth Wicks—dead son's identity was stolen.

"I just can't believe it," Mrs. Wicks said. "After all these years we just don't know what to think. It's terrible. It brings back horrible memories. I just wish our son could have been left alone."

"Tom," the reporter continued, "we also understand that the FBI task force has been receiving calls in response to the suspect sketch they released yesterday afternoon. Hopefully, these breakthroughs will bring a swift end to the terror which has been strangling the Twin Cities these last few weeks."

"Goddamn, *fucking* son-of-a-bitch!" Olivetti screamed at the TV, as the reporter signed off. "Nice of them to decide that it won't hurt our investigation to release the goddamned alias! *Pricks!*"

"You can always count on the press to interfere with your investigation," Carrington said.

"The thing that really pisses me off," Olivetti said, "is that they reported that for only one reason: they wanted to interview the family of the dead kid, and play their *four sentence* reply! They blew a hole in our case so they could drag a cheap interview out of some old people who had *nothing* of relevance whatsoever to add to the story."

"This is probably retaliation for us squeezing off their information flow," Carrington said. "They liked getting all those interviews with the cops before we came in, so now they're going to make us pay."

"And how did they get that license photo so fast? We just got it this morning," Olivetti asked wonderingly.

"They have a faster network than we have, evidently," Carrington answered. "Well, the milk is spilled. Let's clean it up and move on."

"Tina, you have to get over this guy and move on," Shelly Neely said. Shelly worked for Blue Cross, and had occupied the desk next to Tina Sullivan for eight months. They were buddies, and Tina had told Shelly the whole story about her fling with Tony, and how he kept ignoring her. It was obvious to Shelly that this Tony was only after sex, and had said as much to Tina several times. For some reason, Tina kept hoping.

"I know," Tina replied, "but I really thought we'd be right together. I thought he cared."

"He cared about getting you in the sack. You know how men are, but there are better ones out there."

"I'm beginning to doubt it," Tina chuckled.

"Listen, I've found in my *vast* experience with men and relationships, that the best way to get *over* a man, is to get *under* a man, if you know what I mean! So we are going to go out tomorrow night after work, drink irresponsibly, act *totally* slutty—well, you will, I'm engaged—and you are going to get this chump out of your mind once and for all. How about that?"

"You know, it sounds fun." Tina nodded her head decisively. "I'm sick of sitting around the apartment waiting for the phone to ring! I don't deserve that!"

"Right!" Shelly said.

Tony Bauer checked on for the afternoon shift, and was immediately sent to an accident on Highway 3 south of Rosemount. A Toyota Corolla filled with five huge Somali men took a curve wide, and the left front corner of the car passed under the flatbed of an oncoming semi. The trailer's dual wheels passed over the hood and roof of the car. What was left of the Corolla was spit out the back of the trailer like a watermelon seed, and tossed into the ditch. The driver, a man who in life had stood six-foot-six, was compressed into the floorboards between the seat and the steering wheel, and killed instantly. Two passengers in the back were forced into the trunk of the car by the impact, and the one on the left side was actually found in what remained of the car's left rear wheel-well. Surprisingly, the passengers in the right front and right rear were only moderately injured. The ambulance and rescue personnel struggled with their patients' limited English in order to treat them prior to transporting them to the hospital.

The Rescue Squad captain in charge of the scene asked Bauer to call Burnsville's Ridges Hospital, where the patients would be taken, and to have them locate a Somali interpreter. Bauer used his cell phone, and got in touch with an ER nurse, who asked him to call the county court.

"Sorry, Deputy," she said, "we've got Spanish, Vietnamese, Hmong, Russian, and Chinese interpreters, but no Somali, and no Sudanese. And, if you find one, please give him a pager so we can call him day or night."

"You get a lot in?" Bauer asked.

"Shit," the nurse replied, "all the time. They don't let their wives learn English, because women aren't allowed to speak to other men. Then, their children get sick, and the husbands are gone, so the mothers bring them in, and expect us to treat them, but can't tell us what's wrong."

Bauer called the clerk of court in Hastings, who had numbers for Somali interpreters, but they were only available for court with prior notice. Bauer went back to the rescue captain, and told him he'd had no luck.

"I kinda figured," the captain replied. "Well, maybe they can take them to Hennepin County Medical Center. You know, I can remember when we laughed at the way the old Bohunks spoke around here. It's another deal now."

"It sure is," Bauer agreed.

After the crash was cleared, and the State Troopers finished photographing, and measuring the area, Bauer went on his way. It was his last night of his work week, and he wanted to stay as free as possible. The coming weekend might prove to be the defining moment of his crusade, if all went well, and he headed for the back roads to try and lay low for the rest of the night. He keyed his mike to tell the dispatcher that he was clear.

"1130, 10-8."

"1130, copy."

Mike Fitz finished his paperwork, and prepared to head out in his own squad car. He had come to work, and found the copy of the patriot's image tacked up on the information bulletin board. He thought that he'd seen the face before, and it aggravated him when he couldn't place where. He shook it off the feeling, and climbed into his car. As he pulled out of the lot he heard, "1130, 10-8," on the police radio, and slammed on the brakes.

"No fucking way," Fitz said to himself. The voice of Tony Bauer suddenly meshed with the patriot drawing in his mind. *No, that's bullshit*, he thought. *Sure, there is a resemblance, but…that's impossible.* He thought back to all of the conversations he'd had with Tony over the years, and how bright and articulate he'd thought him to be. True, Tony had become more reclusive lately, but it *had* to be the divorce. No, the Tony he knew wouldn't be out there shooting and stabbing people. And certainly not an AFT agent, like the last guy.

The AFT agent was undercover, a nagging voice said inside Fitz's head.

Tony wouldn't do that, Fitz told the voice.

The patriot is a big, strong guy, the voice reminded him.

A lot of guys are big.

The patriot drives a black Explorer.

"Fuck me," Fitz said aloud, and pulled off into a parking lot to think.

Mike Rawlings and Frank Olivetti spent their day tying up loose ends and making their travel plans. They got booked into a Best Western not far from the college, and called ahead to the campus police to arrange a meeting. The director was away on vacation, but a captain said he'd be happy to sit down with them, after Olivetti told him they were going to be scouting the campus for a possible future visit from a visiting dignitary. Rawlings shook his head at that, but didn't say anything. He'd always believed that, when dealing with people, especially other cops, honesty was the best way to accomplish your goal, and not leave burned bridges in your wake. But, this was the FBI's baby, and he reminded himself that he was only along for the ride.

That evening, Rawlings took Mary out to her favorite seafood place. They ate quietly, and Mary sensed that Mike was preoccupied with the case. She wanted to help, but knew that she needed to let him do whatever he needed to. What frightened her was how brutally the patriot had killed the young undercover agent. Was it possible that he had mistaken him for someone he thought deserved death? Could it be that he just didn't care who he killed anymore?

She trusted Mike, and knew he was good at what he did, but she also knew that Mike's days of being able to physically tangle with a suspect were quickly getting past him. She chuckled as she watched him chase a piece of fish down with a gulp of wine, and whispered a prayer that he'd come away from this damned case in one piece.

Mike Fitz called Tony Bauer on his car phone that evening after the calls had settled down, and asked to meet him in the parking lot of a business in Bauer's area. They both arrived a little after 9:30, and pulled their cars up side by side, so they could speak without getting out. Fitz had been wrestling with conflicting emotions all evening, and decided he needed to sound out his friend before he made up his mind about anything. He was a supervisor, which meant he was bound to report any suspicions of misconduct by underlings to the sheriff, and he was a cop, which meant he was sworn to uphold the law, and assist in the capture of wanted criminals.

His dilemma was that, as a road sergeant, he also had to have the trust and respect of his deputies, and falsely accusing one of them of something so heinous would permanently impact that trust with all of the others. To compound that, he was also a friend of Bauer, and had been for 12 years, since they both had worked in the jail, and later were partners on the back roads. They'd been to each other's homes, stood up in each other's weddings, and gone on fishing vacations together. Fitz knew that if he turned Bauer in to the FBI, and was wrong, he would lose this friend forever. He had to know first.

The two made small talk, and discussed the earlier accident. Fitz told him about his summer vacation plans while he formed in his mind how he was going to broach the subject.

"Tony," he began, "what do you think of this patriot business? I mean, people are all over the board about this guy."

"What do you mean?" Bauer asked.

"Well, there's all of this copycat crime, militia groups forming, the government talking about declaring curfews in some areas. Do you think we're headed for some kind of civil war?"

"I don't know, Mike. It seems like the world's gone crazy. People want freedom, but they're lazy, and want the government to do everything for them. They don't see that you surrender your freedom when you stop doing things for yourself."

"So, do you think this guy is doing a service to the country?"

Bauer knew his friend, and had the feeling that Fitz was sounding him out for something. That last question was loaded. Maybe he suspected. Without even realizing he was doing it, Bauer slowly moved his right hand down, and unsnapped his holster

"I'm trying to decide that myself, Mike."

"I agree that the country's lost it's way. Hell, just look around: crime, crazy civil verdicts, burglars suing the owners of buildings they break into, and hurt themselves in, political correctness gone wild. What's the answer? Is selectively killing people the way?"

"I don't know," Bauer answered quietly. He didn't like the way this was going, and wished for a call so that he could leave. *What the fuck are you thinking,* he asked himself.

"Tony, I've always thought you were a smart guy—well-read, that kind of thing. You keep up with current events better than I do. What kind of person can kill so many people like that for a cause?"

"People kill for a lot of reasons, Mike," Bauer said as he stared through the windshield into the dark night. "Some kill for lust, some for greed, some in self-defense, hell, some for $20 worth of crack. I don't think it does any good to judge why someone kills…they do it for their own reasons. Society decides if their reason was just or not." You can talk your way out of this one…he isn't sure.

"Isn't there a better way to bring change, though?"

"I don't know, Mike. The system is so twisted…in theory you can vote out politicians you disagree with. You can be active, campaign for somebody you support, and knock on doors, but the system negates all of that. Politicians have to spend millions of dollars to get elected to a job that pays them $80,000 a year. They get that money by making promises to companies and people with the bucks to get them elected. By the time they're in office, they've sold their souls to so many people they can't even remember who they owe. Campaigns have gotten sickening. They run ads that say that their opponent will ruin the country if elected. They find a topic that's got a lot of voter interest, like health care, tax cuts, or supporting farms, and try to convince people that they will be more con- cerned about them than the bastard they're running against. They throw so much shit at each other that you have to mute your sound every time one comes on."

"Do you think they're all the same?" Fitz asked.

"To an extent they have to be. Everything a politician does from the time he's elected is geared toward getting himself reelected. He has staff people that tell him how a particular vote will impact his voter appeal back home, and how that stance will be criticized in the next campaign. Since most politicians seek office hoping to move up to higher offices, they have to play the game forever. What's the answer? I don't know."

"So, if this has been going on so long, what's new here? Why would the patriot start killing now?"

"He's alive now," Bauer said simply. "This is his time, and this is when he felt it was time to act, I guess."

"You think they'll catch him, or will he go out fighting?"

Bauer turned his head and met his friend's eyes. "I don't know, Mike, but I can say this for sure: he believes that what he's doing is right, and important. He believes that what he's doing will make America stronger for generations to come. A man with that kind of motivation will be hard to stop."

Bauer saw the uncertainty in his friend's eyes, and quietly re-snapped his holster.

Fitz drove home with a sick feeling in the pit of his stomach. His question wasn't fully answered, but he had never really thought it would be. He'd hoped that Bauer would have given him a forceful denial—said that the patriot was crazy, that the guy should be strung up—*something* that would allow Fitz to drive away knowing that he had nothing to fear. Bauer had said nothing that some of the other deputies hadn't said, but, in the end, they all maintained that, fundamentally, what the patriot was doing was wrong.

There was no avoiding the decision, Fitz knew; he had to give Bauer's name to the FBI. He wondered if it would be best to go through his administration, but decided that a direct call would be better. Next, he wondered if he should call anonymously, or if it would be better to tell them who he was. The investigators would have a better frame of reference for his information that way, he knew, but could it ultimately get him in trouble with the sheriff? The safe way would be to go through the chain of command, talk to the sheriff, and let him decide, but Fitz decided he owed his friend more than that. At least the benefit of the doubt. He would call the FBI himself tomorrow, and take his chances.

On the night before he left, Mike and Mary Rawlings made the kind of quiet love that people who've been married for years made. They didn't tear the sheets up, and wreck the bed frame the way they had in their wild and reckless youths, but neither did they just go through the motions of sex. Both knew what the other liked, and each gave of themselves until the other was satisfied, and they lay, quiet and spent, their fingers softly brushing up against each other, and their breathing slowing until only the wind could be heard stirring the new leaves outside their window.

Tina Sullivan slept alone, wrapping her arms and legs around her spare pillow, wondering if she was right or wrong, and wishing that her Tony was by her side.

James Knox lay in the dark of his room, staring up at the ceiling, and praying for the peace of sleep. He hadn't had a drink in three days, and he was feeling the sharp edges of the stark, unrelieved boredom of life without the false comfort of alcohol. He knew that he needed to stop, if for no other reason than to show those around him that his life, which he had lived to such fullness, would not end in disgrace.

Around the metro area, many men, women, and children tried to sleep, each of whom had lost a loved one to the man who called himself a patriot. Each carried the burden of knowing that someone out there, someone who now had a face they could picture, had taken from them someone so important, and had inflicted pain on them so deep, for an ideal that he carried in his head. Some bore the burden as rage, as a parent feels when they have had to perform the unnatural act of seeing the casket containing their child be lowered slowly into a grave. Some bore it as confused depression, as a child feels when they've lost a parent who was one of few constants in their life. Others bore it with the black, empty loss that a mate feels when the person they'd committed to live their life with, was suddenly gone, and the other side of the bed loomed so large.

And the man who had caused it all, slept soundly in his bed, on a quiet street, on a Minnesota spring night.

CHAPTER 39

▼

The patriot case could have come to a much different conclusion, had it not been for one of those quirks of fate that pop up occasionally, and twine themselves around important events in history.

Sir Isaac Newton notices an apple falling from a tree, and begins a line of thought that eventually inspires space flight. Alexander Flemming, a research scientist with a messy laboratory, forgets to wash out a moldy dish, and stumbles upon the invention of penicillin, saving millions of lives. Such was the luck that followed the patriot. Mike Fitz, who went to bed Thursday night after work, intending to call his suspicions in to the FBI the next morning, woke up coughing shortly after falling asleep. He smelled smoke, and heard the distant beeping of a smoke alarm coming from downstairs in his house.

A pinhole leak had sprung in the fuel line of Fitz's take-home squad car shortly after he'd parked it in his garage for the night. A small amount of gasoline had squirted onto the hot manifold and ignited, causing a little fire to flicker around the engine compartment. The fire slowly ate through the plastic and rubber inside the Ford Crown Victoria's engine compartment, and eventually made its way outside the grille to a bag of charcoal that was sitting on a shelf directly in front of the car. The engine fire had burned itself out by the time the charcoal combusted, and lit the shelf, and nearby workbench, on fire.

The Fitz home was well equipped with smoke detectors, but had none in the attached garage, where the majority of home fires begin. By the time Fitz realized what was happening, the wall between the garage, and the split-level home's entryway, was fully on fire. Fitz ran out into the living room, and into a heavy cloud of black smoke that took his breath away. He ducked low to the floor, and could see that his front entry, which was the only door out of the house, and the only way to the downstairs two bedrooms where two of their three children slept, was impassable. He ran back into his bedroom, and screamed for his wife. In seconds, he had her up, and was dragging her to the adjacent bedroom, where their youngest slept.

Fitz and his wife, Wendy, closed the bedroom door behind them, and he tore off the screen and broke the window out, while Wendy gathered their four-year-old daughter, Alicia. Mike lowered Wendy out the window first, and then dropped the now crying and protesting Alicia down to her. He jumped out, landing hard on his right leg, and broke his ankle. Unmindful of the pain, Mike broke into the downstairs bedroom window, which, thankfully, was on the far side of the house and away from the growing fire. He yelled to Wendy to wake a neighbor and call for help while he crawled in to get their other two children out.

By the time the Fitz family was gathered on the back lawn, and the fire department arrived, half of the house was aflame. They cried and watched helplessly as everything they owned was slowly turned into soot and ashes. Neighbors and responding police promised help and shelter to them while paramedics treated Mike's ankle, and the two older children for smoke inhalation.

So, instead of calling the FBI on Friday morning, Fitz spent the next day in surgery having his shattered ankle pinned back together, and worrying about how he would be able to care for his family.

The pieces were now in place, and the end to the patriot case was set.

On Friday morning Mike Rawlings and Frank Olivetti made the two-and a-half-hour drive north to Duluth, a major shipping port at the westernmost edge of Lake Superior. The city of 80,000 lies like a carpet around and up the steep hillsides which frame the southwestern corner of the huge lake. The drive up Interstate 35 from the Twin Cities is fairly boring until the traveler finally and dramatically crests the final hilltop, and the huge harbor and city are revealed below in either spectacular splendor, or choking fog, depending on the city's very changeable weather.

The two investigators paused in their conversation when they saw the view of the deep blue lake, the 1000-foot-long ore carriers lined at the docks, and the city that stretched around and across the bay to northern Wisconsin.

They followed the signs to their hotel, and checked in before heading up one of the city's many hills to the campus of University of Minnesota, Duluth, better known as UMD. They asked directions to the Darland Administration Building, which housed the campus police offices, and soon found themselves in the company of Captain Russ Blanchard, a tall, easygoing man in his late thirties, who invited them to sit down and got them each a cup of coffee.

"So, you two gentlemen are here to scout us out for a future visit, huh?" Blanchard asked.

"Possibly," Olivetti replied. "You must understand, this conversation has to be kept strictly private." Blanchard nodded. "A senior member of the President's staff is planning an upcoming trip to Duluth to meet with some trade officials, and he is interested in touring, and possibly speaking at the college. The President is very interested in making sure that his commitment to education is known on campuses around the country, and he has encouraged his staff to speak at colleges and universities whenever possible."

Rawlings looked at the floor while his associate deftly rolled out the lie to Blanchard.

"I see," Blanchard said. "What is it that I can do for you today?"

"Well," Olivetti went on, "we'd like you to give us the cook's tour, as it were, of the campus, of the speaking facilities, and an overview of how your department handles security for a visit like that. What measures do you take to ensure the safety of a person, say an unpopular person, who is speaking at the campus? We'd also like to have a look at the auditoriums where a speech would be held to get an idea of how we would need to prepare for this visit."

"I'm confused," Blanchard said, "we've had government officials and foreign leaders here before, and the security precautions have always been worked out with the Secret Service. Why is the FBI doing this?"

"The FBI often does some preliminary work for the Secret Service," Olivetti lied. "Since this is only a proposed visit, we agreed to look around for them."

"Would this visit be during the school year or in summer?" Blanchard asked. "That makes a difference in how things would be handled."

"It would be during the year," Olivetti replied.

"So, next fall I guess," Blanchard said, "since this year is almost done."

"In all likelihood, yes," Olivetti told him.

"You know what would be a big help?" Blanchard asked Olivetti and Rawlings.

"What's that?"

"If we actually discussed why you're really here, and stopped feeding me some bullshit story," Blanchard said simply.

"Excuse me?" Olivetti asked.

"Guys, I may be just a simple campus policeman, but I'm not stupid. I know how the government deals with security. I also don't live in a bubble. We get TV up here in the hinterland, and you two have been plastered all over the newspapers and TV for weeks, especially you," he pointed at Rawlings. "This is about the patriot, not some trade official. Now, either do me the courtesy of telling me the truth, or get out and let me get back to work."

Rawlings and Olivetti looked at each other. "Russ," Rawlings said, "I apologize. The truth is, neither of us liked the idea of trying to pull the wool over your eyes, but we were under orders from our superiors. This is a very important case, and a lot of very powerful people are calling the shots now. What we just did was wrong, but it wasn't meant to make you look dumb. It was a need-to-know thing."

"Okay. Well as I see it, I need to know so I can tell you what you need to know. Obviously your superiors don't see it that way, so I'll have to take a few guesses. Since you're hunting the patriot, I'll assume you think he might show up here. And, since I know that Beverly Geary is coming here, and is exactly the type of person the patriot seems to want to kill, I figure you might think she's in danger of being victim number, what is it now? And, since you're playing a cloak-and-dagger game, I figure you don't want anybody, including Geary, to know about your concerns. That means you intend to set some sort of trap for him. Am I close?"

"As Mike said," Olivetti replied, "we're very sorry. Since you've figured out why we're really here, I have to ask for your full cooperation, and a promise of complete confidentiality, or we'll have to walk out and leave you in the dark."

"Whatever you propose I have to run by my boss who, as you know, is on vacation. When this is over, I want to still have a job. I think I should call and run this by him."

"That's fair enough," Rawlings said. Blanchard made the call and briefed his director on what was going on.

When he hung up he said, "Well, my boss, who is a pretty good guy, has agreed to let me use my best judgment. I have a rule about not trusting people who lie to me, but I guess I don't have any option here. I'll promise you my full cooperation and confidentiality. If you screw me over, you owe me a job."

"You got it." Rawlings chuckled.

For the next hour, Olivetti and Rawlings laid out what they hoped to accomplish the next day. Blanchard was concerned about the idea of keeping Geary in the dark, and explained that, as a campus police official, his office was very much under the scrutiny of the campus administration. The university desired a happy, safe, and positive educational experience for their students. Friction often occurred between the campus police, who had to enforce the rules, and an administration who wanted to graduate happy people, who would hopefully make sizable monetary donations to their alma mater in the future. Colleges tend to be populated by mostly liberal-thinking people who would take a very dim view of the FBI using a popular actress and activist in the same way that a fisherman would dangle a tuna in front of a Great White Shark.

Gradually, Blanchard agreed to the plan. He was encouraged when he learned that members of the well-trained FBI Hostage-Rescue Team would be there, and everyone would be in plainclothes.

"Well," Blanchard said, "as I see it, if nothing happens, you guys will go home, and no one will know you were here. If the patriot does show, and you catch him, everyone will be happy. On the other hand, if he shows, hurts Geary, and gets away, my office can blame the FBI, and you'll get me a new, better-paying job. I can't lose here."

Olivetti and Rawlings laughed as they got up to go on a walking tour of the campus and Montague Hall.

Tina Sullivan went home after work to change into bar-hopping clothes. She took the time to put on her tightest jeans, which she referred to as her "Boy-Getter jeans," a lacy, low-necked, top under a snug waist-length red leather jacket, and red-fringed cowgirl boots. Shelly Neely picked her up, and they were joined by another work friend, named Ginger. They ate dinner at a Chinese restaurant because, according to Shelly, "Chinese throws up so much easier than Mexican." Afterward, they went to a bar that was popular with singles, and had a liberal happy hour, and a live band that pumped out good rock.

The three girls had a pretty good buzz going from the tap beer specials by 9:00 p.m., and were talked into switching to "Blow Jobs," a mixture of vodka, Tia Maria, and Kahlua, topped with whipped cream, and served in a shot glass. The drink is properly consumed by holding your hands behind your back, bending forward to lift the shot glass off of the bar, and tossing it back using only your lips. The exercise was proposed by some horny single guys at the bar who were eying Tina's well-stuffed outfit.

After a few rounds of Blow Jobs, Tina found herself dancing with a pretty cute guy named Jason, who was doing his best to impress her by talking about his car (a Beemer), his apartment (gas fireplace, great view), and his job (marketing executive). He left out just enough details so Tina wouldn't know that his Beemer was ten-years old, and dying of cancer, that his apartment was the basement of his parents' home, and that he sold used cars while doing telemarketing on the side. Jason shoveled the bullshit while Tina bounced deliciously off him, trying her best to dance with all the alcohol surging through her system.

Tina wasn't a very experienced drinker, and the booze hit her hard. She was having a great time, and everything Jason said was hilarious to her. She went to the bathroom with Shelly and told her that she was going to leave with Jason, so there was no need for a ride home. Tina staggered out and grabbed Jason by the sleeve and walked him out to the parking lot, saying, "Let's go!"

She and Jason kissed and groped each other a little in the lot, and then piled into his car. As they drove, Tina gagged a little on the exhaust from the old beater. Jason knew he couldn't take her to his place, so he suggested they go to hers. Tina mumbled that she lived too far, and that she wanted to see his view. Jason drove to a nearby lake which he knew was particularly pretty at night, and parked facing the shore. He and Tina began kissing again, and he started to undo her jacket. Things were moving a little fast for Tina, who had thought it would be nice to cuddle in front of Jason's fireplace, and watch the city lights twinkling in the background. She became chilly as Jason had been forced to shut off the car, to insure that they didn't die of carbon monoxide poisoning as they parked.

"Jason, let's go to your place," Tina said, as Jason's hand found her breast.

"But this is so nice," Jason pled, continuing his caressing.

"I'm cold, let's go sit in front of the fire. I'll make it worth your while," she teased.

"Look at the beautiful lake," Jason said, hoping to change the subject.

"Jason, I mean it, let's go."

Jason pressed his lips harder on her, and slid his hand between her legs.

"No!" Tina said, pulling Jason's hand out.

"C'mon, don't tease me. I know you want this," he said, grabbing her crotch again.

"Stop it!"

"C'mon Gina," Jason said, committing the ultimate sin a man on a date can make.

"Gina! My name is Tina, you bastard! Take me back to the bar! Now!!" Tina demanded.

"Fuck you!" Jason yelled. "Get out and walk, you bitch!"

"Gladly!" She stumbled out of the car, as Jason angrily cranked the ignition, causing the old car to shake and sputter before it finally fired, and he drove away, leaving her in the dark park alone.

"Son of a bitch!" she yelled, as he spun out of the parking lot. Tina staggered out toward the road, and had to walk nearly a mile through dark streets before she found a payphone. She called a cab, which took a-half-an-hour to arrive. She had the cabbie take her back to the bar, but found that Shelly's car was gone. She resigned herself to an expensive ride home, and gave the cabbie her address. By the time she got there, it was midnight, and she was drunk, angry, and hurt. She began to cry, thinking about what a disaster the night had been, what an asshole Jason had turned out to be, and how the only man to make her happy was just 15 minutes away in Hastings.

Tina picked up the letter she'd written to Tony and got into her car. She backed out, and headed to Pine Street in Hastings to try to make something out of the night and her life.

Rawlings and Olivetti sat up in their hotel room going over what they'd learned from Russ Blanchard. They had good maps of the campus, and to-scale diagrams of Montague Hall. Blanchard had obtained Beverly Geary's arrival plans from the campus administration office and told them that the university had reserved a room for her in a campus VIP guest suite.

They agreed that if the patriot was going to have a chance to get near her, he would have to do it immediately before or after the lecture. There was a reception planned in an adjoining banquet room, but the general public had not been made aware of that. The college only published the event in their newsletter in order to avoid a crush of people. Geary was scheduled to leave the school early Sunday morning and go directly to the Duluth airport, so Saturday night was likely to be when the patriot would strike, if at all.

Rawlings maintained his belief that Justice Hudson was the patriot's real target, and that his comment about driving to his next target was a ruse, but he concentrated on finishing the work so the SWAT commander and Carrington could make their final plans when they arrived the next day.

They finished and went to the hotel bar for a nightcap before they turned in for the night.

Vince Cushing made his final plans for the morning arrival of Justice Hudson and collapsed into bed at 12:30 a.m. He had gone through all of his precautions several times, walked the Hilton Ballroom over and over, and made more of a nuisance of himself to the other agents than he usually did. Cushing had worked the Presidential Detail for many years, and knew the stress that came from being entirely responsible for the life of the world's most important man. The Supreme Court Detail was a cakewalk generally, but that night Cushing felt as much pressure as he'd ever known. The patriot was a major threat, and he was determined not to give the man an inch of space in which to operate.

An armored limousine had been flown in, and a motorcade was arranged, despite Hudson's desire for a more low-key arrival. U.S. Army Ordinance Disposal experts had swept the hotel room, hallways, and ballroom for explosives, and would do so again tomorrow. Bomb sniffing dogs had "cleared" all of the cars that would be used in the motorcade, and they were now under 24-hour guard. Secret Service agents had been called out from offices all over the country to take over jobs that would normally have been done by local police, who were unacceptable for this job. No press was to be allowed in, and all of the 176 University of Minnesota Law School graduating seniors would be thoroughly searched by hand, and by metal detectors when they arrived. Cushing had a list of all of the names of students and faculty who would be attending the speech and banquet, their backgrounds, and all had been checked in detail.

Cushing knew that he could do nothing more. He forced himself to surrender to sleep so he would be at least somewhat rested for the long day tomorrow.

The patriot sat up in his kitchen getting things ready for the next day. He had emptied his garage cubbyhole, and had his Mini-14 rifle, Browning Hi-Power, knives, and other weapons laid out on the table. He had disassembled and cleaned everything, and was beginning to put them back together. The Hedgehog sat on a microwave stand in the corner, waiting for the patriot's final touches to convert it from something that looked like a fat steel porcupine into something much more benevolent-looking. Normally, he would have done this work in his basement, but the night was hot, and the breeze coming through the kitchen windows was pleasant. He had the newspaper open on the table to a story about the chaos he'd caused. There was a copy of Bill Shire's drawing prominent on the page.

He was deep in thought, reviewing his plans for the next day, and didn't hear the car pull up to the front of his neighbor's house.

Tina was unfamiliar with the neighborhood and too drunk to do a good job of reading the house numbers in the dark. She walked determinately up to the dark house, and was going to knock when she read the house number, and realized that it was wrong. She walked back under the streetlight, looked at the address on the envelope again, and saw that she was off by one house. She walked to the next house and saw a light on inside. *Shit,* she thought, *what if he has a girl in there?* She decided to do a little window peeking before she knocked.

Tina walked around to the back of the house and looked in the door. She saw Bauer sitting at the table cleaning a rifle. She looked around the room to see if there was any evidence that he might not be alone, but saw none. A feeling of safety and love coursed through her as she realized that her trip wasn't in vain after all. She would give him the letter, and, if he was interested in talking, maybe they could discuss her concerns, and she would have her answer. With luck, Tony would comfort her, and then she would know.

Deciding that a bold approach was the best way to demonstrate her strength, Tina quickly turned the knob on the unlocked door, and walked in, much to Bauer's shock and dismay.

"Tina, what are you doing here?" Bauer sputtered as he looked around at his kitchen.

"Tony I'm sorry, but I just had to come over," Tina answered, as Bauer quickly turned over the newspaper picture. "Tony, what's all of this for?" she asked, looking at the arrayed weapons.

"Well, I use these for work," Bauer told her.

"Knives, and what's that?" she asked, pointing to the stun baton.

"It's a police tool," Bauer told her. "Look, let's go into the living room." He steered her out of the kitchen while his mind frantically took inventory of anything else in the house that might be incriminating. They sat on the couch, and Bauer asked her what was wrong. Tina started to tell him about her night, and the whole story poured out: her confusion about their relationship, Shelly's advice to dump him, the bar, Jason, and the park. She started crying when she told him about the jerk leaving her to walk home in the dark neighborhood.

"I was scared and all I could think about was that you would never have done that to me," she sobbed as Bauer took her into his arms.

"Tina, I'm sorry that I've left you hanging. I never meant to hurt you," Bauer quietly told her. "I can't promise you anything even though I'd like to. That's why I haven't called. There's nothing wrong with you. I have things in my life and in my past that make me think I should just stay single. I care about you, but I don't want to hurt you any more than I have."

"But, we're so good together," Tina told him, hoping to change his mind.

"Tina, you don't want me to promise something to you that I can't deliver, do you?"

"No."

"Listen, it's late, and this is a talk we need to have when you're awake and sober. Let me drive you home."

"I have my car here," she said, guiltily.

"Jesus, Tina, you shouldn't be driving like this."

"I know, but I had to see you."

"How did you find out where I live, anyway?" he asked.

"Mike told me."

"Good old Mike. Okay, I'll drive you home, and then get a cab back."

"That costs so much; you could stay with me," she said hopefully.

"Tina, I have a lot of things to do tomorrow. I have to be out of town. It's a family commitment I can't get out of. Look, I'll take you home and sleep on your couch. In the morning, you have to bring me back early, because I've got to get on the road, okay?"

"Okay, but you don't need to stay on the couch. I don't bite…well, much," she giggled.

"I won't take advantage of you in the state you're in. You're drunker than a saloon mouse."

"Okay."

Bauer drove Tina home and tucked her into her bed. He ran some water over his face before he curled up on Tina's short couch. He knew she would come to him in the night, and she did. Bauer knew it was more about rejection and confidence than about sex, and he knew he wouldn't turn her down. Instead, he made a quiet, gentle kind of love to her, so that she knew that he cared for her, and, no matter what happened, she would look back at their time together with fewer regrets.

CHAPTER 40

▼

Saturday June 1, 2002 dawned still and cool in Duluth. The morning sun sent orange rays into the valleys and crevices of the city, and its beams danced off the giant lake, making the surface appear to be covered in diamonds—or broken glass, depending on your mood.

During the night Rawlings had dreamt that the patriot had come into his room, and was standing at the foot of the bed. Try as he might, Rawlings was unable to move, and he watched helplessly as his tormentor slowly raised a handgun and pointed it at him.

"Don't!" Rawlings pled as the gun went off, and he woke to the sound of the alarm clock trilling.

After gathering himself, he and Frank Olivetti rose, showered, and went downstairs for the hotel's complimentary breakfast. Carrington and the testosterone team would be arriving shortly, and they would all meet with Russ Blanchard at 1:00 p.m.

Tony Bauer woke early, and quietly called a taxi to take him home. He knew that Tina would be in pretty rough shape so early, plus he wanted to avoid the inevitable conversation they would have if she drove him home. He hoped that she wasn't hurt too badly, but he was committed to his course. At another time, in another life, he would have been glad for her and for the love she obviously had for him. Now, though, it just wasn't meant to be.

When the cab pulled up out front, Bauer knelt over Tina's bed and kissed her goodbye. She protested a little, but not much, and he was glad that she knew how things were. Now, he could do what he had to do.

Two dark Dodge Minivans pulled into the parking lot of the hotel Rawlings and Olivetti were in. Stuart Carrington got out accompanied by ten very fit, serious-looking young men, each of whom carried a duffle bag. They all went up to the room, and tried unsuccessfully to get comfortable, hotel rooms not being designed to fit 13 large men.

Olivetti and Rawlings showed the layout of the campus and the auditorium to Carrington and Dan Edwards, the head of the Hostage-Rescue Team. Edwards was forty-years-old, and had been an FBI agent for 15 years. He'd been put in charge of this particular HR team two years before, and looked every bit as tough as someone in his position needed to be. Edwards was the Bureau's combat pistol champion for the previous six years running, despite challenges mounted by younger agents who had failed to take the crown from him, more through a lack of experience under stress, than from a lack of desire to win. He was superbly fit, and wore a high and tight crew-cut, which helped send the message to one and all that Dan Edwards was a serious man in a serious business.

The four men studied the information from the college, determined where the danger areas would be, and where men would have to be posted to provide the best coverage.

"It's critical that we blend in," Carrington said, "not only so the college officials and Beverly Geary don't know who we are, but so the patriot isn't spooked. If he is, as we suspect, a cop, or an ex-cop, he'll recognize us for who we are. What can we do about that?"

"All of my guys are pretty young-looking," Edwards said. "We're going to buy some of them college shirts, and hats at the bookstore today to help. Some will have backpacks, and some will dress kind of sloppy. None of these guys are so far out of college that they don't remember how they dressed back then," he said with a grin. "As for you *more senior* guys—I would think that a talk like this would attract a very diverse group of people. There'll be people dressed up, so I think you could get by with suits, or casual attire. We should arrive separately, and sit apart. Now, we brought covert radios and earpieces for twelve; I wasn't aware there would be thirteen of us."

"I can do without," Rawlings said. "I'll hang out with Frank for protection."

"Because of the congested nature of the area, we'll stick to handguns. I want to post a sniper back here," he said, as he pointed on the map to an area in the back of the auditorium near the control room. "Most of these places have dark corners."

"Yeah," Olivetti said. "I remember an alcove—one they would use for storage, or something."

"Perfect. I'll have one man there with an MP5 submachine gun with a laser sight, in case the need for a long shot develops rapidly. Each man will have a stun grenade in case a distraction device is needed. I will roam the lobby area outside of the auditorium throughout the time Geary is there. Once she moves into the banquet, we need to mill around, and appear to be mingling. Do we need passes for this event?"

"Yeah, the campus police Captain, Russ Blanchard, will have everything we need when we get there today," Olivetti said.

"What does he know about this?" Carrington asked.

"Well," Rawlings said, "he saw through our story, and guessed why we were really here. He's a pretty sharp guy, and got pissed because we lied to him. He's promised to keep everything confidential, and he's been a big help so far."

"Damn," Carrington swore. "I hope you're right. Eager locals can really blow a stakeout."

"Eager locals can also keep you from looking like a chump," Rawlings retorted, annoyed at Carrington's superior attitude.

"The long and short of it," Edwards said, "is that we're probably going to be reactive by necessity. I want a couple of people close by the stage, but I think the best chance we have to catch this guy is to keep most of us mobile. The patriot will have a plan, and it's safe to say that he won't be exposed for very long. At a speech everyone's attention is on the speaker—ours has to be everywhere but."

"Are we ready to go to the college?" Carrington asked.

"There's one more thing," Edwards said to Carrington. "As the Agent-in-Charge, you've set our rules of engagement, and you want the patriot taken alive, if possible. As the SWAT commander on scene, I can override them. Obviously, we'd like the patriot alive, but it's my belief that he is too dangerous to take even moderate risks with. There will be no heroics tonight, gentlemen," he said, looking around the room. "The patriot is a stone-cold killer, and he is bought-and-paid-for. Take him down. If you are 100% sure he is unarmed, or incapacitated, and I don't know how you can be, take him alive. If not, nail him. If he does show, he'll be here to commit murder—it's what he does, and he's good at it. All of us *will* go home after this is over."

Vince Cushing's morning started much the same way as Rawlings's. After a light breakfast, he went down to the Ballroom, and made the first of many checks on the speech and reception areas. Hudson's plane was due in at 3:00 p.m., and Cushing would be there two hours early to make sure everything was set.

Outside, the Army bomb technicians were walking a Black Lab and a German Shepard around the hotel, letting them sniff trash containers, delivery vehicles, and flower pots. Later, they would be brought in to go through the Ballroom and reception areas, as well as Hudson's room. This process would happen once more before the evening.

Everything seemed to be going according to plan.

The patriot spent his day in preparation, much as his adversaries did. He loaded up magazines for his Mini-14, and then hid the rifle inside a flat, wide box, which had a picture on the outside of the unassembled nightstand it had formerly contained. He loaded up the 9mm Hi-Power, secured it in his shoulder holster, and left them on the bed, to be put on later, along with his bulletproof vest.

He spent the majority of his time working on the Hedgehog. He put a silver serving platter on his kitchen table, and carefully placed the chicken wire and sparkler-bomb in the center of it. Next, he inserted the seven sixteen-ounce plastic water bottles into the honeycombed structure, and secured them with loose wire, which he had affixed near the openings. He unscrewed the bottle caps, and went to his basement to mix the ingredients which would fill them.

The patriot knew from the teenagers he'd spoken to, and by research he'd done on the Internet, that adding an explosive chemical, such as gasoline, could increase the yield of his bomb tremendously. After careful thought, and more Internet research, he set about obtaining a small supply of polystyrene from a packing company, and Benzine from a friend who used the chemical in his cleaning business.

Polystyrene is simply Styrofoam in its original state. Styrofoam cups and plates are made by heating and bonding polystyrene beads together in a mold, and it is fairly simple to obtain the beads from a variety of locations.

Benzine is a harsh chemical, which is a byproduct of the distillation of alcohol, and is often added to gasoline to boost its octane rating, and is used by chemists, painters, cleaners, and other tradesmen, who need it as a solvent.

The patriot carefully mixed a concoction of 46 parts polystyrene, 21 parts Benzine, and 33 parts gasoline in a pail. He combined the materials well, until it was a thick jelly, known to the military and the general public as napalm.

Napalm had been used in flame throwers and antipersonnel bombs since the Second World War. The Army found that simply using gasoline for these purposes wasn't as effective, since gasoline burned so quickly that it tended to burn off before it ignited the intended target. Also, gasoline is very unstable, and too easy to ignite. Therefore, it can be as hazardous to the friendly soldier as it is to the enemy.

Scientists discovered that by mixing polystyrene and benzine with the gasoline, the resulting mixture was actually much harder to ignite, was safer to handle, and would act as a sticky, fiercely-burning glob, that clung tenaciously to the target. Soldiers in the Second World War used napalm to clear out German and Japanese machine gun nests, and fortified artillery emplacements. Even the stoutest soldier will quickly leave his post when he is faced with immolation.

Napalm got a very bad name during the Vietnam War, when a photographer took a photo of very young Vietnamese children running from their burning village, which had been hit by firebombs. Their skin was hanging from their bodies as they ran, and they were screaming in agony as the napalm clung to them. The photograph was widely distributed, won a Pulitzer, and has endured to this day as an example of the horrors of war.

The patriot took his homemade napalm to the kitchen, carefully ladled it into a funnel, and filled each water bottle. Since napalm is harder to ignite than gasoline, it requires a very hot ignition source, and the patriot was confident that the burning magnesium of the sparklers would be more than hot enough to set it off. He'd practiced with a small amount of the substance in the back yard, and it had performed impressively. When he was finished, he tightened down the caps, and was ready for the next part.

He took the thin plastic dome cover from the meat and cheese tray, and fitted it over the top of the bomb, taking note of where the center fuse-sparkler jutted up. He set the cover back onto the table, and used a sharp knife to carve a hole just big enough for the sparkler to pass through. Then he fitted the cover onto the Hedgehog, and glued the corners down with a strong epoxy sealant.

He squeezed more epoxy onto the plastic cover, and spread it until a tacky, sticky surface covered the top and sides of the bomb. That way, the cover would be less smooth for the last step. He placed an empty ballpoint pen body over the fuse-sparkler in order to protect it from the next step.

The patriot took two large tubs of cake frosting from his cupboard, and opened them. Using a rubber spatula, he ladled a thick coating of frosting all over the now-sticky plastic cover's top and sides. He had practiced this on actual bakery products he'd made, and now was able to do a fairly credible job of making the thing look like a big cake—the kind you would serve to a lot of people.

When the entire dome was covered and the frosting was evenly distributed, the patriot loaded a decorating bag with a different color frosting. He screwed a star-shaped tip on the end, and squeezed the frosting out around the base of the "cake," making a fancy design. He placed some red, white, and blue baking sprinkles on the cake, and finished by affixing a sign in front that had the logo of the University of Minnesota Law School, and the words, CONGRATULATIONS, CLASS OF 2002!, in bold characters underneath.

As he stepped back to admire his work, he saw that it was 4:00 p.m., and nearly time to go. He had one last preparation to make and picked up the phone to call the Allied Delivery Service.

Rawlings joined the FBI agents in a quick early meal, and then rode back to the hotel, where the final assignments were handed out by Edwards. Each man had his area fixed clearly in his head, they donned their college clothes, and prepared for the night. Russ Blanchard had provided all of them with the ID cards which would serve as their invitations to the lecture and reception afterward. Then he set off to accompany Ms. Geary to the college from the airport, a task he insisted upon. He would attend the evening's activities in plainclothes as well.

Rawlings debated calling Mary, but decided against it. It would only worry her. Besides, he was still of the opinion that the real target would be the Justice, and their being here was another wild goose chase—courtesy of the patriot. Instead, he checked his duty pistol—a habit he had definitely fallen out of during his many years as an investigator. Unlike detectives on TV, real homicide investigators are rarely in the type of physical danger faced by other cops. They spend their days talking, questioning, and working the evidence, not in gunfights. Actually, Rawlings only fired his weapon once a year during the BCA's mandated qualification course, and it was fair to say that the Rangemaster was very understanding of what Rawlings did for a living. The course was certainly not demanding, and was handled more as a pro-forma tip-of-the-cap to the rules.

Rawlings found the weapon in good working order, and jammed it into his belt holster as the rest of the men gathered their equipment and prepared to head off to school.

Justice Hudson's chartered jet arrived on time and taxied to the VIP entrance at the Minneapolis-St. Paul International Airport. The formalities of airport security were waived in the presence of all of the Secret Service, and Hudson was whisked away in his limousine within 15 minutes of landing. The motorcade of three cars made good time to downtown Minneapolis, and pulled into the underground garage of the Hilton. Hudson was put in a secured elevator, and taken to his room, which had just been rechecked for bombs and intruders. The room was stocked with the judge's favorite brand of Scotch so he could relax while he gathered his notes together.

Vince Cushing rode the elevator back down and began checking the security details again.

At 5:10 p.m. the patriot, driving a Chevrolet Blazer he'd rented in the name of Gordon Tidwell, another unfortunate soul who'd died in childhood, pulled up in an alley behind the Barger's Bakery in Inver Grove Heights. Barger's was a small family bakery that had served the neighborhood for over 20 years, and the patriot had stopped there many times. He knew that the bakery closed on Saturdays no later than 4:00 p.m., because old Henry Barger, who owned the place and was the baker, would be home spending time with his family before he had to go to bed and rise at 3:00 a.m. to come make the next morning's offerings.

The patriot knew that Barger's didn't have an alarm system, and that the back door had the oldest, most worthless lock in town. The bakery had been broken into several times, but Henry Barger had told the patriot a couple of times that there was no point in installing tougher locks, since the burglars would just do more damage in order to get in. The patriot easily slipped the lock with a piece of rigid plastic, and opened the door to the kitchen. He opened the back of the Blazer, carefully removed the platter holding the Hedgehog, and carried it inside. He looked under the big table that Mr. Barger used to roll his dough on, found large, collapsed cake boxes, and removed one that would be the right fit. He opened the box and carefully put the bomb inside. He removed the pen cap from the sparkler, and then closed and sealed the box with tape marked with the bakery's name.

The patriot went to the little office, found a pad of invoices, and tore one off. He wrote out an invoice to read, "Hilton Hotel—Minneapolis—Law Class Graduation—Special Order," and taped it to the top of the cake box. He settled in to wait.

At 5:30 p.m. a delivery van arrived and pulled into the rear of the bakery. The patriot, wearing a large white apron, which he had found hanging on a nail, greeted him, and made sure that the driver knew where the delivery was going.

"Minneapolis Hilton, right?" the guy asked after consulting with his clipboard.

"Right. They have a big dinner and graduation party for a law school there tonight. This is the cake."

"When does it have to be there? I have other deliveries."

"No later than 7:00 p.m." the patriot told him.

"No problem. Law school graduation, huh?"

"That's right."

"Great, more lawyers in the world," the man quipped.

"I hear you, but they paid me."

"Yeah, and you'll pay them back later."

"Well, maybe not so much later," the patriot told him with a thin smile.

After the man left, the patriot locked up and drove away.

The graduating seniors of the U of M Law School began arriving at the Hilton around 6:15. They had been told to come early for security reasons. They discovered why, as each was thoroughly searched and probed with a metal-detecting wand. One student was taken into a rest room and strip searched when a metal plate in his leg set off the alarm. The Secret Service agents made no apologies as they went about their work and, though the process was tedious, it went fairly quickly.

The guests took their assigned seats in the banquet room, and cocktails were served at 6:45 when the Honorable G.E. Hudson arrived to mingle with the new attorneys. Vince Cushing hovered nearby, his eyes scanning for trouble, as the great man mingled with the guests.

The Allied Delivery van pulled into the Hilton's loading dock and was met by a Secret Service agent.

"What's this?" the agent asked the driver.

"Delivery from the Barger Bakery…its the cake for tonight's big shindig."

"Open it up," the agent ordered.

The driver opened the back, slit open the tape on the box, and lifted the top to show the agent.

"Where did you get this?" the agent asked.

"Picked it up myself from the bakery a little bit ago. Here's the work order." he said, offering the manifest to the agent.

The agent read the manifest and compared it to the invoice. He read the plaque on the side of the cake, and decided everything was kosher. "Okay, I'll call someone down to get it."

In the Hilton kitchen one of the cooks answered the house phone and was told that the cake had arrived.

"Okay," he said, and hung up. "Terry," he called to another, less senior, kitchen worker. Get your ass down to the loading dock with a cart and bring the cake up. It's just been delivered." The cook was happy to handle the matter himself without bothering the head chef, who could be a heavyweight prick when he was under pressure.

Rawlings and Olivetti settled into their seats for the lecture. The auditorium was nearly filled with students and faculty who had come to listen to how wrong the Bush Administration was in dealing with the Taliban in Afghanistan. Rawlings was seated next to a pretty, red-haired coed, who wore a pullover that read, "Saints," and who looked to Rawlings to be about sixteen-years-old. *I am so old,* he said to himself.

Geary began her talk a little after 7:30 p.m., and Rawlings wanted to die by 7:45. Geary's comments and observations struck him as wildly naïve, but the crowd seemed to appreciate her, for they broke into applause, seemingly, after every other sentence. The red-head next to him turned at one point and said, "Isn't she wonderful?" Rawlings agreed that she was, indeed, wonderful.

Outside of the auditorium, Edwards and his men patrolled the area casually, but alertly. Each scanned the faces of passing people to mentally compare them to the Shire drawing as they slowly walked around.

At 8:10 p.m. Justice Hudson finished his talk to a standing ovation. He moved from the dais to the head table, and joined senior faculty members in a drink as a lovely prime rib dinner was served. Vince Cushing moved off to the back of the room.

"What's this?" the head chef asked, looking at the cake.

"That's the cake for tonight," one of the cooks replied.

"Then we have two cakes? There's the one we made over there," he said, pointing to a flat cake.

"You suppose there was a mix-up, or did they want two?" the cook asked.

"Well, I suppose this could have been ordered by the school. It's certainly fancier than the one we provided. What the hell is that on top? A candle?"

"Looks like a sparkler," the cook told him.

"I get it—patriotism, red, white, and blue, all that. Okay. Well, I hope they're hungry, because we've got a lot of cake for dessert."

Beverly Geary wrapped up her monologue at 8:40. She bowed to the applause from the standing crowd and received a kiss from the University President, who led her into the adjoining banquet room. Most of the crowd left, since most weren't invited to the reception, and the members of the SWAT team filed in with those who were. Champagne was served, and Ms. Geary happily raised her glass as she was toasted by a Dean who thanked her for her insights, and her commitment to peace. It was 8:50 p.m.

At that moment, the kitchen crew began clearing the dinner plates and set out the dessert dishes and forks. In the kitchen, the chef looked at the two cakes, and decided that the one with the sparkler was much more festive. Besides, if the school had specially ordered it, it wouldn't do to give them a different one. He wheeled the cart to the door and turned to his assistant, saying, "Do you have a lighter?"

"I think we're out of luck here," Rawlings told Olivetti. "Any word from the Hilton?"

"Nothing. We'd have heard if something happened. I wonder if the patriot took the night off, or went after someone totally different."

"I guess we'll find out soon enough," Rawlings said.

The chef wheeled the cart out onto the floor as red flame danced on the top of the fizzing sparkler. The assembled diners clapped at the display, thinking how nice a salute it was to the guest of honor. The chef pushed the cake to the front of the room so everyone could see it, and then slowly wheeled it around for the benefit of those at the head table before the sparkler could go out.

As Hudson read the plaque, he smiled appreciatively, saying, "What an appropriate thought." The judge cleared his throat, and stood up. "I'd just like to say," he said in a loud voice, "that all of you will be entering a profession in which you will have great opportunity to serve your fellow Americans. Some of you will go far, and I hope that, as you travel whatever roads you choose, you remember that service to mankind is the debt of all Americans."

Hudson's comment concluded just as the sparkler burned down to the icing.

The people in the room were amazed to see Hudson disappear in an ungodly light that was brighter than the sun. The magnesium sparklers fired with a roar, quickly melting the plastic bottles, and igniting the napalm within. The burning gel was carried by the shockwave in a twenty-yard arc. It set fire to three rows of tables, the head table behind, and numerous students, most of whom were blown backward their chairs by the intense heat.

Vince Cushing spun at the sound, but was unable to see Hudson at all—so bright was the teepee-shaped cone of white flame that was now beginning to consume the ceiling tiles. A stampede of people rushed the exits and collided with Secret Service agents who were running into the room. One agent grabbed a fire extinguisher from the wall and sprayed it on the fire, but it only flared and sizzled more brightly. He turned the blast on the front rows of diners, who had been hit by napalm, and whose clothing was now on fire. His actions quickly doused the flames on the guest's bodies, and moved on to others.

"GET OUT!" Cushing yelled above the mayhem. "GET THE FUCK OUT, NOW!!" His words were pointless, since there was a crush of bodies already headed out the door. The room emptied as the fire crawled along the ceiling and spread. Cushing could see the bodies of the men who had been at the head table, and knew that they were dead. Hudson's lower body was partially visible in the curtain of flame, and Cushing knew that he'd failed.

"Fuck!" he yelled, and left both the burning room and the man who's safety had been in his hands.

Stuart Carrington's cell phone beeped at 9:15 p.m. He moved to a quiet corner of the room to answer it, and his face turned pale and angry when he heard the news. He closed the phone and walked quickly to Rawlings and Olivetti.

"He got Hudson," Carrington told them, tight-lipped. "Somehow he got a bomb into the banquet and it went off. It looks like Hudson was killed along with a few others. Several people are injured, and the Hilton is on fire."

"Son of a bitch!" Olivetti exclaimed under his breath.

"Well, you were right," Carrington told Rawlings. "We've been had."

"I'll gather the troops," Olivetti said, and set out to look for Edwards.

"We need to get back as soon as possible," Carrington said. "I'm going to see if I can arrange a chopper right now." He turned on his heel and walked out, leaving Rawlings standing dumbfounded.

And so the hunt goes on, he thought to himself while people laughed and chatted around him.

"Mike," Olivetti said, "Edwards has called in the SWATs, and we're going to head out once everyone's together."

"Okay, I'm going to find Russ Blanchard, and tell him we're taking off. I'll meet you outside."

Rawlings found Blanchard on the other side of the hall, and told him what had happened. Blanchard shook his head at the news, and said, "Shit. That guy's a pure fucker alright. Well, I'm sorry for you, but I'm glad he chose to go there instead of here. I don't envy you, Mr. Rawlings." The two shook hands, and Blanchard left to call his boss to let him know that they had dodged a bullet.

Rawlings walked tiredly down the hall, feeling every year of his age. The prospect of the media storm that was sure to come filled him with dread. He knew that things had gotten so far out of control that fingers would now be pointed, and blame would be laid so the big shots could run for cover, their chair-shaped butts safely protected. *God, I'd rather stay here than go back now,* he thought as he passed a tall, muscular man, in a U of M football jersey, coming in the building. The man passed, and Rawlings had a flash of realization as he walked by, and the two locked eyes for the briefest moment. To Rawlings, time seemed to slow to a crawl, as he turned and looked at the back of the man, who was headed for the reception area. There was something about the face…and suddenly he knew: it was the patriot.

Rawlings reached for a radio, and then remembered that he didn't have one. He had his cell phone, but he didn't know Carrington or Olivetti's direct numbers, and he knew it would take too long to call the airport task force office to get them. He ran back up the hall toward the banquet room, turned the corner, and found, nothing.

Where the fuck did he go? Rawlings thought, looking around for Blanchard, but he was gone, too. *Shit! Shit! Shit!* He pulled his gun, and held it down at his side, behind his thigh. Rawlings slid around the door into the dark auditorium, and moved forward a step when a bright light exploded inside his head.

The patriot had recognized Rawlings as he passed him, and he ducked into the alcove that had so recently hidden the sniper who had hoped to put a round right between the patriot's eyes. He saw Rawlings ease in after him, and hit him hard on the right side of his neck from behind with his heavy forearm. Rawlings collapsed in a heap, his pistol clattering uselessly to the floor.

Rawlings didn't lose consciousness, but seemed to have no control over his body. He wondered if he was paralyzed, and then wondered how the patriot would kill him.

The patriot pulled Rawlings to a kneeling position by the hair, and reached around in front of his face with a knife. He drew the sharp blade across Rawlings's eyes in one smooth movement, being careful to not cut too deep. It would have been so easy for the patriot to cut Rawlings's throat, and a part of him knew he should have, but in the end, he was content to put the investigator out of action. As it was, the effect on Rawlings was devastating.

"Oh, Jesus!" Rawlings cried, as he felt the knife cut through his eyelids, and the blood pour down his face. Immediately he panicked. *I'm blind!! The son-of-a-bitch blinded me! Oh, God!*

The patriot dragged him into the control booth of the auditorium, and threw him onto the floor. He closed the door and dragged a heavy speaker cabinet over to wedge in front of it, in order to pin Rawlings inside while he finished his mission.

Rawlings lay on the floor for what seemed like hours, but was really only a couple of minutes. His split eyelids caused him agony when he tried to brush the blood away in order to see. He felt the sensation coming back to his arms after the nerve stun that the patriot had delivered to him. He groped around the room until his hands found a shirt laying over the back of a chair. He used it to dab the blood from his eyes, and was finally able to see, although poorly, out of his left eye.

Rawlings stumbled to the door, and tried to push it open, but it was stuck. *There's no lock, so something must be sitting against it,* he thought. He gathered his strength, and pushed until he felt the door give a little. He pushed harder, and it finally opened enough to allow him to squeeze out. He groped around for his gun where he'd fallen, and located it under a seat. He grabbed it, stood up, and walked directly into a wall, having no depth perception at all, due to his closed right eye. He felt his way out into the hall and toward the banquet room, his gun dangling from his right hand.

A couple of passing girls saw the bloody-faced man with the gun as he came out of the auditorium, and screamed. Rawlings hoped that their screams would summon help, but they were drowned out by the shrieking of a fire alarm that began going off next to his head.

The patriot had located the reception for Geary. He knew there would be one, and assumed it would be near the auditorium. He'd gone to school here fourteen years earlier, and knew the building well. In fact, as an alumnus, he got a copy of the school paper sent to him that told when interesting guest speakers, like Beverly Geary, would be coming.

He looked into the party, and saw Geary not far from the door. He needed to separate her from the pack, and he knew that he didn't have much time. Rawlings wouldn't stay penned up in that room forever. He walked into the banquet room, and saw the men's room to his right. He went in, and found it empty. He removed the lid from the garbage can, and set fire to some of the paper towels inside. Soon, the can was burning well, and he slid out the door.

Back in the banquet room, the patriot casually walked toward Geary, and the fire alarm on the wall behind her. When he saw the smoke wisping out of the men's room he pulled the alarm.

"Fire!" he yelled, and pointed toward the men's room. "The bathroom's on fire!" People looked and saw the smoke, and began running to the doors. The patriot stepped over to Geary, and took her by the arm.

"I'll get you to safety, Ma'am," he said, as he led the unresisting woman out the door.

Through the thin smoke, Rawlings saw the patriot and Geary leave the room, and walk away from him down the hallway.

"No!" he yelled, but there was too much noise and confusion. Rawlings ran after them as quickly as his poor vision would allow. He saw them disappear around a corner, and he stumbled after them as the alarm shrieked up and down the hallways. He pushed his way through the mass of people, and ignored the gasps as passersby were treated to the very unexpected sight of a middle-aged man with blood all over his face, carrying a pistol in his hand. Rawlings stumbled down the hall and saw them walking toward a lounge. In desperation, he yelled, "Stop! Police! Get down!" hoping that Geary could pull away. Geary heard him, and turned to look back at the sight of Rawlings pointing his pistol at them. For the first time, she realized something besides the fire was wrong, and said, "Who on earth is that?" The patriot grabbed her by her collar, and yanked her roughly around in front of him. He fired three shots at Rawlings, who ducked as he felt sheetrock splatter around his head. The patriot dragged Geary through a door, and into another part of the building. Rawlings cried out in pain when he again had to wipe blood from his eyes with his coat sleeve, and he followed them, cursing, "This is my fucking nightmare, I swear to God."

The patriot and Geary disappeared behind the door of the lounge, and Rawlings ran after them, knowing it could be a trap, but seeing no other alternative. He knew that the instant the patriot had Geary alone, he would kill her and make his escape. Rawlings burst in the door, and found himself looking at an empty room and a slowly-closing door on the other end. "Jesus Christ," he muttered in frustration, and ran to try to catch up. Rawlings burst into an adjoining meeting room, and found himself ten feet away from the patriot, who was holding a now-terrified Geary between them. He had run out of maneuvering room, and there was no other way out.

"Why didn't you stay where I left you?" the patriot yelled in a loud voice filled with frustration. Rawlings recoiled, and his feet went out from under him. He fell over backward, as the patriot raised his gun, just as he had in Rawlings's dream. The patriot had Geary pinned in his arms, using her as a shield, and Rawlings knew he didn't dare fire.

For a moment, Rawlings was certain his life was over, but the patriot hesitated. He knew that this man stood between him and his cause, but something deep inside him told him that Rawlings wasn't the type of person he detested. The patriot had been a cop before his demons had overtaken him, and that part of him was still inside.

"Don't make me kill you," he said to Rawlings, almost in a pleading tone. "Give her to me and I'll leave."

"I can't," Rawlings answered. "You know I can't. Let her go. This is wrong, you know it is."

"I have to stop her," the patriot said, his voice shaking with emotion. "She hates me. She hates America. People like her want to destroy us."

Rawlings knew that in the patriot's mind, the line between his identity and the country had blurred, and that he actually saw himself as America. He knew that the patriot was truly insane, and there would be no reasoning with him.

As the standoff continued, Geary's fear and confusion had sapped her strength, and she began sagging to the floor. The patriot had his left arm wrapped around her waist to hold her up in front of him, but his grip had loosened. He jammed the muzzle of his gun into her throat to force her to stand. Rawlings now had a clear shot at the patriot's head, but his vision was still obscured by the sticky blood clotting on his eyelids.

The patriot began dragging Geary along the wall toward the door, and Rawlings knew he had to risk taking a shot. He would have one chance only, and knew that he would die if he missed. Quickly, he brought his gun up, lined his sights on the patriot's face, and fired. The round went wide, and brushed past the patriot's right ear, missing by a fraction of an inch.

Enraged, the patriot fired back. Rawlings rolled to his right as the gun went off, and cried out as he felt the bullet sear into his left buttock. Rawlings brought his gun up again, and fired five shots wildly over the patriot's head, hoping that he would run, or that the stupid bitch would get down, so he could at least have a slim chance. The patriot took aim, and Rawlings knew he had nowhere to go. Rawlings heard a gun go off, and was surprised to feel nothing. He was more surprised to see the patriot fall over backward.

In amazement, Rawlings turned and saw Olivetti and Edwards in the doorway, with guns drawn. Edwards had fired and hit the patriot in the shoulder. The agents had come back looking for him, and were surprised when they found the smoke and the flashing alarms. Then they heard the shots, and Geary's screams, and they followed the sounds to where Rawlings lay, preparing to die.

The patriot, surprised but undaunted by the blow to his left shoulder, rolled, and came up firing rapidly, his bullets slapping into Edwards and Olivetti, and the wall around them. Edwards felt one round slam into his left shoulder, and he spun to the floor, his pistol clattering under a desk. Olivetti felt a round pass painfully through his right elbow, and he dropped to one knee, but held on to his pistol. He transferred his weapon to his left hand, as Edwards scrambled to retrieve his own gun, saying, "Shit, shit, shit!" Rawlings took advantage of the patriot's distraction, and scrambled across the floor to Geary. His left leg dragged uselessly behind him, but he managed to grab her dress, and pull her down to the floor. Olivetti rose and unleashed a volley of rapid-fire shots, hitting the patriot five times, again knocking him to the floor. The bulletproof vest under his jersey stopped the rounds from penetrating his skin, but the impact knocked the breath from his lungs as if he'd been hit by a baseball bat. In a desperate burst of fierce determination, the patriot made one final attempt to finish what he'd determined to do. He fired once more—this time at Geary—his face a mask of hate as he tried to erase the last name on his list. She was being covered by Rawlings's body, and this last shot hit Rawlings in the back. Olivetti, firing left handed, pulled the trigger twice, this time aiming at the patriot's head. The big .45 caliber rounds struck Bauer in the right eye, and temple, expanding, and mushrooming, before they came out the left side of his head. The man who'd terrorized a city, left so many bodies in his wake, and tried unsuccessfully to unleash a civil war on the nation, was finally silent.

The patriot fell onto a table, and then slowly slid to the floor, his pistol still gripped firmly in his right hand. As he had predicted, the patriot had died fighting, and reaping what he had sown.

Olivetti pulled Rawlings off of the screaming and hysterical Geary, and saw from his pallor that he was going into shock.

"Get an ambulance!" he screamed to Edwards, who was disarming the patriot, and making sure that he was really dead. "Mike, Mike!" he yelled as Rawlings's consciousness slipped away. "Stay with me Mike! Stay with me, goddamn it!"

EPILOGUE

▼

Mike Rawlings woke up three days later in the Critical Care Unit of Duluth's St. Luke's Hospital. Mary was by his side, and she broke into a teary smile when she realized he was finally awake.

"Rest now, Sweetheart," she told him, as she gently touched his bandaged face. "You're going to be okay."

When Rawlings was well enough to have visitors later in the week, Jim Knox made the drive to Duluth, to do the final wrap on his patriot story, and to thank the man who had given him something he didn't think he'd have been able to find on his own.

"How's that monkey?" Rawlings asked him. "Is it still hanging on your back?"

"Well, it's there," Knox said with a smile, "but its claws don't hurt so much anymore. I know I can't do it on my own, so I've been going to meetings. The important thing is that I'm closer now to my daughter than I've ever been in my life. In fact, I'm taking some time off next week, and driving down there."

"You're sure not letting any grass grow under you are you?" Rawlings chuckled.

"No time like the present. Besides, I'm going to be losing my license for a while after I get back, due to that driving indiscretion of mine, so I have to do it now, or not for a long time. Who knows, maybe I'll like the weather there, and see if the local rag needs an old fart to do the crime beat. Think they have those meetings in Arizona?"

"I'm sure they do, Jim, and I'm sure you'll find one."

The following day Frank Olivetti, wearing a sport shirt, with his arm in a sling, came to visit, and filled in the parts that Rawlings didn't know. He told him that the patriot's real name was Anthony Bauer, and that he was, in fact, a working deputy sheriff in Dakota County.

"We were so close on so many things," Rawlings said to Olivetti. "How could he stay hidden for so long?"

"He knew the ropes, Mike," Olivetti answered. "It's harder to hunt game who knows what you know."

"Do we know why?" Rawlings asked.

"Not really. As near as we've been able to piece together, he was considered a very sharp guy by his co-workers. He was known to be politically conservative, but only his patrol sergeant suspected that he might have gone off the deep-end."

"Why didn't he do something?" Rawlings asked, shaking his head. "We could have stopped him."

"Well, once again, the guy's luck held out for him. The sergeant was going to call us on Friday, the day before the banquets, but his house caught fire, and he wound up with a broken leg, and having surgery. He never got the chance to make the call. I swear, Mike, I'd like to have Bauer's luck. If he fell into a toilet, he'd come out with a Lake Trout."

"Did the search of his house reveal anything?"

"Not much. We have his computer, and it looks like he spent a lot of time on right wing sites, and chat rooms. Not much in the way of participation, though, which I think helps explain his luck. He kept his ideas to himself, and didn't blab. We did find a cubbyhole in the wall of the garage where he kept notes and information on his victims. We found a truck he rented under another alias at the college, and inside was the rifle he'd used to do Borgert, a bunch of extra clips, and ammo. He was loaded for bear."

"And the Hilton, how did that fare?"

"Well, the fire did a lot of damage, but didn't spread too far from the ball-room. Hudson was killed, along with six big shots from the law school, and one student. Fifteen other students were burned, and a few were injured in the rush to get out. The bomb guys say he constructed a device out of 1000 ordinary sparklers, and then built it around bottles of homemade napalm. Here's the real kicker: he sent it to the Hilton by plain old messenger service on Saturday after-noon, so he would have time to get up to Duluth, and nail Geary after the bomb went off."

"He nearly pulled it off, too," Rawlings said quietly.

"It was a lucky thing you happened to pass him in the hall, or he would have."

"Yeah," Rawlings chuckled, looking at the tubes and hoses sticking out of him. "Real lucky. I owe you, too, my friend. Seriously, I thank you, and my wife thanks you."

"Well, it was good luck for Geary, anyway, and for however many other people Bauer would have gone after if you hadn't spoiled his plans. You're the real hero, here, Mike, and I'm proud of you. It took real brass balls to go in alone like you did."

"What's that?" Rawlings asked to change the subject, pointing to a bag Olivetti had brought with him.

"This is something we found in Bauer's house. Like I said, we didn't find much incriminating evidence at all, but this was hanging on his living room wall. I thought you might like it as a memento. It's a framed quote from Mark Twain." Olivetti pulled it out of the bag, and held it up so Rawlings could read it.

> "In the beginning of change, the patriot is a scarce man; brave, hated and scorned. When his cause succeeds, however, the timid join him, for then it costs nothing to be a patriot."

"Thank God his cause is finished," Rawlings said.

News broadcast:

"FBI officials in Minnesota have confirmed the identity of the dead man as Anthony Bauer, a twelve-year sheriff's department veteran, and they have announced that they are certain that he was indeed the man who called himself the patriot," the TV news reporter said. "Stuart Carrington, Special Agent-in-Charge of the Patriot Task Force, said that ballistics tests on a handgun and rifle found on Bauer's body, and in his vehicle, were positively matched to deaths of many of the victims. Also found in Bauer's home, were notes and information on his victims. Agent Carrington credited the fine police work done by the members of his task force, and by police and by BCA officials, who had worked the case before the FBI took over. He expressed regret that Bauer was able to defeat Secret Service safety precautions and kill Supreme Court Justice Hudson, but said that he was pleased that his team was able to save Bauer's final intended-target, actress, and activist, Beverly Geary.

"Agent Carrington said in a press statement, quote, 'Americans can once again breath easily, and know that the threat, posed by the man who called himself a patriot, is over.'"

A man sat in his basement in a city and state far from Minnesota, watching the news broadcast. He had a large array of weapons assembled on the floor near him, and he was slowly running a knife blade over a whetstone.

The man, who also thought of himself as a patriot, listened, as the reporter said that the threat was finally over.

"That's what you think," he said quietly.

Acknowledgements

When I sat down to write this book, I decided I would follow the author's rule which warns, "Write what you know." Having lived as a full-time police officer for the last 22 years, I had many memories and characters to draw from. While all of the characters in the story are fictional, some may resemble real people I've known in my past. As I have nothing but the highest respect for my brothers and sisters in the police, fire, and emergency medical fields, I've tried to be fair, and show them in the honest, and therefore, respectable light they deserve.

I am fortunate enough to know some very intelligent and talented people, who helped me with some things which were outside of my experience. They put up with me calling and bugging them with questions and scenarios which, I'm sure, were confusing, since they didn't know what I was writing. Still, they came through for me, and gave the story the ring of accuracy I was striving for.

I'd like to thank Angie Shambour, a former officer, now an Assistant St. Louis County, MN Attorney, who walked me through those parts of the book which deal with the deep end of the law. She also was kind enough to spend a lot of her free time proofing the book for me, and giving helpful suggestions, and I will always be in her debt. She works hard putting bad guys in jail for less money than she'd make by keeping them out. I'm glad she's doing it, though.

I'd like to thank Brian (Tex) Edwards, a crew chief on the Northfield Ambulance service. Tex answered my questions about emergency medicine, trauma scenes, and patient care. I've been fortunate enough to see Tex many times working a bad scene, keeping his cool, and making sure that people who'd gotten one foot into the grave were able to get out and see the sun rise again, which is what folks like him do. He's good at what he does, and I'm grateful he was there to help me. Thanks also to the other members of his crew. They're a fun bunch, and were all very supportive.

I'd like to thank my sister, Sue, for her advice, opinions, and support. She was very instrumental in this story being told, and I owe her. I also owe her son, Brian, and his friend, Gary Jansen, as well as William Kent Krueger, and Don Tubesing, who pointed me in the right direction when the story was finished, and provided some very welcome advice. Also on that list, is Coralee Allen, from Editorial Eyes, who provided the spit-and-polish.

I'd also like to thank my wife, Annette, and our children, Andrea, Brianna, Dan, Matt, and Nathan, each of whom provided the support and encouragement I needed to keep at it. Not once did anyone roll their eyes and say, "Are you writing that book *again?*" when they wanted to use the computer. Thanks to you all.

And finally, I'd like to thank the men and women of law enforcement, the firefighters, and medics who I've been fortunate enough to work with over the years. These people bust their butts every day and night for very little pay, and often even littler support from their bosses to help you. No matter what crisis you may find yourself in at 3:00 a.m., you can always count on these folks to come and pull you out, even if it costs them their life. If you enjoyed the book, please thank one of these people the next time you see them in line at the convenience store…its the least you can do.

—Jim Frie

0-595-33296-X

Printed in the United States
22994LVS00006B/55-78

9 780595 332960